# THE
# THREAD
# THAT
# CONNECTS
# US

*To the oppressed, wherever you may be in this world,*
*God willing, you will one day be free*

First published in the UK in 2024 by Usborne Publishing Ltd., Usborne House,
83-85 Saffron Hill, London EC1N 8RT, England. usborne.com

Usborne Verlag, Usborne Publishing Ltd., Prüfeninger Str. 20, 93049 Regensburg,
Deutschland, VK Nr. 17560

Text copyright © Ayaan Mohamud, 2024

Author photo © Oluwayemisi Oshodi

Cover illustration by Wasima Farah © Usborne Publishing, 2024

A CIP catalogue record for this book is available from the British Library.

ISBN 9781803704517    7941/1    JFMAM JASOND/24

Printed and bound using 100% renewable energy at CPI Group (UK) Ltd, Croydon, CR0 4YY.

MIX
Paper | Supporting
responsible forestry
FSC® C171272

# THE THREAD THAT CONNECTS US

## AYAAN MOHAMUD

USBORNE

# SUMMER
## OLD HURTS, NEW HURTS

In the district of Yaaqshid, Mogadishu, in a villa built in the centre of town, a girl and boy fell in a love that existed only where other eyes could not see them. In the shadows of a balmy twilight, behind the cover of trees, or in glances stolen across the frequent gatherings in that house.

It had an intense, almost wild energy, this love of theirs. Nothing could quieten the raging sense of yearning and longing that clung to the edges of their hearts, that clamoured along their vessels – not even the hours they spent away from each other's company, or the condemnation expressed at the idea of their matrimony.

"A housemaid from a lowly tribe to marry our great son?" The elders tutted and shook their heads. "No, no. There is no logic in such a match."

So the girl and boy had no choice but to pretend they felt nothing for each other, to keep their infatuation secret. But, eventually, even the secret began to bulge along its seams and joints, unable to constrain their love any longer and so, one night, they bound themselves to each other under the eyes of God.

From their fleeting union came many things, but it ended as chaotically as it began, as these intense entanglements often do.

*It wouldn't have surprised the elders, had they known about this love affair made true, but it surprised the girl and boy, and for a long time after, their hearts stopped feeling anything but the contraction of life's beats.*

*Their tumultuous love didn't leave a mark on this world. At least, not one anyone else could see then.*

# SAFIYA

I flip over on my bed, mindlessly clicking on a video on my phone. In the space of twenty minutes, I have covered ASMR, cleaning hacks, Illuminati conspiracy videos and kids hilariously tripping over air.

This wasn't how I expected the first day of the holidays to kick off, but the entire summer stretched out before me feels a little overwhelming. What is someone supposed to do with this much free time?

If I had money and a mother who didn't constantly disappear into herself, maybe I would be heading on holiday someplace far flung where problems don't exist. But I don't have either of those things and so I know that, like every summer before this, I have another unglamorous six weeks ahead of me.

The next video starts playing automatically. Something about spending a dollar in the world's cheapest country, but I stop paying attention when my phone buzzes.

## THREE MUSKETEERS

Yusuf: King Eddy's at 5 yeahhh we still on?

Another chime.

Muna: only if you've done ur chores lol otherwise mum
will fight you

Yusuf: [GIF of a gorilla beating its chest]

Muna: Well done bro good idea!
Gonna forward that to her

Yusuf: NO
Beg u don't gremlin
Gonna clean toilet now brb
@Safiya see you at 5

I laugh under my breath, watching this play out. Muna and
Yusuf can always be trusted to stop me feeling sorry for myself.
I jump onto the chat to send a reply.

Safiya: U two have got to be the MOST dysfunctional set
of cousin-siblings I've ever met

Though the two of them are *technically* cousins, they've
grown up together as brother and sister. Yusuf has lived with
Muna's family since they were both a year old. He'd lost both of
his parents back home in Somalia, because of the war, and was
eventually brought here to be raised by his aunt and uncle.

Muna reacts to my message with laughter.

Muna: well if we're the MOST then guess we're doing
something right

I roll my eyes. Only Muna would think to dig for a compliment
in something intended to be the complete opposite.

Safiya: why are u like this
Ok anyway I'll be outside at 5
catch u later

I switch back to the dollar video. The audio is still playing
through my headphones and it seems as though the guy has
bought street food that isn't quite agreeing with him.

A moment later, it's interrupted by a muffled noise.

"Hello?" I speak into my empty room, pulling my
headphones off one ear. When the knock comes again, I shout,
"Come in!" and jump up, tripping over the pile of laundry I'd
forgotten was on the floor.

To most people, their mum knocking on their door might
seem inconsequential, but here, in this house, it is anything
but. To hear my mum knocking on my door, knowing it means
she is looking for me, wanting to *speak* to me…

Hooyo's knock is not just a knock. It is a quiet miracle.

The door opens slowly, tentatively, and I scramble up from
the floor to see Hooyo standing there.

"Hi, Hooyo," I say breathlessly, rubbing my knee. "Everything
okay?"

11

She blinks once, twice, three times. Opens her mouth and then closes it again. I wait.

I have learned to be patient with Hooyo over the years. I know not to push her too far, to expect too much, because she's too fragile to bear it. So much of the last five years has been dedicated to understanding her and propping her up after my dad left us. I could write a five-hundred-page manual on how to handle Hooyo if I needed to.

There are moments when I try to remember what the precise turning point in our relationship actually was.

Was it when my dad selfishly abandoned us to follow his dreams of extending his business abroad? Or when Hooyo wasted the last of our weekly budget purchasing enough candles to populate a small island because *"They were on sale"* and *"We need this light because your father took ours"*, leaving us hungry for two days? Or maybe when she slept through five phone calls from school attempting to inform her that I'd fainted from said hunger and asking if she'd like to pick her daughter up?

Whatever moment it was – whatever day, minute or second – there came a point where I stopped being her only child and became a parent instead.

But still, I remind myself, whatever Hooyo is, at least she stuck around. At least she didn't leave me and go running to the motherland, sniffing for more money.

Hooyo stands in the doorway, looking smaller than ever. Hollow, like everything inside of her has been scooped out. The dark bags under her eyes bring a misery to her face that makes me want to look away and the once rich, brown complexion of her skin has become ashen. Hooyo's limp hair is laced with grey. She looks as though she has aged a century in the five years since Aabo left.

"Hooyo?" I ask again, trying to tread delicately. "You okay?"

She opens her mouth and I hold my breath.

"Your dad is coming home, Safiya," she whispers, looking down at her feet.

I pull my headphones all the way off to make sure I'm hearing her right. "Aabo is coming home?"

Already my ears are flooded with the rhythmic thump of blood. The chaos of fear and love and hatred.

Hooyo nods but doesn't look up.

I open my mouth to ask the burning questions, but it's hard to sift through the flood in my brain.

*Why is he coming back?*

*Is he back for good?*

*Is he coming to see us?*

Aabo is a topic of conversation that has been too heavy for Hooyo to bear since he left. His name is not uttered in this house. His existence is acknowledged with no words. His life with us is buried in storage boxes in the spare room, while he breathes and lives six thousand miles away.

But even though it might be too much for Hooyo to bear, today I need more. I need to know if what she's saying is really true.

"He's coming back," Hooyo continues before I have a chance to ask anything. Her voice sounds almost completely wilted. "But not for us."

I feel my face knitting itself into a picture of confusion. "What do you mean?"

"He's returning with his new family from back home apparently..." Hooyo replies, a note of hesitation in her voice. She turns away from me. "A shiny new wife and kids."

Then, without another word, she stalks into her bedroom.

I stand there, dumbfounded, waiting for her to come back out; to give me something *more*. To fill in the gaps – to answer the wide, gaping questions in the crater left behind by her explosion.

But when the door doesn't open again, the truth of her words settles like an anchor.

My dad...coming back with a new family.

I slam my own door then, flinging my headphones on my bed.

My hands tremble, and within moments they're shaking violently like someone has possessed my limbs. I slide down the wall, needing to be close to the ground. I'm panting even though I have barely moved, like I'm running a marathon sitting down.

I have gained and lost Aabo again in the space of seconds. The hiccuping starts first, strangely, before the sobbing does. But the hot tears must do something to me because, before I realize it, I'm on my feet again, overwhelmed with wild, choking fury, and I stumble over to my chest of drawers and then my wardrobe, before diving underneath my bed, disturbing the ecosystem of lost and hoarded items, batting away the dust that flies in my face.

Not there.

My eyes scan the mess of my room, trying to find what I need. Somehow, it's all I can think of right now.

I find the binoculars under the third pile of clothes in the corner of the room and pull my arm back to throw them against the window.

I want it to break. I want everything to break the same way Aabo broke us.

# SAFIYA

My phone buzzes later. I ignore it. It's Muna probably, or Yusuf, but I'm not in the mood to speak to anyone.

About ten minutes later, a *crack* startles me. I lift my head from the pillow, wondering if I imagined it, when it comes again from the direction of the window.

For a second, I panic about whether throwing the binoculars did more damage than I anticipated. *What if I actually broke the window?* Maybe there was a delayed reaction and, thanks to the sweltering July heat, the window has given way. And if the window really *is* broken, I know it won't ever get fixed; the landlord won't pay for it and Hooyo certainly can't afford to.

When I examine the glass though, there is only a winding hairline fracture, and no evidence of the kind of damage that would break the bank. I sigh with gratitude, turning back to throw myself face first onto the mattress…when the sound comes again.

"Oi!"

Before the third *crack*, I realize what it is and quickly throw on my hijab. The window creaks as I open it and, sure enough, Muna and Yusuf are standing in my back garden, arms poised to throw more stones. Crossing my arms on the windowsill, I give them both a stern look.

"Do you two realize this basically amounts to property damage?"

Muna grins, letting her stones scatter to the grass. "I think ridding this house of you makes the property better, so where's the damage?"

"Ha ha," I reply drily. "Very funny. What do you want?"

At that, Muna widens her eyes. She makes to grab the stones still sitting in Yusuf's hands, but he creates a fist before she succeeds.

"Safiya, stop stirring shit." His gaze doesn't waver on mine, and even though there are two storeys between us, I swear I can still see the amber flecks in his eyes behind his glasses. "We said we'd go to King Eddy's, right? It's almost half-past five so…"

The unfinished sentence hangs between all three of us.

"I'm not feeling well," I lie.

"I smell BS," Muna replies, narrowing her eyes.

"Well, I smell you," I say childishly, sticking my tongue out at her, and then the both of us fall into a tongue-wagging fight. Yusuf unfurls his fist, accepting that the immediate stone danger has passed.

"Fine!" I huff. There's no way the two of them are going to let this go. "Just give me a few minutes, I'll meet you downstairs."

Once I've changed into a park-appropriate outfit, I grab my phone and step out of my room. I hesitate on the threshold, wondering if there is anything to gain from seeing Hooyo

17

before I leave, but I think better of it. What's the point? If the news of Aabo today has left me spiralling, I can only imagine what it's done to Hooyo. And, as awful as it sounds, I don't know if I can bear her pain along with mine right now.

In the last five years since my dad left, I have taken the time to build my defences. Sky-high walls, moats, barbed enclosures – anything and everything to stop myself from being hurt, from being blindsided like I was all those years ago. And if it all came undone in a single breath, then how good was any of it? If I can't keep a handle on myself, how can I expect to stop Hooyo from falling apart any more than she already has?

My fingers curl around her bedroom door handle but, when I hear the quiet hiccuping, the quivering breaths, I let go and leave without looking back.

Outside, Muna sits on the low brick wall between our houses, donning a wide-brimmed straw hat and sunglasses, like she's in the middle of a photoshoot somewhere tropical. I give her a look before Yusuf rings the bell on his bike, drawing my attention.

"Don't ask," he warns. "You'll get an earful about the sun and tan lines and the eternal hijabi struggle otherwise."

Duly noted.

Muna leaps from the wall, bubbling with excitement. She looks between Yusuf and me, clasping her hands to her chest. "I would like to take a moment to formally announce the beginning of summer." She grins, looping her arm through mine and guiding us both through the iron gate outside my house. "Our final summer as high schoolers awaits! King Eddy's today and for always." She clears her throat. "Even if some people are hell-bent on ruining tradition."

I purse my lips in disagreement.

"What?" Muna narrows her eyes.

"Well, how can it be our final high-school summer? We've still got next year, after exams."

"No, that doesn't count," she argues, as we make our way down the road. Yusuf sets off ahead of us on his bike to the shops. "We'll be college students that summer, since we'll have officially finished with Northwell High."

"Hmmm…not until we get our results that August. *Officially*, we'll still be part of Northwell High until then."

Muna applies pressure to my elbow, gradually increasing it until the discomfort is too much to bear.

"Fine! It's our last summer, weirdo," I mumble, rubbing my elbow. I don't know why I even try to get in between Muna and her traditions in the first place. "You win."

She smiles. "Glad you're seeing things from the right point of view."

We walk in silence for a little while. We're not far from the newsagent's now. I see Yusuf's bike leaning against the shop window.

Muna tugs on my arm. She drops her sunglasses to perch lower on the bridge of her nose, locking eyes with me above the rim.

I don't know how the words line up in my mouth but, somehow, they're there without me having to look for them.

"He's coming back," I say in a rush. "My dad, I mean. From Somalia."

She whistles under her breath.

"With a new wife and kids."

Muna whips her sunglasses off completely then, stopping us in the middle of the road. Her mouth hangs open.

"And before you ask me whether I knew about any of this, or how many kids he has, or when he's coming back, let me just say that I have no idea." I sigh with the relief of getting this off my chest. "Hooyo only told me an hour ago."

"You mean she just found out today too?"

I scoff without meaning to. "Well, yeah, of course. There's no way Hooyo could've kept this from me."

"Unbelievable…" Muna shakes her head. "Do you know anything else? Like is he moving back round here?"

"I have no idea. I mean, his shops are here…" I bite the inside of my lip, welcoming the sting. "If he moves back to live in Northwell then…that would not be good."

We continue our stroll once more. Muna hums under her breath, running a hand along the rim of her hat, as if searching for her next question there.

"Do you think he's going to come and see you?"

I falter, almost tripping on a protruding concrete slab, and we stop again. "I…don't know."

Would Aabo come and see us? See me? When he left, life imploded in a way that left little room for reconciliation. He spent every weekend of that first year attempting to contact us, only to be met with radio silence. I didn't even bother

20

entertaining the idea of closure, because I knew simply picking up the phone would be a betrayal in Hooyo's eyes. Since then, he's never reached out. I can't imagine he would want to try again now, but then I never imagined he would be moving back here with another family.

We stare at each other until a bell chimes. Yusuf waves at us from where he's waiting outside the shop, holding an ice cream in the air like a beacon.

Muna collects herself, sliding her shades back on. "Safiya, I am flabbergasted."

I grimace. "That's definitely the word of the day." We begin walking again. "Also, please don't say anything about this to Yusuf. I don't want him…" I pause, wondering what it is that I'm trying to say. Yusuf and I aren't anything to each other, not really, but I still find myself stumbling over my words whenever I mention him. "I don't want anyone else to know. Including him. Not yet anyway."

"My lips are sealed," Muna says, miming the motion. "I know I'm a big mouth, but I won't say anything until you're ready, promise."

When we reach the newsagent's, Yusuf hands me an ice cream, leaving only one more. He gives Muna a pointed look and she kisses her teeth, stomping inside to buy her own.

At King Eddy's Park, we locate our shared cast-iron bench. The three of us sitting on it at the beginning of summer is Muna's ultimate tradition. Our own version of an Olympics opening ceremony. The bench is warm from the evening sun and familiarly uncomfortable. We sit there, side by side, enjoying our melting ice cream, and Yusuf asks me if I've brought my binoculars – the ones I bring each year, without fail – but I hesitate.

Muna must sense that something is wrong, because she artfully diverts focus as a bird flies overhead.

"Look, a blue tit!" she screeches, knowing full well it's not a blue tit but sticking with our other tradition of painting all birds with the same, silly brush.

The two of them double over, laughing, and I can't help joining in. It's the kind of laughter that's super painful and makes you feel it will be impossible to breathe again and, for a beautiful, blissful second, I forget everything else.

But then somewhere between the giggles I am pulled back into my room, with Hooyo telling me that Aabo is returning home with a brand-new family. I look to Muna and Yusuf, grateful to see them crying too, even if it's with laughter, because it hides the very real and sudden tears that I'm terrified now might never stop.

# HALIMA

## MOGADISHU, SOMALIA

The scent of a newly lit coal fire floats to reach me. I inhale the smoke deeply, wanting the throat-scratching smell to bury itself in my mind. Where I am going, there will be no coal fires.

The thought hurts my stomach, forcing me to lean against the sun-warmed wall behind. Around me, the school courtyard is teeming with kids trying to locate their friends, singing songs or making plans for the evening. The blue and yellow of their uniforms is clear one minute and then blurry the next. I wipe my eyes with the back of my hand, startling when a hand touches my shoulder.

"*Halima, maxaa u oroday?*" Khadija asks, concern heavy in her voice. "*You ran so fast I thought you'd already left school.*"

Her jilbaab billows in the dry wind, making her look like a frilled-neck lizard. I laugh, sadness forgotten for just a moment, and lift my hands to settle the material for her. She smiles, pivoting so she can lean against the wall with me.

Beyond the courtyard, the sprawling savanna looks like a still-life picture. From this distance, it is almost impossible to see the rustling leaves of baobab trees or the swaying grass, but I close my eyes and try to imagine those details so that

I can commit this to memory too.

Khadija touches my shoulder. *"Are you ready?"*

Behind closed eyelids, I sense the blurring again. *I am not ready,* I want to shout. *I will never, ever be ready to leave home.*

She must hear my thoughts because she gives me a squeeze and says that we can stay here for as long as I need. Until the Head, Mr Abdullah, kicks us out, or a hyena jumps over the fence at nightfall to find its dinner.

I know Khadija is trying to make me laugh, to find some light in this moment that feels so very, very dark, and I love her for trying, I do, but I also want to feel like the world is crashing down and burning around me, because it is. My whole world is being stolen from me, and soon I will have to go home to the people who are responsible for all of it.

Just then, Mr Abdullah steps out of his office on the other side of the compound. I peel myself off the wall.

Khadija and I walk together along the dirt road to town. She loops her arm through mine and we walk side by side, the sun beating down on our backs like it has every afternoon before this one. I close my eyes, breathing in this moment and hoping there is enough space in my head for another memory.


Khadija and I part ways at the crossroads. She promises that she will come to my house tomorrow at the crack of dawn to see me and my family off, despite my protests. She shakes her head every time I open my mouth, turning around to wave goodbye over her shoulder and grinning like she has already won. We have known each other for nearly a decade but now, on the eve of my departure, it feels as though we have only just met and been robbed of more time.

*Can a friendship separated by thousands of miles truly survive?* I wonder – and fervently hope.

*Or does time and space force it to become something else, something different?*

Though my heart squeezes with these worries, I try to abandon them for now and turn my attention to the other painful mission I must attend to today.

I turn down the road, sidestepping a cart. A man nearby rings a bell, shouting about his wares. He is selling everything from ripe mangoes to garlic and bananas. The colours gleam strikingly under the roof of his little hut and, when he makes eye contact with me, he rings the bell again and fans a hand over his produce as if it is only for me.

I make my way over, hands fumbling in my pocket for some money. When I reach him, he presents me with a luscious mango, holding it up to my yellow uniform.

*"Yellow for yellow,"* he says with a gappy smile. *"I have never seen such a perfect match!"*

*"I'll take one, please, Adeer,"* I say, happy with the colour theme. *"How much?"*

His face takes on an expression of indignation. *"If a seller gives, it's because he wants to. Not everything is a sale."*

He hands me the mango and shoos me away before I can say anything else. A line is beginning to form behind me, so I have no choice but to leave, taking the gift with me.

I wonder whether I will find strangers in England to be so kind, whether I will find this same openness and camaraderie wherever I go. I have wrestled with thoughts like this in the last few months. They only ever lead to an ache in my chest that feels like it will sit there for ever.

The walk gives me time to sift through the memories that I have boxed away in my mind in preparation for tomorrow; the day that I leave, along with my family, and take a flight to a country that is worlds away from the only one I have ever known.

My mind slowly flips through the treasure I have accumulated.

Warm, sunny mornings. Achingly hot afternoons. Breezy evenings in a city that never takes a single breath. The smell of dhuxul, the heavy presence of that throat-scratching charcoal floating through my house, the streets, marking the beginnings of a breakfast, lunch or dinner. The echoes of the adhaan that linger in the streets during prayer times, forcing you to stop and close your eyes, to step outside the world for a second. The bustling and energetic markets that never feel big enough to hold everyone, to contain the vibrancy of the hagglers, the laughter, the jokes shared between friends and strangers.

I cycle through my treasure again and again, until I find myself standing at the house of the man I have avoided for weeks since I found out I was leaving. My own home, a towering villa on the next road over, peeks above the corrugated metal roof of Abti Haroon's house, but I know I cannot escape there. I have one final agonizing goodbye to make.

I sigh, pocketing the mango, and push open the weathered door to the house. The sound of the neighbour kids shrieking and playing football, kicking up a dust storm in their innocent afternoon fun, follows me inside.

Abti Haroon is sitting in the corner of the small, square house, on his favourite rocking chair. His eyes are closed and his head leans back against a cushion. For a second, I think he might be sleeping, that maybe this is the excuse I need to slip away and disappear, create a false memory of a goodbye instead of experiencing the real thing, but then his eyes snap open. He picks up the cane next to him, sliding it across the floor.

"*Who is that?*" he asks in a sleep-lined voice. "*Maymuna, is that you? Is it dinner time already?*"

I announce my presence in the corner of the room by dragging a gember across to sit in front of him.

"*Ahhh,*" Abti Haroon says, leaning back in his chair again. "*Good to see you, Halima.*" He coughs abruptly, clutching his chest. "*Even if it is one day before you depart,*" he adds wryly.

I drop my bag to the floor, taking a moment to assess Abti. His breathing seems shallow, and he looks frailer than I remember him. He coughs again, lifting a cloth from his lap and holding it to his lips. There is a smear of red when he removes it.

"*Abti,*" I cry, alarmed, leaping to do something. But what is one to do when blood is seen without warning?

He sits forward again, coughing. More blood splatters onto the cloth.

"*Halima.*" He calls me but I am already grabbing a glass to

27

pour some water from the jug at the back of the room. "*Halima,*" he says again, voice not only sounding sleepy this time, but weary. I hurry over and hand him the glass with shaking hands.

"*Abti,*" I whisper, trying to remain calm. "*Are you sick? Do you need me to get a doctor?*"

Abti grabs his cane and smacks it against the gember, indicating for me to sit down. I oblige and wait.

He drinks a swig of water, rinsing his mouth, before spitting into a bucket behind him. Then he finishes off the rest of the water in the cup. I offer to get him some more but Abti refuses.

He leans back in his chair and wipes his mouth with the clean edge of the cloth. "*So, Halima, have you been kidnapped lately?*" Abti enquires conversationally when he appears to have recovered.

I do a double take. From coughing blood to kidnap? Is Abti Haroon delirious?

"*No,*" I stammer. "*Not kidnapped—*"

"*Then where have you been? You are leaving for England tomorrow and I have not seen you in weeks. We have not been able to discuss poetry or school. Have you come to detest me?*"

"*Abti, no!*" I fumble again, uncomfortable with the interrogation. "*I – I could never, there's no way—*"

"*Well, that is a relief then.*" Abti Haroon chuckles. "*For an old man, that is a relief.*"

The familiar pricking and blurring of my eyes returns and then, without any warning, I am sobbing and trying to find an emotional foothold to grab onto that will let me control this wave, but I can't. Abti leans forward, producing a clean cloth, and hands it to me.

When the tears and hiccups subside, Abti and I sit in silence.

"*I want to thank you,*" I say after a while, when I am grounded. "*For everything you have done for me, especially since Aabo died. I won't ever forget you. I won't forget the poetry you've taught me, the Qur'an we've read together. All of it is locked away in my memory. And I'll come back to see you, Abti, of course, whenever Hooyo and her husband let me. I'll save money, I'll do whatever I need to do to come back and visit.*" I take a breath. "*I promise.*"

He laughs warmly, clutching his chest again when another coughing fit sets in. This time, he accepts my offer of a second glass of water.

"*Is that all?*" Abti Haroon asks when he finishes the drink, the corner of his mouth lifting. "*Or do you have more to unleash on my ears?*"

"*Yes,*" I reply, taking in a deep breath for round two. "*Thank you for listening to me and guiding me, Abti. Thank you for paying for my schooling when my parents didn't have much to their name.*"

I hesitate for a moment, wondering just how far a mother's intuition runs. Does Hooyo have eyes in these walls, ears on this ground? I press on, regardless. I do not know when I might see Abti Haroon again and I have to tell him just how deeply my gratitude goes.

"*Thank you for your generosity, your kindness. I am more grateful than you can imagine that Aabo befriended you. That you supported us financially for all those years after he passed away, before Hooyo remarried.*

"*Hooyo told me never to say anything about it. That you wanted to pay for my schooling anonymously but…I just had to say it now, before I leave, because—*"

Abti Haroon clears his throat, stopping me mid-sentence. "Halima, *I did not pay for anything*," he replies. "*Look around, my dear. Does this look like a rich man's castle to you?*"

I frown, taking in the four walls of this room, this house, that I know so well.

"*But Hooyo said you liked to live frugally…she said that you didn't like anyone to think you had more than them.*"

Abti Haroon shakes his head but doesn't try to refute my claims again. He knows that I recognize his truth because he has never lied to me, which is why what he says next steals the breath from my lungs.

"*I am dying, Halima,*" he says matter-of-factly, sitting up as another coughing fit takes hold. "*I will surely have God's mercy if I live to see another year, so I am glad that you have come to see me before you leave.*" He leans his head against the back of the chair, closing his eyes as exhaustion takes over. "*I cannot tell you just how glad I am, my dear, dear child.*"

He sighs heavily before falling into the songs of his youth, and his low, tired voice carries, drowning out the shrieks of children playing outside.

# SAFIYA

They're arriving today, my dad's new family.

That's according to the Somali grapevine anyway, which I'm confident I can trust in the same manner I trust most Wikipedia entries for homework.

In only a few short hours, my deadbeat dad, the evil stepmother and their two nameless spawns will be here, in Northwell, to disrupt the house of cards that is my and Hooyo's life.

I stand at the window, running my hand along the narrow, winding crack. I don't know why, or what I'm waiting for exactly. It's not like I'll be able to see them arrive, but, even knowing this, I'm still rooted to the spot.

I dig a nail into the narrow fissure in the glass, wanting to widen it. If I can focus on this for a few seconds then maybe the other bad thought in my head will disappear. The one that says none of this would be happening if my dad didn't exist in the first place. I pointedly ignore the fact that him not existing also means I wouldn't either.

I stop running my hand along the window and get up to find Hooyo. Today isn't about me. Today is about her and making sure she gets through it in one piece.

A familiar, but bitter and resentful voice speaks in my mind. A voice I know well.

*Every day is always about her.*

I silence it.

In the evening, I find Hooyo in the living room with a mug in her hands. The TV is off and she's sitting on the sofa with her back to the window and a vacant look in her eyes. Just staring into space, lost in some hellhole. One I've repeatedly tried, and failed, to save her from.

I sit down next to her. I don't bother waiting for her to acknowledge me. There's a ninety-nine per cent chance she doesn't even know I've walked into the room.

Seeing Hooyo like this is giving me flashbacks to some of her worst moments since Aabo left. I still remember the day he walked out the door, a week after my tenth birthday. Not because it was the last time that I saw his face before he deserted us, but because of the look on Hooyo's. As if she had lost the only thing sustaining her. She'd fallen against the banister as the door slammed shut, face contorted in agony, like the skin had been ripped off her bones.

It took a lot to pull Hooyo out of the misery she drowned herself in after that but, eventually, it paid off. All the house chores I took on, the weekly hair washes Hooyo reluctantly allowed me to do for her, the countless welfare forms I filled in, the grocery shopping, the lies I told her friends and our neighbours... It took everything I had to juggle these things, to steer us in the right direction and keep us afloat, but we got through it.

When Hooyo's Okay Days began to balance out her Bad Days, it felt like we had reached the summit of a mountain.

I would say the three months leading up to this summer had been the best I could remember since Aabo left. The tragic thing was that it took only *one* day to undo all of that.

I have since learned that there are words to describe Hooyo's unravelling – ones like *severe depression* – but people like us don't believe in that. At least, we're not supposed to.

I still wonder what it was about Aabo's leaving that pushed her to such despair. Yes, he left and yes, he blindsided us, but Hooyo didn't just grieve. She lost herself and became entirely untethered in the process. Maybe I'll never understand, even though I have exhausted myself on so many nights trying to make sense of it. There is one question I always seem to circle back to though: was there more to my parents' marriage than they showed me? Because for ten years, all I saw were two people devoted to each other and their family. A mum and dad who loved their kid. But if there is one thing I understand now as the inadvertent third parent, it is that the truth is always hidden behind closed doors – and perhaps there are a few closed doors in my memory too.

I peer over Hooyo's arm to look into her cup. It's empty.

"Hey, Mama," I say gently, reaching to slide it out of her hands. "Do you want some shaah? I can make that chamomile one you like."

Hooyo looks at me, a little surprised. She folds her legs on the sofa, pressing the cup into my outstretched hands.

"Oh, Safiya. That would be nice. Thank you."

I paint a smile on my face. "No worries. I'll be right back."

Hooyo smiles thinly in response and goes back to staring at nothing. I sigh, standing from the sofa. When I'm halfway to the kitchen, Hooyo calls.

"Safiya?"

I turn around so quickly I'm certain of whiplash. "Yeah, Hooyo?"

Hooyo calling me, saying *Safiya*, noticing me, is something I have learned not to take for granted. I'm grateful when she sees me, even for those brief moments, because it reminds me that I'm not invisible. That I am her daughter and she is my mother. That we exist to each other in this house, at least sometimes.

"Can you use the chamomile tea in the cupboard? You know the blue box, the one I like?"

I let out the breath that had been clamouring in my chest, hopeful. Hooyo doesn't hear me, never hears me – even when I'm right there in front of her, offering a cup of tea – and I need to truly accept that. "Sure, Hooyo," I reply. "I'll use the one you like."

As I pop the kettle on, my phone pings with a text from Muna. She only lives next door and often hops over the low brick wall between our houses if she has something she really needs to tell me. Usually, it's about a piece she's not sure about running in her anonymous blog, Hexpose, or something

34

completely trivial like which colour hijab matches a "banging" outfit she's put together. There was even one time she hopped over, thumped on the door about ten times and said, "Wallahi, it's bare serious this time, Safiya, I'm not even joking." When I'd got her inside and sat her down, she sighed loudly and said that she couldn't find her favourite eyeliner in Boots.

Today though, I know even before reading her message that Muna's not texting about any of that.

## THREE MUSKETEERS

Muna: Stay strong today boo – you and ur mum got this
And I'm here today if you need anything. Even if it's just to beat up your dad lmao
U know my freakish strength gotta be used if we wanna sustain it
And I ain't above being a criminal xxx

I find myself laughing when I imagine Muna's tiny frame holding its own against my six-foot-tall dad. I start typing out my reply as the kettle reaches the end of its boiling.

LOL ur an absolute joker Mun—

I pause, realizing that we're having this conversation in the wrong chat. That she's messaged in the *Three Musketeers* instead of the *Two Musketeers*.

*Why can't this girl spend two seconds checking the group name before she sends her texts?* I groan.

This is the fifth time it's happened, but I also have myself to blame for giving our private chat a confusing name.

## TWO MUSKETEERS

Safiya: Muna!!! Delete the messages in 3M.
I feel weird talking to Yusuf about any of this stuff man
which is why I haven't told him yet idiot
U were meant to text in this one

Her reply comes a few seconds later.

Muna: Oops my bad
but can you just tell Yusuf ALREADY??
& also –
when are u two gonna stop putting me in the middle of
your weirdness
Like I'm not saying I WANT my cousin and best friend to
be a thing but

I can see she's still typing, which means she is not deleting from the other chat.

Safiya: Muna DELETE NOW

Typing…
Another ping.

Yusuf pops up in the Three Musketeers group chat.

Yusuf: Yooo Saf
YOUR DAD IS COMING BACK?!?!
WTF

I look over to the kettle, tempted to drop my phone in there in a bid to escape both chats.

Muna: So...
my bad
lol

Well, at least Muna's finally texting in the right group.

Safiya: Ngl, I'm ready to block ur ass sis

The rest of the evening is uneventful. Hooyo continues to sit on the sofa in the same position, staring into space, but she picks up the remote after some time. She flicks through several channels before stopping on a teleshopping one. I didn't even know they still existed.

I balance a sudoku workbook on my lap, tapping my foot against the coffee table. There are probably a million other things I could be doing but I wouldn't be able to concentrate on any of them today.

Muna's voice rings in the back of my mind too.

*Do you think he's going to come see you?*

I really don't want to think about it, but I can't seem to help it.

I wonder whether Hooyo's forgotten about the fact that Aabo is coming back with his new family today. Maybe the days have all blurred into each other for her. Maybe today is the same as yesterday and the same as tomorrow as well. I hope that's true, because if this is not already rock bottom...I don't know what is.

A part of me worries about whether she can keep it together for her job interview next week – the first she's ever been invited to and the first job I thought she could hold down.

We'd put her name on the list at the Jobcentre for a cleaning job a month ago, just before the news of Aabo hit. I remember how excited she'd been too. To clean toilets, of all things. But the way her shoulders had set in pride and her face in determination when we applied, as if she had already gotten the job, was enough to keep me smiling for days.

That smile was long gone by the time we got the interview email a couple of weeks ago.

I glance over at her. She looks sunken and empty, a bone with the marrow sucked out.

Would she have still looked like this if she'd accepted Aabo's offer of money when he left? If she hadn't spat on his shoes and said, *I'd rather people shit on my grave than take your dirty money, Halane*, and actually *had* taken the monthly stipend he'd offered us?

Five years ago, standing at the door with the sun dipping

below his shoulders, Aabo had looked from his shoes, to Hooyo, and then finally to me. I knew he wanted me to step in and maybe plead with Hooyo, beg her to play nice, at least for me, their only daughter. But seeing him standing there in our hallway – the space where I'd always kiss him goodbye before work or greet him with gossip from school, the space where he'd gifted me a set of binoculars that I treasured more than anything else – I didn't recognize him any more.

And when I looked to Hooyo and saw her angry and resolute, I knew there would be no pleading. Mostly because I didn't want to. I shuffled over to stand behind her, wrapping my arms around her waist and burying my head so I could no longer see Aabo. It was only seconds later, when the door shut behind him, that Hooyo came undone.

After that, money was tight. Since Aabo had been the one sustaining us financially, we lost almost everything overnight.

Our barely-there finances became a chokehold around our stomachs and a war between heating and electricity, but it helped me to believe we were poor on principle. If everyone in the world couldn't be well off, why should we? I'm not going to lie though, it is getting harder to convince myself of that these days.

But I am always grateful for the no-questions-asked kindness of some people in our community. Like when Muna's mum offers meals, at least twice a week, because she's just "made too much". Or when Adeer Ali lets me run up a tab in his shop because he knows how desperately we need it.

I am grateful that their kindness never feels like pity,

a bargaining chip, or a way to dig further into the mess of my family.

I'm not quite sure how we would have ever survived without it.

A knock on the door interrupts my thoughts and Hooyo-gazing. It's quiet, a little hesitant.

Hooyo doesn't stir, only carries on watching a show that I know she's not really watching.

"Someone knocked, Hooyo," I say anyway, closing my unmarked sudoku workbook. "It's probably just Muna. I'll be back in a sec."

I head to the door, hand going straight for the handle, stepping out of the way to let her wade into the house. Usually, by the time she's taken three steps inside, she's halfway through some story.

That doesn't happen today though. There is only a very uncharacteristic non-Muna silence.

I peer around the door.

But it's not Muna there. It's my dad.

# SAFIYA

My heart is no longer following a normal rhythm. There are skipped beats, fast beats, double beats. Blood anarchy.

I feel an urge to put a hand against my chest because I am pretty sure it's about to cleave open, but I resist. I keep my hands locked in position by my sides, praying they don't give anything away.

Aabo stands with one hand against the door frame, the evening sun dipping beneath his shoulders like it did five years ago. To anyone passing by, his posture probably seems casual.

But Aabo's fingers are gripping the doorway. His back is rigid and his shoulders are tense. He doesn't look like a man without a care in the world. He looks like a man trying not to buckle under the weight of whatever he's carrying with him. Guilt, I hope. Along with a healthy dose of regret.

"Safiya," Aabo says softly. His voice cracks and he clears his throat awkwardly. "You don't know how happy I am to see you."

*You can do this, Safiya. Don't let him get to you.*

Aabo's hand gravitates towards me, but seeing my expression, he swiftly lets it drop. Behind him, the cars drive along the one-way road like clockwork, oblivious to how time has seemed to pause on my doorstep.

Aabo gazes at me. He's wearing a pressed white shirt and smart trousers, the same get-up I remember he always wore, day in, day out.

"I've missed you, Safiya," Aabo says, even more softly. He doesn't flinch under my glare. "More than I could ever express... I have dreamed of reuniting with you for so long that it began to feel impossible. But we are here now. I am here now."

I put my hands in the pockets of my hoodie and rock on my feet, trying to ground myself.

He's missed me.

Three easy words. Three weightless words.

*For how long?* I want to ask.

*You called every week for a year,* I want to say. *Then you gave up.*

*Why did you give up?* I want to scream.

"How is your mother?" he asks, this time looking away. "Is she okay?"

It's as though this question lights a fire in me, something that leaves a trail of burning ash where my curiosity had just been.

I keep my voice low, steady. I pause with each word, letting them sink into his skull.

"Don't you dare mention Hooyo again. Keep her name out of your mouth."

And then I slam the door shut in his face.

\* \* \*

When I go back to the living room, Hooyo has gone. I search the kitchen, but she isn't there either. I find her upstairs, lying in bed with the curtains drawn. The mug is on the floor by the bedside table, shattered. I grab a dustpan and brush and clean the shards before they have a chance to hurt anyone.

That night, I lie in bed at the mercy of thoughts hell-bent on not letting me get any sleep. Flipping over for the tenth time, I try to wait them out. When that doesn't work, I get up, turn on the lamp and sit by the window instead, tracing a finger along the winding break in the glass, watching the raindrops land. Some coalesce, growing into bigger drops; one finds its way directly onto the fissure, following it along the curving path to the end.

I shut my eyes, remembering the blinding fit of rage that cracked this window and left the pair of binoculars at my feet. Unbroken, intact. How that moment created the perfect portrait of our family. Aabo: the pair of binoculars able to inflict damage yet remain whole, while Hooyo and I are the glass: fractured but not completely shattered either.

My phone pings with the fifth message from Muna and the third from Yusuf in the last hour alone. They're worried about me, though they normally try their best to hide it. I shoot them both a quick reply before silencing my phone. Muna and Yusuf know, better than anyone, that there are times I can't bring myself to speak about my ugly family history.

I switch off the lamp and get into bed again, rolling the duvet tightly around me.

It's on nights like these, on Hooyo's Bad Days, when I try to understand whether she still loves Aabo or if all her sadness is because she's not done recovering from a years-long heartbreak. I've tried to figure out which it is, but there's no way to tell and there's no way I could ever ask. But, if she still loves him, I wish I could ask why someone as heartless as him deserves her love. And if it was heartbreak, I would ask why my love isn't enough to hold her together – because since Aabo left, I've always been there, holding her hand and drying her tears, picking up the broken pieces of her heart, sometimes even cutting myself on their jagged edges.

I'd just about managed to put it back together, pieces held in place with a little prayer and a glimmer of hope, but suddenly all my hard work has been undone. The pieces are on the floor again, in their hundreds and millions, waiting to be collected once more with energy I'm not sure I have.

And if I'm being completely honest, right now, I'm worried about whether my own heart can hold out too.

Aabo returning with a new family feels like a nail in the coffin of whatever future relationship part of me had unwittingly hoped for. Because maybe somewhere behind the hidden doors of my heart I did hope to get my dad back one day. But now it seems he didn't just leave us for money. He left us to find happiness and he found it elsewhere.

# HALIMA

We walk through checkpoint after checkpoint in this London airport. People ask us questions. A lot of them. I don't always know what they are asking but you can tell what a question is in any language. The words glance off each other differently.

My mother's husband breezes through the checkpoints effortlessly. When they demand, he dazzles with papers. When they prod, he impresses with a smile, a few choice words in this language of theirs, a nod. I try to break apart this smile into its constituent parts because a smile is never just a smile.

His is cunning, impatient, mildly insulted, but I'm sure the people guarding these checkpoints don't see that. I catch my youngest brother's face on one of the papers he shuffles, mine on the next. A part of me wants to leap over everyone, grab my face and rip it up before it's scanned into their system. Before I become part of this place, even if it's just in code.

But too late. The red light dances across my paper face before my arm can even leave my side.

I notice the guards here don't have guns, only papers and computer screens.

Strange.

I've only ever seen people like this with guns strapped across their backs.

Disappointingly, we pass through the checkpoints without incident. Hooyo is beaming and staring into her husband's eyes as if she's found something in them that she has never seen before. She does not even pay mind to her boys, who run around like they're chasing after camels in the countryside.

I call out to them.

*"Kamal, Abu Bakr, waxaas joojiya. You're not at grandfather's home,"* I remind them. *"These are not the legs of goats and sheep you're running around. These are people."*

*"Halima, maku maqli karo,"* Abu Bakr sings, which is a lie because, if he really couldn't hear me, he wouldn't be saying so.

We near the exit of the airport. Even though I'm desperate to leave this bustling place, I am also aware this is the closest I will be to the home I left and the friends I have abandoned. Once I step out of this building, I will get further and further away from the planes that could take me back to Yaaqshid, to Khadija and Abti Haroon. I feel a pit begin to open in my stomach when I realize that, and my steps slow. The air that I breathe in finds its way into my stomach pit, bypassing my lungs completely.

~~I can't breathe.~~

~~I don't want to be here.~~

~~I have to go home.~~

Hooyo is still smiling for some reason. I try imagining that

I'm looking at her upside down and convince myself she is frowning.

We step out into a summer day, but the heat feels like a sham, as if someone is trying too hard to simulate a real summer.

My mother's husband leads us to a minivan. He waves at a man standing outside it and runs ahead to greet him. Hooyo looks a little lost without her husband by her side now, but I don't move to take his place. There is no space for me next to her any more, not like there used to be.

Thankfully, the boys have stopped running around in circles, though they are still oblivious to the groups of people they cut through as they make a beeline for their father. I stare at their bobbing heads, trying to understand for the hundredth time how we are related.

Biologically, I know they are my half-brothers since we share the same mother, but knowing that their other half comes from the man who single-handedly ruined my entire life…it's enough to make me want to disown my sisterhood to these boys sometimes.

They break their formation when they reach the minivan. I'm a little behind and slow down some more. Hooyo reaches the van next. She loads the boys in while her husband catches up with the driver. She doesn't look back at me.

As I near them, my heart quickens, thudding against my chest as if wanting to escape just as badly as I do. The box of my memories shakes in the corner of my mind, and I open it to calm myself, shifting the focus from my steps hitting the concrete to thoughts of home instead.

To the Xamar Weyne market where I spent so much of my youth running around stalls or learning to sew. The scent of my grandparents' home in the countryside…how very different it was to the city air. The poems Abti Haroon would recite whenever I went by his house in the evenings. The way he'd bring the words to life simply sitting in the shade of his courtyard. How he'd recite them until I learned them off by heart because –

*Halima, a poem is not a poem unless it is treasured in the heart.*

Because –

*Halima, a poem can only save you in the dark if you've seen it in the light.*

And also, because –

*Halima, don't disrespect me. Learn these poems,* he'd say, laughing. *Or I'll beat you with this branch!*

I smile at my feet, quietly reciting the lines that come to me, and, for a moment, it almost feels as though I am back in Abti Haroon's courtyard, sitting on a gember, pulling the edges of the sun-beaten cowhide stretched over the seat.

Then I recall what he said when we shared our goodbyes. His coughing, the blood, a death warrant, and my heart almost rips from me completely.

I look up at Hooyo through the open door of the minivan as she buckles her sons in. We lock eyes. I don't know if she can read my resolve this far away, but I hope that she does.

*I am not staying here for long,* my eyes try to tell her. *I am going back home.*

# HALIMA

The drive from the airport is quiet. The boys watch through the window, wide-eyed. Of the two of them, Kamal is the closest. Abu Bakr eyes his seat enviously, but Kamal is too excited to notice.

Hooyo, too, is wide-eyed, sitting with her face pressed against the glass. She blinks slowly like she is afraid to miss another grey building in this suffocating place.

Though we are yet to see much of the city, everything so far looks…restrained. There are no bumps that rock the car to make you feel as if your brain has shifted. Cars follow each other diligently, the people walk on the concrete slabs made for them, and not a single person is standing by the roadside waiting to sell you deliciously ripe mangoes.

It feels unnatural, as if someone is controlling all these people and things with strings, but to Hooyo and the boys it must look like paradise, because their eyes never leave the landscape.

We drive along the highway, across bridges, past some greenery with a body of water peeking through, and then my mother's husband turns to us.

"*Wax yar aa noo dhiman,*" he says with a toothy smile. The boys let out a cheer, Abu Bakr's seat jealousy forgotten.

Kamal strains against his seat belt and asks exactly how long is left.

"*Shan daqiiqo maa noo dhiman, Aabo? Ama lix?*" he demands, swinging his legs at a dizzying pace.

"*About ten minutes,*" my mother's husband replies, before turning around to face the front.

Abu Bakr pulls Kamal's ear and says, "*I knew it was ten minutes all along.*"

Kamal flicks his ear in retaliation. "*Beenta jooji doqon-yahow.*"

"*I'm not lying,*" Abu Bakr retorts, screaming it again and again as Kamal laughs at his reddened ear.

Hooyo looks over to me then. It takes me a few seconds to realize she is looking *at* me, and not past me. She leans over to take my hand.

"*Nolol fiican aa na sugeyso, Halima.*" The spark in her eyes is like a living, breathing flame. It hurts to look at it directly. "*And our new life will be great. I'm going to make sure of it.*"

My mouth opens reflexively to disagree, but Hooyo flinches. Something about that move drains whatever fighting energy I had left in me.

I am tired, so tired, from all this travelling and the loss of my home, and while, ordinarily, I can withstand the pain of seeing my own mother flinch from my hurt, right now, I have nothing left to muster.

So, I nod and squeeze Hooyo's hand. "*It will be great, in shaa*

Allah," I say. "*This new life, yes, it will be good for us.*"

The lies feel like a noose around my neck. I seek quiet forgiveness from God and pray that the angels on my shoulders don't write down my sins.

"*I'm glad you understand, macaanto,*" she says. "*You see, sometimes you need to start fresh in a different place. A new place can change everything – fortunes, perspective, hope. Us moving here for your father's business will be the start of something new, God willing. For all of us. I'm certain of it.*"

I still have Hooyo's hand in my own – her right hand, adorned with gold rings on her second and third fingers. Gifts from her husband to make her look good, wealthy, the wife of a successful businessman, as he parades her now into his town.

I only let my skin touch the unadorned parts of her hand. I try to light that same spark in my eyes. I speak the same sin.

"*A fresh start is just what we needed, Hooyo. You're right.*"

But the subtext? The subtext is very different.

*Hooyo, a fresh start to me is a life without the man you decided to marry.*

*A life with just us.*

*Only us.*


We stop outside a plain house held up on either side by two other houses. It's like that all along the road too. House, house, house, with no space in between. It reminds me of the bodies in the markets back home on those busy mornings and afternoons. But at least, I think to myself, there is an end to those packed bodies. You are not stuck in a crowd for ever, unlike this house, which is stuck here, in the middle. For ever.

I stand to the side while my mother's husband unloads the car. Most of our things have already been delivered, so there are only a few suitcases to bring out. The driver helps with the last suitcase while my mother's husband tries to stop Kamal from climbing into the empty trunk.

Hooyo stands with her back to all of us. Her head moves up and down as she takes in the house, as if it's too large to see in one view. Her husband shuffles to stand beside her, giving Kamal a stern warning first. He lifts her hand, kissing each one of her fingers.

"*This is for you, Rahma.*" He pulls her closer. "*All for you… as it should have been long ago.*"

He says things like this often. He will speak about time as though he has been with us for much longer than the last five years, as if trying to insert himself into the part of our lives that never involved him. When I first heard him doing it, I'd roll my eyes and Hooyo would always snap and tell me to stop being disrespectful to my father. *Your husband,* I'd always correct her. *Not my father. My father died from tuberculosis when I was only five years old, and there is no man that will ever replace him.*

He turns around when he's done being romantic. "*And for all of you, of course!*" he shouts. "*Halima, my daughter.*"

I roll my eyes, glad that Hooyo has her back to me.

"*Kamal and Abu Bakr, my sons.*"

The boys squeal in delight. Abu Bakr looks a little light-headed from all the excitement and leans against my suitcase to right himself.

My mother's husband beams at me, not breaking his gaze. I don't break mine either.

For all his excitement, I give this thing less than a year.

A year for my mother to realize she's made a huge mistake letting us leave our home behind.

A year for Hooyo to recognize that this isn't the dream she thought it would be.

A year until this make-believe act falls apart.

I take comfort in the knowledge that I won't be around to see any of this happening. Even if I don't know how yet, I know I will be long gone by then.


The husband leads my mother into the house first. The boys hang a little behind, following in the same formation as they did at the airport – Abu Bakr, the oldest, first, followed by Kamal.

They don't race ahead, or jostle and shove each other in a bid to claim first touch of the house like they normally would. Even without being explicitly told, they know that their father will not be in a forgiving mood today. Still, I notice their slow legs straining. I imagine they won't last very long.

The husband's focus is only on Hooyo. He watches her as he pushes the door open, as she takes her first step into the hallway, as she stops to breathe in the scent of her new English home. He clutches her hand to his chest like he's a magnet for her skin and gold.

"*Halane*," my mother starts to say, shaking her head in disbelief. "*I can't believe this is ours.*" He beams at her. "*It's…it's so beautiful. Everything. All of it. It's unbelievable.*"

I clear my throat, the fight in me slowly returning. "*You haven't seen any of it yet, Hooyo. You're only standing in the doorway. It could be the worst house ever built for all you know.*"

Hooyo sighs. "*Halima…I had hoped your anger would've drowned in those waters we flew over. Clearly, it hasn't.*"

Abu Bakr looks back at me pityingly. He's only four years old but he understands Hooyo's disappointed tone well.

"*Why don't you go upstairs?*" she says. "*Find your room, get unpacked. Come back down when you feel ready.*"

I splutter in response.

"*Hooyo,*" I say, flustered. "*Really?*"

"*Halima,*" the husband interrupts. "*Waa inaad maqasho Hooyadaa. Soo noqo markaad nasato, all right?*"

At that, even Kamal's head swivels towards me.

Come back downstairs when you've rested, he says to me. Doesn't he know he's the very reason I'll never find rest?

"*This is all your fault,*" I reply. "*You are the reason I am angry, because you have taken everything away from me for a business that means nothing. My home, my friends, my school… I will never forget it. And I will never forgive you.*"

I ignore everyone's looks and grab my purple suitcase, pushing past my skinny brothers. I reach my mother and her husband, still standing in the doorway. They break apart to let me through, my mother to the right and her husband to the left. I consider lingering for a moment longer, to keep this distance between them, even if it's only for a few seconds, but then Hooyo touches my shoulder.

"*Waa ku jecelahay, my Halima.*" She kisses my cheek. "*But I don't love your anger. Anger weighs you down, macaaney. It sinks you into the ground beneath your feet, and then it leaves you drowning.*"

I nod.

"*Okay, Hooyo. Sorry. I'll unpack and come down later.*"

But the subtext? The thing I am really thinking and that I am sure she can read in my eyes anyway?

*It's impossible for me to drown any more, Hooyo.*

*I drowned the minute you brought this stranger, this man, into our home and tried to convince me he would become one of us.*

As I climb the stairs to my room, I catch the beginning of the boys' unrest. Kamal's voice carries the loudest.

"*Why does Halima get to go inside first, Aabo? That's not fair!*"

I grin as I pull my suitcase up, glad to have caused some trouble for the husband. After a little labour and sweat, I reach the landing. There are four doors on this level and the smell of fresh paint makes me momentarily forget about my bag, which makes a soft thud as it falls against the banister. I push open the first door on the left. The hinges give way smoothly, not like the squeaks and creaks of our house in Yaaqshid whenever you did anything, even take a breath. When I step inside fully, I find myself in a bright bathroom, newly tiled with a green and yellow mosaic print. The brightness of it is enough to make me blink a few times.

I run my hand along the colourful tiles. Part of me is

disappointed when my hand comes away clean and not streaked in the vibrant colours that dance across the walls.

My hand floats to the glass box of the shower. It's so transparent that it looks as though there is nothing there. But the glass beneath my hand is solid and real and cold.

It is beautiful.

I'm not sure how long I have been admiring the bathroom, but I realize it has been too long when my mother's husband knocks on the door and peers in.

He smiles at me like he's caught me red-handed.

*"It's stunning, isn't it, Halima?"* he muses, making a pathetic attempt at conversation. *"This bathroom. The tiles were very expensive but I think they were a good choice."* He nods to himself as he says this, letting his eyes roam over his tiled kingdom.

I ask him to show me to my room.

Even though I don't like the husband, I have to hand it to him. The man certainly knows how to do up a house.

He leads me to the first room on the right and gestures for me to enter. He smiles the same way as when he caught me marvelling in the bathroom, as if the two of us are sharing a secret. But his expression now makes him look a little unhinged and overexcited. Teeth and gum on a desperate canvas.

I step inside, pivoting to turn and close the door so that I can get rid of him before any further conversation can take place, but – too late – he's already stepped in too.

I know what he wants from me. He wants me to fall at his feet in gratitude, cry "Thank you, thank you, thank you" until my lips are dry and chapped. For me to shed tears because he has given me the ultimate "prize" and brought me to England. Given me what so many people from home foolishly covet. He wants me to be pliable and easy-going and not so difficult.

My thoughts stop cold.

There is a book on the desk in the corner. I go to pick it up, letting it sit in my joined palms.

My mother's husband takes a hesitant step forward. He stands some way behind but speaks like we are standing much closer. I strain to hear him.

*"I know that you love the poetry of our people the same way I love it, Halima. I've heard you around the house, reciting those verses that your father and Abti Haroon taught you."*

He clears his throat. I angle myself so that he cannot see any part of my face.

*"A good father should know what his children love and don't love."*

Maybe it is because I am too lost in admiring this book and remembering Abti Haroon, but I don't say the words I usually say when he calls himself my father. Maybe holding the words of Hadraawi has softened me temporarily. I don't know.

He walks quietly towards the door, and I turn to close it behind him, to finally get rid of his shadow, rubbing my eyes briskly. That's when I notice my name painted on the door.

*No. 1*

*Halima*

He catches me looking and taps on the number trapped in the painted green box.

57

*"Number one for my daughter,"* he says, with that toothy grin again. *"My first, my eldest."*

And, because his fake kindness is getting too much for me now, I let the default words tumble out.

*"Stop saying you're my father. You're not. You are my mother's husband. My father may be dead, but you will never replace him."*

He leaves without a reply, taking his disappointment with him, and shuts the door on his way out. My name and number disappear.

Then, when it's just me and my suitcase and these enduring paint fumes, something else occurs to me.

*I am not your first,* I should have said to him. *You already have a daughter who is your own flesh and blood and I wonder if she hates you as much as I do.*


I come downstairs after I've unpacked and had some time to recover from everyone else's excitement. The happiness in the house feels too much like carbon monoxide – colourless, odourless, quietly fatal. It is better to be exposed only in small, tolerable doses.

Downstairs, the boys are glued to the TV already, watching cartoons. Though the screen is much larger than the one back home, Abu Bakr is sitting directly in front of it on the floor, head tilted upwards. Kamal lies on the white leather sofa, hands curled protectively around the remote. There must have been a battle for it but clearly Kamal has reigned supreme.

I sit down next to him on the sofa, holding out my hand expectantly.

"*Halima*," Kamal whines, hands twisting like vines around the remote. "*Waa ku tuugaa.*"

Abu Bakr's head whips around to us. A miserable expression sets in on his face. They know what is coming next. They know who always wins.

"*There's no point begging, Kamal. It's not like you understand what they're saying anyway.*" I gesture for the remote again.

"*But you don't either!*" Kamal shouts.

I shrug my shoulders. "*Waxyar aan ka fahmaa,*" I tell him. "*I can say 'Hello, how are you? I am in London today,' as a start. That's more than you, so hand it over, little boy.*"

"*Halima!*" Hooyo calls from the adjoining room. "*Kaalay!*"

Kamal pumps his fist in the air. "*Ha! Hooyo's calling you!*"

"*Don't worry,*" I say, narrowing my eyes at him. "*I'll be back, little brother, just you wait.*"

He gulps and then proceeds to shove the device down his trousers.

It appears that the adjoining room is a kitchen and dining room. Hooyo is sitting on one of the high-backed chairs with the husband across from her. She motions for me to sit down too.

"*Aabo has enrolled you in the local school,*" she says, fingering the gold-lined tablecloth. "*You'll be starting in a week.*"

I shake my head.

"*No, thank you, Hooyo. You told me that I did not have to attend school here if I didn't want to, and I don't.*"

Hooyo wrings her hands, glancing at her husband. *"Unfortunately, there is no negotiation here, Halima. The laws of this land require you to be in a school and you will be. There's nothing else to discuss."*

A short laugh escapes me.

*"My entire life, you've taught me to never go back on my promises. You said that a broken promise is a sign of a distrustful person. Has he blindsided you with this?"* I ask, pointing at her husband. *"Or did you know and willingly lie to me?"*

Hooyo runs a hand over her chin. *"Whatever price I pay for peace, it is a price you've forced me to pay, Halima. Don't make this any harder than it needs to be."*

*"Me?"* I ask indignantly, struggling to make sense of her words. *"We would have had all the peace in the world if you hadn't dragged us here. If you hadn't taken me away from the only home I've ever known, from the place where my father lived and died. From Abti Haroon and Khadija. Any war that we have is because of you, Hooyo. Not because of me. You may not care about where you come from, but I do."*

*"Halima!"* the husband booms. *"You have no right to speak to your mother this way. To either of us. You are here now and you must accept it. Our life cannot be dictated on your terms."*

*"And what? It can be dictated on yours? Just because you're everyone else's shepherd does not mean you are mine,"* I reply, scoffing. *"I will never follow you."*

He takes a deep breath. *"Whether you continue to fight our new path or not is up to you, but do not fight your mother."* He leans over to hold Hooyo's hand, rubbing her knuckles.

"*Everything she does – everything – is out of love for you.*"

My eyes take in their joined hands. The warm and tender look he gives her.

The way Hooyo's shoulders relax.

"*No,*" I spit. "*My* father *is the one who did everything out of love for me. My mother does this out of love for* you."

Hooyo rubs her chin aggressively with her free hand, not meeting my eye. The husband shifts in his seat. I can tell he is gearing up to say something, but Hooyo squeezes his hand. Some silent message passes between them. Something I cannot interpret.

Bloated silence hangs between the three of us, but I sense the husband simmering. After a minute or so, he stands. The screech of his chair adds to the growing tension.

"*Where are you going, Halane?*" Hooyo asks, with a tired smile. "*To work?*"

He grips the chair tightly but says nothing. Hooyo's smile changes. It is no longer tired. Her smile is uneasy, bitter, masking envy.

No one speaks but we all know where he's going. To see his other family who, apparently, are living only a stone's throw away from here.

It's a stone too close as far as Hooyo is concerned. But, as the husband has assured her a thousand times already, he is here for his business, nothing more, nothing less, and, of course, she – his beautiful, second wife – has absolutely nothing to worry about.

Supposedly.

# *SAFIYA*

## HEXPOSE
## Musings of The Investigative Hijabi

### September Edition
### Editor's Letter

Welcome back, fellow Northwellers!

Hope you've stocked up on your mental well-being over the holiday because it's about to get thrashed this coming year. Though no one can say for certain whether we'll be subjected to more of Mr M's urinary charm (yes, sir, some people caught that fountain you decided to spray in the Astro when you thought no one was looking) or Miss D's violent self-maiming (I am, of course, referring to that horrible eye injury sustained during her particularly impassioned reading of Shakespeare's Macbeth), I'm sure there's lots more in store for us.

Regardless of what comes next, I wish everyone good luck in getting through another year at Northwell High. And don't forget, when times get tough, HEXPOSE is always here to lend a helping hand and distract you with the latest scandal. Please do send through your stories throughout the year – I'll be sure to investigate!

On a final and more positive note, let's welcome a new student to NWHS this year: Halima Omar. She'll be joining Year Eleven this month and is coming to us all the way from Somalia. Let's do our best to make her feel at home with us.

Signing off here and leaving you all with a little bit of the HEXPOSE magic to get you in the mood for September. As always, I hope our exposés put a hex on you.

**HEXPOSE Editor-in-Chief**

I shut the laptop. Hard.

"Are you serious?" I ask, pushing the computer aside.

Muna must have known this is exactly how I would react, because she's standing at the other side of the room, sandwiched in the tiny space between the wardrobe and wall.

"Whaaaaaat?" she drawls, pivoting further into the minute space. "Can't hear you, friend."

I sigh, clawing my face. The pain helps stop me from exploding all over her bedroom floor.

"Seriously, Muna, why would you put that bit in? You know that's just going to draw attention to the whole situation and that's the last thing I need right now!"

She whimpers dramatically.

"Stop acting all feeble. You messed up. How are you plastering my dad's other daughter all over as front-page news?" I cross my arms. "At least look me in the face and act like a big woman, Miss Editor-in-Chief."

Muna shuffles around with a faux-timid expression.

"Shhh," she whispers, conspiratorially. "Someone might hear you."

I roll my eyes. "No Northwell teacher is lurking around your bedroom, all right? Relax. Your secret identity is safe."

I avoid adding "for now" even though she deserves a little paranoia.

"I know." Muna grins, extracting herself. She sits down cross-legged on the blue fluffy rug in the middle of the room. "I was just trying to distract you."

"Well," I snort, "mission not accomplished."

"I know," she says again, this time more solemnly. She picks at the blue fluff, twirling it between her fingers. "And I am sorry, Safiya. Really, I am. But you know I had to, right? Journalistic integrity leaves me no choice." She grimaces. "The news is out there anyway. It's not like it's the beginning of summer when you had just found out. And the piece doesn't even say that she *is* your sister, just that she's coming to Northwell High this year…"

Muna pauses, and holds my gaze, biting her lip.

"What?" I groan. "Spit it out. You can't possibly say anything that will make this worse."

Muna throws her hands in the air, shedding all traces of hesitation. "Well, have you considered that Halima might not even be the terrible person that you think she is? Just because your dad is evil doesn't mean she is! Who knows, Saf," she says, "maybe your sister hates him as much as you do."

"Don't call her that." I narrow my eyes. "She isn't my sister, she isn't anything, and are you seriously trying to *rationalize* this to me?"

Muna opens her mouth, closes it. Scrunches up her eyebrows. "No?"

This is the first time Muna's journalistic pursuits have put us in confrontation with each other. She set up Hexpose three years ago in a bid to centralize all the school drama. The journalism society that she'd initially joined wasn't cutting it, so Muna promptly broke free and experimented with an anonymous blog – *Northwell High Unfiltered*. When her first three months of reporting grew a huge readership, she rebranded it as Hexpose. And while some people over the years have tried to dismantle it – teachers and students alike – and one year a competing parody blog was even set up, all in all, it's been a pretty successful endeavour.

Hexpose has always reported on everyone else's gossip, but never ours. Yusuf and I are the only people who know Muna is behind the legendary keyboard and I'd always thought being the friend of an anonymous blogger would afford me some type of protection. But I know thoughts like that are slippery, because if I start thinking that...then what I'm really saying is that Muna may not have my back, when I know that's completely and utterly untrue.

Still, reading this in print stings. It's only been a few days since I overhead this horrible news – that Halima would be violating my school territory this year. I had been in the back aisle of Adeer Ali's shop as I caught the tail-end of an auntie gossip session and instantly froze. When I came to my senses, I legged it from the shop as quickly as I could and went straight over to Muna's, though only Yusuf was home.

"Why couldn't he have picked any other school in this borough?" I screamed at Yusuf about four times, before transitioning to "How the hell am I supposed to survive an entire year with her?" and then finally landing on "This is the worst nightmare anyone could have inflicted on me."

Eventually, the anger dissipated but I was left feeling defeated.

"What can I do?" Yusuf had asked, handing me a glass of apple juice when I'd calmed down. "Shall I drive her out of school? Banish her to the wilderness? Toss her on a boat and send her back home?" He slapped the kitchen counter for emphasis. "Tell me what, Saf, and I'll do it."

"No." I'd laughed, still aggrieved but starting to feel better. "But I appreciate the thought, Yusuf."

"Saf..." Muna starts again now, breaking through my thoughts. "I know this is hard to accept, but her being in school

66

probably isn't going to change anything for you. Everyone's just going to go about their business, same as always. You won't even be in the same class since our form is full."

The logical part of my brain knows this, but the other part tells me that this one girl coming to my school will be the end of my life as I know it.

In the years since Aabo left, school has become a sanctuary. Northwell High is a break from the crappiness of my life because there I am just Safiya. At home, there are other layers I wear. Ones like Abandoned-Safiya, Fatherless-Safiya, Caretaker-Safiya. I am a lot of Safiyas, living in my house with my mother, but never Just-Safiya.

And now, with Halima joining school, I'll be Broken-Family-Safiya in the one place I've always been able to shed the skin of home.

"And," Muna continues, building her argument, "everyone new always gets a shout-out in Hexpose. So you could potentially argue that *not* mentioning her in the letter would have been a bigger call for attention."

"You really do have a way with words, you know. You're like a manipulative little snake."

"Don't I know it," she says with a sigh. "A blessing and a curse."

Muna rolls off the floor to sit at the vanity. "Anyway," she says, clearing her throat. "Moving on. I wanted to show you my new Eid lippy for tomorrow. It's this banging soft pink colour, right—"

"Actually," I interrupt, smiling at the seed of an idea that's beginning to take shape in my head. "Since you've basically thrown me under the bus for your little Hexpose agenda, I think you owe me one."

"Oh?" she replies, a little nervously. The fear sets in when she realizes where I'm going with this. "Oh no..." Muna whispers. "Please. Please don't make me do it, Safiya. You know that shit makes me sick to my stomach."

I lie down on the rug more comfortably, burying my face in the blue fluff.

"Thanks to you and your Hexpose stress, my muscles have all seized up, so I'm going to need you to crack my back for me, Muna, and make sure you get that big, juicy knot right at the top."

This year's Eid-ul-Adha prayer is once again at King Eddy's Park. Hooyo and I enter through the south gate along with swarms of other people. As usual, the narrow walkway to the congregational prayer further down is swallowed up by all the Eid-goers. Little kids run around like they own the place, tripping over each other and the extravagant clothes that are too big for them. Then there are the elderly people who are given a wide berth out of respect, creating the illusion that they have all the space and time in the world to walk the path. Eventually, when it feels as though we've barely moved, Hooyo and I give each other a knowing look and bypass the path, walking across the grass towards the main congregation in silence.

Compared to everyone else, Hooyo and I haven't really

dressed up. I'm wearing the same outfit I wore last Eid – a simple black abaya with a forest-green hijab – and Hooyo is wearing a black jilbaab, the same one she wears everywhere else.

Around us, however, it's a different story. There is every colour under the sun. Embroidered shawls, intricately designed abayas and beautiful shoes to match. People with henna-coloured hands that bring their gestures to life. I keep my head up, training my eyes on everyone else, because if I can't see myself, maybe I can pretend that I am not wearing the dead clothes that I actually am.

Still, that solution comes with its own problems. With my head up, I get an unobstructed view of all the curious looks when people notice the unstable divorcee and her broken-up daughter walking by. Hooyo and I rarely make appearances together so, when we do, it doesn't take long to come under the microscope. People will usually see me around, if it's running over to Adeer Ali's shop or hanging out with Muna, but a me-and-Hooyo duo is a rare occurrence. Rare enough that people don't even bother hiding their interest.

I catch sight of some of the usual gossip-hungry suspects and give them a wide berth lest they decide to corral us before prayer.

I grip Hooyo's hand, holding it firmly between us. After a few moments, the shaking in her hand lessens.

"You've got this, Hooyo," I whisper under my breath, still looking ahead. "Just twenty minutes then we're out of here."

She grips my hand tighter.

It had been nothing short of a miracle when Hooyo had agreed to Eid prayer in the park this year, even though we've gone every year since they started offering it at King Eddy's.

At first, Aabo's abandonment had made it a simple decision. Yes – she would go to the park. No – she would not go to the mosque where he had taken us every year before then. Yes – she would weather the stares and whispers so long as she was outside, in a place where it would be impossible to feel trapped. No – she would not stay behind to catch up with old friends and share gossip that somehow grew another head with every retelling.

But I knew this year would be different, thanks to Aabo coming back. Though I was sure he'd take his shiny new family to the mosque instead of King Eddy's, it was enough for me to worry about the stares and whispers. They were bound to be even worse this time. We both knew that, so when I asked Hooyo, expecting a categorical no, I was surprised by her silence. Then she floored me with:

"Okay, Safiya. We will go."

I decided not to push my luck by asking why. I just let the tentative gratitude sink in and went off to iron our clothes.

In the years since Aabo has been gone, Eid celebrations have taken a new form in our house. We pray, we come home. We eat dates, drink sparkling white grape and elderflower juice. We share silence, punctuated with brief reminiscences and nostalgia for happy memories – *sans* Aabo, of course. Eid is when I get a little bit more of Hooyo and so this day is all the more special for it.

It is not like the stares don't bother me, or that it's easy seeing everyone else dressed up while I stand beside them in my shabby clothes. But, for me, Eid has always been about something greater than all of that. It is about devotion and sacrifice and the belief that, no matter what, God comes through for you. Even if it is not in the way that you expect. Lately, I've had trouble holding onto that, but coming to Eid prayer reminds me of it. It gives me hope, and, right now, I need a lot of that.

"Salaam, Idil!" comes a shrill voice from somewhere to our right. Hooyo's hand becomes instantly limp.

I quicken my pace, nudging Hooyo lightly to match it.

King Eddy's is always noisy, I tell myself. Easy enough for a voice to lose itself in the rumble of general conversation, right?

There is nothing to worry about.

"Idil!" The call is banshee-like now and impossible to ignore. It draws another group's attention to us too.

Game over. We stop walking.

I flick my gaze over to Hooyo. She looks forlorn and tired. I slide my game face on. It'll be up to me to steer this conversation and prevent it from hitting any icebergs.

The usual suspects – Habaryar Shukri and Habaryar Binti – walk hurriedly and determinedly over. They're panting by the time they reach us, though it would be wishful thinking to imagine that could ever deter them.

Habaryar Binti, the taller auntie with a gap between her teeth, grins like a lunatic. She leads the conversation in Somali as usual and I mentally prepare to reply in my standard combination of a broken mother-tongue and English.

"*Eid Mubarak, Idil and Safiya,*" Habaryar Binti purrs.

I swear I see a forked-tongue snake out of her mouth.

"*How have you both been? I'm sure the news of…*" She pauses, glancing around furtively as if trying to keep a secret, though it's all a charade since her volume is going entirely in the wrong direction. "*Well, the news of Halane's return…with a wife and several children it seems! It can't be easy. For either of you, of course. I pray everything has been amicable between you. What a shame it would be to see a family like yours fall apart.*"

Hooyo sags a little into my side. Habaryar Shukri notices the movement and opens her mouth to say something that I'm sure would make the situation infinitely more unbearable so I interrupt.

"*It's going well actually,*" I reply. "*Everything is going well.*" I pause, backtrack, and attempt an improved imitation of confidence with my slightly shaky Somali. "*I'm not sure why anyone would think our family is falling apart since we've never been stronger.*"

Habaryar Shukri purses her lips. "*We are glad to hear it, Safiya. And how has—*"

A hand touches my shoulder. I whip around, wondering what third devil I'm going to be dancing with today – then I see who it is.

"*Come on, you two,*" Muna's mum interrupts. "*I've saved us a spot over there. Sorry to steal them away so rudely, sisters, but I've got something time sensitive that I need to discuss.*"

We are enveloped in the warmth of Habaryar Zainab's arms as she shepherds us to the tarp with all the grace of a hero.

Being with her feels a little like being cocooned in a Zorb ball; seeing the world but knowing it won't touch you.

"*So, Zainab,*" Hooyo says quietly, "*what was so urgent you needed to whisk us away?*" There is a hint of humour in her voice that I didn't think I'd be hearing today.

"*Ah, you know how we get at this age, Idil. Thoughts are here one minute and gone the next, so who knows!*" Habaryar Zainab chuckles. "*I'm sure it will come back to me soon.*"

Hooyo smiles widely, and I don't know if I imagine it, but I'm sure her back straightens just a little.

I notice Muna standing near the edge of the tarp, along with both of her sisters. When we're close enough, we remove our shoes and head across the plastic.

I greet Muna's mum properly now that we've escaped the vultures, wrapping her in a huge hug. "*I missed you, habaryar. See tahay?*"

"*Good, my love. Alhamdulilah,*" she replies with a smile that isn't pitying but feels like an acknowledgement of all the crap I've had to go through lately. "*I've missed you too, though I'm sure we've seen each other almost every day this summer.*" She winks, squeezing my shoulder, before turning her attention to chat with Hooyo.

"So," Muna's older sister Nasra says, lightly punching me on the shoulder. "I don't get a hello now? Damn, Safiya." She looks me up and down disapprovingly. "Seems like your generation is getting more disrespectful by the second."

"Piss off!" Muna laughs. "Don't you have your own friends to go and see?"

73

Nasra turns to give her younger sister what I assume is going to be an earful, but I cut in.

"You're right, Nasra." I nod, trying to be as deferential as I can. "Us Gen Zers don't know how to speak to the elderly. No disrespect intended, of course."

Nasra bursts out laughing. "Touché, my friend. Glad to see that hanging around Muna hasn't taken away your edge." She freezes, looking over our shoulders. "Well, seems like you guys have got your wish. Hanan's just arrived. Catch you losers later."

"Wait!" Muna calls.

"What?"

"Take this one with you," she requests, pointing to their younger sister Luul. "She can catch up with Hanan's sisters. They're around the same age, right?"

To be completely honest, I had forgotten that Luul was even standing next to us. That's how quiet the girl is, but I guess she balances out their family. Nasra and Muna steal all the noise that exists in their house and if Luul were the same…

No. The thought is too chaotic to imagine.

The congregational prayer begins. Everyone lines up shoulder to shoulder, facing the direction of Mecca. We must look mad to all the other park-goers. The daily runners and tennis players, the parents who find refuge in the park every summer with their high-spirited kids. But, standing here, under the canopy of this greenery, I stop feeling the eyes of all those people. Instead, I experience a transcendence that makes me feel like I'm see-through. Like I'm floating and capturing something that makes my insides brighter. But the sensation, whatever it is, is fleeting, because it always disappears after I pray and, try as I might, I've never been able to find it anywhere else.

Above, the birds and squirrels chase each other through the overhanging sycamore trees. They stop when the melodic reading of the Imam reaches them, but only for a second before they return to the dog-eat-dog politics of the park.

The Imam concludes the prayer and, after the duas are read, everyone stands to disperse. The morning prayer marks the beginning of Eid and it's the rest of the day that's set aside for celebration with family and friends.

In my case, it will be just me and Hooyo for today. Though Muna invited us to her family's get-together, I opted to keep Eid the same as it has been for us lately: at home, away from all other happy families.

I look for Hooyo, relaxing when I see her walking with Muna's mum towards the gate. I follow behind with Muna and her sisters.

"Yooo!" a voice calls out. "Wait up!"

Yusuf jogs up to us. He's in a grey thobe and wearing his signature Air Maxes. I can't lie, the look is working for him, but I know better than to pay him that compliment. I would never hear the end of it.

"I kept calling you guys," he complains, breathing hard. His glasses fog, replacing his eyes with smoke. "Like for a full minute almost."

"Calling *us* or calling Saf?" Muna grins. "I feel like the distinction is low-key important."

*I want to disappear into the ground and I want it to happen now.*

"You're right, gremlin, I wasn't calling you," Yusuf hits back at his cousin. "I didn't get to catch Safiya before she left the house yesterday. Just wanted to say Eid Mubarak." He turns to me, still moving at the same pace but walking backwards now. "Eid Mubarak, Safiya."

"Thanks." I smile a little awkwardly since I'm still processing how Muna could lob me under the bus like that. Thankfully Yusuf begins walking normally again so I drop the smile. "Eid Mubarak to you too."

He clears his throat. "A little birdie tells me you've got a secret, you know."

"What?" I blink in confusion, slightly startled by this segue. "What are you talking about?"

He grins. "Something called the Two Musketeers, I believe?"

"What?" I repeat, panic beginning to twist my ability to speak coherently. "Who? What?"

"Thank your good friend Muna for leaving her phone lying about. Slightly shocking behaviour from a seasoned investigative journalist, I have to say."

Somehow, in less than a second, Muna's presence next to me disappears. She's gone, melted into another crowd behind us. I can't fault her for running away, because the bus that she drove has well and truly destroyed everything now.

"Look, Saf," Yusuf says, putting his hands in his pockets. "It's not that deep. I just know there's a lot happening with your dad coming back and I'm here for you, is what I'm trying to say.

I don't care about some knock-off group chat as long as you're good. That's all that matters." He stops speaking abruptly, as if his tongue has suddenly dissolved. I open my mouth, curious about what was left unsaid, when I'm reminded of what *did* happen the last time Yusuf spoke without holding back. I'm sure he's thinking of the same thing too. Of the memory that is almost seven years old now. When he had ridden his bike in front of my own, in this very park, letting Muna pedal away without us, and said: *I'll marry you one day, Safiya. I don't know when but I know I will.*

He had said the words quickly and fled, not giving me a chance to reply and, for weeks after, he had refused to look at or even speak to me. Anytime we occupied the same orbit, even briefly, he would run off, as if I was carrying a deadly disease.

It has been years since then but sometimes I'll think about that moment. When I feel like everything around me is crumbling, I'll remember the certainty in his eyes, the lack of hesitation in his quiet voice. I'll remember that someone wanted a future, a whole life, with me.

But after, when the sun sets on that thought, which it inevitably does…I find myself wondering why my dad could never be as sure about my mum.

I sneak a glance at Yusuf – at the once eight-year-old boy who made wild promises in the park. He's never been just the boy-next-door. Never been unassuming, unexciting, predictable. Because, if he were, would I feel this unsettled around him? Unsettled *by* him? If he blended into my life like wallpaper, would I still be aware of his every smile, waiting for his dimples to rise into it?

If he was to me what Muna is, would eight-year-old me have dreamed of that same future with him? And would fifteen-year-old me be quietly holding onto some fragment of it?

"Umm…" Yusuf's voice wobbles. "Safiya?"

I snap back to the conversation.

"Sorry," I say quickly. "Lost in thought. You're right, Yusuf, and I'm sorry. I don't want you to think we're cutting you out. There's a lot going on, you know and—"

*And I can't talk to you about any of this because it's too deep and the two of us are better when we're not deep. At least, it's better for me.*

"I know, I know," he replies hurriedly, craning his neck to look at something further ahead.

I narrow my eyes at him. "Hey. I'm trying to give you a proper apology and you don't want to hear it?"

His Adam's apple bops up and down. "Nah…it's not that," he whispers. "Safiya, don't get mad, okay?"

I throw my hands up. "Yusuf, I'm not getting mad. I'm trying to apologize. Why are you making this so hard?"

He blinks fast, as if his vision has suddenly become misty.

"All right, I might be wrong…" He hesitates, still blinking and looking ahead. Yusuf almost has an entire foot on me, so he's got a view I will never be able to reach without heels. "But I have a feeling that's your dad over there."

When I hear him say those words, the connection between my brain and feet falters. I stumble and then stop right in the middle of the path. Yusuf stops too and the crowd instinctively bends and folds around us, as if we're rocks rooted in a fast-flowing river.

He opens his mouth to speak but I put a hand up.

"Wait." I try to think rationally even though it feels like someone's thrown a fishing net over my brain. "I need to find my mum." The thought is like a siren in my head. A command that silences everything but the need to find her in this river.

"What can I do?" Yusuf asks, adjusting his glasses. "I can distract him, maybe—"

"Nothing." I shake my head. "Please, nothing from you."

The "from you" slips out too easily and I want to tell him that I don't mean it, that I'm stressed by a situation that should never have come to pass, but then I see his face fall – crumpling so quickly in a way I've never seen before – and something in my stomach pinches, making me feel a little sick.

I dodge past him – needing to get away from him and get to my mum. I cut through groups of people at intervals, jumping in and out of the river until I find Hooyo. There are some tuts and whispers, but I block all of it out.

It's Hooyo's shoulders that I notice first – twin sloping lengths in a perpetual state of sorrow and shame. I would recognize those shoulders anywhere.

"Hooyo," I say, breathless, grateful. I pull on her arm. "Let's go this way."

If I can get her to turn around right now, walk with me to the exit on the other side of the park, neither of us will have to lay eyes on him. But we're closer to the south gate than I realized and the second I pull on Hooyo's arm is the same second that Aabo comes into view.

He hasn't noticed us yet, caught up with pulling a young boy out of a ditch he has wandered into, but the woman standing next to him gasps and calls his attention. He turns around a moment later, young boy in tow. The woman – who I have now clocked must be his wife – stands next to another small boy and a girl who doesn't look much older than me.

"*Halane*," the woman says.

I can read her lips.

*It's her.*

Beside me, Hooyo's face freezes in utter disbelief. The new wife's finger zeroes in on us. Habaryar Shukri and Habaryar Binti elbow their way towards the drama, lingering at the periphery, inhaling the turmoil in the air.

No one speaks. No one moves.

We are tethered to this moment, this exact hour and minute and second, all of us. But every spell can be broken and, when the initial shock lessens, I grab Hooyo again and guide her away from this mess.

The walk home is a blur, though thankfully Hooyo and I have most of our faculties in check. We remember to press the button at the traffic light and wait for the green man. We avoid the smear of fresh pigeon shit on three pavement slabs. We veer away from the roadworks by our house that are missing a couple of safety barriers.

We reach home.

The tremor that disappeared when I held Hooyo's hand is back. I can see it, from all the way across the room. She stands in the middle of the living room, staring at the floor – whether to pull herself together or orientate herself, I don't know.

Eventually, when it looks as though she is not going to move, I bring over a fresh set of clothes and help her change out of her jilbaab. Her body responds to my gentle encouragement even though I can tell from her eyes that she has disappeared again.

When that is done, I guide her to the sofa and wrap a blanket around her. My sudoku book is still lying on the coffee table from my last failed attempt and, because I know I'm going to be here a while, I grab it and focus on the boxes and the numbers that will fill them.

Later, Hooyo stands from the sofa. I'm not sure where she is going but, when I hear the toilet door open and shut, I allow myself to relax and lose myself in my nine simple numbers, waiting for her return.

I lose myself so completely that it takes too long for me to realize Hooyo hasn't returned yet. If I had to guess, I would say it's been about twenty minutes. The fact that I don't hear any water running makes me throw the book off my lap and run across the hall to the bathroom.

I knock on the door.

"Hey, Hooyo. You okay?"

No answer.

I shake the handle, but the door is locked. I knock louder,

attempting to keep the desperation out of my voice.

"Hooyo! I need the toilet. Can you hurry up, please?"

When I don't hear anything the second time, I don't bother trying for a third. I jam my fingernail in the lock, using all the force I can muster to open it.

A few moments later, I have the door open. I rush in, stopping short when I see Hooyo sitting on the toilet lid.

"I was desperate to pee," I say feebly. "Sorry."

I am grateful that it's a lie we're both happy to accept.

Hooyo stands and leaves, making her way back to the living room. I turn to follow when I notice a drop of red hit the floor.

For a second, I am furious. For not realizing that she had hurt herself. For accepting that she was fine.

But then another drop hits the floor, and another, and another.

I follow the trajectory upwards to find that I am the one bleeding. The fingernail that I jammed in the door is mangled, blood dribbling off the side. I pivot to the sink and open the tap to numb the stinging pain I feel inching its way up now that the adrenaline is wearing off.

# HALIMA

In the hallway, I lie in wait for Hooyo as she puts the boys to bed. The creak of her footsteps on the floorboards alerts me before the door opens. She exits backwards, stepping quietly to avoid startling Kamal. He has always been a light sleeper and, if he wakes, then Abu Bakr likely will too.

I have timed this perfectly. The husband is not around, giving me the space that I need to unravel the uncomfortable, impromptu encounter at the park today with the husband's first family. If there is anything that will make Hooyo question our relocation, entice her to drop her plans and fly us home, it must be this. And then I will get what I want too without having to hatch an escape plan.

"*Hooyo*," I whisper.

She startles, surprised by my nearness, before fixing herself resolutely where she stands. Hooyo plants her feet widely and crosses her arms. She transforms herself into the trunk of a tree with an invisible network of roots under the surface.

I try to read her the way I used to, to see if there is something behind her eyes that will give away her secrets. Because, since the day her husband walked into our lives, I have been convinced that there is something she refuses to let slip. Either that, or he's got my mother under some type of sihr. Black magic is a real phenomenon, even if the horror stories people share only sound like nightmares for children.

"I just put the boys to bed," Hooyo says, with a weary smile. "Are you going to sleep soon, Halima?"

"I think so." I nod, thinking over my next words. "I'm a little exhausted after everything that happened today."

Hooyo stares at me impassively. She shifts, crossing her arms a little tighter. Her defences are up, as they usually are around me.

"You know, in the park," I continue. "Seeing...the two of them. His wife and daughter."

Their existence, when I first learned of it almost three years ago, did not come as a shock to me. I remember Hooyo had mentioned in passing one day that the husband would be making a quick trip to England, to deal with some urgent matters. He would be back soon, she said. He had a family, a daughter and ex-wife left behind, she'd added quickly. But he was going for business. To tie up loose ends.

But what alarmed me more than the revelation itself was Hooyo's reaction to his leaving.

She asked every day how long he would be gone, where he would be staying, who he would be seeing. I watched her anxiety swell right until the moment she bade him goodbye at the front door.

"Look after your mother," the husband had said to me.

And Hooyo, instead of reciprocating with a similar

84

sentiment, had simply replied, *"I'll be waiting for you."*

Granted, it was the first time he would be leaving since they'd wed two years earlier, but it seemed as though Hooyo no longer knew how to exist without him.

Or maybe she was afraid he would never return.

*"That woman is not his wife,"* Hooyo replies breathlessly now, dropping her arms. *"She used to be, but she is not any more."*

I look down at my feet, faux apology written all over my body. *"Sorry, Hooyo, that's not what I meant."* (Except that it was.)

Hooyo sighs. Recently, she has begun to lose patience with me much more quickly. What used to be lengthy conversations have now become fleeting and guarded.

*"I'm going to sleep, Halima."* She raises an eyebrow. *"I suggest you do the same. Goodnight."*

She turns on her heels, roots now completely dissolved, the light of contained annoyance in her eyes flaring – but then she hesitates.

She turns back and walks over to me. Hooyo wraps me in an embrace, before pulling back to give me a kiss on the cheek. I kiss her forehead in return, the way I have always done. A sign of respect and, always, a sign of love.

But because it has been so long since either of us have done that, the very action is my undoing. I pull Hooyo back into our circle and hold her there. She must sense my need because she grips me tightly, rocking me gently, as my tears flow.

*"I know this is hard, macaanto,"* Hooyo whispers. *"The hardest thing we have ever done, but we will get there. We will make this place our home."*

When I hear this, my tears stop just as suddenly as they started.

That night, I call Khadija, desperate to hear something of my life that has stayed the same. My mind does not stop to think of the time difference, where she might be or what she might be doing but, miraculously, she picks up on the fourth ring.

For a while, the both of us are silent. I listen to her breathing, the intermittent static that interrupts our connection. I imagine her face. Her brown eyes and full cheeks. The chip in her bottom tooth. I try to imagine myself beside her, but the image distorts.

*"Halima, are you well?"*

I grip the mobile tighter, thinking of Hooyo's certainty. *We will get there. We will make this place our home.*

*No, I am not okay,* I want to say. *I won't be, until I am back where I need to be.* But instead, I simply say, *"I miss you."*

Khadija sighs. *"I miss you too. Nothing is the same without you."* She groans. *"Especially not mathematics. I need you to carry me through that class, like you have always done."*

*"And I need you for this infuriating language."* I laugh. *"They speak too quickly for me! I know you would understand all of it. You always did."*

*"Maybe I should fly over there too,"* she jokes. *"It would be the best of both worlds, right?"*

I do not laugh at that, and she must sense my reluctance to joke about any of this because we both fall into silence.

86

When my eyes start to burn, and I reach the edge of sleep, I tell Khadija goodbye.

"*Halima, I am sorry about the joke,*" Khadija adds. "*You know I did not mean it that way.*"

"*I know,*" I reassure her. "*I just think everything is too…raw right now. It all hurts. This place hurts, I hurt.*"

"*I know,*" she repeats. "*And I will always be here for you. Through all that hurting, whatever you need.*"

We say goodbye properly then and I let my mind take me far, far away from the nightmare I am already living in.

Hooyo throws herself into making breakfast the next morning,

The boys sit patiently for all of five minutes before they begin foaming at the mouth. Abu Bakr asks five times when his pancakes will be ready. To his surprise and delight, on the fifth go, Hooyo passes him the steaming plate, his anjeero folded and topped with a healthy drizzle of olive oil and sugar.

I make the shaah whilst Hooyo is cooking. The thing that boils the water is apparently called a *kettle* – a cheat appliance that does the job for you. It seems wrong to me that the power bubbling through the water should come from the flick of a switch and that I only stand there and watch as it reaches the end of its process, not assessing myself whether it is the end but having to listen for the *click* after a few minutes that tells me so.

If I had any choice in the matter, I would have done it the way we always have. Maybe not sitting on a gember, over a coal fire, but at least using a stove-top kettle. Hooyo had shut that idea down promptly when I raised it. She said that we would use what has been bought for us by the husband and nothing less.

Our hallway conversation from last night knocks around in the back of my mind. I had wanted to unsettle Hooyo, remind her that life – if we are to remain here – will certainly be messy and complicated with the husband's second family around. But, watching her now, standing over the cooker, trying to get to grips with its buttons and dials, I realize I have my work cut out for me. Clearly, Hooyo is not giving up easily.

When everyone's nearly finished with breakfast, Hooyo says, *"We are going shopping this afternoon."*

Kamal wastes no time pumping his fists in the air. *"Yes!"*

*"What are we going to buy, Hooyo?"* Abu Bakr asks. Of the two of them, he is the one who likes to get beneath the surface the most. Kamal, on the other hand, is happy to accept almost anything at face value.

*"School clothes,"* she replies, grabbing her last bite of anjeero and using it to mop up the escaped oil and sugar on the plate. *"School begins in a week and we need to make sure you all look the part."*

Kamal pumps his fists again on cue.

*"Oh yeah, oh yeah, oh yeah, oh yeah."* His entire body shakes along to a catchphrase he's learned off the TV already.

*"Who's going?"* I interrupt.

*"All of us."* Hooyo smiles, standing up from the table. *"Your father included."*

And, because I could never roll my eyes with Hooyo looking, I shut them briefly for a second and roll them to do myself justice.

I head to my room in a bid to shore up on some sanity before the shopping trip this afternoon. If I can build my reserves now, maybe we can all get back home today unscathed.

I lie on the floor, stomach first, and flip through the poetry book the husband gifted me. With every few pages, I rip one out, scrunching it up and dropping it on the floor. I look up when I hear rustling.

"*What's this, Halima?*" Abu Bakr asks, unfolding the papers. He has sneaked in without my realizing. He lies next to me and looks them over.

"*Not your concern,*" I say, a hint of warning laced in my words.

I use this tone because it's normally enough to scare him into disappearing, but this country we have waded into has given my brothers a newfound confidence. My usual tactics are beginning to fail and I don't have fresh ones yet. He squints at the pages, attempting to make out the words. I ignore him.

He'll get bored soon enough, I tell myself. He always does.

"*These are the English pages!*" Abu Bakr shouts, triumphant. He waves them in the air. "*All of them, they are in English.*"

I sigh. Further conversation with my little brother is not what I wanted.

"*Yes,*" I say, tearing out a new one. "*They are.*"

He grabs the newly ripped sheet out of my hands before I can scrunch it. I let my head flop onto the open book in front of me.

He makes a noise of confusion and then shakes my shoulder.

*"Halima, can you help me? I don't know what this letter is. Aabo taught me, I think, but I forgot."*

*"Well, if your father taught you the first time, maybe he can teach you again now,"* I whisper into the book. He shakes my shoulder again.

*"If I teach you the letters, will you go away?"* I snap.

Abu Bakr nods his head vigorously.

*"Fine."* I sigh, defeated. Annoyed because the only way to win is to compromise which, in many ways, amounts to defeat. *"Let us start with the song then."*

And then we rattle off the ABCs together, cycling through them once, twice, and by the end, five entire times. Abu Bakr sidles even closer and asks me to read some of the words on the page. I glance at him from the corner of my eyes, poised to give him a nudge, remind him that our deal is done, that he needs to go now and give me my space back, but something makes me hesitate.

Maybe it is his nearness, or the fact that I can see the light birthmark underlying his jaw. The one that marks him as my brother, as son of my mother, and helps me to forget who else he comes from. Or maybe it is the sugar from breakfast that has gotten to my head. I do not know what it is but, for some reason, I do not push him away.

So, I read him the words of Hadraawi, one of the greatest Somali poets to have ever lived, in the words of a language that I do not want to speak. And I butcher the words, I do, but something about it sounds magical too – the fact that I can read the same words in a different tongue.

We read the wrinkled pages slowly. Abu Bakr breathes in and out through his nose, concentrating as hard as he can.

We travel to the uniform shop by bus instead of using the car parked outside the house.

"This is your new home," the husband explains, glancing at me over his shoulder. "So you will need to understand how things work here." He points across the road. "There are buses every few minutes at those box shelters. When the bus arrives, you get on and tap your card. Then you press the button when you want to get off. It's simple," he says. "The whole thing runs like clockwork."

It is the worst comparison he could have used really. Like clockwork. Why would anyone want anything so regimented?

Unsurprisingly, the boys are eating all of this up. They are fascinated by anything and everything. From the loud red that violently paints all sides of the bus, to the pattern on the seats that they cannot seem to get enough of. They all sit at the back, happily chatting away, but the joy in the air makes me feel nauseous.

I stand away from them, nearer the middle of the vehicle, tipping my head towards the open window.

From a pushchair nearby, a little girl makes a repeated grab for me. When she successfully latches on, I swat her food-stained hand away.

The girl bursts into tears. Her mother gives me a look I can only describe as death itself.

"You baby," I try to explain in English. "She…she…she touched…"

I give up on trying to find the right word and instead act it out for her, but her withering gaze only intensifies.

A bell rings from somewhere and suddenly my mother's husband is next to me. He speaks rapidly, and though I can't make sense of everything he is saying, I know he is apologizing on my behalf.

"*Why did you tell that woman that I'm sorry?*" I ask when we disembark. "*I'm not sorry. That baby grabbed me like I belonged to her.*"

As if trying to incense me further, he chuckles.

"*Halima,*" he replies, in that pacifying tone of his. "*One thing you will quickly learn is that here you are expected to apologize, even when it is not your fault. And especially,*" he adds, "*if it involves a baby.*"

I scoff. "*Every time I learn something of this place, it feels like my head might just fall off.*"

The husband bends to pick Abu Bakr up.

"*Well, I would suggest you screw it on tight from now on.*" He chuckles again and my anger flares. "*If you are not careful, you may just lose it.*"

He turns, leading the way to the uniform shop, before whirling around, the ghost of a smile on his lips. The smile of a man who thinks that, after a long struggle, he has won.

"*This country has a lot of new rules, Halima, and you will need to learn them all if you're going to survive.*"

"*Not all of them,*" I mutter under my breath. "*Just enough to get me back home.*"

Of course, my mother's husband does not need to know that.

We are at the front of the queue now. The next ones to be admitted inside the store.

I'm looking down at my shoes, watching the ants veer away from the soles, when I sense something shift… I feel my skin rise with goosebumps, and I become certain it is the same thing I felt shiver along my spine days ago, when we came face to face with the past of my mother's husband. That feeling of being unsettled, of being stripped down by someone's eyes. The feeling of someone else's dread made real on your skin.

I look up to find the girl from the park standing there. She stands at the door, frozen, her gaze locked on all of us, but also somehow only locked on her father. She clutches a bag that looks the emptiest of all the bags we have seen coming out of the shop today, but holds it to her chest as if it is the most precious thing in the world.

I try to read her the same way I read my mother. Anger is there, shimmering on the surface. She is not shocked, like she was the last time, caught unprepared in a sea of people. No, this time she is angry. Fingers twitch, nostrils flare.

And I know it is anger because I have felt that way before.

When I first saw this man who parades himself as my family's saviour, as my mother's husband, as a man trying to fill the shoes of my dead father. A father whose memory has been blurred by tuberculosis and eleven years of loss, but a man I know the husband would never measure up to, in any way.

Her fingers twitch again. I notice a bandage tightly wound around her left thumb and a speck of blood that seeps through.

My mother's husband speaks cautiously, poised for rejection again.

*Good*, I think. He should be eternally rejected. Why should this man get everything he wants, at the expense of everyone else?

"*Salaam, Safiya.*" He clears his throat awkwardly. The boys look up at him, surprised by their father's inability to speak. "*You look well. Have you finished your shopping for today?*"

Safiya's stony expression should be answer enough for him, but the husband is obviously not a smart man.

"*I was hoping we could, perhaps…if you're free, of course… that we could see each other. For a meal, perhaps, or a coffee. Whatever you are comfortable with.*"

He broaches the topic tentatively, like one does when walking into a dim room, stretching their arms ahead of them before they allow their body to follow.

"*Or if you came by the house for dinner, it would be nice…for all of us to get to know each other.*"

Safiya is still frozen, still twitching, still breathing hard. She pinches her hurt thumb for comfort. A few more drops of blood seep through.

The husband scrambles for something in his pocket. He finds his wallet and slides it out, counting a few notes of cash. He leans forward to curl the money into his daughter's right hand and, for a moment, I think she has accepted his cowardly offer but then she unfurls her palm, letting the papers float to the ground.

Kamal is the first to break composure, diving for the fallen notes. Abu Bakr follows his lead. They run into the shop like scattered moths.

She spits her words out, her Somali understandable but a little broken, a little shaky.

*"If I don't trust anything that comes out of your mouth, why should I trust anything that comes out of your hands?"*

Next to me, Hooyo gasps. I resist covering her mouth with my own hands. *This isn't our fight*, I want to tell her. *This is business between a father and his daughter, let them be.*

But Hooyo doesn't seem to understand the situation the way it should be understood and I see her preparing to speak. Probably to say something in defence of her stupid husband, who is the reason we are all in this tangle to begin with.

Thankfully, Safiya stalks off before Hooyo has a chance to make things worse. The three of us enter the shop to find the boys.

I stay by the door when we enter, watching Safiya walk away through the glass. I watch the angry girl get smaller and smaller until she is almost gone. Then, at the junction, she looks back.

My heart pauses for a moment, wondering if she can see me this far away.

Someone comes up behind me. I slide out of the way to let them pass. They gaze at me curiously, eyebrows raised in question.

*Keep on moving,* I'm tempted to say. *This has nothing to do with you.*

But I remember the words of the husband then. There are different rules here. I cannot speak the way I would if I was home because this is not home. That much has always been clear.

So I give them my best imitation of a Western smile instead.

# SAFIYA

Something makes me look back. The instinct to bolt is strong but this feeling is stronger.

I stand at the junction, not crossing the road, but looking back to the place where, for the second time in ten days, I have been blindsided.

I know now that I'm no longer safe in my own town. That I cannot exist here without coming face to face with the father who left and stopped looking back, abandoning me with a mother who stayed but never sees me.

I feel powerless in my tribe of one against their tribe of five – because I am on my own, I know that. Hooyo and I may live in the same house but, even in the same room, there are still walls between us.

No one tells you how difficult it is to be a one-woman tribe though. They make it sound sexy – independent girl doing her thing with not a care in the world. Invincible and indestructible, and in need of nobody.

It's an easy lie to wear, but it's a heavy one to carry.

I look back to find that girl – Aabo's stepdaughter – staring at me. Standing behind the shop door, still and scrutinizing.

I wonder what she sees when she looks at me. If she sees that facade of invincibility, or if her eyes catch what's beyond it.

I hope it's the former.

A couple of days later and the official start of the new school year has arrived.

I pack my bag, getting ready to head out, and knock on Hooyo's door before I go. Today is too important to leave anything to chance.

When she doesn't answer, I step in anyway, wrinkling my nose at the sour smell.

Hooyo is bundled up under the duvet. I know she isn't sleeping from the way she breathes, but her eyes remain firmly shut.

I bend down, running a hand over her hair. "Hey, Hooyo," I whisper. "You've got your interview this afternoon, remember? For the cleaning job?" She doesn't stir.

"It's at two o'clock. I've got school starting today so I won't be around, but I need you to go. Please." Hooyo grunts something, turning over in the bed.

"Just say *okay* so I know you're hearing me, Hooyo. Then I'll leave you alone, promise."

I wait a beat, then another, then –

"Okay."

I sigh with relief. "I'll text you to remind you as well. And I've left your clothes ready downstairs, along with a copy of your CV." I bend down again, this time to kiss her cheek.

"I love you, Mama. Good luck for today. I know you can do this."

I finally leave – trying to push the worries down, so I can at least attempt to look forward to the first day of Year Eleven – and wait for Muna outside the gate of her house, five minutes earlier than we're supposed to meet. It's a tactic I've employed almost every day since we started secondary school after realizing that she has no concept of time. The bedroom she shares with her sisters faces the street and I have subtly encouraged her to assume that she's late anytime she sees me waiting outside.

Do I feel guilty about this psychological conditioning? No.

Will she ever know about it? Not if I can help it.

The door opens, and I wait for Muna to hurry out, coffee in hand (because, in her opinion, every budding journalist, even fifteen-year-old ones, must be breathless and frazzled, and clutching their morning coffee if they're to be taken seriously), but it's not her. Yusuf steps out, holding the door open with one arm whilst pushing his bike out with the other. He has his eyes trained on righting the wheels, so he doesn't notice me straight away.

I take a deep breath. "Hello there," I say, trying not to overthink this.

Yusuf and I haven't seen each other since Eid prayer in the park. Since he offered to help me find Hooyo in the family affair that spilled out for everyone to see.

I had squashed his kindness without batting an eyelid but the guilt that set in afterwards grew like an ache.

He hadn't sent anything on the Three Musketeers group chat since that day. No memes, no check-ins, nothing. My own fingers had itched so many times, tempted to message something light, funny, to make us both forget about how easily I'd dismissed him, but I couldn't bring myself to do it.

I look down, clearing my throat. "Looking forward to the first day of our last year?"

Yusuf glances up, startled and then nonchalant. He shrugs his shoulders, mounting the bike. I hold the gate open for him.

"Might be."

Yusuf and two-word sentences are infrequent. He's making me work for this.

"I never thought we'd get here," I continue conversationally. "You remember, in Year Seven, when we first started and we said it would take exactly three hundred and sixty-eight years to reach today?"

Yusuf bikes through the gap, coming around to stop opposite me.

"Perhaps."

A stepdown from two words to one. My hopes for a painless reconciliation flatline then. It must show on my face, how uncomfortable this all is, how desperately I wish not to be at odds with him, because he gives a small smile, half-dimples finally revealing themselves.

"Pretty sure we said it was three hundred and sixty-nine years though." He rings the bike bell lightly. "So your maths must be off on that."

I laugh, a little too loudly. "You're so full of it."

"We both are." Yusuf grins.

His eyes look like hot chocolate – not the instant powdery kind but the real kind made with rich, melted chocolate on the hob.

My stomach squeezes and comes close to flipping, so I say the first thing that comes to mind to distract myself.

I extend a hand. "Your glasses, please."

He obliges.

"You should really consider cleaning these for the first day of school, Yusuf," I say, wiping the lenses thoroughly with the edge of my hijab. "How are you supposed to see anything with all this dust and dirt?"

I hold the glasses up to the light, assessing my handiwork. Happy with the results, I hand them back.

"Don't worry, Saf…" he says with a small frown as he slips them back on. "I always see the important things."

My stomach engages in a fully-fledged flip then and I discreetly wrap an arm around it. Fifteen-year-old Yusuf may not be as direct as eight-year-old Yusuf, but his words are still sometimes heavy with unsaid sentiments.

He rides away before braking abruptly and looking over his shoulder.

"I don't know if you're stressed about that girl starting today…" he says, scratching his head. "But you don't have anything to worry about. Northwell High is a big place. I'm sure she'll have a tougher time of it than you." Yusuf looks away. "Anyway, see you in form. I've got to catch Mustafa by the shops." He waves goodbye with a two-finger salute and then he's gone.

My stomach transitions from flipping to dropping. I'd been so preoccupied with smoothing things over with Yusuf for the first day of school that I'd inadvertently forgotten about the bigger problem: my dad's stepdaughter.

Muna comes out a moment later, Thermos in hand. She throws her shawl aggressively over her shoulder as she strolls through the gate.

I push thoughts of Halima aside. She will not infiltrate my day, my thoughts, my anything, because Northwell High is Just-Safiya's territory. I refuse to become any other Safiya as a result of her presence.

"First of all," I say with a smirk, "I know you're late because you were trying to dig out that shawl even though it's still *summer*, but what's up with you? You look ready to choke someone with it." I take her hand, looping it through my arm.

Muna rummages in her pocket for her phone. "Look," she huffs. "*Look* at this, Saf."

I peer at the screen. The profile is of an account called BANTRxpose.

"And?" I ask. "They haven't been active in years, Muna. I thought we'd moved past this. I thought you'd healed from the trauma."

"I'm not having those dreams again," Muna insists, pushing the screen in my face. "It's really active again this time! The bastards are back," she growls.

"Okay, language, please." I bat her hand away, scrolling through the profile properly.

The entire account was wiped clean almost three years ago,

but I notice a new post has been added today. A screenshot from the Hexpose Editor's Letter. Most of it is cropped out apart from a single paragraph.

On a final and more positive note, let's welcome a new student to NWHS this year: Halima Omar. She'll be joining Year Eleven this month and is coming to us all the way from Somalia. Let's do our best to make her feel at home with us.

Three devil emojis have been added to the corner of the post. Halima's name has been circled in red.

"Bastards, indeed," I mutter under my breath. So much for hoping my dad's new stepdaughter would just fade into the background.

Muna throws her hands in the air, misinterpreting my reaction. "Now you get why I'm so aggravated! I can't believe this dumb BANTRxpose has returned to ruin Year Eleven." She pulls on her shawl. "I couldn't find the idiot last time but I'm not having this again. I will find the person responsible and I will end them."

We cross the road. Yusuf and his best friend Mustafa stand outside the newsagent's on Cromwell Hill. As per usual, Mustafa is stocking up on his weekly supply of gum, chocolate bars and halal Haribos, ready to sell them to hordes of peckish teenagers come break and lunchtime.

I stay silent.

"Don't worry, Safiya," Muna says gently, rubbing my arm.

"Your favourite investigative hijabi is on the case. No conundrum too small, no challenge too big. I will not cower before a smokescreen. Not today, not ever. I promise you, BANTRxpose will be exposed once and for all."

Muna interprets my silence as concern for Hexpose. I do not correct her.

We get to form a little early and stake out some good seats. Yusuf trails in not long after with his friend in tow. They head to our table at the back, pull chairs out and make to sit down.

Muna puts a hand up. "Uh, no."

"What do you mean 'no'?" Mustafa replies, insulted. "Do you own this table?"

She smiles sweetly, looking at Yusuf. "Cuz, collect your friend and sit elsewhere, please. Saf and I do not appreciate sitting with a certain type of energy."

Muna's rule at school is that she doesn't interact with family if she can avoid it. Because she and Yusuf have always had to share the same spaces, she likes to step out of those spaces as frequently as possible.

Mustafa floats his head in front of Yusuf, answering before he can. "And what kind of energy would that be, Muna? Bad boy energy? I happen to think a lot of people would be attracted to that sort of vibe."

Yusuf and I catch each other's eyes and stifle a laugh. These two have had a back-and-forth thing for a while and it only serves to make the rest of us uncomfortable.

"Just go, Mustafa," I reply. "You know this chick be unstable anyway." I indicate Muna. "Dangerous for anyone else besides me to get too close."

They give in without any more trouble. Mustafa throws me a free pack of sweets, but I know he's only doing it to get under Muna's skin.

"I'm dealing with crippling stress and this dumbass is trying to pick a fight," Muna says, kissing her teeth. She extends a hand to dip into my open packet.

I slap it away. "Oi. Get your own. Your boyfriend has a whole blazer full of them."

She mimes strangling me with her shawl. The bell rings before I manage to fake die.

# HALIMA

Hooyo and I walk past the main gates of this prison school to a smaller one on the other side. She pushes it, expecting it to give way easily, but it stays shut. She tries again, shaking the bars more violently with each turn.

If I did not know any better, I would say Hooyo was just desperate to be on time for our appointment, but I know she is only desperate to be rid of me.

I try not to take offence. I'm aware I have not been the most pleasant person lately and really I am just grateful Hooyo is the one accompanying me to the school office today. That had been another battle in itself, but eventually persistence won out. Now, the husband is sitting in the car having dropped us off, remaining firmly outside.

Someone strolls over to us as Hooyo shakes the bars yet again with a force I'm certain could split metal.

The man chuckles, stopping to press a button on a silver box we hadn't noticed. He is wearing a bright yellow jacket, accessorized with a small radio. An identity card hangs around his neck.

He opens his mouth and says some words. *Confirm, identity, buzz, love,* with some more in between. I clutch some and lose others. I nod in partial understanding. I think if I had noticed him sooner, I could have focused my mind and ears and held onto his every word. But surprise and comprehension do not go hand in hand. I make a conscious effort to be more alert from now on.

We hear static from the box and wait for something to happen.

Hooyo bristles. *"Did that man just say he loves me?"* she whispers, looking over her shoulder at his retreating back.

*"I think so,"* I reply. The word "love" had definitely been thrown around (if I remember correctly, something along the lines of "all right, love?") and that is certainly a word no one could misunderstand.

Hooyo shakes her head. *"There is no shame in this country, i s there? No shame at all."*

The static from the box transforms into the voice of a tired woman.

I concentrate. Focus my mind and ears.

"How can I help you?" the box says.

Hooyo and I look at each other. I step forward. The words are all jumbled in my brain but I try to squint through the fog.

"Uh…I am Halima. I am starting new school today."

If Khadija could see me now, I know she would be howling on the floor. Of the two of us, she was always the one to pick up languages quicker. Though we would both hear and learn the same words, her mind was always lightning fast and, in no time at all, she would be conversing, spelling, contemplating in that new language.

Whenever we did our homework together, she would practise with me. Sitting in our favourite bustling café around the corner from school, the strong wafting scent of qawxo warming our noses, Khadija would be patient as I copied the words that tumbled out of her mouth.

"One moment, please," comes the tired voice before a persistent buzzing sound begins.

Hooyo cautiously puts a hand against the gate and pushes again. It swings open this time and she steps inside. She holds the gate for me but I can't seem to move my legs as easily. This prison we are walking into, it's not a prison for her. Hooyo will be able to walk out of it, just as easily as she is walking in now, but me? I will need to stay in this place for as long as they have a right to keep me.

We are guided into a dingy office that reeks of urine. The smell is so strong that I am convinced someone must have used a corner of this place to unload their bladder at some point. A woman – not the same as the one with the tired voice – motions for us to sit down, indicating the two mismatched chairs opposite the desk.

"Hello, Halima and Ms Mohamed. It's lovely to finally meet you both," she says with a wide smile. She cranes her neck to look beyond us. "If I'm not mistaken, I believe Mr Aden was due to be here as well? To help facilitate our conversation and, I suppose, ensure we're all on the same page. Will he be joining us?"

Hooyo's gaze swings to me expectantly. The woman notices and follows suit.

"No," I reply. The fog is still there over my words, but I find them. I will always find them wherever my mother's husband is concerned. "He is not coming."

Her owl eyes blink at me, awaiting what I assume is clarification regarding his whereabouts but, when nothing else comes, her smile becomes pinched with awkwardness.

"Okay, well...perhaps we'd better get started then." She shuffles a few papers on her desk. "I'm Ms Devlin, your head o f year, Halima. I'd like to start by extending a warm welcome for the first day of what I hope will be a great year for you at Northwell High. We're so excited to have you join us. I have no doubt that you'll thrive here and my job is to help you do just that."

I lean forward without realizing, as though I can physically catch the words that flow out of her mouth. I am understanding the exchange so far, but barely. My mind and ears must be exhausted from all the focus, because I begin to lose some of the phrases that pass her lips.

"Now I know...first time in an English-speaking... Halima...organized support...easier." She takes a moment to glance over a sheet of paper, before leaning back in her chair. "Going to...assess...level...and...support...your classes. Until...comfortable...of course."

Ms Devlin taps something into her computer before turning her attention back to us. "Did that all make sense?" she asks.

I try to shake the fog away from my brain. I may not be able to speak this language the way Ms Devlin can, but that does not mean I am completely slow to catch on.

"It is okay. I can understand but takes time." I stop short of breaking into a triumphant grin. That is the most English I've strung together since coming here. Khadija would be proud.

Ms Devlin smiles on my behalf. "Wonderful! That's great to hear, Halima." She turns her attention to Hooyo. "Thank you for bringing Halima in for her first day. We have your husband's contact details as the primary relative, so if there are any issues we'll get in touch." She stands up and extends a hand. "We'll take it from here, but it was so lovely to meet you."

Hooyo nods, standing to shake Ms Devlin's hand. She shoulders her bag, understanding her cue to leave, and heads for the door. When she pushes down on the handle, Hooyo pauses.

*"You're going to let your mother leave without a goodbye?"*

I laugh under my breath. Affection under coercion is one of Hooyo's favourite approaches though, secretly, I am glad. It means she is not ready to say goodbye either.

I walk over and give her a crushing hug. She kisses me on the cheek and I kiss her forehead.

Then, she walks free of this prison.


Ms Devlin seems to have mistaken my understanding her for complete fluency, because she is now talking so fast that I begin to worry about enough oxygen getting to her brain.

110

I focus enough to capture the salient points and brush the fillers aside.

"We have your timetable ready," she says, waving a sheet of paper in front of me. "Your form tutor will go through it and explain. You'll have a buddy for the first week."

Ms Devlin takes a sharp left down the corridor. My feet skid on the floor as I try to keep up.

*My God*, I think to myself. *Even mosquitoes do not fly as quickly as this woman walks.*

"Lessons in maths, English, sciences, history, Spanish, art, PE, ICT and religious studies. We'll squeeze in some one-to-one English language support too."

A staircase appears out of nowhere and Ms Devlin leaps onto it. I feel my breath start to get away from me.

"I think you will do fine. You understand and speak some English – it won't take you long to pick it up at all."

I take a deep breath and cut in before she can start another explanation. "It's far?" I ask. "Where we going?"

"Almost there now," she says with a laugh. "I'm sorry. I should have warned you about the size of the school."

It turns out Ms Devlin is telling the truth because after another turn, she stops at a door.

"This one. Form 11C." She knocks on the door. "Just give me a minute." Then she walks in, letting the door slam shut behind her.

I take a moment to survey the hallway given the fact that half of the school appeared blurry as we sprinted to get here. The corridor is long, with four identical doors on either side and a few posters on the brick wall.

Ms Devlin steps out a minute later. She shakes her head in exasperation.

"I got the wrong room," she says. "Can you believe that, Halima? In my own school, I've got the wrong room. Terrible, isn't it?"

"Yes," I reply. "Terrible."

She laughs.

We proceed to walk to the right room, which I pray is not another sprint away.

# SAFIYA

The last few stragglers find their way into class. Our form tutor, the same one from last year, Ms Birch, trots in with a large cardboard box, but all I can think about is the fact the bell has rung. That means I'm safe. That means that this class belongs to me, and only me, because Halima Omar must be somewhere else and, at least for now, I can breathe a little easier.

"It's planner time," Ms Birch sings. "Time for a new year, my fresh-faced Year Elevens!" She drops the box onto her desk and points to her unsuspecting student of the day. "Chop, chop, Kyle. These planners aren't going to hand themselves out, are they?"

Kyle begrudgingly stands, sauntering over to her desk. He grabs a stack of planners and tosses them violently across to the closest table, only stopping when Ms Birch turns around to locate the source of his latest victim's yelps. When she turns her attention to the board again, Kyle throws the next planner. This time it hits Mustafa's head.

"Shit! What the hell is wrong with you, Kyle?" Mustafa cries, rubbing the back of his skull.

Ms Birch whips around. Mustafa lowers his head,

whispering under his breath. Most of us can still hear him though, including Kyle. "Absolute twat, man…"

"Miss, did you hear that?" Kyle sniggers. "He called me a twat! That's got to be an L1."

Ms Birch opens her mouth to tell them both off when there's a knock on the door. Ms Devlin, one of the year leaders, pokes her head in.

"Hi, miss, do you mind if I borrow you for a second?"

"Of course, I'll be right there." Ms Birch breathes a sigh of relief. I'm sure she's glad to take her referee hat off for a second. She leaves Kyle with strict instructions not to go tossing any more planners at people before she steps outside.

After a few minutes, Ms Birch returns, but she doesn't let the door slam shut behind her. She holds it ajar, clearly waiting for something. Everyone faces her, wondering what's happening, because it is obvious that Ms Birch is walking back in with a different energy. She has a rare smile on her face and is clearly no longer bothered by the Kyle and Mustafa drama.

She pulls the door back a little more and there, suddenly, stands the bullet I thought I'd managed to dodge, staring straight at me.

My senses hit the floor. I am reeling and I can barely feel Muna's hand on my arm, hear her calling my name, or meet the looks of pity that Yusuf throws my way. I can't hear what Ms Birch is saying either, because it feels as though my ears are full of water.

And yet I have a strong sense of the bullet that's shot through the room. She moves, closely following Ms Birch, sitting down at the only table with a free seat, opposite Yusuf and Mustafa, and next to Leanne. When she has sat down, she glances at me, but I can't decipher her expression.

Is she smug? Disgusted? Equally distraught? I don't know.

Ms Birch stands at the front of the room and points to her, smiling. I can't hear her properly, but I can read her lips.

"This is Halima, everyone. She's new to the school and will be joining our form this year. I want everyone to go around the room and introduce themselves so we can make her feel welcome."

I stand. The screech of my chair is enough to penetrate the water in my ears. My mouth feels dry, like I haven't had anything to drink in days.

"Miss, I don't feel well," I manage to croak out. "Can I go to the toilet?"

Ms Birch stops her smiling. Concern colours her face. "Of course, Safiya." She pauses, assessing me. "Muna, do you want to go with Safiya and make sure she's all right?"

I must look bad, I think, if she's suggesting somebody else joins me. She isn't usually so lenient with these requests.

In the toilet, I sit on the lid with my head buried in my hands. Muna's feet shuffle beneath the door, walking all the way in one direction before pivoting and going the other way. She doesn't knock on the door and ask me if I'm fine. She just lets me be.

Alone in the stall, my thoughts are quiet. Strangely, nothing fights for attention in my mind. There is only a story that Aabo told me growing up.

It was one I heard more than a few times, but it felt different to all his other stories because of what happened the first time he shared it. I remember the way his eyes had filled with tears and how he gazed at the ceiling for some time before he could look down again.

It was a story about his best friend, someone who he loved more than anything in the world. They were inseparable growing up, he'd said that first time, as I sat on his lap, plucking at his henna-coloured beard.

He and his friend would wander endlessly in the markets as kids, spend hours watching the ocean, spend even longer measuring the tide by the water lapping up their legs, run and chase each other all day in his family villa – because what else was there to do on a hot day in Yaaqshid when you lived in a house that had so much to explore?

"But, Safiya," he'd said gravely as I toyed with his beard, "*growing up is a dangerous myth. You don't gain the freedom that you're promised in the way you expected. You gain a different type of freedom and, with that, sacrifices sometimes need to be made.*"

I remember pulling my hand away from his face. I was only around six or seven years old then, but I was old enough to understand the heaviness that came with a word like "sacrifice".

"*What are you talking about, Aabo? What happened? Did you stop being friends with each other?*"

He smiled a little sadly and looked up at the ceiling as his eyes began to get misty.

He said, yes. When they got older, things changed. The world interfered and they could no longer be as close as they once were.

His parents believed his friend had been a bad influence on him, even though Aabo felt his friend had changed his entire world for the better. That his friend had made him happy.

I shook my head, looking up at the ceiling along with him.

"*Sorry, Aabo, but if you or Hooyo didn't like Muna and Yusuf, I wouldn't stop playing with them. I might pretend to, but I wouldn't really.*"

I saw the corner of his mouth go up. "Well…" He smiled ruefully. "*I tried that too, but it didn't work. Eventually, it was too painful to see my friend everywhere and not be able to talk to them, to not be the way we used to be, so I left. I flew away and came here to London. I married your mother and then we both found you.*"

I frowned then, new understanding piecing things together. "*I'm only here because you and your friend stopped being friends?*"

I remember the thought had made me uncomfortable. Like him coming here and finding me wasn't a choice, it was because he'd run away.

"*Well, yes, but I am grateful for it because look at what Allah led me to! My beautiful wife and beautiful daughter.*"

He looked down at me, eyes shiny, and hugged me close. "*What more could I ever want?*"

It's that last part that has run circles in my brain ever since Aabo left, because when a person says something like that, it means one of two things.

That they are certain, beyond a shadow of a doubt, about

the answer; that they already have everything they could ever need. Or that they are uncertain, questioning themselves as they speak, hoping for an answer to spring forward from elsewhere.

And I think to myself how lucky Aabo was to run away from his problems. How cowardly it was, and how easy, because that's something I won't ever be able to do. The four walls of this toilet are solid enough, but I know I won't be able to hide behind them for ever.

Since our bags are still in class, Muna and I have no choice but to head back to form before the period one bell rings. I get the bright idea to send her in alone to retrieve them for the both of us, but then I think…why? Why am I so scared to walk into *my* classroom? I was here first after all. This is *my* territory. I will not let Halima steal this away from me.

Ms Birch makes a beeline for me once we're back in our seats. She squats down next to our table.

"Are you feeling any better, Safiya?" She taps her long pink nails against my desk. I stare at them, wondering how teachers are allowed to get away with the very thing someone like me would get dragged for before I even stepped a foot past the school gates.

I shrug my shoulders. "Just a bit of period pain. I'm fine now."

My lying-to-teachers go-to has always been a fall back on period pain. *Why haven't you finished that poster on the periodic table yet, Safiya?* Period pain. *Why can't you run those three laps around the track, Safiya?* Period pain. *Why are you wearing your jacket in class, Safiya?* Period pain, sir. It makes me feel cold sometimes. You know how it is, right?

I can't lie, that one got me in trouble.

"Excellent. Glad to hear you're feeling better." Ms Birch stops tapping her nails and stands. "I wanted to ask whether you'd mind taking on a special job for me? I think you'd be the best person for it."

Muna cuts into the conversation, leaning in closer. "What's this special job I hear of? Something that a four-time school councillor may be able to help with perhaps?"

"No, Muna." Ms Birch laughs. "I appreciate the school spirit, but this is a different kind of assignment and, anyway, you're already busy with enough extra-curriculars." She zeroes in on me and squats once more. I can smell the coffee on her breath and I don't like it. "What do you say, Safiya? It wouldn't involve much, and it would only be for a few weeks."

I think it over for a moment, assessing my bargaining power. "Do you think that little something might help with college applications? Because if we're discussing favours here, I need a real good recommendation, miss."

I try not to sound desperate even though I am. College applications are just around the corner and my grades have been slipping for a while now. Between keeping Hooyo alive, and doing everything else around the house, there hasn't been all that much time for studying.

While I've never been one to sign up for optional school

activities, this might also be a worthwhile opportunity to take my mind off Halima and the nightmare playing out right before eyes.

"Of course," she replies unhesitatingly. "There is no question about it, Safiya. It'll go straight in your recommendation letter."

I pretend to mull it over, though my answer is pretty obvious. "Then, sure, happy to do it."

"Excellent!" Ms Birch stands again. "I know you will be the perfect person to be Halima's buddy—"

"*Excuse me?*" My voice reaches an octave I've never heard before. "This is about that girl?"

"Yes, it's about *that* girl," Ms Birch says, raising her eyebrows. "Not only is Halima a new student, she is also adjusting to a new country. You're likely in the best position to offer support in this transition, given your similar backgrounds. I don't want to inconvenience you, but I really think you're the best person to do this, Safiya."

"I'm not," I splutter. "Ms Birch, I refuse—"

It seems like Ms Birch hasn't even heard a word I've said, because she looks over her shoulder, to the other side of the classroom. "Halima?" she calls out. "Halima?"

Everyone in the class looks over to our table. Halima straightens, taking a deep breath before replying.

"Yes, Ms Bitch?"

Oh my gosh.

*Oh my gosh.*

Beside me, Muna is creasing. The whole class erupts into laughter alongside her. Yusuf and Mustafa, sitting opposite

Halima, have lost it too. They pump their fists against the table in disbelief, tears streaming down their faces. Yusuf holds his stomach as though to stop his intestines from spilling out. Halima takes in the unfolding scene in bewilderment. She glances at Ms Birch, who now looks as though she could slice through a block of wood if rage were a physical thing.

This isn't the first time Ms Birch has had her name substituted with that word and on the last three occasions it's happened, the culprits were given enough detentions and demerits to last a lifetime.

After that, people stopped making the mistake of joking about her name.

"I want you to pack your things, Halima," she says through clenched teeth, walking back to the front of the class, back ramrod straight. "Now! The rest of you have three seconds to stop talking before I start handing out lunchtime detentions!"

Halima packs in silence. I notice the way her eyes harden when she looks at Yusuf and Mustafa.

Ms Birch sits at her desk and sighs, rubbing her temples. I don't blame her. We've barely started the new school year and there's already too much going on.

"Safiya?"

I snap to attention. We're seconds away from the bell ringing and if I can make it out, I'll be free. This whole fiasco has diverted Ms Birch's attention from what she's just asked of me, but I sense the spotlight turning in my direction once more.

"Can you please accompany Halima to Ms Devlin's office?" Muna inadvertently yelps at this instruction, grabbing my arm.

"And don't worry about being late. I'll make sure to tell your Spanish teacher."

In that moment, I regret coming back to form more than I've regretted anything in my entire life.

# HALIMA

I curl my fingers around the school diary, distorting the metal rings. The laughter builds and builds. The boys in front of me lose all control, consumed by their sniggering. But if it was only them, I would be able to handle it. I just do not know how to handle a tsunami of this.

The laughter in the class halts when the teacher threatens them. I let my fingers around the rings loosen, watching the indentations disappear.

I know what the teacher is going to say before she says it. Anger settles around her head like ash from a volcano. It's as clear as day, even though I don't quite understand what has caused the eruption. That is why my hand is already picking up my bag before she tells me to do so, but I do not expect her to say what she says next, and I know the girl who she says it to does not expect it either.

The rest of the class watch on curiously. I read the question in the air.

*Why Safiya?*

Their question is mine too. Why is Safiya being painted as if she is something to me? Why can't anyone else, bar the two fools opposite, lead me to punishment?

Ordinarily, I always make a point to clarify matters such as this, but I know I cannot step out of line now. There is no margin of error here and if I do anything to worsen this situation, it will take longer to climb out of Ms Birch's bad books. There is no future for me here beyond the days it will take me to get back to Mogadishu, but I would be silly to think those days could be spent in blissful time-wasting if she despises me.

I stand, keeping my head up.

Some of the students look at me as if they couldn't care less. Others smirk. Some look at me with pity and it is those pitying glances that grate on me the most because it means they think I am weak. That they think the new foreign girl cannot handle herself. That she has walked into a territory where she doesn't understand the rules and where not knowing them can land you in the kind of hot water I am in now. But what they don't know is that I am a quick learner. That I learn what I need to survive and what I need here is respect because, in its absence, my humiliation is for the taking and that is one thing Abti Haroon always warned me about. It is dangerous to let anyone make a fool of you, to let them paint a picture of who you are before you have had a chance to paint it yourself.

I may be new to the scene, but I know how to paint a pretty good picture, and that is exactly what I intend to do.

I follow Safiya out of the classroom, keeping a respectable distance between us. She walks fast, perhaps expecting to lose me in this jungle of corridors, but I keep up, making sure to quiet my breathing as much as possible so she does not hear my panting. I look down at her hand, remembering what was there last time, but the bandage is gone.

She stops at the door I walked through only a short time ago and knocks.

"Come in!"

She pushes the door open but doesn't hold it for me.

The putrid smell in the room hits me again as I step inside. Somehow, it's even worse than before. Safiya imperceptibly wrinkles her nose too.

Ms Devlin sighs, closing her laptop. "I've just had an email from your form tutor." She raises her eyebrows, gesturing for us to sit. "Seems like we've gotten off to a bit of a rocky start, Halima, but she does understand this probably stemmed from mispronunciation more than anything malicious, so nothing to worry about there." Ms Devlin pulls a face.

"Ms Birch wanted me to explain the situation to you without the pressure of your curious colleagues listening in. You must – and rightly so – be a little confused by the reaction to using *that* word…" She gives a small chuckle. "But to give you some context, the word 'bitch' is actually an offensive and derogatory term, and quite insulting. So I hope that explains why Ms *Birch* sent you down here in a flurry." She taps her fingernails on her computer. "I must say though, this awkward incident was miraculously good timing for other reasons."

Safiya points to the door behind her. "Ms Devlin, sorry, but I really need to go. Ms Birch told me to drop her off and

125

leave. I can't be late to Spanish—"

A lie, obviously, but one that has my full support.

Ms Devlin shakes her head. "Don't worry about all that, Safiya. I'll give you a note to explain why you're late." She indicates the seats again and we both reluctantly sit down. "It's great that you're already here too. Ms Birch mentioned that she'd elected you as a buddy and, unfortunately, there is more that I must ask of you today." She shakes her head, staring hard at her laptop. "I received an email explaining there won't be any language support for you, Halima, for some time. It could be days, it may be weeks. Our language support teacher has taken sudden sick leave." She rubs her temples, like Ms Birch did upstairs. "The best laid plans…" Ms Devlin sighs.

"No problem," I say, wanting to end this conversation as quickly as possible. "I will wait."

Safiya appears startled when I speak, as though surprised I have a voice. Or maybe because I can speak this language of hers. Not as well as she can, of course, but enough to get by.

"Yeah, Ms Devlin, that's calm," she agrees, standing up to leave.

Ms Devlin interrupts her escape. "No, that's not *calm*, Safiya. Halima will need some help with her English as she settles in to Northwell High."

Safiya shrugs her shoulders. "I really don't see how that's my problem."

The frustration is starting to set in for her. Ms Devlin can see it too.

"Let me be clear. I know, Halima," she says gently, placing

her hands flat on the desk and looking to me, "that this incident in form was an accident, a simple misunderstanding, but this issue of language support is something we do need to address."

I wonder whether I should correct her and tell her that it was not an accident. I did call Ms Birch that word, but only because the boy opposite told me that was the way to pronounce her name. I had not asked him for any advice. He happily volunteered the information. I vaguely recall the girl beside me had squirmed in her seat when he'd said it. It was subtle, but a sign that should have made me realize that he might have been a snake.

Still, I know when to keep my mouth shut. One thing I have learned is never to go crying to someone else about your problems. It only becomes a problem when you can no longer handle it yourself.

Someone knocks on the door, interrupting Ms Devlin.

Her brow furrows. "Come in," she calls.

The door opens and a man steps inside. He looks sheepish, rubbing his cufflinks as he stands in the doorway.

Safiya and I lock gazes. She looks as if she is about to throw up and I don't blame her. I feel that same wave of nausea and the man is not even my father.

# SAFIYA

I don't stand when my dad walks into the room. In fact, I don't even acknowledge him. I'm not sure if Ms Devlin can sense that anything has changed, that the air is suddenly popping with tension but, if she can, she does a pretty good job hiding it.

"Sorry, sir, can I help you?" asks Ms Devlin. "I didn't think I had any meetings scheduled this morning..."

Aabo steps into the room and the whole space shrinks. "Apologies, Ms Devlin, I'm Halane Aden. I was due to attend with my wife and Halima this morning." He pauses and meets my gaze.

*Don't say it.*

*Don't you dare say anything.*

When Aabo upped and left, I didn't waste any time expunging his name from my school record. He is no longer linked to me in this building or its records and I would prefer it to stay that way.

"I was regrettably caught up with some urgent matters earlier, but I realized Halima had forgotten to bring along one of her school forms. I was in reception when I thought I saw her step into this room." He looks at me again, confused. I turn away. "I hope I haven't overstepped."

"How timely!" Ms Devlin all but squeals. "I was planning to call you straight after this meeting with the girls, but this is far more convenient. Please, do come right in, Mr Aden. I've got Safiya, Halima's buddy for the next few weeks, with us too. She and Halima share a similar background so we thought it might make this unfamiliar environment for Halima easier to navigate."

She rushes to pick up a chair from the corner and places it next to Halima, who is now stuck in the middle. Her leg has been jumping up and down from the moment we entered the office but the frequency of it intensifies now. Aabo sits and, when everyone is settled, Ms Devlin catches Aabo up on news of the missing language provision.

"The loss of this support deals a very big blow…" Ms Devlin starts, but she's lost me. How am I supposed to concentrate on her words when I'm trapped in this hellish room with Aabo and Halima? The very two people I've been trying so hard to cut out of my reality?

My subconscious detaches from real-time then. I only hear static whenever someone opens their mouth, as if I've switched onto a different radio frequency entirely. I nod when I feel expected to, like when Ms Devlin locks onto me with her owl-like eyes and pauses, or when my dad and Halima nod too.

At some point, Ms Devlin calls my name, filtering through the static.

"Sure," I say, on reflex. "That's fine."

Those few words are clearly enough to appease her because she dismisses us shortly after.

I head out of the door first, not conscious of my body moving but aware of the fact that I need to get out, right this minute, before I melt onto this floor.

When I step out of the room, a hand touches my shoulder.

"Safiya," my dad says quietly, shutting the office door behind him. "Thank you."

"For what?" I reply curiously, turning to face him.

He rubs his cufflinks before he answers, as though for good luck. "For helping your sister," he replies. "For agreeing to help with her English in class until…they find someone more permanent."

The laughter bubbles in my chest before it makes its way out.

"Aabo," I say, when I get a hold of myself. "Be serious. There is no way in hell that I am doing anything to help either of you. I said what I said in that room to get out of there, but if you believed any of it for a second…" I try to swallow it, but a laugh jumps out of me again.

Aabo looks taken aback, shocked that the good luck he hoped for hasn't arrived. Halima turns her head a fraction to the side. I had forgotten she was still here. I can tell she's laughing but I can't tell whether she's laughing with me or at me.

"I want you to listen to me carefully, Safiya." Aabo's voice is measured, but his bottom lip quivers. "I know there is a lot for us to work through, but—"

"No, you listen to me!" My voice bounces off the chipped brick walls in the admin block, but I don't care. If my dad wants to do this here and now, we will.

"You haven't stopped to give a crap about me for years and now you turn up with these strangers and, what? Expect me to welcome all of you with open arms? Smile like you haven't broken apart your actual family because you were too weak to stick around?" I point my finger at Halima. "I don't care about her because she is not *my* family, she's yours, so don't start shoving her down my throat because, guess what? I'm going to spit her right back out!"

I turn on my heels, ready to walk away before the itching in my eyes transforms into tears that I would rather hide than let my dad witness. But then I stop, twisting back to him before I can second-guess myself.

"Why are you even back here anyway?" I ask, trying to speak through the lump lodged in my throat. "It can't be because you wanted to reconcile or reunite or whatever, because you would have tried *way* harder before now, so what are you really here for?"

Aabo looks down at his shoes like I've sucker-punched him. He doesn't need to give me the answer because I already have it. I've known it from the minute Hooyo said he was finally returning, after all this time away.

"Well, I hope your businesses and money and success and everything you've worked so hard for all crashes and burns."

Aabo looks up, holding his anger at bay.

"And when you lose everything, I hope you remember that

it was Hooyo that got it for you in the first place. You'd be nothing without her."

I go to Spanish, alone. Muna takes French so I won't see her until next period, which is a relief. I'm not sure that I could handle her interrogations right now.

Halima finds her way to the class ten minutes later and introduces herself. She doesn't mention me, only sits where the teacher points, which, thankfully, is on the other side of the classroom.

The conversation from the hallway plays repeatedly in my head, as hard as I try to block it out. I hear none of Mr Fraser's usual reminders on correct tense or warnings that people throwing around the word *puta* will be receiving an automatic after-school detention. All I hear is Aabo's voice ringing in my ears.

*Safiya, thank you.*

When I close my eyes, all I can see is the gratitude and *relief* that set in on his face when he said those words.

*Thank you.*

Somehow, all in the space of an hour, and on the first day of school, everything has become about this girl. What she wants and what she needs. What's good for her and what's not. It's a bloody Halima-day parade and I'm sick of it.

I glance across to her.

She looks even more like my dad's daughter than I do, with her long fingers, dark complexion and high cheekbones.

Halima must sense my wandering gaze because she starts to look my way. I whip my head back to the board before she notices.

The rest of the school day drags painfully. All I can think about is getting home and putting the train wreck of today firmly behind me.

My phone buzzes in my pocket at the end of the final lesson. I peek at it underneath the table as I'm packing away.

An email. From the company Hooyo was meant to interview with today for the cleaning job.

I hold my breath as I click on the notification.

*It's good news*, I think. *It has to be.*

But it's not a job offer. It's a notification of application rejection.

Turns out Hooyo didn't even go to the interview after all.


We head back to form at the end of the day for final registration. Yusuf jogs up to me and Muna on the stairs.

"Hey, Safiya," he says. "What happened this morning with the new girl? Did she get in trouble with Ms Devil?"

I roll my eyes. "Ms Devlin's not even that bad. Not compared to the other head of years anyway. I don't know why everyone calls her that."

He shrugs his shoulders, fastening the top two buttons of his shirt and fixing his tie. Ms Birch is a stickler for proper uniform, and no one wants to get in trouble during the last fifteen minutes of the day.

"Did she get in trouble though?" he asks again, more insistently. "For calling Ms Birch that?"

I jump the last two steps on the staircase, about to ask why he's so interested in any of this, when Muna cuts in.

"It was you, wasn't it?" She kisses her teeth when he grins. "You're the worst, Yusuf. Dragging an innocent girl for no reason. What's wrong with you?"

I realize then that Muna is right. I think back to the morning, remembering the hardened look in Halima's eyes when she locked eyes with Yusuf and Mustafa.

I shake my head, pushing our class door open. "That was a little below the belt, Yusuf."

His head bobs back in surprise. "What? I thought you'd be gassed that new-girl-who-is-not-your-sister would get into trouble on her first day."

"I'm not saying that it wasn't funny..." I say over my shoulder, walking to my seat. "Just that it was a bit savage."

Yusuf looks at me uncertainly, as if he can't quite believe what I'm saying and, to be honest, I can't either.

We take our seats in class and, for the last few minutes of the day, I close my eyes and attempt to erase Halima from my memory, try to erase her very existence from my knowledge entirely, despite the fact she is sitting only a couple of tables away from me.

All I want is blissful ignorance. The thing I never even knew I had until the beginning of the worst summer of my life.

# AUTUMN: PART 1
## SMOKING GUNS

*The girl scrubbed her heart down, fervently and meticulously, when she bid goodbye to the boy, her love. She watched as he travelled across land and sea to be rid of the pain and anguish that almost ripped them apart whenever their eyes met across the courtyard or the narrow hallways of the villa. So strong was this pain that the girl did not sense the mark that their love had left with her until it was too late.*

*And the boy fell into the arms of another girl not long after, in this new land. One he did not love, but one who seemed to please everyone around him given, as it was, that she did not come from such a lowly tribe.*

*There is logic in this match, the elders agreed, when the boy accepted this new union. It is as we wished. May Allah bless your marriage!*

*The elders blessed the boy – now a man – and his new wife with wealth, in riches and in children. They blessed them with peace, with love. With patience and grace. They blessed them with for ever, though it must be said that even blessings cannot revive something already destined to be dead.*

# HALIMA

In the month that I have been here, I fear that I may be well on my way to swallowing my mother tongue. The strange and flimsy language of this country comes to me now more easily than I would like to admit, and while I have yet to lose my grip on the Somali I came with, the worry is still a gnawing ache in the back of my mind.

I ache so deeply for the music of home. For a mother tongue that colours everything vibrantly and envelops effortlessly. For words you need to work at, and *really* work at, for them to sound right. For sounds that come from the deepest part of your chest and that lighten the load when you breathe them out.

But here, in this country…words roll off in calm waves. Not the crashing, unpredictable ones I'm used to. It is clear no one speaks with their body either. Hands don't fly the same way, the eyes never come alive.

Sometimes, when I lie in bed at night, my soul feels like it is no longer breathing. Though that doesn't surprise me any more. How can a soul breathe when its lifeblood disappears? I need the salty and dusty air of home. I need it to live.

Really, I do.

I sink into my bed, letting the duvet engulf me, wanting to disappear into the cotton fibres. A sigh pushes me further into the mattress and I feel my mobile dig into my thigh.

For the tenth time, I check that the battery is fully charged, the ringtone is not silent, and my internet connection is steady. Though I have had this phone for years, since the husband purchased it as a bribe for my affection, I find myself worried that I have forgotten how to receive a call. Khadija and I have spoken regularly since I have been here but what if something goes wrong today for the one call I've waited so long for?

Khadija is the only one with reliable enough internet access, the only person who can help me easily connect to what I've left behind; if today does go wrong, I am not sure my heart will be able to bear it.

I turn over on my side, cradling the mobile close, waiting for the telltale vibrations. Soft morning sunlight glints through a gap in the curtains, creating a warm glow in the room. A slant of light dances across my face. I close my eyes, preferring darkness for now.

The phone vibrates in my hand twenty minutes later than scheduled. I scramble to sit up. A protest builds in my throat as I prepare to berate Khadija for being this late, after all the waiting and rescheduling we have had to do in these last few weeks, but when a familiar face fills the screen, those protests die on my lips.

"*Abti Haroon*," I breathe, feeling sharp pinpricks in my eyes. His dark and weathered face looks blurry with the poor connection. I wait for the picture of him to become clearer and, when it does, I gasp.

Abti Haroon's rounded face is all angles now and his once sun-kissed complexion appears ashen. A smear of blood underlies his bottom lip. The camera is readjusted and I get a glimpse of Abti lying on his bed. He looks emaciated, collarbone stark beneath his skin, as though close to erupting through the surface, and his chest heaves dangerously fast. A sheen of sweat covers his forehead. Khadija's arm comes into the frame to dab his face with a towel.

I turn the camera away from my face. My throat constricts with the effort of not making a sound, but the waves are gaining momentum. The pinpricks in my eyes sharpen even more and silent tears begin streaming down my face.

"*Halima*," Khadija calls anxiously. "*Are you there? Has the connection dropped?*"

I quickly wipe away the evidence before turning the camera back around.

"*Yes, I am here.*" My voice comes out thick and I cough, hoping neither of them picks up on it. The lump in my throat feels impossible to speak around but I try. I do my best to inject some semblance of normality into my voice, because this is what Abti Haroon needs. He needs me to be strong, like he has been for me all my life. He does not need me to be crying, weak, unable to hold myself together.

"*Bring the phone closer, Khadija,*" Abti Haroon says so softly

I struggle to hear him. "*I need to hear her voice.*"

Khadija obliges. The screen zooms into Abti Haroon's side profile. I bring my legs up to my chest and smile as brightly as I can, praying some of that false brightness bleeds into my words.

"*Halima,*" he wheezes, "*my dearest girl…how I have longed for us to speak.*" He shifts slightly in the bed. "*Bless you, Khadija, for bringing her to me. You do not know how grateful I am for this moment before I depart this world to meet God in the next.*"

I close my eyes, blinking hard. "*Abti…don't say that, please. You are not leaving this world, not yet.*"

He grunts, a trace of admonishment in his tone. "*Be careful with the words that you use, Halima. You know I have always taught you that we are not—*" He coughs violently, and the phone shakes, falling to the floor. I feel as disorientated as the screen I stare at, holding my breath, waiting.

Abti Haroon's side profile returns with Khadija's help. He wipes his lips with the back of his hand before continuing.

"*Remember, we are not the planners of our lives, Halima. There is only one and that is God.*"

"*I know,*" I reply, exasperated. Abti Haroon always likes to play the God card. As if I do not understand or accept the concept. "*But, Abti, I only mean that you don't know when it is your time either. You make it sound like it will happen imminently, but you could still live for another five or ten years. You do not know—*"

"*Halima.*" The solemnity in his voice gives me pause even though I want to keep speaking and never stop speaking. I

141

know what he will say, what he will try to force me to acknowledge.

*"The doctors have told me I am dying. The blood that pours from my lips is not make-believe, it is my life source finding its way back to this earth. My lungs are not what they used to be, and they are beginning to fail."* I catch the edge of his smile. *"And yet, all I feel compelled to focus on is the good. All I want to hear and breathe and think of are the blessings that God has bestowed upon me. Should I not be a grateful slave in life and approaching death? Please, Halima, even if you do not want to, humour me. Tell me of your life, your adventures, of the new world you inhabit. I want to hear everything. Could you give me that at least? As a favour for this old, dying man?"*

This time, the waves come crashing in full force and there is nothing in my power to hold them back. The once silent tears become wailing, weeping, howling ones and, while I struggle to bring myself back to shore, Abti Haroon soothes me in the way he has always done. He recites the enthralling poetry I grew up hearing, that he made it his mission to teach me, the words imprinted in a mind that has never failed him and has never ceased to amaze me. And when I gain control once more, Abti Haroon stops, letting me paint him a picture of the new world I have come to live in unwillingly.

Soon after, exhaustion creeps in, overwhelming his body. Abti Haroon falls asleep to the sound of my voice and stories, leaving me alone with Khadija. She steps away from the bed to sit in a corner of the room and his light snoring follows her.

*"How bad is it, Khadija?"* I ask. *"I need to know, is Abti's*

*condition truly as bad as he says?"*

Khadija's face is shrouded in darkness so I cannot read her expression.

*"Halima..."* She sighs, shifting her head to look at his sleeping form. *"There is a word that his granddaughter Maymuna said the doctors are using..."* She pauses and, in the dim light, I see her bite her lip. *"Cancer. You remember this word from our studies? It can be deadly and, in his case, it has already found its way into his lungs. Apparently, it is too far gone for any doctor, let alone the ones in this country, to do anything about it."*

I let the words sink in before I say anything. *"How long does he have left?"*

*"Months, maybe weeks..."* Khadija pauses, looking to Abti Haroon. *"But one thing is for certain, Halima – he will definitely not live to see another five or ten years."*

We are silent after that. Khadija and I have known each other for long enough that the absence of speech is not awkward for either of us. She does not try to comfort me, and I do not ask for it. Our friendship has always been of the quiet sort. We are there for each other, without question, but neither of us need to speak or shout to show it.

In this moment, I am grateful for her more than I have been in my entire life. For letting me sit in my sadness, for not forgetting about me even though I have moved thousands of miles away, for trying so hard to make this video call with Abti Haroon work. And the sadness hits more acutely when I realize that I have one friend at the edge of this world, close to leaving it for ever, and my other friend – who I have known and loved for over a decade – is sitting by his side when it should be me in her place. When it was me who never should have left home to begin with.

That night, I try to fall asleep but, after several hours, I am nowhere close. I pull the covers over my face, replaying the conversation from this afternoon. It is all I have been thinking about since ending the call with Khadija.

*My lungs are not what they used to be.*

*Cancer.*

*Months, maybe weeks.*

*The doctors have told me that I am dying.*

After waiting so long for today's call, I feel robbed. How can it be that things have deteriorated so rapidly? When I last saw Abti Haroon, he had said he would be lucky to see another year. Even then, a part of me believed he was exaggerating – perhaps self-diagnosing a dreadful illness when he might have something milder – but now, in the space of an afternoon, we have gone from a year to potential months, even weeks.

A spear of something – anger, maybe frustration – shoots through me when I think about that lost time. In between Abti being unwell, transferred to the crumbling, dingy local hospital, and Khadija and I not being able to find a good moment to speak, no one has had the opportunity to tell me this terrible truth.

And now, in the face of it all, my attempts at getting home seem utterly pitiful. All I have tried are my usual below-the-belt tactics: slipping in needling comments to inflame Hooyo's thinly veiled insecurity about the husband's second family; or reminders about home and how that is truly the only place we belong; and, as a desperate attempt once, something about the weather and how the cold in this country – come winter – would not spare Hooyo's old bones. After all, she wasn't young and neither was she used to the savagery of the season.

I sigh, pushing thoughts of defeat aside, and open my mind's memory box for comfort – my carefully curated treasures of home.

Khadija, the scent of dhuxul, the ringing call of the adhaan. The vibrancy of the crystal-blue Indian Ocean and the feel of grainy sand between my toes. The sweetness of mangoes and papayas, the juice of those heavenly fruits trickling down my chin. The poetry of home that lives in my bones, and, of course, Abti Haroon.

In the sixteen years that I have known him, he has become a sort of father figure in my life. Besides Hooyo, he is the last living connection to my own late father. Aabo's family had disowned him when he wed Hooyo thanks to tribal disputes and Abti Haroon, the quiet, good-natured neighbour, grew to fill that space left behind. Abti Haroon was a friend, a mentor, a life-instructor of sorts for my own father and, when Aabo passed away, their friendship became my inheritance. I grew up hearing stories about Aabo, of the poetry he too was so enthralled by, of enchanting tales about our homeland.

The husband, when he arrived, could never live up to him. Abti Haroon was wise, contemplative, lyrical, funny. He had lived so much of life, had seen so much, and he was patient. He really cared, despite living with so little. I always thought it was a mark of the great man he was that he chose to live with nothing even though he could have had everything. Then I remember what he said to me the last time I spoke to him.

*Look around. Does this look like a rich man's castle to you?*

My mind falters. I sit up, replaying that exchange.

Abti Haroon did not pay for my private schooling. Not even a single dollar. So why did Hooyo tell me that he had for all those years?

Before Hooyo married the husband five years ago, she had no source of income. No family abroad, no inherited wealth since she had been born into a poor family from the countryside. My own father had been a poor man too, she said, whenever I asked about him and his side of the family. *His parents, your grandparents, they want nothing to do with you either.* They had been unhappy about his marriage to Hooyo, about how they had eloped, but, more than that, about their conflicting tribes.

And yet...I went to the most expensive schools in the city. We never worried about food, rent, about keeping ourselves out of the sun or rain. For a long time, I assumed if Abti Haroon was paying for my schooling, he was financing everything else too.

I shut my eyes, lying down again. I won't be able to sleep tonight, but it will be for a different reason now.

Why did Hooyo lie to me all those years? And why did she use Abti Haroon to do it?

\* \* \*

146

The next morning, I leave the house at the same time my brothers do with Hooyo. The husband is already gone, pulled away to his business, which is just how I like it. A morning free of him and his hovering and his constant chatter.

When I reach the main school gates, I make my way to class by the only route I know. There must be other shortcuts, but I would rather this than ask anyone for help. Safiya was assigned to be my guide when I first started here, but it wasn't something either of us wanted. Now, she goes her way and I go mine. We do not intentionally cross paths and, if the husband ever asks how it's going – which he does from time to time – I tell him that the arrangement is working out splendidly. Of course, since there is no Safiya to corroborate the story, he only ever sighs and shakes his head when he hears the layered sarcasm in my voice.

Ms Birch is much easier to convince, even with the sarcasm. But I have come to realize that is because her questions are only a formality and, truly, she does not care.

I pass by the third fire extinguisher on the wall along my route – an indication that I am only one turn away from the classroom – when something catches my leg. I tumble forwards violently, grainy floor magnifying, and crash into someone.

Hands grip my arms. Firm, but not hard enough to leave a bruise. A shoulder leans against my chest, holding me upright. I look down. This person I have crashed into is bent at the knee. They have swooped in at the last second, closing the small gap between me and the floor. Their face is blocked by the way they are angled, but I know who it is.

Safiya pushes me up and I lean on the fire extinguisher to gather myself for a moment. She stands from kneeling, dusting herself off.

"Oi – got ourselves a little Wonder Woman over here!" someone hollers.

A few snickers go around.

"Nah, nah, I'm actually serious you know…" the same voice says again. "You got quick reflexes, Safiya. I'm impressed."

I turn around to locate the voice. I recognize it as someone from class, though I am not yet certain of everyone's names.

"Stop being an idiot, Kyle," snaps Safiya. The laughter dies as the tone shifts. "And you better not try playing this game again or, I'm telling you now, Ms Birch will be the least of your problems."

The *ooooh*s replace the silence, building until Kyle clears his throat.

"You saying you're her little guardian angel now?" He sniffs, looking Safiya up and down. "Didn't peg you to be such a dead ting."

Safiya throws her head back, laughing, but it seems forced. When she recovers, she glances at me. Her gaze is ice-cold and calculating, and I can tell she is weighing up her words not just for Kyle but for me too.

"I'm only going to say this once," she replies, lips curled. "I'm not anybody's guardian angel, but you better hope and pray that you have one the next time you try chatting to me like that."

Muna steps in then to grab Safiya's arm. Her other friends,

Yusuf and Mustafa, move to stand next to her too. Between the three of them, they have created a human force field with Safiya in the centre of it.

Ms Birch comes out a moment later to ask what everyone is doing outside of class, and then they are all trailing inside, whispering, whispering, whispering, until it is only me left outside of the door, alone.

An island of a girl who used to be a country.

By the time I return home, my unease is rippling at full force. I sense the undercurrents of rage, feel the exhaustion from last night stinging my eyes, and I know these things are on my face, plain as day, for anyone to see. But when Hooyo notices me in the hallway, she only gives me a wan smile and disappears into the kitchen. I hear the fridge open and shut. The rumbling of the kettle. Hooyo is not coming back out to find me.

I blink, and I am back in the school hallway from this morning with Safiya. I see the force field that formed around her. She did not call for help but it still came. Help and love and support flocked to her, the same way flowers turn to the sun. Unbidden, instinctive. Without question.

But me? I am an island. I come home and even my own mother ignores me.

The boys are glued to the TV in the living room, watching cartoons. The husband is not around. If I am to capitalize on this opportunity, it must be now because, for too long, he has had a monopoly on Hooyo. Exercised some unholy control over her and the words that come out of her mouth.

He is the reason we are here and the reason I cannot go back, regardless of how much begging and crying I wish I could do about Abti Haroon.

But I need the truth now, desperately. I have to know if what Hooyo and I had before the husband came into our lives was real. That it was built on truth and trust and respect. Whatever our relationship is now, I need the comfort of knowing, at one point, it was perfect.

I zoom past the living room, not wanting to draw the boys' attention, and step into the kitchen, shutting the door behind me. Hooyo is standing at the cooker, heating dinner for the husband, which means he will be home soon. I need to get this over with before that happens because, if there is one thing I know, him being here will stop me getting the answers that I need.

"Hooyo," I say, leaning against the door. "Intee ka timid lacagteena?"

Hooyo almost drops the wooden spoon. She recovers quickly but, in that simple movement, I know that this question has struck a nerve.

"Halima, what do you want from me?" Hooyo says with a sigh. "Don't you have schoolwork to be doing or Qur'an to be reading? Stop wasting your time."

She mixes the food in the pan vigorously and the smell of it hits me. The earthy scent of lamb, the oil, the cardamom and cinnamon. Oodkac, the dish that she first taught me to make, nearly a decade ago, when it was only the two of us.

Another reminder of the life lost once her new husband came into the picture.

"*I want to know, where did all our money come from back home?*" I ask again. "*Who paid for everything? Who paid for my schooling?*"

*Clang. Clang. Clang.* The spoon bounces off the edge of the metal.

"*You know, before you married that man.*"

Hooyo shifts, turning away from me completely.

"*Because…*" I continue, holding tighter to my resolve. "*Before we left, Abti Haroon told me it was not him, though for years you insisted it was. You always told me that he was wealthy, only posing as a poor man, that he helped us out of the goodness of his heart. But that is not true, is it?*

"*And I know that our family was poor. Abkow and Abooto barely had enough to feed themselves, let alone feed their only widowed daughter.*"

Hooyo's back stiffens. I stand up straighter, zeroing in. The answers are here, I'm sure of it.

"*I know that they were so poor in the countryside that they sent you off to work for a wealthy family in the city. Because it was better for you to find good work as a housemaid.*"

Hooyo turns off the cooker. She places her hands on the counter.

"*And I know that my father died a poor man, that his family wanted nothing to do with us, because that is what you told me. So where did all our money come from?*"

Hooyo slams both hands against the countertop.

*"Halima, stop it!"* she shouts.

The move is so quick, so aggressive, it makes me jump. The handle of the door behind me shakes a moment later. I hear Kamal's muffled voice and grab the handle to make sure the boys won't push themselves in.

*"Enough is enough!"* Hooyo shouts, still standing with her back to me. *"Where is the respect I raised you with, Halima? Because questioning your mother is not respectful, it is shameful."*

*"It is not shameful to ask questions,"* I reply, drawing out my words slowly.

I think about Abti Haroon and what he would say if he was here. What he would tell me if I was back home and I went to him about any of this, or if he overheard our raised voices through the open windows and came by the house to give me his no-nonsense advice.

But I do not have to think for too long because the only thing Abti Haroon does is turn to the words of God or the words of poets if he wants to give advice, and I know what words he would share with me if he decided to turn to Hadraawi.

I say the words I might have held back from speaking on a different day, but it is too late for regrets now.

*"It is not shameful to ask questions, Hooyo,"* I repeat as I detach myself from the door. The handle has stopped shaking. *"It is shameful to lie."*

I walk up to her where she stands, facing the wall. She is motionless.

I lift my hand to her shoulders and she flinches.

"*Please, Hooyo.*" My voice comes out choked. "*I just want things to be how they used to be.*"

Tears escape from the edges of my eyes but I do not move to wipe them. In this very moment, it feels like I am frozen too.

"*I do not care where the money came from. I want you to know you can trust me. You can always trust me.*"

Hooyo opens her mouth to speak. I hold my breath, not wanting to disrupt anything.

"*It came from me.*"

Though Hooyo's mouth is open, the words are not hers. They are his. He is here.

Hooyo whips around so fast that it takes a moment for my hand to register it is no longer holding anything.

My mother's husband stands in the doorway of the kitchen with Kamal and Abu Bakr tucked away behind him.

"*The money came from me, Halima. Your mother reached out to a mutual friend of ours and I decided to give her the money you both needed, which covered your schooling.*"

His gaze leaves mine for a moment to meet Hooyo's. It is quick but long enough for me to notice there is something in it.

I cross my arms. "*And why on earth would you do that for someone you never even knew? Tell me, were you bankrolling half the widows in the city?*"

He shrugs his shoulders. "*I had money saved up and my friend was always good to me. When she said that your mother needed help, I didn't question it. It was always meant to be a loan,*" he adds. "*Never a gift. But then…*"

153

He looks at Hooyo and smiles.

*"Well, then we fell in love, and the matter was closed."*

It does not pass my scrutiny that his smile is not matched by Hooyo. Hooyo looks relieved but a little sick too.

I open my mouth, prepared to shut down his entire defence with a single point – that Hooyo has never had a single friend she would be prepared to ask that much of – but I stop myself.

Clearly, the question that I thought was straightforward has a much more complex answer. Neither of them will give up the truth, but I also know that the more you search for it head-on, the more slippery it becomes. The quicker it evades you and disappears. Whatever this is will need to be coaxed out in a different way.

Though, even without answers, this conversation has been illuminating in more ways than one. Because now I know that whatever exists between Hooyo and the husband was never simply pure, unadulterated love. What has hung between them, from the very beginning, are the heavy dollar signs of debt.

I place my hand back on Hooyo's shoulder.

*"See, Hooyo,"* I say in my gentlest voice. *"I wish you would have just told me that sooner."*

# SAFIYA

If there is one thing Kyle Peters has always been able to do, it is get under people's skin.

After the fiasco this morning, I can't seem to forget the words he threw at me. It wasn't the fact that he called me a dead ting. No, if those kinds of insults bothered me, there is no way I would've survived at Northwell High for as long as I have.

It was the other thing he said – that he probably didn't even think twice about – that's got me in a tailspin.

*Guardian angel.*

I had looked at Halima when he said that. A wave of bitterness came on so strong I wouldn't have been surprised if I had pounced on her, landing a punch right there and then. I couldn't stomach the fact that someone could imagine I would stand up for her, the girl who has taken my place as a daughter, who walks around these hallways like she owns the whole damn place.

If I had been more alert, I wouldn't have stopped her from slamming into the ground, but my instincts had kicked in. My head had overridden my heart. I'd seen Halima falling and, before I could even process what saving her would mean, I'd skidded across the floor and taken on her weight.

The ideal scenario would have been me quietly slinking away and pretending the whole thing hadn't even happened, but then Kyle opened his stupid mouth. I knew he'd been the one to trip her up because that's always been Kyle's MO and, when he didn't contradict me, I knew I was right.

I breathe a sigh of relief at lunch, grateful to have some distance from Halima, even if it's only for thirty minutes.

Muna and I grab some food and claim our favourite table at the back of the hall. It's during this window of the day that we do most of our Hexpose dissections. Muna is in the middle of discussing an alleged scandalous mural drawn on the wall in the boys' bathroom when she stops speaking mid-sentence.

"What?" I say, mouth full of shepherd's pie. "Finish your story then. What are they saying it is?"

When I notice she's no longer looking at me but looking past me instead, I twist in my seat to follow her gaze.

"Those two are going to try and sit here with us, just watch," she announces.

True to her prediction, Yusuf and Mustafa make their way to our table, lunch trays in hand.

"Mind if we sit here?" Mustafa asks sweetly. Yusuf doesn't even bother to ask, only pulls up the chair next to me, sits down, and begins shovelling food into his mouth.

Muna interlocks her fingers, leaning her chin on her hands. "Mind if you don't?"

Mustafa gasps. "That's no way to speak to your man, is it?"

Muna grimaces. "You don't even know how full of—"

Before she can finish her sentence, someone slams into Mustafa from behind. He manages to keep a hold of his tray, but the cake and custard sloshes around violently, leaving more than half of it collecting in a pool on the table.

We all know who it is even before we hear the laugh. Kyle makes a run for it a second later, disappearing into the crowd. Mustafa slams his tray down and makes to chase after him before Yusuf stands and pulls him back, nearly choking on his food in the process.

"Bro," he splutters. "Not even worth it with that prick. Don't do it."

Mustafa breathes heavily, probably beyond ready to beat the crap out of Kyle, but I sense the tension start to slowly diffuse. I give Muna a look while the boys aren't watching.

Her eyebrows do a little dance in response.

The two of us have always been able to read each other, and not only on a superficial level – sometimes we can almost sense exact thoughts. It doesn't always work, but it works this time.

*I don't want that boy getting any ideas! He's too delusional.*

I shrug, pursing my lips. *Haven't you ever heard not to kick a man when he's down? Let him sit. Lunch is nearly done anyway.*

So that's how Yusuf and Mustafa end up having lunch with us.

The four of us sit in awkward silence. I'm almost done eating, though Muna still has most of her food left to finish. Clearly, Mustafa bothers her more than she cares to admit.

I decide to be a good friend and draw attention away from her. "So, Mustafa. What's up? Business been good to you?"

He chews his food for longer than seems necessary, swallowing dramatically before he replies.

"Can't say too much about that to be honest." He eats another mouthful. "You know what they say about an entrepreneur never revealing their secrets, Safiya."

"I thought that was only about magicians."

He shakes his head, drinking a swig of water. "Trying to tell me they aren't the same thing?"

"Yes." I smirk. "But I do see you regularly stocking up at Cromwell so I assume you must be turning some kind of a profit."

"What's this? You're keeping tabs on me?" He frowns, pointing a finger in Yusuf's direction. "You'd be better off keeping tabs on your own man. I think my girlfriend might get pretty jealous otherwise."

Muna pushes her tray away then, plate practically licked clean. I hide my smile.

"Personifying air is not the way to go," she interjects, pointing a fork at him. "Take my advice on that."

"Damn." Yusuf nearly chokes on his food again, slapping Mustafa on the back. "She just used English Literature on you, mate."

Mustafa grins. "My girlfriend gets feisty when she's jealous. I like it."

Muna splutters in response. I lean forward, drawing attention away from her *again* to help her save face. "To circle

158

back to your earlier point, Mustafa, yes, I do keep tabs on my man, but I can multitask. I'm sure an entrepreneur like yourself understands that skill pretty well."

Yusuf, as expected by this point, chokes for the third time.

Since I *rarely* play into the whole Yusuf-and-Safiya thing, when I do, it never fails to take him by surprise. Sometimes it's just for fun, especially when Mustafa is also trying to get under Muna's skin, but other times…

Other times, I don't know. Maybe a part of me imagines that, in some alternative world, Yusuf really is my man. And it definitely feels safer to joke about it than say it for real.

"I do." Mustafa nods, matching my mock-serious tone. "And, to circle back to *your* earlier point, Safiya, business has been good but, I've got to say, there have been a few…issues cropping up recently. Things that might cut into profits, reduce my customer base. I'm keeping tabs on that though since I, too, can multitask."

He winks at me and I can't help but laugh, finally breaking composure.

"What do you mean?" Muna asks anxiously. "What is it, Mustafa?"

Mustafa rolls his eyes. "Calm down, Miss Editor-in-Chief. I'll tell you what you want to know, don't you worry."

*Oh crap.* Since when does Mustafa know that Muna is behind Hexpose?

Muna swivels to face her cousin, though Yusuf is already cowering with his head underneath the table. If he was smart, he would've already made a run for it.

She stands, slamming her hands against the table. "Idiot!" she screams. "You told him? What the hell's wrong with you—"

"Mr Khan's walking behind you and looking this way," I whisper.

"…O lovely cousin of mine," she continues, with an instant smile. "What the hell is wrong with you, O lovely cousin of mine, is what I meant to say."

Muna sits down.

"Please, Muna, don't be angry," Mustafa pleads, more earnest that I've ever heard him before. "I kept harassing him about it last year when I was convinced it was you and he has the worst poker face, you know that." He pauses. "I'm sorry. I shouldn't have even said anything, but it kind of slipped out."

Muna stares him down hard. The bell rings and I see the relief that sets in his eyes. Mustafa will be escaping with his life today.

We deposit our trays and head to the quad for the afternoon assembly.


Once everyone is registered, Ms Birch leads us in, indicating the rows we are supposed to fill. Somehow, I've ended up sitting between Mustafa and Yusuf instead of next to Muna.

I turn to my left to see Yusuf grinning. To my right, Mustafa wears a placid expression, and, beside him, Muna stares ahead, stonily.

"Keep trying to tell my guy he has no chance," Yusuf

whispers after stealing a glance in Ms Birch's direction. "I think he just likes messing with her too much."

I turn to reply before stopping myself.

What I want to ask is what makes him think that his chances with me are any better because, even though he's only ever said it once, I know he thinks that he has one.

Yusuf has always been there for me, has always been solid and dependable. He's been the guy who will turn up when I haven't even noticed how close the loneliness and sadness have got to chipping away at me, the guy who will buy me a Magnum every Friday of the summer with his tiny allowance because, according to him, what good is a summer without quality ice cream? The guy who will make the deadest jokes, not to see me laugh, but to see me cringe in horror instead.

But ice creams and jokes can only do so much, because the loneliness and sadness never go far.

And the thought that I always come back to is this:

How can anyone trust love?

Because, in my experience, love is deception. Love is wild. Love has no rules.

It can pack its bags in a second and disappear, never to be heard from again.

And then you're left with nothing but depression.

Yusuf cocks his head, waiting for me to agree with him but, in a strange turn of events, Kyle saves me from having to respond. He turns around to look at us in the row behind, making a whipping sound effect. Yusuf shoves him, forcing him to turn around. Thankfully, he doesn't restart the conversation.

I catch myself wondering what everyone else must think of us. The ones who create ships and ship names, the people who have called the both of us *Yufiya* for as long as I have been at this school.

I'm not stupid. I have always known that love stories are different for people like us because we live by different rules. We're not like Caprice and Marcus, who'll find any empty hallway during break and lipse each other until their faces are numb. Or Rianna and Luke, who can hold hands for what seems like every minute of the seven hours we're stuck at school.

Ours is a quiet kind of ship in a quiet kind of sea. Not in raging waters and whirlwind currents. Ours is a ship held together by faith. A belief in something different. I mean, that is, if we had a ship at all.

I'm not quite sure it makes sense, to be honest. Not the believing in something different, but the belief in love stories at all.

On the way home from school, Muna catches me up on Mustafa's entrepreneurial concerns.

"It's edibles," she says with a grimace. "Apparently, a few people in the year have been taking them and Mustafa only found out about it because he overheard some idiot on Cromwell Hill. And, of course, in true capitalist fashion, Mustafa doesn't even care about the *actual* drug problem, he's only worried that people will stop using their limited pocket money to buy his stuff."

I whistle low. "Wow...wasn't expecting that."

"Me neither," Muna replies. "I can't believe no one's messaged Hexpose to say anything either! The level of disrespect from my schoolmates, my comrades-in-education. Can you believe it?"

"I know you want me to say no, but actually, yes." We stop outside our houses. "I can believe it. This is serious."

"Exactly!" She sighs, perching on the brick wall. "This is serious. Now, between this and BANTRxpose acting up again, things are getting out of hand."

I lightly shove her to make space for myself on the wall. "Acting up again? You mean after that one post you showed me last month?"

Muna slides out her phone. "Look. Another new post from today. You're partly in this one too actually. At least, your leg is."

My heart sinks when I see the picture. My bent leg on the ground. Face hidden behind the falling body of another. Halima's body, from this morning.

*Fresh off the boat and still can't walk on land LOL*

"Why won't these people leave me alone?" I groan.

"Leave you alone? Don't you mean leave Halima alone? This is proper savage."

"Savage or not, there's nothing I can do about it." I hand back the phone. "And to be honest, all I see is something that draws further attention to her, which potentially draws further attention to *me*. It doesn't make it easier to forget my dad either. Every time I see her face, I see him as well."

163

Muna goes quiet then and I do too. We sit on the wall, swinging our legs, occasionally tangling and then untangling them. We sit until our bums hurt and then some more.

A loud knock on the window behind is our signal to say goodbye. Muna's mum draws the curtains back to wave me and Muna inside, but I gesture to my own house.

"Are you sure?" Muna asks, eyebrows knitted in worry.

I look across to my house. Lately, it has grown incrementally harder to step foot inside it. Each time I cross the threshold I find myself assaulted with disappointment over Hooyo missing her job interview.

I knew, logically, that Aabo returning with his new family would undo the work of building her up again, but seeing it fall apart so easily – like a breath of wind to a dandelion head – made me realize I am still not enough to keep her together.

Going to Muna's house would do nothing to quell that pain though. In fact, it would probably stoke it.

I'm tempted, but I shake my head.

Muna envelops me in a crushing hug.

"I love you, Safiya," she whispers to me fiercely. "So much."

My arms, limp from surprise, promptly recover. I squeeze her back. "I love you so much too."

We sway from side to side and I close my eyes, wanting to be this happy, feel this steady and safe, for ever.

A wolf whistle from behind forces us apart and we see Yusuf straddling his bike.

"A tad jealous, are we?" Muna smirks.

Yusuf's gaze flicks between us before landing on me.

"Perhaps," is all he says. His unblinking, hot-chocolate eyes are on me.

"Whatever, gremlin." Muna chortles, diffusing the warm sensation that was beginning to make me feel very, very unbalanced.

And, because there is something seriously wrong with me, I echo her exact words and say, "Whatever, gremlin" too.

Yusuf spits laughter. "I really don't know what I did to deserve you two in my life." He wheels his bike past us, giving me a salute from the doorway.

As I watch his retreating back, and then Muna's, all I want is to echo those words too.


After school the next afternoon, I check on Hooyo, who's napping on the couch. It takes me longer than it should to realize that the house is freezing cold. The absence of warmth means that I haven't instinctively removed my jacket like I normally do when I get home from school. Hooyo hasn't got a blanket either. When I touch her ankles, she's frozen.

I pop the heater on before covering her with two thick, grey blankets and then go upstairs to make my afternoon prayers.

Noise from Muna's house carries from near my wardrobe but I tune it out, the way I've taught myself to do all these years. It's a reflex now, not to pay attention even if, with a little concentration, I could probably make out every cough, conversation and snore.

Though when I was younger and the pain of seeing Aabo

walk away was still so raw, I would press my ear against our shared wall sometimes. Not to eavesdrop, but to simply listen to the love and laughter of a family only a couple of metres from where I stood. I used to pretend that I was with them instead of in my silent house, with my present-but-absent mother, living with a loneliness that felt like a second skin.

Of course, the door to their house was always open to me, but it felt wrong being there all the time to siphon from that joy. As if I'd only be using them to dispel my sadness, like some kind of emotional bloodsucker.

I shut my eyes, sharpening the reflex again. Then I locate my binoculars, grab some cash from Hooyo's purse, and the water bill from the table that's long overdue, before heading out.

Maybe I can't be at Muna's house, but I can sure as hell be anywhere else but here.

# HALIMA

I watch my mother like I have never watched her before. I watch as she eats, I watch as we clean the kitchen after dinner, I watch her as she watches her sons and husband. I watch her not watching me, avoiding me, as if I am something that might blind her if she looks at me directly.

Even when I want to stop, I can't. It is a compulsion. This feeling that if I continue, things will begin to make sense. That the answers will be there, written on her face, even if she doesn't want to speak them.

I turn my gaze away from Hooyo to him now, the husband, and I hope he can feel the intensity of it.

He is the man who took everything from me, and I hate him for it now, more than ever before, because there is a gulf between me and Hooyo where there never used to be, in the shape of him. Because now I know he had his claws in my life long before I ever realized. Because now I know the truth.

That Hooyo was never really mine – mine alone, anyway – to begin with.

\* \* \*

After school the next day, I walk home instinctively. While the map of Northwell High is still somewhat fuzzy in my mind, the walk to and from it has always been clear, and I find myself outside the house without realizing.

A worrying thought flickers in my head.

*Have my mind and my feet grown too comfortable here? Do they know these concrete steps too well?*

But I try to bury it before the sinister idea takes root.

My hand goes automatically to my pocket for the keys, to the lock, to the handle, before I stop. I undo it all, locking the door again, and back away from the house.

I am not ready to watch Hooyo right now, to participate in another infuriating iteration of our dance. I am not ready to see her lie to me again or pretend that I am not hurting.

I head to the park instead, the one place I remember that is not so grey in this dull place.


It was around three weeks ago that I was last here. I was happier then, I remember. More certain that us moving here would be a failure and that I would be returning to the motherland swiftly. I am still certain, of course, but what is certainty without an escape plan? It is a donkey without a cart, a key without a lock.

Useless.

But the countdown I initiated when I first landed here is still ticking away in the back of my head. And the conversation with Abti Haroon the other day has only sped it up, made me more determined to get home and be where I need to be. Because if Abti Haroon really doesn't have long left, then neither do I.

Though without cash or a credit card, my options are severely limited. I may have only travelled once before in my life but I know the journey requires money...and a *lot* of it.

Even if I miraculously source enough to cover myself, what about Hooyo and the boys? Could I really leave them behind, with a man who I am now certain is keeping my mother hostage over a decade-old bribe?

I groan under my breath.

My escape plan has just become infinitely more complicated.

*King Edward VII Park*, the plaque outside the gate reads. A park fit for a king it seems, but I am a little sceptical. I do not remember this park being anywhere near as magnificent as the plaque seems to suggest, though, in fairness, I do not understand this country's royalty or standards anyway. Maybe a park littered with all kinds of trash and teeming with commoners is more than adequate for an English king or queen.

I head in and begin walking around the perimeter. From where I am, I cannot even see the edges of it, which means that this park must be huge, much larger than I realized when we came here for Eid. It also means that I could circle this entire area without getting close to another human, which is exactly what I need.

All I want is a few minutes of serenity. The kind of peace that I took for granted back home. Like in those minutes between Fajr and sunrise when the city would begin to wake though not yet ready to thrum with life. Or in those seconds after a long heat-filled day when the boys would be so tired that they would fall asleep on top of each other and I would realize what it was to find silence.

But even that kind of peace was nothing compared to what I would find with Hooyo in those evenings when it was only the two of us. When we would reminisce and gossip and laugh and cry. When we would just talk and talk and talk until I was sure there were no words left to speak in either of us. And when she would tell me the stories about my late father – stories of how they met and fell in love and bound themselves to each other under the eyes of God – I did not feel as though I had lost anything at all. How could I when Hooyo felt like everything I could ever want or need?

Yellow and orange leaves lie in heaps all through the park, like quiet little fires. I bend to pick one up, running it over my hands.

I am halfway along the perimeter when I first notice some of the kids from school. They have their backs to me, shouting to a couple of their friends on the swings. I walk by, still holding onto the leaf though I pull my hand into my jacket to obscure it. I may be foreign to this season they call autumn, but I am not foreign to the kinds of things that appear strange, and clutching a single yellow leaf would likely fall into that category.

I am almost past them when I hear someone call out.

"Yo!" the one that's not on the swing shouts. "Freshie!"

I maintain my pace, ignoring the sniggers that follow.

"Where you running off to, freshie?" Another shout, but a different voice. "Back to the boat that you came on?"

They laugh again as I struggle to understand what the joke is. I came by plane, not by boat. Should I correct them, I wonder?

"Dumb girl can't even understand us," a girl says, laughing.

By this point, the leaf is crushed in my hands.

If anyone back home had dared to speak to me in this way, I would have had them floored in a second. When did I let myself get this spineless?

I whirl around and think of the only word I know that holds power in this language of theirs. "You, bitch," I say, simply, finding instant satisfaction in seeing them splutter.

I see then that one of the boys holds a phone in his hands, recording. He leans back against the swings, drawing in air in huge gulps, body shaking like a leaf as he sniggers. The girl eyes him with a scathing expression.

I turn on my heels to leave, thinking about how my bad luck just keeps on coming. The one place where I thought I would be able to find some peace is the one place where all these hyenas happen to converge. I reach the edge of the tennis courts when my bad luck reaches dizzying heights.

Safiya, sitting on a bench, holding a pair of binoculars, and staring right at me.

# SAFIYA

A shiver crawls up my spine and I pull my jacket tighter around me. Unfortunately, with a broken zipper, the only protection I have against the cold is to physically hold both ends of it together. An awkward look, but what else is there to do? With little cash at home and a lot of demand, it's not like I can buy myself a brand-new wardrobe, or even a functioning coat.

Logic would tell me to get the money from my dad, but pride wins over it. Pride will not allow me to ask my dad for anything, not even a crumb.

I perch the binoculars on the bridge of my nose and scan Eddy's, finding comfort in the magnified view of this familiar landscape.

Muna, Yusuf and I have always loved these binoculars. We grew up spying on people all over town using them and we've launched the beginning of every summer for the last eight years with them too, birdwatching and people-gawking in the park. They've been a fixture of our friendship since Aabo first gifted them to me.

I still held onto them when he left. As painful as the reminder was, the binoculars grew to mean something more.

Something that represented the silliness and ridiculousness of The Three Musketeers.

But now with Aabo back…the pain is starting to get a little stronger, and a lot more difficult to ignore. I wonder how long before I finally let the binoculars go.

I spy Marissa, Yash, Adam and Lauren by a cluster of oak trees. The group migrate to the playground for the swings and I track their movements as if they are a new species of bird.

The group's attention focuses on something outside of my field of vision. I swing the binoculars slightly.

Halima.

An urge to fling my binoculars to the ground climbs like a vine around my arms. But, even hyping myself up, I can't do it. It makes me hate myself even more.

I observe the unfolding scene with mild and reluctant interest.

Halima strides past the playground gates with the same air of confidence I've noticed at school. Her left hand disappears into the sleeve of her jacket as the group's attention zeroes in on her. Though she is yet to look their way, it's obvious she not only senses them, but also their interest in her presence.

Then the shouts start. Yash kicks it off but I'm too far away to catch any of it. Adam chimes in too before pointing his phone at Halima. Lauren adds something to the mix – presumably an insult because it's quite clear by now that this interaction is not a friendly one – when Halima whirls around. Though I only see the back of her head, Lauren's reaction tells me everything I need to know. Halima has said something provocative. Adam and Yash burst into convulsive laughter and Halima strides away, seemingly intent on shutting down the episode.

My eyes swing back to Adam still holding his phone and I'm reminded of my conversation with Muna less than an hour ago.

Does this have something to do with BANTRxpose?

First the devilish re-editing of Muna's Hexpose letter from last month -- then Halima ends up in the year leader's office.

A slyly captured picture of her fall from just this morning and now…this strange incident with Yash, Adam and Lauren.

BANTRxpose hasn't been active in years. Not since the account mysteriously went quiet after spending two months ripping off Hexpose. Though everyone had known it was a parody account, it hadn't stopped people from jumping on its bandwagon.

BANTRxpose had reported on pointless, inconsequential news like Mr Khan being spotted buying haemorrhoid cream or how many hairs a student had found in their lunch.

But Muna's readership took a hit. Her numbers dwindled until only a smaller portion of loyal readers remained. She'd never been able to find the owners behind BANTRxpose but, when it suddenly all went quiet, everyone eventually moved on.

BANTRxpose starting up again now doesn't seem like a coincidence though. Especially since its only two posts feature Halima. The one person who, at Northwell High, just happens to be the bane of my existence.

I shake my head as if to physically short-circuit my brain and erase these thoughts.

I do not care about Halima, I remind myself, and, if BANTRxpose is turning its sights on her, then what does it have to do with me?

I stare ahead through the binoculars, waiting for her to obscure my vision once more as she walks past, and then away from me, but nothing appears. I see the same clear blue sky, beginning to darken with sunset. Then I hear shuffling. Sense it. A body redistributing its mass on the bench beside my bag.

Wait.

Maybe she doesn't recognize me. Maybe she can't tell who I am with these binoculars covering half of my face. Maybe she's just sitting here because there's nowhere else to sit.

Maybe.

"I have question," she says, shattering all my maybes with those three words.

Her English is heavily accented, but the words are clear.

I wonder, for a moment, why she is speaking to me in a language I'm certain she hates. Or does she think I'm so British that I can't properly speak our mother tongue? She wouldn't be completely wrong, I guess, but the assumption would still sting.

"I have question," Halima says again, not even ten seconds later.

I hold myself back from scoffing. Does this girl seriously think I'm going to be chatting with her?

"Your dad," Halima continues, undeterred. "He know my mum for long time."

I push my binoculars further onto my face. The edges dig into my orbit. "*Iga tag,*" I grit out in Somali.

She laughs. Her laugh is full of delight and surprise. I want to slap that laugh right out of her mouth.

"*Oh, you would like to speak Somali!*" she says, letting the English go. "*I thought all of you here were only Somali by blood, not by tongue.*"

Of course, I can't speak it perfectly but, since it's me that has got the ball rolling in this direction, I can't lose face now.

"*What I am and who I am has nothing to do with you,*" I say, letting the words loose cautiously. "*Leave me alone.*"

Halima sighs, shifting on the bench again. "*I want to, trust me. I want nothing more than to leave this entire country alone and go back to where I came from. But I need something from you first.*"

Disbelief bubbles into laughter and I drop the binoculars from my face.

"*And how am I supposed to help ship you off?*" I ask when I recover.

"*You are Halane's daughter, treasure chest of secrets,*" Halima replies simply. "*I have a question and you could have the answer.*"

I grit my teeth at her brazenness. Coming to me to dig up secrets on my own father? What does she think this is? Family espionage?

But then I consider the motive underlying her words…

Halima wants to get back to Somalia. She's made that clear enough.

My mind zooms through a million questions.

*Why?*

*Does she hate my dad?*

*Does my dad hate her?*

*Do they all want to leave and go back? Or just her?*

No. I put a brake on those racing thoughts.

I will not get sucked into the black hole that is Aabo. I have spent so long trying to drag me and Hooyo out of that despair and I refuse to let him back in.

Still, I can't help but think her request over, tentatively skimming the edge of that hole without falling in.

*What could it mean?*

Could the answers I give – provided I even have them in the first place – help her disappearing act?

And if Aabo and his new family leave, would it give Hooyo a chance to have more Okay Days? Start to get back to the good place she was in before they turned up?

"I'll answer your question, but then you need to leave me out of it," I say in English, dropping all pretence of fluency. "Got it?"

Halima nods, eyes flaring with barely contained excitement. "Got it," she repeats before turning on the bench to face me directly. "*Your father knew my mother long before they were married. They had a mutual friend apparently. Did you know about this?*"

I shrug my shoulders coolly, despite the fact it feels like the air is dangerously thinning out in the wake of her question. "Maybe."

Halima eyes me. "*Is there a chance you know who this mutual friend might be?*"

"My dad had a lot of friends. Am I supposed to know which

ones he shared with other people?"

She nods. *"Can you give me any of their names? There could be some that I recognize."*

I stand up brusquely then, packing the binoculars away and shouldering my bag. "That's the end of question time."

*"But,"* she protests, standing up too, *"I need to know—"*

"No," I snap. "You asked for *a* question. Not multiple questions. I'm not a bloody genie."

Halima bristles, crossing her arms.

"Just remember this," I warn her. "We are not friends and we are not family. Don't try speaking to me again."

Even though I physically distance myself from Halima, I still feel her nearness in her questions that circle my mind and the revelation that nearly floored me.

Halima claimed Aabo knew her mother long before they were married. Which would mean that he didn't miraculously fall into a stranger's arms when he upped and left for Somalia. He was going back to someone he knew.

My mind shoots to the only logical conclusion: that Aabo must have been unfaithful in his marriage to Hooyo.

A swirl of anger rises inside me then and I feel myself teetering closer and closer to the black hole I was so determined to stay away from. But I pull myself back from it when Halima's face floats up in my memory.

These words…coming from the girl who became my father's fake daughter.

Why would I ever listen to or believe anything she has to say? Only God knows what her real motives are.

The bottom line is Halima can't be trusted. I might have been silly enough to give her the time of day, but I won't be making the same mistake twice.

I head to town with the cash from Hooyo's purse and go to Adeer Ali's shop with the overdue water bill safe in my pocket.

Adeer's Ali shop has, thankfully, always been our lifeline. I've known him since I was little and, after Aabo left, he never once batted an eyelid at our climbing tab or asked me to leave an item on the counter if I ran out of money to pay for it. He's a kind, cheerful man with greying hair and three silver teeth, and he's an absolute blessing. There is no way Hooyo and I would have been able to get through the last few years without him. There were times he'd even pretend I had paid off a debt when I was sure I hadn't. I always kept a meticulous diary of all our income and outgoings – and knew it all off the top of my head too – but there were times he was convinced the balance sheet was clear.

*"Are you calling an old man stupid?"* he'd ask if I ever protested.

I would get flustered when he said that because he was basically goading me to say something unintentionally disrespectful.

*"No, Adeer, but—"*

*"Ah, there's no buts here, Safiya. Only yes, Adeer, and thank you, Adeer, and see you later, Adeer."*

I tried my best to never let the tab creep too high, only ever using it when we desperately needed, but I was grateful the lifeline existed. A safety net for if I ever felt things slipping away, getting a little out of control. Knowing it existed made life that bit easier.

The shop door makes a tinkling sound as I push it open.

"Hey, hey, hey," Adeer Ali sings when he spots me. "Is that Safiya the boqorad I see at my door? A queen at a poor man's door? A miracle before my eyes!"

I grimace, looking down at my feet as I walk to the counter. Adeer has refused to drop this Queen Safiya joke since I walked into his shop almost ten years ago in a princess costume for school.

"Please, Adeer, when are you going to stop calling me that? You're the only one who finds it funny," I say, sliding over the water bill along with a twenty-pound note. "And you don't have a sense of humour."

Adeer lets out a roaring laugh, banging the counter with his fist. A customer in a nearby aisle jumps.

"See," he says, wagging a finger at me. "Only a queen could go around insulting people like that."

I laugh, heading to the aisle at the back where the eggs are. "Well, the boqorad needs to get a few things so I'll be back in a second, Adeer."

I snake through the shop to reach the furthermost aisle when something blue catches my eye.

Sanitary pads aren't on the list for today, but I think back to the last time I got my period, exercising some quick mental maths of my cycle. It's a little hopeless though since my period has been super erratic lately. Still, there aren't any at home and the emergency stash in my school bag is empty. I check my pocket to count the remaining cash. I only have a fiver. The pads will have to wait.

I take my things to Adeer when I'm done and hand him the money once he's rung the items up. He returns a few coins. My hand automatically pivots to the green charity collection box and I drop them in one by one.

"Adeer, thank you so much for being patient," I say gratefully as I grab the carrier bag. "I'll get the rest of the money to you soon, promise."

I don't bother asking how much the tab has run up to because the number is already flashing in my head, the same way it always does when I step into this shop.

£43.47.

A reminder of how much there is choking what little Hooyo and I have to begin with.

"No! No! I don't want to hear it, Safiya." He waves his hands in protest. "The matter is closed and I won't hear any more on it."

"Closed?" I repeat, frowning. "Adeer, what are you talking about?"

He waves me away again like I'm an annoying fly. "No, I don't want to hear anything else, okay? Khalas. It's done."

I place the bag back on the table.

Most of the time, when Adeer magicked away money, it was small amounts here and there. Not the *entire* tab.

"Adeer, I don't know if you're joking but Hooyo and I are paying you back." I pause. "For everything," I add, in case that wasn't clear the first time.

Adeer sighs. Thankfully, he doesn't start up again with the intense gesturing.

"Safiya," he says softly, leaning down on the counter. "Trust me. There's nothing to be paid. The debt is finished."

"Finished? What do you mean, finished?"

"I mean that your father has settled it." Adeer Ali looks as though he doesn't want to be giving me this information. "He settled it weeks ago and left a little extra on there too."

"My dad?"

I'm aware that a lot of what I have said in the last minute has just been repeating Adeer Ali's words but I'm not sure I have any more of my own left.

"Yes, Safiya, your dad," Adeer repeats. There is a palpable layer of guilt in his voice. "I'm sorry, but when a man wants to protect his family, look after them and look over them, I must let him. I cannot stand in the way of that.

"I'm sorry," he adds again, after a moment. "I wanted to tell you but I was hoping your father would tell you first."

I want to put a fist in my mouth and scream. Kick the crisps stand and swing from the fluorescent lights. Curl up into a tight ball and not let any light through.

I pick up the bag again and leave instead, not bothering with a goodbye.


When the cold air hits my face, I regain some composure. I walk home unhurriedly, trying to process what I've just heard.

Aabo paid off our tab at Adeer Ali's shop.

Aabo snuck behind our *backs* to give us money.

I'm not sure it's possible to reverse anything of this situation but, if there is one thing I know, it's that I can't tell Hooyo. She has been in a passive, barely-here state ever since Aabo and his entourage arrived and while this news would shake her out of it, it would be for all the wrong reasons.

No, I can't tell her. I know that. I just don't know how I'll ever be able to look my dad in the eyes again. Charity is one thing. Forced charity crosses a whole different kind of line because it disrespects. It violates the boundaries and protections that me and Hooyo have worked so hard to put in place. It dissolves our barriers of no contact, no money, no love. And now, our clean break from him five years ago is no longer clean, but marred.

I pass by my dad's butcher's shop at the end of the street. The first business he opened in this country after my mum finally convinced him to stop feeling sorry for himself almost fourteen years ago. I remember the story of their life perfectly.

Sixteen years ago, Aabo was new to the country. Distraught, struggling to adjust, he hit rock bottom. Until Hooyo. Though they had been promised to each other years before, their love story was instant and it seemed he was revived. They married and, for a time, he was able to recover from the homesickness he carried with him from Somalia. But before they became pregnant with me, something seemed to pull Aabo back into his pit of despair and he sought comfort in too many bad things. In khat and cigarettes, in too many vices that a new husband and father should not have found himself with. In the second year of my parents' marriage, they struggled. Hard. And yet, somehow, Hooyo brought him out of it again.

I walk quickly by Aabo's shop, ducking my head. There is almost a zero per cent chance he's in there, but I can't deal with *almost* tonight because the stain of forced charity is still bitter in the back of my throat. And, given what happened the last time I saw my dad, I don't trust myself to be calm around him.

Against my better judgement, I find myself thinking about Aabo, Halima and the rest of their family. Their overflowing wealth, the pitying way they must look at us. About how full their bellies must always be, how bathed in peace, instead of anxiety.

How easy it must be for him to throw money at his problems and how pleased he must be with himself tonight. A bit of cash to exonerate him of his sins.

My hands ball into fists and I stuff them into my pockets.

There seems to be no escape. School, the park, Adeer Ali's shop. Safe haven is out of reach. Perhaps it doesn't even exist any more.

But then Halima's face floats up in my memory. She'd seemed so serious about running away and digging into Aabo's past… Is there a chance that any of what she'd said today had been true?

I see Habaryar Binti and Habaryar Shukri turn the corner and walk in the direction of my dad's butcher's shop. I pull my hood up so it obscures my face and hope it is enough to let me return home unscathed.

Ten minutes later, I'm home. Hooyo lies on the sofa, in the

same position as before. She's awake now, watching the news with the television muted. She doesn't say anything as I walk through to the kitchen and neither do I.

I find myself wondering whether Hooyo would notice if I never came home. If I went missing, how long would it take before she realized? Probably a couple of days, I think, and even that might be a generous estimate.

I change out of my school clothes before returning to the kitchen to fix us an oven pizza dinner. Grabbing the remote from the coffee table, I turn the volume up, then flick through the channels to find something that isn't an hour long run of people failing obstacle courses or a dry quiz show.

"Where did you go today?"

My head snaps from the television to Hooyo.

"Where did you go?" she repeats, pointing to the clock. Her voice sounds scratchy and unused. "You came back after school and then left again."

I consciously swallow the bite of pizza in my mouth so it doesn't end up going the wrong way.

Did Hooyo hear the thoughts in my mind? I wonder. Or does she pay more attention to my comings and goings than I realized?

"I went to the park," I reply once I'm certain the immediate choking risk is gone. "With Muna," I add. "I went with Muna."

Though I don't remember when it started, there came a point when I began using Muna's name as a shield. If Muna was there, it was fine. If Muna was with me, I was safe. Of course, Muna doesn't know that I use her name like that.

"Hooyo, can I…" I stop. "Can I ask you a question?"

I want her permission first. Maybe it's the fact that she's willingly speaking to me that's made me brave enough to ask. Hooyo nods, eyes swinging away from the screen.

I take a breath and just say it. I don't want to give myself a chance to second-guess anything.

"Did Aabo ever know that woman he's married to? Like… before he left?"

Immediately, Hooyo stiffens. A rod lining her back instead of bone.

"Sorry, I know I shouldn't even be asking…" I put my plate down. "And I'm sorry for bringing it up but…"

I stop myself there.

What am I doing? Why am I asking these silly questions? He left. That's the beginning, middle and end of the story and asking stupid questions because some annoying girl got into my head—

"I knew."

Hooyo's voice comes out softly, belying the metal that has hardened her shoulders.

"What?"

"I knew." She shudders, closing her eyes. "About the woman, the children. I knew before I knocked on your door, Safiya. I knew he married five years ago when he left and…I didn't tell you." Hooyo opens her eyes. They're swimming with tears. "He came to see me a couple of years ago…I'd heard things before then but nothing concrete. When he came…he confirmed it was all true."

My mind and body disassociate. A numbness sets in.

Our barriers of no contact, no money, no love. Everything I did, for Hooyo, for us.

He called every week for a year before he stopped. Hooyo had said we didn't need him or his meaningless words. I never picked up.

He knocked on our door a month ago. I chose Hooyo. My mum who was hurt, who was destroyed. I slammed the door in his face.

I have chosen my mum time and time again but, when it mattered most, she didn't choose me.

"I'm sorry, Safiya," she says, her voice hoarse now. "I'm sorry I didn't tell you sooner."

Hooyo wipes away her tears and stands. For a moment, I'm tempted to believe that she's going to hug me. That she'll hold me close and tell me that the only people we need are each other. That she is sorrier than I could ever know for lying to me for all this time.

But she doesn't do any of that. She leaves her dinner mostly untouched and retreats upstairs. For the first time ever, I hope she stays there.

# HALIMA

It appears I am becoming too much for Hooyo to bear because the first thing she tells me when I return home from the park is that she and the husband have enrolled me in the local weekend dugsi starting in a few weeks.

"*Not just you,*" Hooyo says, leaning into the open fridge. "*Your brothers are going too.*"

She stands hidden behind the door for longer than seems necessary.

"*Sounds good.*" I smile, pulling out a chair to sit. "*You know, Hooyo, I've really been missing my Qur'an lessons since we moved here.*"

My dissent – while therapeutic for me – is probably not going to be an effective tool in leveraging, persuading and, ultimately, escaping. I *need* Hooyo onside if I'm going to convince her that we have to go home. To convince her that she can exist without the husband and does not owe him any money, love or loyalty.

Hooyo shuts the fridge, eyeing me cautiously as she pours a dash of milk into her qaxwo.

"*Well, that's good to hear,*" she replies, coming to sit at the table.

*"I'm sorry that we haven't been able to organize it sooner."*

*"No, it's all right. These things take time, I understand."* I drum my fingers on the table as she sips her coffee.

*Ask. Ask. Ask.*

I will it in my very bones. I need Hooyo to voluntarily take us down the path I am desperate for.

*"So how was your day today?"* Hooyo asks.

My face erupts into a grin.

*"It was good,"* I reply, stilling my fingers. *"All my usual lessons. An unseasoned lunch. And then…"* I sigh. *"There was Safiya."*

Hooyo pauses mid-sip. *"Excuse me?"*

*"Well, we found ourselves together at the park after school and we got to chatting. That's why I'm a little late coming home, actually."* I shimmy my blazer off and hang it on the back of the chair. *"We were just gossiping."*

*"Oh?"* Hooyo replies, putting her cup down.

*"Nothing bad, Hooyo, really."* I shake my head. *"Mostly about her father."*

Even across the table, I swear I hear Hooyo grind her teeth.

*"Oh, and the mutual friend you mentioned,"* I add, slapping my own forehead in mock-irritation. *"I'm forgetting too many things these days."*

*"And what did she tell you?"*

*"Well, I promised I wouldn't say anything…"* I bite my lip. *"She made me say wallahi. But I can ask her next time. She says she wants to meet again since she has a lot of daughterly wisdom to impart. Apparently, it's not easy sharing family ties with Halane, though that doesn't exactly surprise me."*

Hooyo drinks the rest of her hot coffee in three gulps and stands.

"*Halima*," she says, pinning me with a pointed look. "*While I can't tell you to stay away from anyone, I can warn you against speaking out of turn. Safiya may be your father's daughter but even family can't always be trusted.*"

"*Like this family?*" I nearly mutter, but I remember the spirit of dissent I am trying to quash and think better of it.

# HALIMA

Since the new weekend dugsi is only a few roads away from where we live, Hooyo tasks me with the responsibility of leading my brothers there and bringing them back in one piece.

"*But what if I lose them?*" I ask, bending to find one of Kamal's lost shoes behind the rack.

Hooyo cracks a rare smile. I catch it in the mirror as I stand, missing shoe in hand. "*Well, I suppose you will just have to find yourself another place to sleep tonight then, Halima, because no brothers means no entry back into this house,*" she says, pulling Abu Bakr's hood tighter around his head.

"*You would rather have me homeless?*"

Hooyo laughs, and it's as if a part of her is surprised she can still make the sound.

"*I would rather have all of you or none of you,*" Hooyo quips, not letting me bait her. "*Now, let's get you out the door. I do not want you late for your first day. Does everyone have their books?*"

"*Haa, Hooyo,*" Kamal shouts as he attempts to push his head through the letter box. "*I packed it, like you told me to.*"

"*Well done,*" Hooyo says, leaning over to pat him on the

head. *"You're a good boy, Kamal, always listening to your mother."*

I glance at Hooyo, wondering who those words are truly meant for. Hooyo does not usually make those kinds of throwaway comments and it felt like that one was sharpened, cocked and aimed straight for me. But when I look over at her she has gone, heading towards the kitchen, as if we are already afterthoughts.

I turn to find the boys' eyes glued to me.

*"What?"* I ask.

Kamal curls his hand around the door handle. *"Are we going now?"*

*"Yes,"* I say, putting my own shoes on. *"Of course we are. Open the door."*

He pulls it open before immediately shutting it again. *"It's raining,"* he says uncertainly, biting the edge of his lip. *"A lot."*

*"What are you?"* I laugh. *"Fire? Do you think a little rain will put you out?"*

He squares his shoulders, not happy with the suggestion that he is nowhere near as tough as he likes to think he is.

*"No, but I want my umbrella,"* Kamal says, crossing his arms. *"I don't want to get wet."*

I lean over to look outside myself. The rain is coming down in a drizzle, not the full force he makes it sound like.

*My God…*I think. *England is truly making these boys more delicate by the second.*

I know I cannot say anything like that to them though, so instead I open the door wider and say to them:

"*A little rain never hurt anyone now, did it? Especially not two grown, brave men like you.*"

Kamal and Abu Bakr all but trample each other to get out the door first.

At the weekend Islamic class in Northwell Community Centre, I deposit the boys in the young children's section before making my way to the registration desk to pay the monthly tuition. I pocket the receipt and turn to see three girls at the foot of a staircase who look about my age. I try my luck and follow them.

They lead me to a room upstairs. I find there are already about fifteen girls there, in groups of three or four huddled around the room. Whoever the teacher is, she is yet to arrive.

My eyes scan the carpeted space to find a corner I can claim for myself, somewhere that can give me a physical excuse not to engage in conversation. My eyes catch an attractive option as someone walks past, blocking my view.

It takes me longer than it should to recognize her. Although, in fairness, I've rarely seen her alone. She has been attached at the hip to Safiya from the moment we met.

Muna's head whips in my direction like a dog that has suddenly caught a scent. She narrows her eyes. In warning? In hatred? Likely both.

I sidestep her, moving to claim a spot at the back just as the teacher walks in; a small, elderly woman, shrivelled like a date.

The hour-long lesson crawls at a snail's pace and when it finally concludes, I am the first to leave, heading downstairs to collect the boys. The other girls trickle down the stairs, chatting away like before, but the looks that I get from two of them, then four, and then five, makes me think that something has changed. And when, finally, one girl has the gall to point directly at me, I decide to confront her.

"Why you looking at me?" I ask.

Her friends flock to circle her but, with the aloof manner they hold themselves in, I think perhaps they are not her friends. Perhaps they are just outsiders, vultures circling for dead meat.

To her credit, the girl does not bat an eyelid. The look of surprise that registered on her face when she saw me striding towards her is gone, replaced by a cool, shuttered expression.

"You're on BANTRxpose again," she replies unhesitatingly. "I wasn't sure it was you at first but now I am."

My face inadvertently betrays me. I feel my mouth and forehead trying to twist into neutrality, but it is too late for that. She knows that I do not know what she is talking about, that I have no idea what this BANTRxpose is or why I am in it.

Someone shoulders their way into the middle. A particularly eager vulture here to disrupt the gossip ecosystem most likely.

A few people grumble in annoyance, but when they see who it is, they quieten.

"Show me," Muna orders, arms crossed against her chest, stepping into the space like a self-appointed ringleader.

Without missing a beat, the girl pulls out a phone, clicks on a few things and then angles the screen towards us. Everyone leans in to get a better look.

On the screen is a picture. Of me. Except that it is not. My face is not my own. It is debased with the ears of a monkey and the tail of a donkey and with licks of fire in the background.

A couple of the girls suck in a breath. Others quietly snigger. One coughs.

Without prompting, the girl scrolls through a few other pictures of me. All similar but corrupted in different ways. I stop looking. My eyes are beginning to burn, as if the flames from the pictures have leaped into my orbit.

Muna opens her mouth as if to speak. Either to the girl or to me, I am not sure. But a conversation is not something I want to be entangled in right now. Especially with someone I trust only as far as I can throw them.

"Thank you," I say to the girl pointedly, before going to collect my brothers.

I do not look back but, if I had, I would not be surprised if my anger and shame had left scorch marks where my feet touched the earth.

# *HALIMA*

I am not waiting long for Abu Bakr and Kamal. They exit class, bounding with the kind of excitable energy I do not have the patience for. My head is still swimming with the pictures the girl showed me on her phone, flames still fanning in my vision. I blink a few times, but they refuse to disappear.

As we make our way home, I hear Kamal mention something about a new friend, but my mind is working on too many things to process what he is saying.

*These pictures of me, who took them?*

In them, I am wearing my school uniform, but my eyes never meet the camera. They are taken from the side, a few from the front, none from the back. Whoever took those photos did so underhandedly, but effectively.

*Who hates me enough to waste their time on such a thing?*

Because whoever did all of this must have a burning hatred of me. Something so deep as to warrant this kind of action. Taking my pictures and altering them, making me look more beast than human, is not something I imagine would be done lightly. With this logic, there can only be one plausible answer.

Safiya.

But my mind pulls me in a different direction when I think of the boy who tripped me up.

Kyle.

What if all of this is simply child's play and not a calculated act for a calculated agenda?

Then there are others. The quartet at the park. The ones who told me I'd arrived in this country by boat, as if I had simply waded ashore. Who recorded me and have likely already distributed the video.

And the word that I keep circling: BANTRxpose.

Whatever it is, it is not a word in the English dictionary.

Abu Bakr pulls on my hand, drawing me out of autopilot mode. We are at a crossing, not far from home, but how we have got here is anybody's guess. I have no memory of the walk from dugsi.

"*You can't cross yet,*" he says, exasperated. "*The green man isn't here!*"

I avoid rolling my eyes. I know he is only regurgitating whatever he has been taught at that school of his. I cast my eye to Kamal holding my other hand to ensure I haven't accidentally misplaced him.

Though I want nothing more than to stop thinking about the pictures and the flames and the donkey tail, one last thought pushes its way up.

*Why does it suddenly feel like there is a fresh target on my back?*

Abu Bakr tugs on my hand again.

"*What, Abu Bakr?*" I snap. "*Why do you keep doing that?*"

Someone catches my eye on the other side of the road.

*"Isn't that our sister?"* Abu Bakr asks, left eye squinting in question.

My mouth opens to answer but I hesitate. I cannot tell him no. That she is his sister, not mine. That answer would open the door for too many questions because the boys do not understand the way I do. They are too young for that. To them, we are all family. To them, we are all connected.

*"Maybe,"* I say instead, even though I know it is her, and the woman walking beside her is definitely her mother.

Kamal slows his pace. *"Can we say hello?"*

*"Maybe another time,"* I reply through clenched teeth.

*"But we are her brothers,"* Abu Bakr insists. *"We have to say hello."*

I breathe through my nose. *"They look busy. You can ask your dad to introduce you another time."*

*"But—"* Abu Bakr starts again.

*"No,"* I tell him. *"No more talking."*

He deflates, folding in on himself as if his muscles have atrophied.

*"How about I tell a story instead?"* I try, changing tack.

I feel the edge of my lips curve into a smile. If there is one thing I know how to do, it is to distract these boys when all they want to do is push and dig.

*"Sheeko sheeko, sheeko xariir…"* I begin.

And so, with a little effort, the spell is broken, but I still find myself watching as the strolling forms of Safiya and her mother recede in the distance, trying to unpick her, the daughter of the man I hate most in this world.

While I know how much she despises her own father, I wonder how much of that rolls onto me.

Am I collateral damage for being associated with him? Have I been caught in the crossfire of BANTRxpose because of it?

Safiya and her mother are near the junction, on the edge of disappearing, and I realize that while there is much I do not understand about her, and much more I never will, there is one thing that I do feel certain about.

Safiya knows what it means to walk alone.

Because, while she walks only inches apart from her mother, she holds herself as though there is no one worth trusting beside her. I recognize the wiring in her shoulders, the tension in her neck, the stiffness in her legs. I recognize all of it because I see myself in her.

There is an ocean of difference between us but, in this, we are the same. Daughters without mothers, and daughters without fathers too.

At home, Abu Bakr talks Hooyo's ear off well into the evening. Nothing she suggests piques his interest or seems to divert him. Not the ice cream she invites him to eat, the TV she tries waving him away to, or the picture book she begs him to read. The headline is Abu Bakr's First Day at Dugsi and, for the rest of the evening, Hooyo will be Abu Bakr's only, and unwilling, listener.

I head to my room to complete some homework. There is a sheet of paper with all kinds of symbols and chemicals that

I am meant to decipher with Safiya's help but, of course, that is out of the question. For both of us. And with this new BANTRxpose strangeness – whatever that is – I am even more inclined now to stay out of her way.

I refuse to seek out any trouble when I have bigger things to worry about, like saving my family from the husband and getting back home to Abti Haroon and Khadija.

Upstairs, the door to the master bedroom is slightly ajar. I pass it on the way to my room. The husband's voice floats to my ear. Strained, low. Purposefully low. I continue walking but, when I reach my room, I slink back, pressing my ear close to his door.

*"I need a few things from the boxes I left behind in the spare room, Safiya and…"* the husband says, voice wavering. He coughs before continuing. *"And I would love to see you, if you're free, of course. We have a lot to catch up on and…and I have a lot that I need to speak to you about."* Another waver. *"Okay, wa alaykum salaam."*

A moment later, I hear the shower running in the adjoining bathroom.

I cannot quite explain what happens next, but my legs propel me into the empty room. I pick up the husband's mobile. There is a passcode lock on it. I punch in random numbers, dropping it onto the bed after a few unsuccessful tries.

The shower is still running so I make the most of the short time I have to spy in my mother's room. I have never stepped foot in here, but the conversation with Hooyo in the kitchen a while ago has put me on edge. There is a story here that Hooyo wants to keep hidden. One about money, lies, blackmail.

Hearing that the husband had financially supported Hooyo in a big way had been a difficult pill to swallow. All those years she'd lied and told me Abti Haroon had been the quiet hero – schooling me and feeding the both of us.

But aren't most untruths birthed from an innate desire for survival?

And what was Hooyo's desire after losing my father, her soulmate?

To keep a shelter over her family's head. To ensure her daughter's belly was full. To provide her daughter with the education she herself never had.

Hooyo did what she had to for us. And the look on her face after the husband walked into the kitchen that evening – one of nausea and relief – had been all the confirmation I needed that something deeply wrong was at work in their supposed love story.

I do not know what I am looking for. Some ammunition maybe. Evidence of some sort. Perhaps something that I can fashion into a wedge, to drive the husband away, and get us a one-way ticket home in the process.

I rummage through both bedside tables, paying attention to the sound of the running water and the faint conversation that carries from downstairs. I check everything as thoroughly and stealthily as I can, then move onto the chest of drawers and finally the wardrobe but find nothing of interest. Only clothes and more clothes. No smoking gun. I am not sure what a smoking gun would even look like but I'd hoped it would be obvious.

I sit down at Hooyo's dressing table. Though the shower is still running I know logic says my business in this room is done. I have not been able to find anything and I won't be able to explain myself if I am caught.

Hooyo's table is on the cusp of overflowing with perfumes and jewellery. I thumb the necklace stand, the gold bracelets encrusted in all kinds of vibrant gems, the gold earrings in her jewellery box. Gold, gold, gold, everywhere I look. I remember the single gold ring that Hooyo owned before she married this man, the one that sat on her right hand. A simple band that she wore day in, day out. The ring my father gave her, she said, when they were first married.

She does not wear that ring any more.

I comb through her jewellery with renewed energy now, trying to find it. She stopped wearing it the second she re-married and replaced it with a bigger, gaudier one. She had changed it quickly, without a second thought. I remember wondering then whether she had even loved my father at all. How could she, if she was so willing to replace the only ring he had given her?

It does not take long. Though I have not seen the ring in years, I would recognize it anywhere. I find it tucked away in a corner, the edge of it slipping into the gap created by the foam insert. I slide it out, trying to avoid disturbing the placement of the other pieces. I do not know how particular Hooyo is about the positioning of her rings but I would rather not find out.

I'm pushing the insert back into place when I notice

something peeking out. A slip of something white. Papery. I pull the edge of it gently.

The peeking piece of white turns out to be something larger, folded into a tiny square. I unfold it once, twice, each time wondering whether this thing, this paper, whatever it is, will be the smoking gun I am looking for. It feels like nothing in my hand – the weight of a feather – but smoke is weightless and this could be it.

The unfolded square is a creased photograph. Lines criss-cross all over, obscuring details. I squint to see if I can recognize anything, leaning back to hold it under the light.

That's when I gasp. I feel the chair wobble beneath me and sit properly before I fall and incriminate myself. My eyes scan the photograph again.

Two women stand together in a dusty courtyard, a grand house looming behind them.

The woman on the left looks happy, radiant, staring into the lens of the camera with absolute certainty, with confidence just shy of arrogance. Her smile is infectious, full teeth and all gum. I find myself smiling just looking at her.

Hooyo's youth almost leaps from the photograph. I recognize the sharpness of her jaw and the soft arches of her eyebrows. Her large eyes and narrow shoulders. I recognize every part of her because I know my mother like I know no one else.

I turn my attention to the other woman, the one gripping Hooyo's waist as if she needs my mother to simply stand upright. Her lips are curved, bottling in laughter that I am sure must have slipped out the moment this photo was captured.

Her eyes dance in mischief, head angled slightly downwards as though unwilling to share her secrets with the camera.

I stare at this woman, pulled by some unexplained magnetism, until it clicks.

I grip my mouth. No air in or out, but I feel smoke filling my lungs anyway. The photograph is not on fire, nothing is on fire, but something must be because the heat floods my back and my face so quickly that it feels as though I am burning.

"*Halima?*" Abu Bakr's voice cuts through, dousing it. "*Maxaad sameynee?*"

He stands in the open doorway, left eye squinting in question like it always does whenever he is confused. I watch him hear the shower and realize his father must be in there. Then his right eye squints too.

"*Nothing,*" I reply as calmly as I can.

I stand, moving so he won't be able to see the open jewellery box. I fold my hands behind my back.

"*What are you doing?*" I counter.

"*Me?*" he splutters. "*Nothing.*"

The shower stops running. Abu Bakr and I cock our heads in the direction of the bathroom at the same time, noticing the new silence.

"*Let's go,*" I whisper, hoping to keep the anxiety out of my voice. I do not want him to realize that I need to be out of this room before his father steps back into it. "*Let's go play a game, Abu Bakr, okay?*"

He squeals in delight, un-squinting both eyes.

"*Yes, yes, let's play! I'll tell Kamal too!*"

He is off at lightning speed without waiting for me to say more. I deftly rearrange the jewellery and close the box as quietly as I can.

Then, I pocket my smoking gun and run.

# SAFIYA

The house is freezing cold when Hooyo and I return to it from our neighbour's, but it's not just from a lack of heating. Some of it flows over from the icy tension between us.

Hooyo hovers awkwardly in the living room. Her nervous energy and guilt pricks at my skin; eyes roaming over me.

I can't remember the last time Hooyo was on edge about anything because, for the last five years, Hooyo has been a solid ghost. Almost here, but not quite. But her watching me like this, wondering whether to apologize again for her years of deceit about Aabo and his second family, is actually making *me* uneasy. Though it's been weeks since she admitted to her lies, the betrayal still feels too raw. I'm still not ready to forgive her and I don't know if I ever will be.

Thankfully, she disappears to her room, and I let myself relax. My stomach growls the moment I do, reminding me that I haven't eaten properly since we'd spent most of the afternoon at our neighbour Habaryar Anab's house, paying our respects. The news of her sister passing away from cancer had rocked the entire community a few days ago and there was no way we could *not* go, even with things being so tense between me and Hooyo.

There had been a small spread at their house, but it seemed wrong to be stuffing my face, even if I was starved. I nibbled on a few things, out of politeness, of course, but I didn't want to go overboard.

Unfortunately, we'd been caught by Habaryar Binti and Habaryar Shukri outside the house just as we were leaving. I had been holding my breath that we might manage to return home untouched by any such interaction, but our luck ran out.

*"On your way home?"* Habaryar Shukri had smiled. *"How sad that we've missed each other."*

I opened my mouth to speak the regular niceties and haul us out of there when Hooyo interrupted.

*"Not sad at all, Shukri."* Hooyo looked to me. *"Everything happens for a reason and everything has an appointed time."*

I wasn't sure if Hooyo was speaking to me or Habaryar Shukri, but I didn't waste any time thinking it over because my mum isn't someone who makes sense. She's too busy being irrational and selfish and incomprehensible.

The bell rings as I bite into my cheese toastie. I sigh, putting my sandwich aside, and head to the front door, pausing when I realize it's not the doorbell. The sound is shrill, more tinkly. A tune?

I follow the melody to the living room, around the sofa, to the display cabinet. The flashing lights of the dusty telephone docking station almost makes me laugh. I haven't heard the home phone ring in a long time. I peer at the display which shows a saved contact.

Dad.

I don't pick up. The shrill phone continues singing. Then, the line goes quiet and the screen flashes.

*1 voicemail message.*

My Aabo-reflex tells me to delete it immediately. Get one over on him by refusing to give his message the time of day. But curiosity wins. Aabo will never know whether I've listened to it anyway.

*"As-salamu alakyum, Safiya."*

His voice comes out the way it has always sounded. Familiar, a little gravelly, self-assured. It seems wrong, somehow, that his voice should make him sound human because he can't be. How can a human do to their family what he has done to us?

I sigh, sitting down to lean against the sofa. I wonder if there'll ever come a time when seeing him or hearing his voice won't be triggering for me.

*"I hope you and Hooyo are well,"* he continues. *"I just…I just wanted to see how you were both doing."*

In an instant, his voice loses that self-assuredness.

*"I know that we left things on bad terms the last time we spoke, Safiya, but…that is not what I want for us. You are my daughter, and I am your father, and we are family. We are all family, even if that is difficult to accept right now."*

Aabo coughs, clearing his throat.

*"There is something else I wanted to discuss with you,"* he says, edging closer to the truth behind his call.

*"I need a few things from the boxes I left behind in the spare room, Safiya, and…I would love to see you, if you're free, of course.*

*We have a lot to catch up on and I have a lot that I need to speak to you about."*

His voice wavers.

*"Okay, wa alaykum salaam."*

The phone clicks off.

When I am confident that his voice won't unexpectedly jump out at me, I grab the phone and navigate the screen until I find the button I'm looking for.

*Delete voicemail message? Press 1 for yes / 2 for no.*

My finger finds the number I want swiftly, and then the message is gone, just like that, as if it never existed.

Muna calls me on Sunday evening as I'm getting ready for bed. I waddle over to my phone, pyjama trousers circling my ankles. I'm either too slow or she's too impatient because there's a sudden knock that reverberates through our shared wall.

"Calm down!" I shout back. "I'm coming."

I pick up the call. As if she can see the expression of displeasure on my face, she says, "Listen, Safiya, don't be frowning at me. You know I always knock if you aren't picking up by the fourth ring. Saves me having to call you a second time."

I roll my eyes. "Don't say '*always*' like you've done it before. You know I *always* pick up within a socially acceptable time frame."

She sniffs. "You should really be thanking me since you've got an incentive to pick up from now on."

I laugh. "Are you really trying to condition me into getting the phone when you ring? If that's the case, you can speak to my voicemail from now on."

My stomach clenches at my own words, a clamp extending around my middle. It's the reminder about the voicemail…the one that I've just deleted.

I divert the conversation.

"Anyway, how was your weekend?" I ask, putting the phone on loudspeaker and pulling my trousers up. "Anything exciting?"

Muna snorts. "I mean, if you can call seeing *your* sister exciting then, yes…sure, that's probably been the most exciting part of my weekend."

"Well, that sounds nice. I'm glad you had such a good time."

Muna doesn't respond. I know she is waiting for me to sweat, to come out and beg for details but, clearly, she doesn't realize how little I care.

"Ughhhhh!" she groans a minute later. "You're so annoying, Saf, do you know that? I hope you know that."

I hear shuffling in the background before Muna comes back on the phone.

"Anyway," she continues, stretching out the word and still sounding mildly disappointed, "I was going to say I saw your stepsister prancing around at dugsi yesterday. You know she genuinely tried to give me a heart attack because I was walking over to Fatima and then, suddenly, she was just *there*. I don't even know where she came from, man. It was a little creepy. Gave me horror movie vibes."

The way Muna tells this story, I know she has made it sound a thousand times more dramatic than it probably was and, usually, I would be laughing at this point too – because Muna's stories are always laughable – but this one today isn't funny. This story today actually makes me kind of sad.

A lot changed when Aabo left but one of the biggest things, after losing my dad to a whole other continent, was losing dugsi too. Muna and I had spent almost our whole lives going to those weekend study classes at NWCC but, when Aabo left, Hooyo couldn't afford it any more. The monthly cost wasn't all that expensive but, in the grand scheme of things, dugsi was on the chopping block.

Our entire lifestyle changed virtually overnight, but the thing that really hurt was losing those weekend classes. Losing that sense of community, that connection to everyone else trying to understand their faith together. I have learned the hard way since that it's not the same trying to figure things out by yourself.

I switch the conversation for the second time in as many minutes.

"Cute story but I'd rather hear what's happening with BANTRxpose, to be honest. Anything new on that front?"

When I finish speaking, I realize that I haven't succeeded in diverting anything. I've only gone and drawn Muna into further conversation about Halima Omar.

Muna sighs. "I wish," she says. "BANTRxpose is getting on my last nerve. At least when they were active before, they were posting about a variety of news. Pointless news, but, still, it was all different. Unpredictable. All they seem obsessed about this time around is Halima! Their latest post is a video of her at King Eddy's where Yash and his lot are goading her. Like, come on, can you shake things up a little?"

My eyes go to our shared wall and I can almost picture her: back against the wardrobe, head turned to the ceiling, eyes tightly shut. I can see her shaking her head in that way of hers that makes it feel like the whole world must be burning down. Of course, for her, the whole world *is* burning down, even if it's only in her head.

Muna has always prided herself on knowing everything about everything and, above all, being the first to know it. This whole situation has torn into her in a way that I've seen few things do but, knowing her, she will never admit it. No, Muna will keep digging away until she gets the answers she wants.

And, this time, it's in my best interests that she uncovers the truth because the quicker BANTRxpose is shut down, the quicker Halima will stop getting thrown in my face.

"Still, at least there's something to be grateful for," Muna continues. "They haven't reported on the edibles situation Mustafa mentioned and, let me tell you, Safiya, that is a story I *need* to break. My recent blog numbers have really taken a hit."

"Well, if I hear anything, I'll be sure to let you know," I say. "Trust me, I want BANTRxpose to disappear just as much as you do."

I hear scuffling in the background. Muna's voice gets distant for a moment before she laughs into the line.

"So, Yusuf's saying you're not replying on Three Musketeers and, to quote him exactly: *stop being a dead ting with a dead phone.*"

"How about you tell your cousin that I'm a big girl with big girl problems now? Texts kind of aren't on my radar any more."

Muna howls. "Oh my god, I beg you tell him. Wait, let me put you on speaker—"

"Bye!" I shout into the phone before swiftly pressing the end button. I think that's more than enough social interaction for tonight.

# SAFIYA

Sleep does not come easy. Even when I jump into a hot shower after an hour of tossing and turning, it refuses to come. Even with counting a thousand sheep, eating another toastie, and watching three different ASMR videos, I am nowhere closer. I can't remember the last time I experienced this level of insomnia. I drag a hand over my eyes, letting out a groan. My phone vibrates with a notification. Fajr. Time to pray. I try to leave my exhaustion in bed as I get up to do my wudhu.

I knock on Hooyo's door to wake her. Usually, I give her a gentle shake even though I know she won't get out of bed. It has been months since she last prayed but I still hold out hope that one of these days, she'll spring right up. That the both of us will stand side by side, in that moment of darkness before sunrise opens its eyes, and pray together, the way we used to, before everything soured.

A soft light streams through the crack of her bedroom door before I've got it all the way open.

*Hooyo must have left her lamp on*, I think to myself, but when I open it fully, my eyebrows almost disappear into my hairline.

Hooyo is already awake.

The soft light is not from a forgotten lamp but from one purposefully switched on. She is sitting on the floor, on a prayer mat I haven't seen for a long time, prayer beads in hand.

She gives me a small, tired smile. The kind of smile that makes me feel as though no time has passed since we last saw each other during these pre-sunrise hours.

"Have you done your wudhu?" she whispers.

*Why are you whispering?* I almost ask. *There's no one else here.* But I stop myself, nodding instead.

"Shall we pray together then?" she asks, still whispering.

I blink, take a beat, survey the room, wonder what kind of sorcery this is. Am I dreaming?

Hooyo rises, indicating for me to stand to her left and lead. She gives my hand a squeeze and I almost jump at the touch, so unused to feeling my mother's skin on mine. She must sense my surprise because she lets go immediately, eyes downcast.

I don't want the awkwardness lingering any longer, so I start praying. I let the words tumble out of the deepest parts of my soul, the parts that I only ever feel when I'm standing here like this, invoking something greater than anything else in this world.

To most people, I know this would probably not look like anything more than spiritual yoga. A few repeated movements against the backdrop of Arabic words. But to me? To me it's like a breath of fresh air in a smoke-filled room. A few minutes beyond the prison of life in something that feels like heaven, or close to it.

*   *   *

215

Afterwards, I head back to my room, before pivoting at the last second. I quietly shut my door behind me, and tiptoe past Hooyo's room to the end of the landing.

I flip the switch on in the spare room. The light flickers for a few seconds, as if unsure about whether to commit, before it steadies.

Sunrise peeks through the blinds, reminding me that I don't have time to waste. School is in a few hours, and I am pretty sure I've misplaced my planner again. If I don't bring it in for form, Ms Birch will definitely have my head.

I pull forward the box nearest to me. I don't know what I am looking for since Aabo wasn't specific on the phone. I'm not quite sure why I'm here at six in the morning. It certainly isn't to do my dad's bidding. But when I was standing beside Hooyo, shoulder to shoulder in prayer, I was reminded of how little I know her. How easily she lied to me and continued to lie. How much I now distrust her.

And all I keep thinking is how different life might have been if I'd been selfish too and picked up the phone in that first year Aabo called and kept calling.

Maybe he would have explained things to me in a way I could understand. Maybe he would have apologized and tried to rebuild our relationship.

Maybe he would have told me he loved me, that he would never stop loving me. That I wouldn't stop being his daughter, wherever he ended up in the world.

But, regardless of what might have happened, the present, the *now*, is in my hands. I refuse to let anybody else lie to me and that starts with finding whatever was important enough for Aabo to call about.

I fan out the items from the box, skimming through.

A notebook sits at the top. Opening to the first page, Hooyo's handwriting jumps out at me. The block letters, the mix of capital and lower case. I'd recognize it anywhere. There is no one else in the world that writes as bizarrely as she does.

I read the words she's written on the front. It's in Somali so it takes a moment for me to translate the first part of it.

*Bookkeeping for Halane Aden*

I flick through. Everything is neatly laid out in Hooyo's signature style. Monthly outgoings and incomings for…Aabo's fledgling business, it looks like.

Another notebook. I mindlessly brush my fingers along Hooyo's sentences, realizing that these scribbles are business-related too. At the back I find a list of contacts: names, phone numbers and email addresses all meticulously laid out.

I turn my attention to a thick, black binder. Most of the papers stored appear to be in business-language again which, unfortunately, I am not fluent in. I skim over the pages, pausing every so often to scan more specifically. I stop on one such page about halfway through and my breath catches.

A list of investors for Aabo's first business: H. Aden Butchers.

Several names on it I recognize, including Adeer Ali, Muna's dad – Yasin Mohamed – and…my mother.

Idil Ahmed.

*Twenty-five thousand pounds.*

I sit down on the carpet, crossing my legs.

My knees feel weak from kneeling for so long. Or maybe they feel weak from having my legs cut out from under me because now Hooyo's heartbreak makes more sense. Now, Hooyo's unravelling seems like it was inevitable, because when Aabo walked out, he didn't just take himself. He took her life savings too – everything she invested in him beyond her love.

I have always echoed what Hooyo said about Aabo; a parrot imitating what it hears without any thought for context. How much he owed to her, how much she built him up, and how little gratitude he had for any of it. It's what I threw back at Aabo when I saw him in Ms Devlin's office. The way his face had crumbled, I thought it was only because I was spitting venom at him. I hadn't realized any of it was real and how deep Hooyo's truth ran.

I close my eyes…

See my mother's words writing my father's life.

I try to remember Hooyo's history, find some explanation for how she could ever have afforded this – even if it was a decade ago. And then I recall the stories she would tell about the land she once owned. Land passed down from her grandfather to her father, and finally to her. Land she once told me she'd sold to give us a better future here. A revelation I never questioned.

The world feels slippery all of a sudden, even though I am still sitting on the mottled carpet.

I turn my attention away from the notebook, needing to look at something else, anything else, but there's not much more in the box except photographs.

Most are pictures from Somalia, a mix of black-and-white and colour. I don't recognize many of the people in them, but there are a few I do. My grandparents on my dad's side, both of whom have since passed away. Aabo's countless sisters and, in one photo, his youngest brother, who died from a fever and rash that nobody could make sense of at the time.

I sift through the photos slowly. I've never had the chance to go back home to Somalia but looking at these photos makes me feel like I've been there. Even in this tiny room with its peeling wallpaper and musty smell, I feel like I'm right there with them, with this family I never got to meet. In a few of them, I even make out the towering house in Yaaqshid that Aabo used to speak so much about. His ancestral home, he called it, even though his own father had built it only a decade before he was born.

Another grainy photo, set outside Aabo's house, but this one doesn't have him in it.

It's a photo of Hooyo, her arm wrapped around another woman who is grinning into the camera. I try to place her, flicking through the mental catalogue of our crazy family tree. I am sure she isn't any of Aabo's sisters – I know what each of his seven sisters looks like and she doesn't fit the images in my memory, but…there is a familiarity that nudges me, makes me feel like I've seen her before.

The sun climbs through the blinds, reminding me that time is not on my side. Northwell High will be calling soon. I drop the photo on the growing pile next to me and move on.

It takes me longer than it should to realize the next photo

isn't one of my dad's old ones. The faces staring back at me should be ones that I recognize instantly.

On a simple level, I know that it is me, Hooyo and Aabo. The three of us at King Eddy's Park, my pink bike with its training wheels stationed in front of us. I even vaguely remember this day, although the details are fuzzy.

But the strangeness is like an itch I can't get rid of. The three of us wearing smiles that feel like a sham now.

My eyes start to burn with the hours of lost sleep, but I blink it away.

I am down to the last item from the box. A small booklet with tulips on the cover. I open it, ready to take a quick glance then throw it on the pile too, ready to be done with this whole night and box-searching mission, but something flutters out, landing on the floor. It looks like a Polaroid. I sigh with exhaustion, looking a little more closely under the flickering light, and, when I do, I realize that it's not a Polaroid.

It's an ultrasound scan of a baby...

Dated months before I was conceived.

# HALIMA

Why this school insists on a portion of mandatory physical activity, two times a week, is beyond me. It clearly is not enough to chain us to our desks for seven hours a day. No, now they must subject us to a different kind of torture.

It has been a couple of months but I am yet to adjust to this *PE*. The loud, raucous changing rooms, the incessant whistle-blowing that our teacher, Mrs Farrant, seems too happy to engage in, the running around in the cold air and light rain. It is all too much.

The worst thing is that this *PE* is not an individual sport. It is a "team" activity according to Mrs Farrant, which means that while I can escape the boys from our class for those hours, I cannot escape the girls.

I change into my school mandated outfit and leave the gym through the double doors to stand with our assembling class. As usual, Mrs Farrant eyes my uniform. For the most part, it is up to par with school code. That is, if you ignore the knitted scarf and gloves I wear to protect myself from the biting cold everyone else seems immune to.

Ironically, it wasn't that long ago I was convinced that

Hooyo would be the one to succumb to the cold.

Mercifully, Mrs Farrant looks away first, reaching for the whistle around her neck.

"Girls!" Mrs Farrant screams. Her voice reaches a pitch that I did not think was humanly possible. "You've got five seconds to stop gossiping and get yourselves out here, or you'll be cleaning those changing rooms you seem to love wasting so much time in!"

She blows the whistle once with each number she reaches in her countdown. I retreat a few steps out of concern for my aural well-being.

The rest of the girls trail out. A few of them roll their eyes, but Mrs Farrant either doesn't seem to notice or care.

When their eyes roam over to me, I do notice. Whispering sparks in one cluster before spreading to another and another and another, until all five huddles of girls are speaking under their breath and indiscreetly flicking gazes at me.

Only one, Leanne, looks uncomfortable. She gives me a small smile.

The two of us have sat at the same table in form class for a couple of months now. I wonder if she feels some kind of misguided loyalty. But Leanne has misread the situation. I need respect, not loyalty, and so I turn away from her smile.

Even without it being spelled out, I know this must be connected to the profile the girl from dugsi showed me.

BANTRxpose.

An anonymous, cowardly person – or persons – holding some wildly inappropriate obsession with me.

My initial suspicions had been Safiya or Kyle, the latter not only due to the tripping incident but because he also seems to be a persistent thorn in everyone's side. But now, I wonder whether it could be any one of these girls.

The last to arrive are Safiya and Muna. As always, they are joined at the hip, although today Muna appears to be almost holding her friend upright. Safiya looks like someone has wrung her completely dry. Her eyes do not meet anyone else's as they walk towards us, but I see the dark circles around them that suggest she did not find any sleep last night.

I wonder if my own eyes appear like that. The photo I found in Hooyo's jewellery box robbed me of most of my rest and I had been in such a rush this morning that I hadn't stopped to properly appraise myself in the mirror.

I was tempted to confront Hooyo at one point in the night. But I held myself back, because you do not confront someone who has lied straight through their teeth before and who would surely do so again. And, given where I found this photo to begin with – hidden in Hooyo's jewellery box – I know that she would not give me the truth easily.

Whatever is going on, Hooyo certainly knows much, much more than she is willing to share with me. The photo I discovered is incontrovertible evidence of that. And if there is one thing last night helped me realize, it's that Hooyo does not need saving.

What I need is to escape *from* her.

I look to Safiya again, wondering what secrets she knows and holds. If she has the answers to the questions swirling around in my head.

I tried to seek answers from her once before without success. I'm not sure if I would fare better a second time.

Mrs Farrant blows the whistle for the eighth time in a lesson that has not even begun yet. She indicates the football pitch on the far end of the field. We follow her there like sheep. Then, she drops the equipment bag on the floor and begins drilling orders.

"You, Leanne, take these cones and set up the pitch."

She dips back into the open bag.

"Here, Rianna, hold onto these bibs. You'll be captain for your team."

Mrs Farrant grabs another set.

"Safiya."

*Blows whistle.*

"Safiya! Yes, thank you, Miss Sleepy, glad we've got your attention now. Here, take these bibs. You'll be captain too."

The captains begin picking their teams. Rianna chooses Leanne. Safiya takes Muna. Then Huda and Mary disappear. Natalie and Sakina follow. The girls around me slowly thin out until it is only me left.

The choice reverts to Rianna, who is now forced to pick me. She does not seem unhappy about it, which makes me feel a little bad since I plan on maintaining my zero-contribution streak. I take the bib she offers me, putting it on and arranging my knitted scarf elegantly on top of it.

Everyone positions themselves on the pitch. I follow Rianna's direction, standing where she points. "You'll be a defender," she says, whatever that means.

Mrs Farrant blows the whistle.

Chaos ensues. A flurry of orange and blue across the pitch; screams and laughs. I look down at my chest to remind myself what I am. Team Blue.

A few minutes in, I realize that we, Team Blue, appear to be losing. Quite a few of the Oranges have kicked the ball past Leanne, who is standing a little way behind me between two cones. I can tell we are losing because Leanne looks dejected every time it happens and because some of the other Blues tell her to *fix up* in a way that doesn't sound very friendly.

Another ball heads Leanne's way, this time led by Safiya. She is spearheading the attack, although it is a concerted effort. Muna and Mary flank her on either side, protecting her from the Blues.

*She's made a very swift recovery*, I think to myself. The girl looked almost comatose before.

Rianna points wildly at me. She is shouting something too. If I had to guess, likely an instruction to intervene and halt the ball but, from the determined and almost vicious looks on the faces of that trio, I know that is not something I want to be involved in.

I wave my hands about to Rianna, trying to exaggerate the uncertainty on my face. Hopefully she'll believe this language barrier I'm trying to erect and leave me be.

The three girls swoop past. I look to Leanne, feeling sorry for her. She looks small, standing there all alone.

Safiya, Muna and Mary run with renewed energy now that they have crossed into enemy territory. There is nothing to

225

stop them and they know it. I am admiring their powerful legs when I notice something.

I squint, unsure, the muscles in my eyes pinching, and then my legs start carrying me forward before I have even fully understood what I am about to do.

Still, I do feel something in me hesitate as I run straight for the trio.

*We are not friends and we are not family*, is what Safiya said the last time. *Don't try speaking to me again.* But one could argue this is technically not speaking. Technically, this is wordlessly saving her from embarrassment, a distinctly different situation.

Then I have a flash of memory, of hands that caught me when I was tripped in the corridor weeks ago. Hands that could have washed themselves of me and been idle but chose to save me instead. I realize then that my decision is already made. It was made the moment I started chasing after her and it is too late to stop now.

I keep my eyes locked on her back, pushing my legs faster, faster, faster. We are nothing to each other, but I owe her what she once gave me. I owe her decency. At least, just this once.

I hear Rianna screaming my name in encouragement. "Yes, girl! Go on, Halima! You got this!"

I suppose to her, it looks as though I am chasing after the ball, but I do not have enough air in my lungs to tell her otherwise.

I reach Safiya just as she is a couple of metres from the goal, whipping off the knitted scarf around my neck at the same time and stretching it between my hands. I angle it so that I can wrap it around her hips and hopefully get out of the trio's way before I cause any actual disruption.

Wrap and run, is the plan. Wrap and run. But Safiya stops abruptly, like a train that has run out of track. She prepares to kick the ball past Leanne, bringing her right leg backward to gain momentum. There is not enough time for me to process.

I crash into her as her foot kicks the ball. Safiya falls face-first with the impact and I tumble on top of her. The ball veers off course and sails through the air to hit Leanne on the head.

Mrs Farrant blows the whistle three times in quick succession. The game comes to a grinding halt.

# SAFIYA

Dirt in my mouth. Grass in my eyes. A weight on my back, crushing my chest.

Those are the only things I'm aware of in the second after I suddenly lose sight of the goal in front of me.

I try to catch my breath, but it's hard work. Muna screams something that I catch the end of. Hearing her eases my anxiety a little about what's going on even if I really, really can't breathe right now.

"—Get off her! Get off!"

The pressure on my back moves and I realize then that it's a person. Someone must have fallen on me.

The weight shifts again and while I still feel crushed, my chest rises and falls more easily now. I take in air in huge gulps, lifting my chin so I don't accidentally eat more mouthfuls of pitch.

Mrs Farrant blows a whistle and I sense people step back. I can't actually see anyone since I'm still face-down on the ground but I am grateful for the space. Even if none of this was my fault, it's still embarrassing.

Finally, the weight rolls off me completely. I push myself up on my arms but they feel shaky, like the ground beneath me is vibrating.

I'm on my hands and knees when I feel something around my waist. Then, tightening.

Looking down, I see the ends of a scarf hanging between my legs. I glance to my side to see Halima leaning back on her heels. She grimaces when our eyes meet.

Muna squats, blocking my view. "Are you okay?" she asks, still breathing heavily from our coordinated goal attack. "You fell pretty hard, you know. Any head injuries, cuts, dizziness?"

Mrs Farrant blows her whistle. She doesn't follow it up with anything but we understand the language of the whistle well. Muna scuttles away to the periphery along with everyone else.

Mrs Farrant chuckles as she comes into view. "Thank you, Muna, for those wonderfully probing medical questions, but I'll take it from here."

She kneels, looking from me to Halima. "You girls feeling dizzy?" I shake my head. Halima does the same.

"Feeling sick?" We shake our heads again.

"Anything that feels like a broken bone?" A final shake.

"Well, excellent," she says, standing back up. "Let's go about starting this game up again, shall we?"

The whistle follows once more with directions from Mrs Farrant for everyone to resume their positions. She returns to tell me and Halima that we won't be playing. There is a lot me and Mrs Farrant butt heads about, though this instruction won't be one of them.

Halima stands, clearly feeling steadier than I do, and a sudden desire to bring her down courses through me, because what she did doesn't feel like an accident. How could it be when one moment she's standing hundreds of yards away, looking totally out of it and, the next, she's got me eating dirt? Halima may be new, but she's been around long enough to know how to play football.

Her legs stop in front of me. I look up to see her hand extended.

Is this girl concussed? The ridiculous peace offering is enough to give me the momentum I need to get up on my own. I stand on shaky legs and walk off the pitch, Halima trailing close behind.

When I reach the sideline, I sense that same tightness around my waist again.

"Huh," I whisper, staring down at my body. I'm not sure who I am talking to, but the words seem necessary in that moment. "I guess she is genuinely concussed."

I move to undo the scarf around my waist. The scarf that I *know* was around her neck only moments ago.

*Do not get into it with this girl, Safiya,* I tell myself. *Do not do it. You don't have the energy or the patience.*

But when her hand grabs mine, I lose it. Is she seriously trying to stop me from taking this off?

"What's wrong with you?" I scream. "Leave me alone!" I add, shoving her.

To her credit, Halima bounces back quickly from the shove, looking unbothered. She holds up both hands in surrender.

"You can't," she says simply, keeping her hands where they are. "You need to wear."

I laugh. "Oh, really?" I reply, hands going to undo the knot that she's tied well. "And why not? Why can't I take *your* scarf off *my* body? Please, enlighten me."

"Because blood." Halima points to my bum. "Because there is bleeding."

# HALIMA

In the hallways of Northwell High, I attempt to follow the directions I have been given to find the nurse's room. I take the wrong turn three times and find myself outside the same computer room I walked past several minutes ago.

When I eventually locate it and have the required sanitary pads in hand, I begin the arduous task of trying to navigate my way back to the toilets near the changing room.

Once there, I slide the contents under the cubicle to Safiya, who murmurs a very quiet, very reluctant "Thank you."

I linger by the door, hand on the handle, wondering whether I am meant to stay or go.

What is the socially acceptable manner of handling this type of sensitive situation, I wonder? Especially when it involves a girl who hates your guts and whose father you hate more than the devil itself.

Cleaned up and in clean clothes, Safiya steps out to find me hovering by the door. She keeps her focus on washing her hands.

"This does not make us friends," she says abruptly, hands under the dryer. "We are not friends."

I scoff.

"Saaxibteey, keep your friendship." I pull the door open, no longer on edge. "And the scarf too."

# SAFIYA

If home were a haven, I would have gone to the nurse's room and demanded to be released there but, as life would have it, home is more of a hazard right now. So I have no choice but to consign myself to an afternoon of cramps, chloroplasts and coastal erosion.

In geography, Halima sits at the other end of the classroom. Neither of us looks the other's way.

My abdomen seizes in a cramp and I reflexively double up over the table to hide my discomfort.

The unpredictability of my period has truly been my downfall today. Not only did it cost me a goal in the game, it also brought Halima and me face to face in the most embarrassing PE display ever witnessed.

Half the school must know what happened by now. I groan into my blazer, praying for my painkillers to kick in.

I try being positive and count my blessings instead, but it's a struggle.

Halima may have been the only person paying attention to my backside, I tell myself, so at least the visual count is low. And, though we both took an awkward tumble, I suppose I must be somewhat grateful for her quick thinking. Even if it did give me a scraped knee and two skinned elbows in the process.

Mr Khan dismisses us for lunch. He tells us we have an emergency assembly before final period, but most of the class are already gone, sprinting for Friday fish and chips.


A different energy thrives in the canteen today. It is the excitement only experienced at the end of the week, when even the boys forgo football to enjoy a hot meal. And it's even more intense today given it's the last day before the half-term break.

As expected, Yusuf and Mustafa are at the front of the line. The boys have never been one to drag their heels on a Friday afternoon.

Halima is not too far behind them. I catch myself staring at the back of her head, looking away before Muna or anyone else notices.

A commotion ensues. A babble of displeasure and disgruntled sounds. Someone must be trying to cut the line. This happens at least once every Friday, twice if we're lucky. Whoever the culprit is, they are almost invariably hauled away to the back of the hall to sit with the group that Muna and I call the "Friday Hooligans": a collection of kids foolish enough to misbehave where a supervisor can catch them.

Muna elbows me. "Look," she says. "Seems like Kyle's gunning to join the Friday Hooligans two weeks in a row."

I pull my attention to where she points.

Kyle walks determinedly past the snaking line and it seems as though he's heading towards Yusuf and Mustafa, but he stops before reaching them.

To everyone else, the moment is quick, barely a second long, but, as I see it, it seems to stretch for ever.

Before The Moment: Kyle saunters to the front of the line, seemingly appearing out of thin air.

The Moment: he turns around, viper-quick, and lands a solid *thwack* on Halima's forehead.

After The Moment: Kyle disappears, his exit followed by scattered laughter and *oofs*.

Beside me, Muna gasps, covering her mouth, but I am frozen.

Halima does not do herself the disservice of appearing fazed. She does not drag a hand across her face to soothe her reddened skin. She only looks resolutely ahead, as if nothing has happened.

A few paces behind, my stomach is in turmoil. I try to tell myself it's cramps, but cramps do not come with a twisting guilt that stretches into your blood and makes you feel like your cells are playing a beating drum inside of you.

Around us, the sniggers continue. Snippets of conversation, including a word that I've heard too much of in the last ten seconds for it to be inconsequential.

I tap the girl in front of me on the shoulder. "What's this about BANTRxpose?"

Muna isn't paying attention. She cranes her neck forward,

trying to catch the last dregs of the drama, so doesn't hear what the girl has to say.

"There's a new post about that girl. Halima, I think her name is," she says, pointing ahead. "It came up like an hour ago. Some joke about her hairline. Probably why she got slapped." She frowns. "Have you not seen it yet?"

I ignore her, casting my eyes to the front of the queue again. There are no teachers in sight. Not yet anyway. But they'll be drawn to the scene soon enough, to the scent of misbehaviour, as all teachers are. *They'll come and sort this out*, I think. *They will. They have to.*

Halima stands stiffly in the line. The few people around her seem to have stepped back slightly, as if repelled.

I look away and my eyes catch Yusuf's. Beside him, Mustafa is speaking fast. Too fast for me to lipread but, to Yusuf, his friend's speech must be unimportant because he only stares at me. He doesn't smile, laugh, react. He pushes his glasses up the bridge of his nose, a nervous gesture.

In that instant, it clicks.

It's him. Yusuf.

Everything that has happened since Halima started here, the timing of every post from BANTRxpose.

*I'm sure she'll have a tougher time of it than you anyway…*

Words that Yusuf said to me on the first day of school. Words that I thought he meant generally, never in any targeted way.

But then…

Then I recall our conversation back in the summer. When

237

I'd run over to his house, looking for Muna, but found him instead.

I'd raged about Halima joining Northwell High and he had comforted me with words I never imagined were a promise.

*"What can I do?"* he'd asked. *"Shall I drive her out of school? Banish her to the wilderness? Toss her on a boat and send her back home?"*

I remember the first post. How it came after it seemed my whole world fell apart at Eid.

Then nothing on BANTRxpose...until Kyle tripped Halima, until I caught her, and then, suddenly, another post that Muna alerted me to.

*Fresh off the boat and still can't walk on land LOL,* it had said.

And now? Now the PE incident.

Halima bringing me down, embarrassing me.

A post that goes up tearing her down only hours later.

All these instances, all these memories and connections...

New realization slips into place.

If this is true...

Then Yusuf must have been the one to set up BANTRxpose all those years ago too.

A parody account to torture Muna that died after two months? Of course, it must have been him! Of course, he would pull that kind of a prank.

But the BANTRxpose from three years ago was never what it is now and, clearly, neither is Yusuf.

I pull on Muna's arm.

"Did you know about this?"

Muna must have known. At least, she must have had her suspicions. Not only is she Hexpose Editor-in-Chief, but she and Yusuf *live* together.

Why hadn't she said anything about it?

"What?" Muna says distractedly. "What are you talking about?"

"Yusuf! Did you know that it was him this whole time?"

"Girl, I don't even know what language you're speaking—"

Through the few bodies between us, I see Halima's shoulders start to shake. The turmoil in my stomach grows and grows. There is no teacher in sight.

"That stupid page!" I shout. "Are you telling me you had no idea Yusuf was behind it?" I lean against the wall for comfort, letting the cold seep into my shirt.

"Hold up." Muna's eyebrows furrow. "*Yusuf* is behind BANTRxpose? Are you kidding?"

For a split second, doubt creeps in. About the theory that I have strung together, the conclusions I have drawn, everything. But then my gaze flicks to Yusuf and he must see something because the excuses are written on his face. He heads towards us.

My thoughts circle BANTRxpose. Its inception and disappearance three years ago.

BANTRxpose is the only thing that Muna has allegedly never been able to get to the bottom of. But what if that's because she already knew the truth? That Yusuf was behind all of it? And what if the two of them are using it now as some twisted way to protect me?

"Did Yusuf tell you to hide this from me? Is that why you didn't say anything?"

Muna frowns, registering the anger creeping into my voice. "No," she replies, shaking her head slowly. "I would never do that, Safiya." She touches my arm. "You know that, right?"

My head swims.

Lies, from the people I love.

The people who decided that having my back meant destroying someone else. But that's not the friendship I knew. That's not the friendship I signed up for. Now, I don't know what to believe.

I may not be Halima's biggest fan, but no one deserves to be treated this way, and if this is all happening because of me, then I have no choice but to shoulder the blame and fix this.

"I don't know anything, Muna!" I shout. The girl I'd tapped on the shoulder looks over at us, excited by the prospect of a fight. "I never thought that your cousin would be messing with an innocent girl, but look!"

Muna's eyes darken. "His name is Yusuf," she replies. "He may be my cousin but don't you dare throw that in my face. Trust me, I'll deal with him if any of what you're saying is true, but you of all people should know why he'd do this."

"Excuse me?"

"Safiya, we've known each other too long to be playing games. If this is true, you *know* why Yusuf did this and you know that it has nothing to do with me."

I can't believe this. How dare she try and make this about me?

I am *not* the one who has lied and hurt someone. And I am definitely *not* the one who claims to be the best investigative journalist around.

I breathe, not thinking through my words because there is no space in my head to process any of them, but I have the presence of mind to at least whisper what I say next.

"If you were better at your job, I'm sure you would've figured out it was Yusuf before me. Maybe then we wouldn't even be here. But Hexpose couldn't even catch what was right under its nose." I shake my head. "You can't bark on about journalistic integrity if you're not even a decent journalist."

Muna reels back. Her eyes widen and I see myself in them for a moment. Wild, angry, hurt, like she is too.

"And if you were a decent *person*," she spits back, "you would stop letting Yusuf pine over you so he could move on. So we could *all* move on."

I flinch from her words, feeling a lump rise in my throat, and, for a moment, I am on the outside looking in, seeing something splinter between me and my best friend.

Movement catches my eye in the periphery. Halima, walking away from the lunch line. Perhaps it's the light but her eyes look shimmery.

I don't know what to do, what will happen or what *has* happened, but all I do know is that right now, Halima has nobody. Because of me, she exists in this school singularly.

I forgo my fish and chips, jumping out of the line to take her arm, leading her to the toilets near the changing room where, for the second time today, we find ourselves together.

# HALIMA

With my back against the wall in the toilets, I sob and sob and sob. My chest shakes with the weight of humiliation, but the tears do nothing to lessen it. Hot tears run without letting up, and I use my hijab to catch them, pushing the material against my eyes to try and absorb them before they escape.

Safiya sits on the floor next to me. She tries to draw me into a hug, but my body seizes at her touch and she hesitates.

I look up at her, my face contorted, because I am feeling too *much*. She meets my gaze unflinchingly and simply says – "I'm sorry."

I stiffly lean into her embrace after a moment, wary, but so grateful to be letting go. She soothes my forehead, rubbing gentle circles into the skin.

I close my eyes and think of home. Think of Abti Haroon and Khadija. I think of and dream of love.

In the afternoon, Ms Birch leads the class to an emergency assembly in the quad hall. She insists on everyone sitting down in alphabetical order even though, most of the time, she lets the class sit in the order they want. Unfortunately for me, alphabetical order puts me squarely between Leanne and Kyle.

I brace my hand when I've sat down. It is unlikely Kyle will try anything in this heavily supervised space and because he no longer has the element of surprise but, just in case, my hand is prepared. I hold it in a fist that leaves crescent moon indentations on my palm.

The tension in the air is thick for an assembly. Teachers line the hall; most of them look on edge. Ms Birch wrings her hands, then crosses her arms, and then wrings her hands again before biting a nail.

The doors open. Three uniformed police officers enter, along with Ms Devlin. Heads turn on cue. The room feels stifling all of a sudden, and silence blankets us all.

I see Kyle move and lift my fist in anticipation, but he only bends down, rummaging in his bag. I remain on high alert until he resurfaces and sits in his chair properly, where I can keep a close eye on him. After a few moments, I lower my fist.

"There will be a bag search," Ms Devlin says, without any preamble. "For illicit substances in light of recent concerns about marijuana distribution."

A bag search? The physical searching of bags? For all students? What on earth are they looking for, aside from pens and paper?

I snort. Though I knew I was right to call this "school" a prison, I did not anticipate it would turn out to be a joke too.

# SAFIYA

Back in the classroom, everyone waits in anticipation for the police officers to arrive and begin the bag search for Form 11C. Ms Birch does her best to keep the speculation to a minimum but thirty teenagers waiting for someone to get caught will *always* speculate. It is their natural disposition. Ten minutes later, the knock arrives.

Only one of the officers walks in. He introduces himself as Officer Matt Broderick and asks everyone to open their bags, put their blazers and jackets on top, then step away from their seats.

There are seven tables in the classroom. Officer Broderick makes his way through each one until there are just two remaining.

Table Six: Caprice, Marcus, Kyle, Amina.

Table Seven: Mustafa, Yusuf, Leanne, Halima.

Kyle looks antsy, more riled up than usual, which isn't a great look to project when a police officer is searching you for drugs.

Officer Broderick clears Table Six, inviting them to sit down.

At Table Seven, Leanne is the first one cleared. Then Yusuf. Then Mustafa. Halima is the last one to be searched but, by this point, the entire class has relaxed. The show is over as far as Form 11C are concerned. Nothing to see here.

Officer Broderick puts Halima's jacket and blazer aside, having checked them both. He opens her bag, pausing almost immediately. Placing his hand into the gap, he pulls out a small transparent bag, grimacing.

Edibles.

# HALIMA

Beside me, Leanne gasps first, before I have had a chance to truly appreciate the magnitude of the situation.

My eyes meet Safiya's across the classroom. I do not know where else to look. I do not understand what is happening.

"Pack your things, Halima," Ms Birch instructs, sighing. "The rest of you, sit in your seats and stop gawking."

The police officer holds the incriminating bag of sweets in the air, inspecting them.

*What are they?* I want to ask, but I know it is in my best interests to keep silent.

Ms Birch walks over to me, bending her head close to mine. "Halima, go straight to Ms Devlin's office with Officer Broderick, please. This is serious. Your parents will be called in."

I nod, shouldering my bag, and make to follow the police officer to the door. A chair scrapes the floor loudly.

"Ms Birch," Safiya says breathlessly. "I'm going too."

Muna grabs her hand, but Safiya shakes it off.

"No," Ms Birch says decisively, shaking her head. "You can't, Safiya, I'm sorry. I understand that you're Halima's school buddy, but this is a private and serious matter—"

"She's my sister," Safiya responds, packing her bag. "I'm pretty sure that makes me family and automatically invited to all private and serious matters."

The whole class erupts then, gasping and openly gaping in the aftermath of Safiya's revelation. Ms Birch stands speechless.

Within seconds, Safiya is beside me and I feel something in my chest contract. Something I haven't felt in a long time.

I turn to find her eyes again, searching for a flicker of regret for speaking those words publicly, but I find only resolve and a fierceness that I am not sure how to interpret.

Then we exit the classroom together to meet my fate.

# AUTUMN: PART II
## WINDING THREADS

*The man returned to his love, many years later, in the place where their love first came to be. Though he worried about things left behind, in this return, he was sure.*

*Together, the man and his love sewed a new life for themselves; a life they had envisaged once upon a time when they stood together under the cover of trees.*

*The two tried to bury things in that neatly stitched life, right from the beginning. Anything that might ruin the pretty seams they had pulled together.*

*For the man and the woman, it did not matter that there were secrets in the air. So long as they could still breathe, so long as the new tapestry of their life had no holes, so long as their love remained true and strong, then all would be fine. All would be well.*

*However, it cannot be said that questions did not linger in their minds, even as they tried to convince themselves of this, and there was one, in particular, that seemed difficult to ignore…*

*How many secrets could they safely bury before the tapestry of their life finally unravelled?*

# HALIMA

Sitting in Ms Devlin's office, I replay what happened in my mind.

I knew there was a problem when the police officer pulled that pack of sweets from my bag with a grim expression. I had never seen them before, but to me, they looked innocuous. Sweets I would buy for my brothers if they begged hard enough, or that I might come across hoarded in a corner of their room.

But the ones the police officer removed from my bag were clearly not as harmless as they appeared. The grim expression, the scattered, sharp intakes of breath, the silence that seemed to gain even greater depth – all of this pointed to something else.

I tried to cast my mind back to the assembly that we'd just had, to see if any clues lay there, but I could not remember a single thing. I had been too busy focusing on Kyle.

The scandal in the classroom felt palpable. Suffocating.

But Safiya's distorted voice cut through the tension. Her voice travelled to me as if we were separated by glass, though there was a word I caught that stayed with me.

*Sister.*

I was sure of it.

At least, I was for a second.

Now we sit together in our head of year's office, Ms Devlin at her desk, legs crossed, the picture of calm. I remember what happened the last time I was here, so I am prepared for what comes next.

My mother's husband arrives, along with my mother. Hooyo sees Safiya first and hesitates. Something between her and me stretches dangerously in that moment, becoming painfully taut.

The husband sees Safiya next. His face becomes the sun.

Of the three of them, only Safiya remains unflustered, probably because she's had time to prepare herself.

To my surprise, an "independent" translator is also whisked in. Hooyo gives this translator – an older Somali woman – a single withering look before turning her back on her.

By the end of it, there are nine people in the room. Me, Safiya, Hooyo and the husband. Three gun-less police officers. Ms Devlin. The translator.

It starts with fireworks. My mother's husband jumps into action, fists shaking, spittle flying. Startlingly, none of this is directed at me.

"How dare you accuse my daughter, who still does not know much of this country and this school, of single-handedly distributing these drugs to your pupils?" he demands, slapping the arm of his chair for emphasis.

Ms Devlin and the police officers are finally able to interject as the fireworks slowly die out.

MS DEVLIN: "No one is accusing Halima of doing this single-handedly, Mr Aden."

OFFICER BROWN HAIR: "But we have been aware of marijuana distribution starting as far back as July of this year, coinciding with the summer holidays, which is around the time your family moved to the UK."

OFFICER MOUSTACHE: (Nods.) "There is a bigger picture here clearly."

OFFICER BLUE EYES: "One that we intend to get to the bottom of. Other players are likely involved, so our focus is not only on Halima. It is not unreasonable to consider that, if she is involved, she may have been taken advantage of, given the circumstances."

MS DEVLIN: "It does mean that we will continue to investigate, with the help of the police. Unfortunately, for the time being, we do need to act on the facts that we have gathered."

MY MOTHER'S HUSBAND: (Shifts in his seat.) "And what action would that be?"

MS DEVLIN: "It would mean suspending Halima, effective immediately, once the half-term break is over. But please rest assured that we would still appreciate your attendance at parents' evening once the holiday is over. It's important that we stay committed to Halima's academic progress."

The translator makes a show of looking to me and clearing her throat. "We've not even heard Halima speak yet."

Then all eight pairs of eyes are on me. Though my mind

feels scrambled, I process enough to know it is time to defend myself.

"I did not do it," I say, shaking my head for emphasis. "Not my sweets. Not me."

At home, I lose my defenders. My mother first, and then the husband soon after, following her lead.

"So," I say to Hooyo in the kitchen. "Was all that defending me for show? You have acted like I do not exist since we returned. Do you really think I did what they are accusing me of?"

Hooyo stares at me squarely. I can feel that she is gearing up to say a lot. I wish that I had kept my mouth shut and not tried to pick another fight.

"It is hard to believe someone who has been plotting to make this move a disaster for all of us since the moment we arrived." Hooyo puts a hand up to stop me from cutting in. "Before you try to deny it, know that I am your mother, Halima. I know how your mind works. I know you would do anything to leave this place and go back to Mogadishu, stubbornly unwilling to accept the fact that our lives are here now, that they will never be how they used to be.

"I know you but, these days, I do not know what lengths you are willing to go to. How much of a mess you are happy to make in the hope that it lands you back where you so desperately want to be. So, until the police conclude their investigation, I have no answers. I do not believe you, but I also do not believe the accusations against you. We will wait to see what happens. Until then, at least one of *your wishes has come true – you will not be returning to that school you keep swearing is a prison."*

Hooyo turns to leave, placing a hand on the door. It is only then that I notice her hand is shaking.

*"You are to give me your phone tonight, Halima. No more mobile. No more Khadija and Abti Haroon until all of this is cleared. And no more talk about going back home. Maybe losing your connection to your friends in Mogadishu will finally give you the space you need to accept your new home."* She sniffs. *"Still, your mother is not entirely without a heart. I will keep in touch with Maymuna and let you know if Abti Haroon's condition changes."*

I take a grounding breath. I do not want accusations and a lifeline. I want trust. *"Are you going to hold this over my head for ever, Hooyo? I told you it wasn't me. I've told you a thousand times already."*

If Hooyo was a mother who listened, I would tell her what I know. About BANTRxpose and the grief it is causing me. About how I've come to realize this situation is likely connected. That someone is targeting me, though I have no one to definitively point the finger at. But I am itching to point it at Kyle, the boy who conveniently rummaged in his bag – and probably mine too – only moments before everything went so horribly wrong.

Hooyo shakes her head, but it is not the kind of head shaking that follows a fair fight.

*"I don't know where my Halima has gone,"* she replies, eyes unblinking, holding her gaze steady. *"Seething, vindictive… none of it is you, but that is all I've known since we've come here.*

*How am I to know what's true any more?"*

Those words feel like a slap to the face. The pain is fresh, instant, and the tears spring to my eyes quickly. Too quickly for me to repress.

I run upstairs, ignoring Abu Bakr's call for me to join him in the living room. He screams one last request, his high-pitched voice following me up the stairs, before he gives up.

My bedroom door is already open but there is an anger building from somewhere inside of me – this kind of frenzied frustration that grows with each step – and so I slam the door back with the kind of force that leaves it rocking on its hinges, until the momentum slowly disappears and the door stills, taking my anger with it.

I turn my attention to the wrinkled square underneath my pillow, unfolding it.

Hooyo's beaming face stares back at me, in open defiance of the sorrow sinking my heart.

Hooyo, who I no longer recognize.

Hooyo, her lies captured in a photograph.

# SAFIYA

I duck into Adeer Ali's shop at exactly 5.05 p.m. on Saturday evening, when I know he will not be around. His nephew takes charge for the weekend evening shift, which means I can continue avoiding him like I have done since he confessed his traitorous behaviour. I don't know when I'll be able to forgive and move on, but I know it's not now. I am still too angry and hurt that he helped my dad worm his way back into our lives. Especially when he knows all Hooyo and I have been through.

I grab a basket and make my way around the store, mentally totalling the cost with each item I pick up. In the chilled foods aisle, I grab some milk. When I turn around, I see Halima.

She stands a metre or so in front of me, a basket in hand too.

"Hi," I say, startled. I was not expecting to see her so soon after yesterday's incident.

"Hi," she replies, equally startled.

The silence after that feels oppressive and very uncomfortable. Clearly, Halima doesn't know what to say either. Or how we are supposed to act now we've put a spotlight on our connection and gone out on a limb for one another.

Eventually, the lack of conversation becomes too awkward and we shuffle past each other in the aisle. But then:

"Safiya?" she calls.

"Yes?" I reply, turning back.

"I was going to the park. You...want to come?"

My face must give something away before I've even had a chance to digest the request, because Halima clears her throat and jumps in with a retraction.

"Don't worry. You must be busy—"

"No," I cut in, without thinking. "I'm free."

I wait for my good sense to activate and berate me for agreeing to something that probably won't end well. After all, Halima is my dad's stepdaughter. She's symbolic of everything that destroyed my own family.

But no regret sets in.

Halima smiles.

"You go ahead and buy your things. I'm almost done," I tell her. "I'll meet you out front."

She nods and disappears.

I put the milk back in the fridge, making a mental note to pick some up later, and feel myself hesitate as I shut the door on the cold air.

Have I agreed to something stupid? What am I doing voluntarily spending time with Halima?

But then I think about yesterday – the debacle in Ms Devlin's office – and wonder if Halima is just looking for someone to talk to.

I imagine what Muna would say. Whether she would think this was a good idea or not.

Then I remember I don't have anyone to talk to either.

# *HALIMA*

We walk half a lap around the park before any conversation begins. I feel compelled to break the ice, since I'm the one who has dragged us here and subjected us to this, but I have no idea where to start.

How was my invitation received? I wonder.

Does Safiya think I am desperate for her company? That I am keen to play happy families after her defence of me yesterday?

But then I realize those are not the right questions to ask. Not when I don't even understand my own motivations for inviting her.

"How are your friends?" I ask, deciding to begin with a neutral topic. At least for now, it might be better to avoid all discussion of family. Hers and mine.

Safiya sucks in a quiet breath and I know, immediately, that I have asked the wrong thing. This ground is not neutral and, too late, I remember what happened yesterday, right before Safiya's admission in class. When Muna extended a hand to reach for her and she batted it away.

"That's complicated…" she replies quietly. "But I think you

261

deserve to know Yusuf was the one behind targeting you with all the BANTRxpose stuff. I didn't know about it until yesterday, otherwise I would have…" Safiya trails off, crinkling the plastic shopping bag in her hand. "It wouldn't have happened if I had known, anyway. That's all."

I pause to let the revelation settle in me. I was so sure it had been either Safiya or Kyle for most of it.

But, if this is true, what would have driven Yusuf to demonize me in the first place?

When Safiya crinkles the bag again, it hits me.

The simplest yet greatest motivation in this world.

Yusuf did this for Safiya and, catching the expression on her face, the way her eyebrows and mouth dip in disappointment, I think she knows that too.

I dig into my shopping bag to retreat from this very unneutral territory and offer her a choice between three different sweets.

"That's a lot of sugar," she says with a smirk, selecting the sour ones without hesitation. "Are you sure these are legal, by the way?"

"You are not funny." I scowl, taking one for myself. "They are for my brothers. They're obsessed with them."

She laughs, disappointment slowly waning. "How old are they?"

"Four and three years old," I reply, once I've recovered from the bite of sourness. "Abu Bakr is the eldest boy and Kamal is youngest."

"What are they like?" Her eyes twinkle with questions.

"Super annoying or very manageable?"

I open my mouth to answer with the truth – that they are annoying, hardly manageable, cartoon-obsessed little tykes – when I notice we are on the very ground I thought was unneutral.

Family.

But Safiya's eyes glimmer with curiosity for the brothers that are also hers and it feels wrong to keep them from her. So I share everything about them and she smiles and asks for more and more and more.

My mind briefly thinks of home. About Hooyo, who must be wondering where I am, especially when I no longer have my phone to contact her with.

I imagine what would happen if she saw me with Safiya again, but I do not care. For the first time since coming to this country, a small part of me feels settled and no longer angry.

# *HALIMA*

Like yesterday, Hooyo asks me where I am going when I leave the house.

*"For a walk,"* I tell her.

*"Again?"* she repeats, narrowing her eyes. *"In this weather?"*

*"What's wrong with this weather?"* I reply with all the nonchalance I can muster. *"Plus, it's not like I even have friends I can speak to. You saw to that when you took my phone."*

The husband shakes with laughter, slapping his knee.

*"You think that is funny?"* I snap.

*"I just didn't think it would be the approaching winter that would soften you to this country, Halima. If I'd known that, I would have moved you over here a little later."*

Before I have a chance to answer him, Hooyo cuts in.

*"Halima,"* she says, standing to come closer to me in the hallway. *"I thought you'd like to know that I spoke to Maymuna's mother this morning. She says that Abti Haroon seems to be doing a little better now. Isn't that good news?"*

I gasp with relief, feeling tears spring to my eyes.

*"Really?"* My voice shakes with emotion that threatens to overwhelm me. *"She said that?"*

"*Yes, he had a bout of infection that he's recovered from and is beginning to eat a little better. It's small steps but they are getting there.*" Hooyo envelops me in a hug. "*Alhamdulilah.*"

I embrace her hard. "*Can I speak to him?*" I whisper into her neck. "*Please?*"

Hooyo's hands pause their comforting on my back. "*Let's give him some time to get back on his feet, hmm? We can see how you get on at parents' evening too. If things go well, maybe we can consider reinstating phone privileges.*"

Something in me hardens when she says that and I pull away.


At the park, I find Safiya by the tennis courts, a pair of binoculars hanging around her neck. We begin our walk around the perimeter in silence, before heading to sit on the cold park bench.

"I am going home," I say aloud to her – without even a hello – surprising myself. The words feel good, reassuring, and I realize that while I have had the thought for months, I've never said them aloud and so I say it again, just to hear myself. "I am going home."

"What, now?" Safiya peers at her phone.

I shake my head. "Not my house. I am going back to Somalia."

"Pardon?" Safiya's eyebrows shoot up. "You're leaving? I was under the impression this was a permanent relocation."

I shake my head. "I am going back to see my friend Abti Haroon."

"By yourself?"

"Yes."

"How?" is her entirely reasonable follow-up question, but I have no idea how to answer.

"I don't know yet," I huff. I am trapped in a prison of the husband's making. "But I need to go." I swallow past the stone caught in my throat. "Abti Haroon…he is sick. Really sick. He is better now, a little, but I have to see with my eyes."

Safiya nods solemnly, fingers skimming the binoculars on her lap. "I'm sorry to hear that. I hope he gets better soon."

I fidget with frustration, wishing that I had the means to escape right here, right now. Wishing I could fly back home with only a click of my fingers, or blink and magically find myself in the heart of Mogadishu.

"You know," I add after a moment. "I have hate for your dad. A lot. For flying here and bringing me. Taking me from my home."

Safiya bites her lip, staying quiet, and I wonder if that is my cue to apologize. Have I stepped too far? Misunderstood the situation with her father?

"I hate him for bringing you too," she whispers, staring at the boundary of the park. She sniffs. "And for leaving us."

Catharsis.

That is what this is. The both of us sharing how much we hate the one man who is responsible for the two of us being connected here in the first place.

"Can I hear about your friend?" Safiya asks, still looking away. "He must be pretty solid if you're still holding onto him."

My face breaks into a smile. Abti Haroon, solid? Him and

Khadija are the only two people holding me together. My heart is with them and I am counting down the days until I can be reunited with it once more.

My mouth opens and my stories spill out. Everything about Abti Haroon and my father, the poetry they raised me on, Khadija and our shenanigans.

I tell Safiya about my home, its overwhelming beauty, and its overwhelming people. The chaos of the markets, the heat, the warring scents of charcoal and cooking spices that carry in the air. I tell her that it feels as though everyone in the city is your family, that everyone might as well be some long-lost cousin.

I tell Safiya it is the only home I have ever known.

She listens to all of this without speaking, but my words must do something to her because she faces me directly as I tell her my stories, one leg on the bench, leaning on a bent elbow, eyes wide.

When I am done, Safiya is a flood of questions. I laugh in surprise, caught out by her interest. I answer them all and, when I'm done, I turn on her.

"Tell me your life," I say. "Everything."

# SAFIYA

When the tables turn and Halima asks about my life, my friendships, the city I've spent all my life in, I hesitate.

It's not because I have nothing to say, but that I cannot speak about any of it without mention of Muna or Yusuf.

I can't seem to stop thinking about that canteen incident. How I'd got pissed off at my best friend for a relative stranger. I wonder what Muna would think if she saw us speaking like this.

Would she think that I've replaced her? That I was so unaffected by our blowout I moved on and simply found a new person?

Would she think I hate her?

The words we threw at each other that day had been awful, though mine were the ugliest. Muna had only said the truth, but that truth, centred on Yusuf and his motives, did something to me and I lashed out.

I wish I could pretend that I don't remember what I said, but I do. Every horrible word of it.

How could I have suggested that Muna had kept the truth

about BANTRxpose under wraps? Even if the culprit was her cousin?

The messaging of that accusation had been clear: it was me saying I don't trust her.

And if someone had pointed their accusing finger at me, there's no way I would have taken that lying down either.

I shut my eyes, pushing away the bad and drawing out the good. Finding my solid people in memories.

I tell Halima about the great times with Muna and Yusuf. About Northwell. About the time all three of us spent a summer vlogging because we were certain we'd become breakout influencers. And then the time we accidentally dozed off after sunset at Hyde Park and returned to find Muna's mum had called the police a grand total of ten times.

I tell her all about our silly antics, dodging the unpredictable London weather, and exploring the city together.

Halima grins and laughs at some of my stories, shakes her head at others. She asks me about my mum, and then I shake my own head, indicating no.

We may have briefly discussed Aabo, but family is still a domain neither of us have fully waded into. It feels too intimate and makes me feel too vulnerable. And a conversation about Hooyo isn't something I want to get into, especially with Halima.

Since that morning when the two of us prayed Fajr together, Hooyo has been asking questions. A lot of them, mostly about me. She's been waking up early in the morning, making me breakfast. Grocery shopping, looking for jobs.

Hooyo is acting unlike herself and I can't help but feel wary of it, waiting for everything to become undone, like it always does, and for me to have to step into her shoes and take responsibility again.

What would happen if I forgot how to wear them? If I had no choice but to put the shoes on after Hooyo inevitably flings them aside, but they no longer fit?

No, Hooyo being more present isn't something I can accept without caution, but I'm not sure there is anything else to do but be ready to catch her when she falls.

"What are we doing this for?" I say, more to myself than anything.

Halima sighs. "No ideas."

I burst out laughing, accidentally dropping the binoculars I'd forgotten were on my lap.

Halima purses her lips. "I don't laugh at your Somali," she replies, unamused. "And you always say that phrase anyway."

"It's 'no idea'," I correct, grabbing the binoculars off the ground. "Without the 's'."

We sit in silence for a while, getting up when the sky begins to darken to go our separate ways.

# HALIMA

I return home from seeing Safiya and barely catch my breath before Abu Bakr pounces.

"*Halima! Halima!*"

He pulls on the back of my jacket violently, almost choking me.

"*Halima!*"

I pull from the front, trying to counteract his attack.

"*Abu Bakr!*" I swing him around so he stands in front of me, detached from any articles of clothing, and rub my sore neck. "*What is wrong with you? That's no way to greet people!*"

As usual, he is undeterred by my scolding.

"*Do you know what I found?*" he asks in a sing-song voice.

I sigh, peeling off my jacket. If I go along with whatever this is, maybe it will end quicker.

"*No, I don't. What did you find?*"

"*I found another picture, like you did!*" He digs for something in his shorts and holds it behind his back, playfully.

I bend down to undo my shoelaces, pausing midway when I process his words. "*What do you mean, like I did?*"

Abu Bakr throws me a sly grin. "*In Hooyo's box,*" he whispers, trying to compose himself. *"I found a picture."*

I kick off my shoes before picking him up and throwing him over my shoulder.

*"Come on, little brother."*

I take the stairs two by two, praying that Kamal doesn't come looking for him. *"Let's go somewhere quiet so I can hear all about it."*

Abu Bakr squeals in delight, squirming against me.

I throw my brother onto the bed and shut the door behind me. His hands are empty and I start to worry that whatever he had has fluttered to the staircase, ready to be found by Kamal or, worse, Hooyo.

Abu Bakr lies on my bed, limbs splayed. He stares at the ceiling as if there are stars there.

*"Look, Halima. I'm an* Ok-tow-pus."

He starts moving his limbs, as though swimming against the current of my duvet. I sit on my desk chair, clearing my throat.

*"Okay, little brother, where's the picture? Can you show me?"*

His arms and legs continue to move, creating further creases on my bedding. He stays silent.

*"If you don't show me…"* I sigh. *"Perhaps I'll just have to take the batteries out of the remote."*

He shoots up, a bolt of lightning. *"No, no!"*

*"Then show me."* I smile sweetly.

*"Fine!"* His face contorts in anger as he shoves a hand down his trousers. *"Here, take it! I don't even want it any more."*

Abu Bakr throws the picture onto the bed and then shuffles off, slamming the door on his way out.

I pick up the picture he has left face-down. It is a small photograph, like the one I found in Hooyo's jewellery box. Creases snake all over this one too, a mark of how tiny Hooyo has tried to make it. In the hope of hiding it? Forgetting it?

I hold it up to the weak winter sun streaming in through my window. The light hits it the wrong way at first so that I cannot make out any faces. I readjust so there is more glow than glare and see my mother as before, young and beautiful. Sharp jaw and soft eyebrows. Large eyes and narrow shoulders but, this time, no smile. No joy radiating off her like in the last one. Here, she stares blankly into the camera, holding a hand to her pregnant belly.

There is an arm around her shoulders. I follow it to the face it belongs to, meeting my father's gaze.

His face is angled slightly higher than the camera so that it looks like he's jutting his chin. His dark skin, rich and deep, is marred by the worry bunched on his forehead. He looks deep in thought. Or deeply unhappy.

My father looks nothing like me. I have always known that, but today this realization hits me hard. There is everything different about us. From our complexion to the contours of our noses, the shape of our ears. I know I look more like my mother's husband than him, but there is something we share that no one can ever deny, and I hold onto that truth every day.

Our blood.

# HALIMA

Dogs roam freely in King Edward's Park, darting and zigzagging past shrivelled trees. Some are on leashes, chained to their owners. I hurry past whenever they get too close, trying to make myself as unenticing as possible to an animal that seems to find almost everything enticing.

It is funny, I think, drawing my scarf tighter. When I first came to this country, seeing these dogs as pets, as human companions, threw me. But, now? Now, three months in, these sights are becoming normal to me.

In Mogadishu, it was goats I would see most days. Cows, cats and camels too. None of these animals were pets, mind you.

It seemed pretentious to me when I first moved here. People strutting outside with a chain in their hand as if to say: *Look at me, look at this beast that I have conquered.* Dogs are wild animals in my experience, not meant to be broken, which is why I keep a fairly respectable distance from them and their owners whenever I find myself occupying the same space they do.

I am a little earlier here than I should be but I would rather shiver in this formidable weather than in the presence of my mother. Hooyo's declaration this morning made the house a rather unwelcoming space. She was standing at the kitchen sink, washing her hands, when she made it.

*"Don't forget, we have your parents' evening after this holiday break, Halima. To discuss your progress and your…setbacks."* Hooyo's lips immediately thinned at that word. *Setbacks.* *"We will go. The both of us, along with your father, and I want you to think long and hard about how you plan to conduct yourself."*

*"Is that necessary?"* I asked, trying not to let agitation creep in. *"We've already seen too much of that place. I don't want to go back for more. And you've taken my mobile away, Hooyo, is that not enough punishment? The fact that I can't even speak to the two most important people to me back home?"*

*"What is necessary or unnecessary is not your choice,"* Hooyo replied. *"Not when you decided to make friends with the wrong people. Not when you decided to exercise recklessness instead of good sense. I warned you about Safiya. That even family can betray you. But you didn't listen."*

I doubt Hooyo truly believes the husband's daughter is connected to this drugs scandal, but I know she is yet to recover from seeing Safiya by my side in Ms Devlin's office. And it probably doesn't help that I have positioned Safiya as someone Hooyo should worry about. Someone who knows things about the husband that she likely doesn't want me hearing.

But, even without all of that, Hooyo has always been insecure as the husband's second wife, and me associating with the daughter who takes first place in the family tree bothers her, even if she would never admit it.

I remove my gloves and fish the photo out of my pocket, wanting to see if my mother looks any more familiar now that there is some time and distance between us, now that I am no longer in a house that feels like a once dormant volcano on the edge of erupting, when a scuffle catches my attention. I look up and see Safiya. Then I swiftly push the photo into my pocket, out of sight.

We may not be enemies, but we are certainly not friends. If I asked for truth, I do not think it would be freely – or easily – given.

# SAFIYA

I notice the absent look on Halima's face first, then the photo in her hand. She stands near a tree, seemingly oblivious to the world around her. When I accidentally step on a branch, she snaps to attention, noticing my curious gaze. She slides the photo into her pocket, swapping it out for a glove.

We walk without speaking, feet crunching against the icy grass, before sitting down on the bench. The same one we found ourselves on all those weeks ago after Yash and his friends hounded Halima, and the same one that belongs to the Three Musketeers. Or maybe the One Musketeer now with everything that's transpired. I don't really know what Muna, Yusuf and I are to each other right now. I still haven't spoken to either of them since my fight with Muna in the canteen when I realized Yusuf was behind BANTRxpose.

Although it's not for lack of trying from Yusuf. After the incident, he wasted no time texting and calling until I decided to block him. Then he pivoted to knocking on my front door instead. When I realized it was him, I told Hooyo to ignore it. Normally, asking Hooyo to do anything is just a formality but, for some reason, she decided *this* was the time to start paying attention.

Now, Hooyo opens the front door every time Yusuf knocks – which is usually twice a day – and instead of having my back and telling him I'm sick or out of the house, she tells him the truth.

*"I'm sorry, Yusuf, Safiya is still not up to talking with you."*

The first time Hooyo did it, I was angry. But by the second and third and fourth time, I found myself at the top of the stairs whenever he knocked, trying to catch his words or a glimpse of him and attempt to understand how we got here.

I've thought about reaching out to Muna a million times, but I haven't been able to bring myself to do that yet. Every time I replay our fight, the possibility of coming together seems further away.

I sink further into the bench, thinking about this last week. Seriously…what the *hell* have I been doing?

Not only have I *not* been speaking to my best friend, but here I am, also fraternizing with the enemy and driving a knife deep into my mum's back.

I know Hooyo would only ever see this as a betrayal. Me, speaking to the daughter Aabo chose over us. The daughter of the woman he abandoned us for.

But, as wild as it sounds, it dawns on me that that might not even be the worst thing about the situation. It doesn't escape my notice that this, talking to Halima, is exactly the kind of thing that Aabo would approve of. The kind of thing that he would encourage.

It is that realization alone that makes me want to bolt. Make a run for the south gate, head home and never look back.

Pretend that I have not spent the last week speaking to this girl, my *should-be* sworn enemy, right here in this park, in this place where our bad blood first came to be. Where we first locked eyes on each other in the middle of summer after that fateful Eid prayer.

Though when that scene plays in my head now, I visualize it differently. I see Hooyo, frozen, but not out of shock. I see her paralysed out of fear for the potential disruption in our lives if the truth about her contact with Aabo were to emerge. I see her retreat into her shell and become dangerously undone because she is too weak to face her lies. I see *her* betrayal and I am absolved.

Hooyo's already stabbed me in the back. What does it matter what I do?

Halima's voice cuts through the noise in my head.

"Safiya," she says abruptly. "I have question."

I turn to look at her as she fishes for something in her pocket.

"Do you see this?" she asks, holding a photograph up to me.

I'm only looking for a split second before I process it and then my breath catches.

# *HALIMA*

Safiya's eyes flick across the photo of our youthful mothers. Her face remains impassive but the catch in her breath gives her away.

She has seen this before.

"Do you know," I press, "why this exists?"

Safiya extends a hand, reaching for the picture. I hand it over. She holds it close to her face and I count the seconds before she speaks again.

*Ten, eleven, twelve…*

Eventually she sighs, passing the photo back. "Sorry, I thought I recognized someone." She shrugs her shoulders, but there is no apology in the movement. Only a lie. "I've never seen it before."

This is the first time either of us have been dishonest with each other. Of course, there have been moments we've evaded questions, but this is different, I can tell.

"Where did you find it?" she asks, too curious for a girl who claims to have never seen it.

I shrug my shoulders then too. "Just on the floor as I walked over earlier. I suppose someone accidentally dropped it."

We sit in silence for another couple of minutes before we make our excuses and go our separate ways.

I walk the route along the high road to get home.

My mind is still full of the lie Safiya told me, but I need the headspace to try and think clearly.

I take out the photo I showed her of our mothers, and the second one Abu Bakr found of my parents, desperate to understand the woman in both these shots.

The truth is, in the last week – with the drugs affair and forging a strange, new relationship with Safiya in the aftermath of it – my plan to dig deeper into the family lies has been completely derailed.

But seeing the photo that Abu Bakr found yesterday has sharpened something in me once more.

Since finding out the husband had been the one financing our life after Aabo died, I knew that more of Hooyo's secrets lay buried elsewhere, but I never imagined anything like this.

That Hooyo *knew* – knows – Safiya's mother.

Suddenly, all her envy makes complete sense. Whatever they were to each other, it certainly left a lasting mark. One that Hooyo has shrouded and painted over, but one that has finally been revealed, as all truths are.

I had not recognized Safiya's mother straight away. Though her younger version possesses all the same physical qualities, the weighty sadness that I have become familiar with doesn't feature in the snapshot of her youth. She looked a much happier person, and a lighter one, without it.

But surely Safiya would have recognized her own mother, even if she couldn't place mine, so why did she lie?

Is it because she knows the truth that explains the past? What it is that connects our mothers and why I have never been told about it?

For so long since moving here, I was convinced that the husband was keeping Hooyo under his thumb. That there was something else at play in their marriage. But now I can see that Hooyo has been involved in these secrets from the very start, with knotty lies that are slowly starting to unravel. My mother may not be under the influence of black magic, but the devil is still hard at work here. If I am going to leave, it won't be with her or the boys.

My focus is gradually returning in the wake of my conversation with Safiya and all I can think about is how easily the people in my life lie to me. Of course, Safiya and I do not owe each other anything, but the sting of her deception still hurts, as much as I am desperate to deny it.

And it dawns on me now that if Hooyo cannot be trusted, how can I believe anything she tells me about Abti Haroon?

For weeks now, I have had determination but no plan. No concrete or plausible way of fleeing this country. But now a seed of an idea is germinating in my mind…

An idiotic, criminal, unforgivable idea but one that just might work if I can bring myself to try.

# SAFIYA

I stare at the photo for longer than I should do.

When I first found the picture in Aabo's boxes, I had recognized my mum immediately but felt some niggling familiarity about the other woman.

Now I know who it is. It is the mother of the girl sitting beside me. The girl who holds an identical image.

I bite my tongue before any words fly through my mouth.

*Hooyo lied to me again.*

Keeping a secret about Aabo's new family is one thing, but the fact that she knew Halima's mother is completely unforgivable.

How *does* she know her? How far back does their history go?

As far as I know, Halima's only seen Mum once, at that Eid encounter in summer, so maybe there's a chance she doesn't know who the other woman in the photo is. But that doesn't make any sense, because why else would she show this to me?

Is she trying to trigger me into opening the Pandora's box of our family secrets?

Does she know about the ultrasound picture? About the

theory that has crossed my mind and has started to solidify further with the photograph?

My thoughts tornado through the rational portion of my mind, but I try to calm it.

Whatever Halima's motives are, I will not let her draw me into anything. Not until I have something more to go on.

So I tell her, *Sorry, I thought I recognized someone. I've never seen it before.*

And I see the way her face changes when she hears the lie. How effortlessly she switches to untruth too.

I don't know what this means for us, but I can't worry about any of that now because there is someone I need to go and see. Someone who can help me make sense of all of this.

I stop by the newsagent's on Cromwell Hill, hoping I don't bump into anyone I know, especially Mustafa. This place is his favourite haunt, his one-stop shop for stocking up on goods for his school hustle. I've got nothing against the guy, but he is Yusuf's best friend and I would rather continue avoiding both him and Yusuf for now.

Inside the shop, I grab Muna's favourite: Kinder Bueno. Though I don't see the appeal, it's never stopped her from trying to make me fall in love with her confectionary obsession. She hands me a piece every single time she buys one, without fail.

A few minutes later and I'm standing outside Muna's house, like I have done a million times before, but the doorstep today feels unfamiliar and a little foreboding.

"Please don't be Yusuf," I whisper as I take the plunge and knock. "Please don't be Yusuf."

I am banking on a guess that he will be at Mustafa's house, because that's where he spends most of the holidays, but if I'm wrong I'll be facing two awkward conversations today.

The door swings open.

"Salaam, Safiya!" Muna's sister Nasra cries, pulling me in for a hug. "Oh, I've missed you. I've really, really missed you." She detaches, holding me at arm's length. "Tell me, has there been trouble in paradise?"

I roll my eyes, stepping into the hallway. "You know full well what's going on."

Nasra mimes zipping her lips. "I am not at liberty to discuss what I do or do not know. That much, I can tell you."

I break into a laugh, so grateful that she is the person to have opened the door. As I take off my jacket, I realize she's already dressed to go out.

"Where are you off to?" I ask.

"Catching some friends," Nasra replies, bending to tie her shoelaces. "Hanan and a few of the other girls." She straightens, giving me a knowing look. "She's in her room, by the way, and don't worry, nobody else is home."

Nasra gives me a hug goodbye and then leaves, shutting the door behind her.

I make my way up the stairs, deliberately avoiding the creaky steps. I stand outside the bedroom Muna shares with her sisters, ready myself to knock, hesitate, and then almost—

The door swings open, revealing a smug-faced Muna, wearing her favourite orange baati and worn-out bathrobe.

"It's going to be like that then, is it?" she scoffs.

I drop my fist, sheepish. "What do you mean?"

"You, Safiya Halane Aden," she starts, punctuating every word with a finger jab, "randomly throw a little hissy fit over something I had no idea about – in the *canteen* of all places – and proceed to ice me out when my dumbass cousin does a terrible thing because he's in love with *you*, then come to my house, stand outside my door a week later, and don't even have the decency to run in and grovel for forgiveness?" She narrows her eyes. "You should be doing the most, my friend. Like hiring a skywriter to apologize or buying me a bouquet of flowers, or even—"

I throw my head back, laughing, and then I can't stop. It's only when I feel my cheeks getting wet that I realize my eyes are tearing up from all this laughter, but, still, I can't stop. It comes and comes and comes until, suddenly, I realize I'm no longer laughing and crying but simply crying. The tears run without pause, and I start to worry that this endless crying will leave me dried up; a nasty Safiya-prune.

Muna grabs me, steadies me, and guides me into her room to sit on her bed. She sits too and holds me close, pulling my head onto her lap.

When I am well and truly done with my emotional display, I'm too embarrassed to move. To pick my head up from underneath Muna's hand and explain what happened.

*I* don't even know what's happened. Whatever this is, it's not me. Safiya is not the one who breaks, who falls apart at the sign of trouble. Safiya is the one who glues everything back together. Who holds everything in alignment, who tries to stop the world from tumbling into chaos.

If I'm falling apart now for no reason, what hope is there for me and Hooyo keeping it together?

I dry my face with my headscarf to avoid leaving any snot streaks on Muna's clothes and pull myself to sitting. I stare at the wall. Muna's eyes meet mine in the vanity mirror opposite.

She doesn't say anything but her warm gaze lingers on mine, unwavering. Muna doesn't probe me for answers or jab at me with any more fingers. She just looks at me, and, in her eyes, I see everything she is beneath her exterior of journalism, shawls, drama and light-heartedness. I see everything that the rest of the world doesn't see.

I see my friend. The one who has been here for me for ever. Who listens without judgement to everything plaguing my family. Who hates cracking my back but does it for me anyway. Who is obsessed with Kinder Bueno and who wants me to be obsessed with it too. Who loves me. Who is more than a friend, more than family. Who is my everything.

"Sorry," I say, sniffling, plucking a tissue from the bedside table. "I didn't even realize how much I missed you until now."

Muna smiles. Her hand crosses the gap between us to clasp mine.

"I missed you too, Saf." She squeezes my fingers.

I know she's waiting for me to find my words, to explain this uncharacteristic burst of emotion, but I don't know that I have them. After a stretch of silence, I force myself to swallow the uncertainty and speak.

"That whole thing with Halima... Honestly, I don't know what happened that day. When Kyle came for her in the lunch line, there was just so much running through my mind, but the biggest thing, the thing I couldn't shake, the thing I never expected to even feel, was guilt, you know." I cross my legs on the bed. "After the whole football incident, I felt so bad when Kyle came and slapped her out of the blue like that. Then," I sigh, "it was anger. When I realized it was Yusuf who was behind all those horrible posts about her. When I thought you must have known about it since you single-handedly manage Northwell High's Number One Ladies' Detective Agency." Muna kisses her teeth at that and I grin, reflexively, before the smile falls away again. "I'm sorry, Muna, genuinely. I know you wouldn't have let Yusuf get away with that if you had known and I should have come to you sooner to apologize but the longer it went on, the more difficult it was to speak about any of it, and I didn't want to risk seeing Yusuf and hearing whatever he might have said..."

I swallow, imagining what that conversation would even look like. Yusuf has always had a habit of making his feelings obvious with me. He's been that way for years. And I know that he would love nothing more than for me to reciprocate it – any part of it – but now it's clear that he and I are no longer on the same page. Maybe we weren't ever on the same one to begin with.

Because how could he – the boy that I have known for over a decade – do something so messed up? How could he do that to another person, regardless of who they are or what hurt their presence causes me?

What does that say about the type of person he is? And what does it say about me, for never seeing this side to him?

Muna pointing out Yusuf's motivations in the canteen set something off in me. It ballooned that guilt and made me feel like an idiot for ever feeling anything for him.

But it scared me too; I'm not sure I'm ready to admit what those feelings are yet. Even to myself.

"I was tired as well," I continue. "Of thinking and feeling. And, on top of that, Hooyo had started acting differently at home." Muna raises her eyebrows and I try to find the words to explain how my absent mum somehow became a more present one overnight.

"It's hard to explain…but Hooyo had started waking up every morning for Fajr, cooking me breakfast, asking me how I was, cleaning the house…and it was jarring. She's even picked up the Qur'an more times in the last week than she has in years."

"Isn't that a good thing though?" Muna's eyes soften. "That she might finally be getting better?"

I shake my head. "Yes… No. Maybe…" I sigh. "The thing is, Muna, I know faith. I know it's capable of working miracles when people find their way to it again, but I don't know Hooyo any more. I don't trust her. So if I start to believe she is getting better…it'll just hurt even more when she falls apart again." I take a deep breath. "But that hasn't been the only thing."

I bite my lip, trying to quell the swell of unease that has been building since that night Aabo called and left his voicemail. Since the night I unpacked the life he left behind five years ago.

"There are things my parents are hiding from me. Stuff I don't understand." I think back to those faded, almost weightless papers I found under the flickering yellow light of the spare room. The ones that said my mum was more than the wife who stood behind my dad whilst they were married. That said she was the woman who made him.

"I found a scan," I add, meeting Muna's wide eyes again in the mirror. "Of a baby that I knew nothing about."

I take a deep breath, exhausted by all the words I've had to say. Looking at the shock scribbled over Muna's face, I realize it can't get any worse so I say the thing that has been circling my brain for a while now and has solidified since seeing Halima today. The thought that has probably been there all along, beneath the anger and shame I've been hauling around since Aabo moved his family here. From the moment I locked eyes with her and saw my dad's face reflected in hers, and from the instant I saw the photo in her hand.

I uncross my legs, gripping my thighs with sweaty hands. "I think Halima might be my actual blood sister."

This time, it is Muna who falls into hysterical, breathless laughter in my arms.

# SAFIYA

"Are you okay?" Muna shouts once she regains composure. "How does that even make sense? You guys are the same age!"

"What does age have to do with it?" I reply, incredulous, and slightly insulted at the reaction to my deepest, darkest thought. "It's not like we're twins. We don't have the same mum."

Muna's eyebrows knit in confusion.

"All I'm saying is that it's not impossible. Yes, she's the same age as me but I don't know how many months apart we are. Do you?"

The lines on Muna's forehead deepen. "What are you saying exactly, Safiya?"

I stand, needing to move and kick-start my sleeping muscles.

"I'm saying," I try again, "that *maybe*, just maybe, she's my dad's daughter too."

"And how would that have worked? You guys were born in two different countries!"

I walk to the wardrobe and back, tracking the same path on the carpet, watching the fibres sweep under my feet.

"Yes, but before my dad was *here*, he was *there*."

"He was there?"

"In Somalia." I pause in the middle of the room. "Which would mean she's older than me."

Muna jolts forward, waving her hands in the air. "Hold up. You're starting to sound like a conspiracy theorist. How are you telling me that your dad fathered a child back home and then jumped on a plane to have another one here too? It sounds ridiculous."

"Look, I know it's wild but there's something here, I'm telling you. My dad moved here from Somalia around eight months before I was conceived and the ultrasound I found was dated a few months *before* me. There's no way it's me in the scan, it doesn't add up." I fish for the picture in my jacket and hold it up to her face, triumphantly. "I found this photo in the boxes my dad left behind too. A picture of my mum *and* Halima's mum. Halima had this exact photo too. So does it really sound impossible now? There's no way all these connections are coincidences. It must be like statistically impossible or something."

It's only when I see Muna's face lose its confusion that I realize my mistake.

"What do you mean, Halima had this photo? Is she the one putting these ideas in your head?" Muna gives a disbelieving snort, blocking my path. "Safiya, you're not going to like my version of events but here is how I'm spinning this story, okay? Your mums were probably in a photo together because everyone knew everyone back then in Somalia. That's how the community operates if you've paid attention at all these last fifteen years. They probably met at some random get-together, took a picture to commemorate it, and then completely forgot about it.

"Also," she continues, softening her tone, "the ultrasound scan you're referring to might not be Halima."

It takes me longer than it should to understand what she means. But, if Hooyo and Aabo lost a baby before they had me, why have they never said anything about it?

Muna puts her hands on my shoulders, grounding me. "I know you're trying to make sense of this the only way you think you can but, Safiya, spinning these stories, expending your energy on these unsubstantiated theories…I'm sorry, I would not be your friend if I wasn't being real with you, and I would not be the Number One Lady Detective if I let you run wild with your ideas."

*What if she's right? What if I am letting myself fall head-first into suspicions that I can't back up?*

But even if that's true, Hooyo and Aabo have still been keeping big secrets from me.

I shut my eyes.

Why can't my life be as simple as everyone else's? I don't want a dysfunctional family. I don't want deceitful parents and disappearing fathers. I don't want to be alone, stuck in this sticky web of confusion.

Muna squeezes my hand and I open my eyes.

I'm not alone. I have Muna. I'll always have Muna, I realize.

"You're right," I groan. "Of course you're right! My brain has probably just gone haywire without you keeping me in check."

Muna drops her hands with a grin, perching on the bed

293

again. "Ditto, my friend. I've lost almost all my sanity since we stopped talking. Slightly scary because it was somewhat precarious to begin with."

"Well, let's try finding it again." I lie down on the floor, letting my muscles sleep again. "How's Hexpose going? I haven't seen you post anything lately."

Muna points to a corner of the room, to a pile of shawls I hadn't noticed when I walked in. "I have three words for you my friend: Hexpose is dead."

I frown. "What do you mean?"

"The shawls – my journalistic identity, my badge of honour – are gone, Safiya." Muna covers her eyes with her arm as if there is any sun to be shielding them from. "I'm getting rid of them. I don't deserve to wear them after failing to expose BANTRxpose. My own cousin was behind it and I didn't even know." She sighs deeply. "You were right, Safiya, I'm not a decent journalist. I'm not even a half-decent one."

The sting of my own words hits me. I think again of how I lashed out at her in the canteen. How easily a few words hit my best friend in the place it would hurt the most.

"You know I don't believe any of that for a second, Muna," I whisper, sitting up from the floor. "I was just reacting in a really horrible way. There's no one in Northwell that's half the brilliant reporter you are."

"But I'm not sure that's true any more… Part of me hoped someone might tip me off about the edibles scandal so that I could at least break that story but…nothing. Obviously, everyone knows Halima had nothing to do with it, but people are staying real quiet." She flips over on the bed, burying her face in a pillow.

I crawl over, kneeling next to the bed. Before she can react to my nearness, I pull the pillow out from under her. She gasps, flipping around and making to form a line of defence, but I hit her with the pillow before she can get to it.

She cowers, squealing. "Stop it, Safiya! Stop it! What's wrong with you?"

"I'll stop once you agree you won't flush your lifelong dream and years-long project down the toilet. Halima needs you because she's been *suspended* over this. Do you understand?" I hit her a few more times for emphasis. "Do you?"

"Oh my God, fine! Just stop! I don't know why you're getting violent with it. I wasn't completely serious anyway."

I halt the attack, throwing the pillow across the room for good measure.

"I'm not heartless, you know." Muna narrows her eyes. "Principle dictates that I at least *try* and help someone wrongly accused. Even if that person is planting ideas in your head."

I roll my eyes. "Don't make me grab that pillow again."

I collapse onto the floor, leaning into the plush carpet. Muna joins me.

"Talking about being heartless and matters of the heart…" She nudges me. "Have you spoken to Yusuf?"

"Have *you*?" I retort.

"Well, obviously," she replies. "I do live with the guy. But if you're asking if I've *talked* to Yusuf…then, yeah, I have given him a piece of my mind, and then some."

I stay silent.

"I mean," she presses on, "what he did to Halima was out of order, obviously, but to think that he could stab *me* in the back like that and get away with it? Absolutely not." Muna guffaws. "I saw fit to sentence him to three months of toilet cleaning duty, in exchange for my silence with the parents."

When I don't respond to that either, Muna comes closer and pulls my ear. "Hello? Earth to Safiya? Can you hear me?" she shouts.

I twist away, laughing, but sober immediately when I recall her line of questioning.

"No," I reply truthfully, playing with a small hole in my jumper. "I haven't spoken to him. I know I'll have to at some point but…I don't know, Muna. I'm not ready yet."

"Say no more." Muna nods seriously. "He's with my parents right now anyway. They won't be back till tonight so we've got the house all to ourselves."

Muna and I talk late into the evening, only pausing when the grumble of her family car outside jolts us both into alertness. We share one brief look before scrambling.

I throw on my hijab, grab my jacket, and run down the stairs, hastily shoving my feet into my trainers. Muna follows, anxiously hovering around me.

"Hurry!" she urges. "Hurry!"

"What do you think I'm doing?" I hiss, hopping through the hallway with one shoe on.

When I hear the beep of the car locking, I falter, but only for a moment.

Then I'm in the kitchen, fumbling for the lock on the back door, running outside into the weedy garden, and finding a foothold on the stump of an old tree to propel myself up and straddle our shared fence.

Muna waves a frantic goodbye from the kitchen door, disappearing inside to greet her family.

The fence bites my thigh. As I move to swing myself over, a voice calls out, interrupting my escape.

"Didn't take you for a runner, Saf." Yusuf emerges from the left of the house, from the side gate shrouded in darkness. He moves closer but I'm too afraid to budge.

He stuffs his hands in his pockets. "Can we talk?"

I stare ahead, through the gap between our houses, waiting for something or someone to swallow me whole.

"Please?"

I open my mouth but can't find the words. The fence is starting to hurt my leg though, so I know I need to decide and fast.

I abandon my escape, reversing the movements that got me onto this fence, and then I'm standing in front of him. My heart beats loudly, as if there is a metronome somewhere inside of me.

"Speak," I say, because I don't trust myself to say anything more.

Yusuf appears to have been caught out by my acceptance because he opens and closes his mouth several times before he can actually speak.

"I saw your shadow in Muna's window," he says quietly.

"I mean, I could tell there was someone in the room with her. Not that I know what your shadow looks like. Or that you have a distinctive shadow or anything." He clears his throat. "But I guessed it might be you."

"Well done," I reply drily. "Are you looking for a gold medal?"

"No, no. That's not how I meant for it to sound." Yusuf scratches his head.

"Tell me," I press, sensing the anger and disappointment I've been burying rise to the surface, "is this the kind of sleuthing skill you've built with BANTRxpose? Did you go underground for all these years so you could strike at the right moment? Use your prowess against an innocent girl you thought would be an easy target?"

"Safiya, no, you know that—" He stops, starts again. "That's not why. I don't know why. I mean—"

"No, I don't believe you!" I cry. "Because none of this makes sense. I can't understand why anyone, *especially* you, would do this." I shake my head. "I mean, is this whole 'nice-guy' personality a facade then? Have you bullied other people before?"

Yusuf flinches.

"Just tell me something, Yusuf!" I shout. "Because I have tried to understand what would possess you to go *this* far and I can't!"

"I don't know!" he bellows, burying his head in his hands. "I don't know, Safiya…I saw the way all this drama with your family was eating you up, and…something happened. I thought maybe if Halima was getting dragged, you would be less stressed, less worried...that it might make you feel less bad. When I say it out loud, the logic doesn't make sense. I mean, none of it makes sense, I know that. There isn't any kind of excuse or defence I can use..."

Yusuf takes in a shuddering breath and looks up at me. "But I swear to you, I had nothing to do with Kyle or anyone else getting involved. That wasn't me. I had no idea it would go that far."

"Are you kidding?" I scoff. "You start a smear campaign and you think those idiots at school won't jump on the bandwagon?"

He opens his mouth to reply but no words come out.

"You know what..." I laugh. "I don't even care any more. I don't care about your excuses or your lies. Just leave me alone, Yusuf." I shake my head. "Because honestly, if this is what friendship looks like, I don't want any part of it."

Yusuf lets out a frustrated groan, squatting to the floor. He shoots up again after a moment, letting out a long breath.

"I love you, Safiya!" he shouts, panting slightly, a tinge of desperation in his voice. "*That's* why. And I don't mean just friend love but...real love."

Yusuf slides his glasses off, rubbing his eyes, and I'm glad he does that because the weight of his declaration leaves me unbalanced, forcing me back a step.

My heart, which was already beating loudly, kicks into overdrive and, for a moment, I can sense nothing but the storm inside my chest.

I take a deep breath in, trying to fill my lungs, but the gulps of air do nothing to help. Even though we're outside, I feel suffocated all of a sudden. Like we're in the heart of a fire that's stolen all the oxygen.

"I mean, I tried not to…" Yusuf whispers, sliding his glasses back on. "I tried convincing myself whatever I was feeling was a stupid crush, because what kind of predictable idiot falls in love with his cousin's best friend? A friend who also happens to be their next-door neighbour?"

I know there is a ground beneath my feet, but it doesn't feel that way any more.

"I'm probably going to wake up tomorrow morning and think this was a dream, because I can't believe I've said any of this to you." Yusuf brings his hands together in front of his face. I read the panic in his eyes, intensifying with each passing second. "Safiya, please. Say something. Say anything, I'm begging you."

The storm quietens to a rumble but everything inside me still feels chaotic.

What am I supposed to say?

That Yusuf isn't the only one to feel a crush in our years together and wonder if it might be more? That he isn't the only one terrified about the prospect of love or admitting it?

That eight-year-old me also once dreamed of a future with him before I came to understand the pain of love and loss?

What would I say if I could?

*I think I love you too, Yusuf.*

*I think – but I'm not sure – because I have always tried to keep a lid on those feelings.*

*I'm not sure…*

*But I know that I love your presence.*

*That I need to look up to see you smile.*

*That you can read me in an instant, like a book whose story you know like the back of your hand.*

*I love that you are always here for me, without question.*

But I don't say any of those things.

Regardless of what I think or feel, I can't love freely or easily. I can't wear my heart on my sleeve or come out with the words like Yusuf can.

There have been very few stable people in my life over the years and, though Yusuf has always been one of them, the fear I've carried with me since Aabo left is this: what happens when the guy stops being dependable?

When he stops being so solid and begins to disappear instead? Becoming fuzzy and translucent, becoming *less*, until all of a sudden, he's halfway across the world with a new wife and kids?

What happens when the guy who you've known for ever becomes someone you no longer recognize?

And, as much as it hurts to admit, I *don't* recognize Yusuf right now. The kind and gentle boy I grew up with would never do something like this to Halima.

I hold his gaze, wondering if the Yusuf I thought I knew is still there, but the panic in his eyes is too deep to see beyond.

Whatever reasons he had, they won't ever be good enough, but it's not my job to make him feel any better about it.

The ground that disappeared beneath my feet moments ago begins to return. In fragments, in snatches, until I've found solid footing once more.

"You've said a lot of words tonight, but do you know the biggest one you've missed out?"

He shakes his head hesitantly.

"Sorry. You never said sorry. Not just to me, but to Halima too."

The metronome in my chest quietens.

Then, I leap onto the stump, hop over the fence, keeping my bruised heart safe.

That evening, I jump into the shower, cranking the temperature up as high as I can tolerate and wondering if it will be enough to wash away the pain along with the dirt.

Yusuf's words sit on a track circling my mind. All I want is to push them off course.

*Safiya, I love you.*

*I love you, Safiya.*

*Love, Safiya, you, I.*

I close my eyes, thinking of that word.

Love.

All the heartache it has caused. Everything it has razed.

My dad said he loved us and then he left.

Yusuf says he loves me. Then he purposefully hurt someone else in the name of that love.

So what does love mean? Because, from where I'm standing, it seems like a word that slips too easily from people's lips.

And that makes it very, very dangerous.

Yusuf said he targeted Halima because he thought he was

helping me. Even if that was true, all it did was draw more attention my way. If he'd known me at all, Yusuf would have understood how desperately I wanted BANTRxpose shut down because I couldn't bear to have Halima constantly thrown in my face. And ironically, all it ended up doing was bringing us closer together.

I throw on a towel when I'm done, wrapping another around my dripping hair. Stepping into the hallway, I flinch from a waft of cold air and almost collide with Hooyo. She smiles sheepishly, stepping back to give us both some room.

"You washed your hair?" Hooyo points at my towel turban. "You know, there's a mask I made you could try next time if you like. With shea butter and olive oil."

"Oh…" I secure my towel tighter around me. "Sure. Thanks, Hooyo."

I hurry past to get to my room, away from this biting draught.

"Wait, Safiya," Hooyo calls out before I disappear. "I wanted to tell you…I have a job interview next week."

That stops me dead in my tracks. "Really?"

Hooyo nods, eyes twinkling. "Yes, they called this afternoon to invite me. Another cleaning one that I applied for."

I almost lose my grip on the towel entirely. My mouth opens to ask all of the questions bubbling away, but I hold back. It's no use getting my hopes up. Hooyo has pulled the rug out too many times from underneath me.

Believing Hooyo is not worth the heartbreak. That is one lesson that no one has ever needed to teach me.

"That's great, Hooyo." I smile. "I'm so glad. Really. I hope you get it."

"Me too, macaanto, me too." Hooyo beams. "I'm telling you, things will be different from now on, Safiya. They will be better, for both of us. I promise."

I nod, with the barest of smiles, and escape to my room.

After my nightly prayers, I kneel on the floor, pulling Aabo's box out from underneath my bed like I have done every day since I found it.

The picture, the ultrasound scan, the diaries. The story of my parents' life, pieces of a kaleidoscope that keep shifting before I can put it together. It would be easier if I could ask Hooyo about any of this, but the one thing I can't do is accelerate her falling apart.

Muna almost convinced me to drop this crusade today but there are just too many mysteries.

And Muna should understand, shouldn't she? A budding journalist, someone with a thirst for the truth. Muna has always been an ambassador for evidence-gathering, a poster child for journalistic integrity. Establishing all the facts before diving in. And that's exactly what I plan on doing, even if the *how* is still up in the air.

I clear the floor of the clutter that's accumulated over the last few days, noticing the binoculars that have slid out of my open bag. I reach for them, fiddling with the focus wheel.

I don't know what it is about these binoculars that makes me keep coming back to them. It's not as though I want to be so attached, to keep thinking about the person who gave them to me, when all I want is to pretend they no longer exist.

I remember when Aabo first gifted them to me, after returning home from one of his business trips. I must have been about seven years old then. He'd put me squarely on his lap, listening to my stream of questions, and, in answer, he had simply pulled out the binoculars. They were heavy, black and lined with grey.

"I want you to have these," Aabo had said, presenting them in his open palm. "To see the world when you are older and wiser and ready to step out into it. A curious little girl like you should always have the tools she needs to explore."

I remember protesting that that was too far away. I wanted to see the whole world now, I didn't want to wait to be old and wise.

Hooyo had laughed, listening to our exchange, which only upset me more.

"You'll be ready once you are ready, Safiya," Aabo had said, squeezing my arm, "but until you are, these," he lifted the binoculars to my eyes, "will help you see the most of the world right here, around you."

I found myself staring at a much closer version of Hooyo suddenly, and gasped. Hooyo laughed again, Aabo chiming in too, both of their joy mingling together.

Mostly, in the years since, I have found some small piece of that world in sharing the binoculars with Muna and Yusuf, but I don't know why I'm holding onto them any more. To see the rest of a world I'm sure I will never get a chance or the money to explore? To hold onto some fragment of a happy memory, a mother and father who I thought would always love me and love each other?

I sigh, turning them over to give the lenses a quick wipe, when I notice something. I perch the binoculars on the bridge of my nose, staring at the web that descends over the view of my room.

There is a pull in my belly then, something a little like regret, though it's swiftly replaced by relief.

The binoculars are broken.

It looks like dropping them in the park with Halima has done the trick.

My cracked window, from the beginning of summer, has finally received justice.

# *HALIMA*

Number one on the Monday morning agenda: locating my mobile.

I wash my face with cool water, rubbing the sleep out of my eyes. Now that the holidays are over, Hooyo is off on the school run with the boys and the husband has gone to work, giving me a window of about twenty minutes to find it.

Slinking into the master bedroom, I make a beeline for the jewellery box that I know so well before doubling back.

A mobile is not the same as a photograph. It cannot fit in there the way Hooyo's other secrets can. I survey the room, eyes zeroing in on the bedside table. I open the top drawer with no luck. The second drawer also holds no secrets. But in the third...my mobile sits solidly between Hooyo's socks.

I press the power button but the screen only flashes with the battery sign.

"*Halima?*"

I whip around, sliding the mobile into the pocket of my dressing gown. The husband stands in the doorway, frowning. "*What are you doing in here?*"

"*Me? What about you?*" I throw back at him. "*Last I checked, this is not your workplace.*"

His frown deepens at my caustic reply. "*I forgot my wallet.*"

I reach into the open third drawer. "*I forgot my socks. Now, we both have reasonable excuses.*"

I stalk past him before he can pull me up on my disrespect and hurry to my room, rummaging under the bed for the charging cable. I connect the mobile and sit on the floor, waiting for the sound of the front door. For someone who claims to be here for a forgotten wallet, the husband is taking far too long.

Five minutes later and he is finally gone. I switch the mobile on and wait for the internet to connect. There are eleven missed calls from Khadija. I return them even though I know it is futile because she will be at school, and likely in her mathematics lesson if I still remember our timetable correctly.

I slump to the floor. How am I supposed to last hours more without speaking to her or Abti Haroon?

There are other things I need to discuss with Khadija too, like my desire to return home. See if she has any ideas beyond the only criminal one I've come up with, and if her family might be willing to put me up, at least temporarily.

But then an idea occurs to me. I scramble up and call the one other person who could lead me to my oldest friend. If I can't speak to Khadija, at least I might be able to get through to Abti Haroon.

The line rings and I wait with bated breath.

What if his granddaughter's internet for the month has

run out? Or her phone is broken? What if she is busy visiting a friend on the other side of town?

Each time the loud, high-pitched whine of the line pauses, my heart skips a beat. I know the call will die, that Maymuna will not pick up the phone and it is not her fault, of course not, but—

"*Hello? Who is this?*" Her voice is distorted but it is undeniably her.

"*Maymuna!*" I shout into the mobile, putting it on loudspeaker. "*It's me, Halima!*"

There is a delay as my words reach her and then her voice warms.

"*Halima, my love, it is so good to hear your voice. How are you, sister? How is the family?*"

I can feel myself grinning from ear to ear. Tears prick my eyes and I lean forward to try and wrap myself in this moment for as long as possible.

"*Good, we are all doing well, Alhamdulilah. How are you all? I cannot tell you how much I miss every single one of you.*"

The line clicks and my stomach lurches. This call cannot give out before I can speak to Abti Haroon.

"*We miss you too, my darling. Mogadishu is a lot less sunny without you and your fiery disposition.*"

My head falls back as I laugh. "*Well, don't worry. I might be back home sooner than you think and I will remember to bring that fire with me.*"

If I speak my hopes into existence, they will have no choice but to come true, right? Maybe all I need is to speak my dreams, because how else do dreams see the light of day?

Maymuna gasps. *"When? When will you be home? We can delay the arrangements if you are not far out, Halima. There is nothing that would have made Abkow Haroon happier."*

The line clicks again. A precarious wobble in the connection. *"What are you talking about, Maymuna? What arrangements?"*

I hear my own words echo back to me. Her reply takes longer to come this time.

*"The funeral arrangements, of course. Abkow wanted everything to be done swiftly when the time came but I know that he would have wanted to wait for you. Halima, you were the source of so much…of…his joy…friendship…purpose…life…death—"*

And then the connection clicks for the last time and I lose Maymuna.

I lose Maymuna and I have lost Abti Haroon.

I said that I would see him one last time.

He said that it would be a miracle if he made it to the end of the year.

But I did not truly believe him, because he was an old man, often more serious than he needed to be.

Now he is dead and I have nothing.

The pricking that threatened my eyes mere minutes ago transforms into razor-sharp knives and I cry everything of myself onto the bedroom floor. I cry until I am heaving and then I run to the bathroom and throw up all over the colourful tiles of the husband's kingdom.

\* \* \*

Hooyo returns home at some point and finds me in the bathroom. She starts to say something about parents' evening before she notices that I'm on the floor. Then she sees the mobile next to me.

"*Where did you find that?*" Hooyo exclaims. "*Halima, I expressly forbid you from using this phone.*"

She bends down to retrieve it as another sob racks through me.

"*Halima,*" Hooyo says anxiously, leaving the mobile and kneeling beside me. She puts a hand to my forehead but finds no fever. "*Halima, what is it? Are you sick?*"

She runs her fingers through my hair and I close my eyes. I think about the last time we were this physically close without any tension. But those thoughts birth other memories about home and Abti Haroon and my stomach contracts painfully. I lean over the toilet bowl once more but I am only retching at this point. There is nothing left for me to lose.

Hooyo combs my hair with her hands and the gentleness, the coolness of her fingers, brings tears to my eyes once more.

"*He's gone,*" I sob, my words echoing in the bowl. "*Abti Haroon… Hooyo, he is gone.*"

Hooyo gasps, pulling me back to face her and, for a moment, I am surprised to see anguish there. Pain. Emotion.

"*Oh, my girl,*" Hooyo breathes, wrapping her arms around me. "*I am sorry. I am so, so sorry.*"

Hooyo cries into my hair and the warmth of it spreads over my scalp. She reads the duas for patience, for all encompassing despair, duas for death. Words of healing and remembrance.

311

"*Inna lillahi wa inna ilayhi raji'un*," she says.

*We belong to Allah and to Him we return.*

I cling to those words tightly, try to bury them in my heart, but something else is soldered around my chest, something that tries to stop those words from sinking in.

"*He was a good man,*" Hooyo whispers. She sniffs, pulling back to look at me. "*A brilliant and good man who your father loved so dearly. Who loved you like his own daughter.*"

I shake my head, new waves of sadness peaking. "*I should have been there,*" I say, through heaving breaths. "*To say goodbye.*"

Hooyo places a hand over my damp cheek. "*He knew, Halima, how much he meant to you. He would never blame you for not being there. God takes us all at an appointed time...there isn't anything you could have done, my darling.*"

*It's your fault,* I want to say. *I blame you for my not being there.*

But instead, I dry my tears, grab my mobile, hug Hooyo once more, and go to my room.

Before I realize it, I am punching in the numbers scribbled on a piece of paper and calling Safiya. The phone rings once before I hastily cut it off.

No, I do not want her. I do not need her.

She is another reason. Another person to blame for the fact I am still in this country.

I have been too caught up in Safiya and the mystery of my mother's secrets and in trying to break Hooyo away from the husband, but none of that matters now because Abti Haroon is dead. I should have just focused on myself and figured out the means to run away, because if I had, I wouldn't be on the

312

receiving end of this news. I would have been there, as it was happening. I would have said goodbye to Abti and I would have kissed his cheek and read him poetry and seen him smile one last time. I would have said goodbye to the one person who loved my father like I did.

I would have.

I would have.

I would have.

More tears. More hiccuping sobs.

They are endless because, the truth is, I have no one to blame but myself.

# HALIMA

In Ms Devlin's office for the fourth time, I await my reckoning.

Beside me, Hooyo sits with her hands folded, and next to her is the husband. Kamal and Abu Bakr attempt to sit quietly in the corner but their laboured breathing carries to me. I know they must have so many questions but they're doing quite well, I think, in temporarily quashing their curiosity.

"We've given this a lot of thought over the half-term break, Halima," Ms Devlin begins, "and we've liaised with the police too."

Hooyo shuffles uncomfortably in her seat. All she wants is the news that her daughter has been absolved of any wrongdoing. To see my suspension lifted.

All I want is to dissolve. To withdraw in every sense of the word and escape from this room, because none of this matters. Not in the face of life or death. Not without Abti Haroon.

"This meeting was initially called to discuss home studying arrangements given your disciplinary action, but the good news is that we're putting all of that to rest. We've suspended another student in light of new information." Ms Devlin leans forward, smiling benevolently. "Another pupil has come forward with a damning video which means your suspension is lifted, Halima. Effective immediately. There won't be anything to go on your record, of course."

My mother's husband claps his hands. "That's great news! Isn't it, Halima?"

Hooyo, realizing now that this meeting is exactly what she'd hoped for, smiles too. She squeezes my arm and leans in to whisper, "*All our duas have been accepted, Halima, Alhamdulilah.*"

I smile faintly at all three of them. "Yes, that is great. Thank you."

The lie rolls off my lips easily because, after all this time in this country, I know I'm supposed to say what people want to hear and never what I am thinking.

"We've also got the long-awaited update about your language support, Halima," Ms Devlin continues. "Our teacher is returning from sick leave so we can hopefully set up some sessions with you soon, probably in the next couple of weeks."

She smiles. "And before I let you go, I also would like to sincerely apologize for the strain this must have put on you and your family," Ms Devlin adds, softening. "It must have been a really hard week having to deal with the prospect of the suspension. I'm glad it's all been resolved now."

Ms Devlin shakes my hand and then stands to escort us to the hall. "Parents' evening is just kicking off so hopefully you'll be able to fit your meetings in before the big crowd arrives."

To Hooyo and the husband, she says, "I'll send a letter home confirming we've withdrawn Halima's suspension. Thank you so much for coming in."

Ms Devlin promptly dumps us in the hall then disappears. The next chapter of this miserable evening begins.

The carousel of parents' evening is in full swing.

I tune out for most of it. I am sure no one has anything good to say anyway. I have probably been too slow to learn, too clumsy in my understanding. No doubt the teachers think that I have not tried enough and, if I have, I must still be falling short of the mark. I feel a pang of sadness when I think about what my life looked like only a few months ago.

The dugsi I would walk to, only a few minutes away from the house we lived in – a huge villa we moved into once Hooyo remarried. The hours I would spend sitting with a wooden tablet, rewriting letters of the Arabic script over and over again until they were perfect.

Abti Haroon. The stories, the poetry, the laughter.

Everything that made my life and everything I lost.

I am adrift in those memories until someone shakes me. Kamal pulls my shoulder, alerting me to the fact that everyone at the table is staring at me. My mathematics teacher, Mr Croft, grins.

"Halima, I was telling your parents I have never seen a student pick up mathematical concepts as easily as you have." He points to a sheet of paper, indicating the scrawls at the top. "Look, you got sixty-three per cent on the last test we did.

Sixty-three per cent!" Mr Croft shakes his head. "You have excelled beyond my wildest expectations, Halima. I'm incredibly proud of your progress and there's still so much more for us to do to push you even further."

Hooyo beams, awash with a mother's pride. Her husband slaps me on the back. Abu Bakr and Kamal copy him, each of them smacking me in quick succession. Each hitting harder than the last.

My stomach drops. Mr Croft's praises are just another reminder of me slipping into a life I never wanted.

We stand, finally finished with this appointment, and begin winding our way through the crowd, when my mother's husband comes to an abrupt stop. Hooyo narrowly avoids bumping into him, but the boys trip over each other, oblivious to the hold-up.

Safiya and her mother stand in front of us, pillars in the fast-moving traffic of the school hall. I am pulled again into that memory of summer and Eid prayer in the park, the last time all of us crashed into each other.

Safiya catches my eye. A sense of inexplicable relief begins to fill me; one that makes me momentarily forget about this school circus and everything that I have lost. My face stretches and I realize too late a smile is settling onto it.

The edge of Safiya's lips start to curve into a smile too but, before it goes any further, I wipe mine off my face as quickly as it came on. I look away from her and let my eyes focus on her mother instead.

She looks better than the last time I saw her, standing

confidently with her arms by her side, not gripping Safiya desperately.

"*Salaam, Halane,*" Safiya's mother says, tone curt.

My mother's husband almost does a double take, hearing her speak. I notice Hooyo stiffen out of the corner of my eyes.

His reply is stuttered. "*Wa alaykum salaam, Idil.*"

"*So this is the family you brought back with you.*" Safiya's mother looks over each of us, her gaze lingering first on my mother and then, on me. "*And what a beautiful family it is,*" she says with a smile. "*Seems like your children take after you. All the spitting image of Halane Aden.*"

Safiya's face contorts in shock. I do not know much about her mother but, from the look on Safiya's face, this does not seem like something she had been expecting.

"*Even the eldest.*" She nods her head in my direction. "*Your stepdaughter, correct?*"

My mother's husband opens his mouth, closes it, opens it again. He nods.

"*And, Rahma…it has been too long.*" Safiya's mother smiles at Hooyo. It is a wide one, but it does not feel sincere. "*You are well?*"

Hooyo shoulders her bag. She is thrumming with discomfort. "*Yes, thank you,*" she replies.

"*Good.*" Safiya's mother nods. "*Because I recall what a delicate disposition you once had and, of course, this country and its customs take some adjusting to. I've been here a little over sixteen years, so I know that well enough.*"

My eyes catch Safiya's. The questions racing through me are the same ones I find in her eyes.

"*I think we should get going, Halane,*" Hooyo says, snaking her arm around her husband. "*It was so lovely to see you, Idil and Safiya.*"

We make our way forward, moving through the sea of students and parents rushing frantically for their next appointment. As I pass Safiya, I see her eyes, wide as saucers, on my mother's back.

*What are you thinking?* I want to ask, but I don't.

Safiya can't be trusted. No one can be trusted any more, including me. Not after I became recklessly distracted with secrets and lies and lost everything because of it.


The next morning, I wake up tired, but focused.

I read my morning duas and pray. I think about my resolve to return home all those months ago. How it slipped through my fingers because I gave up the fight. Unknowingly accepted and melted into life here.

I sneak into Hooyo's room while she is downstairs making breakfast for the boys and open her jewellery box. I do the unforgivable but ask Allah for forgiveness anyway.

I take the pieces of jewellery I have seen Hooyo wear the least – including the gold ring my father gave her – and pocket them.

The train this family is on is running out of track, with all the tension and untruths I can feel building and building. I will not be around for the crash and boom, for the destruction that I know is not far off.

I am out of here. I am going back home because, if I could not be there to say goodbye to Abti Haroon, I will certainly be there to bury him.

# SAFIYA

Blindsided, yet again. That's all I can think on the walk home with Hooyo.

With Halima's suspension, I never expected that she would be at parents' evening. So why was she there, with her whole family in tow too?

Those seconds seem like a blur now, but I remember looking up, my eyes finding Halima's without thought. She'd started to smile and I did too. For a fleeting moment, it felt like it was only the two of us, together at Eddy's. Until we both remembered what happened the last time we were there and the secret that pulled us apart: the photo that revealed our mothers once knew each other well.

My mind fills with the tense conversation shared in the school hall. The things Hooyo said. The look that passed over the faces of Aabo and his wife. It was enough for the suspicions I held to find a foothold again. The ones that Muna convinced me couldn't be true. That there is an ugly truth buried deep in my parents' history. One that has everything to do with Halima and me.

I glance over at Hooyo as we cross the road, wondering

what today would have looked like if we hadn't gone to parents' evening.

"We don't need to both go," I had pleaded this morning. "Trust me, they don't say anything important, Hooyo. I'll go by myself like I normally do."

Hooyo flinched, drawing in a long breath before she replied.

"I know you've had to go alone for some time, Safiya, and I am sorry for that, but we're going together now and I am not changing my mind."

When we turned up at school, it felt disorientating. Like I was walking into somewhere foreign and not the place I've spent four years of my life. I was already expecting the worst, so when the horror show kicked into full swing, I wasn't surprised. Ms Barker started it off with geography.

"Safiya, I won't beat around the bush. Your result on the last test was concerning. There are a lot of gaps in your knowledge that you'll need to plug before your GCSEs this summer."

Mr Hughes pushed it further with Spanish. "*¿Qué pasa contigo, Safiya? Tu español fue más mejor!*" As proof of the point he was trying to make, I couldn't even translate those words.

But it was Ms Birch who was the nail in the coffin. "Safiya, I've had a look at your recent results and spoken to some of your teachers. It looks like things have been slipping. I know that you applied for sixth form here but, without hitting your target grades, there's a big chance that our admissions team will reject your application."

Hooyo looked at me, not bothering to hide her shock. To her credit, she recovered quickly.

"Safiya will get the grades," Hooyo said simply. "One hundred per cent."

Ms Birch smiled politely at that, but the doubt in her eyes flared.

So, in all fairness, things were already going horribly before we came face to face with Aabo and his family.

Now, after hearing what Hooyo had to say to them tonight, I have more questions than ever, things I'm not willing to let slide.

Aabo knew Halima's mum, long before they were married. Then there's the picture of Hooyo embracing her. An embrace that appears friendly, familiar, nothing like the frostiness shared between them today. And the ultrasound dated before me. A baby I've never heard about.

I glance at Hooyo again. At the woman who I thought I knew.

The answers I'm searching for are not far off now. I can feel it.

The only problem is…I think I'll need Halima's help to dredge them up.


The next morning, I text Muna and arrange to leave early so I can avoid seeing Yusuf. I got lucky yesterday since he was sick and didn't come into school, but that's unlikely to be true two days in a row.

I creep out of my house when Muna's ready and immediately begin power-walking, dragging her close behind. It's only when we reach the newsagent's that I let us take a breath.

Muna buys her chocolate and grabs me a Lucozade. As we leave the shop, I realize what she's got on.

"Hey! You're wearing your shawl again."

Muna rolls her eyes. "Don't be so dramatic, Safiya. It's just a shawl," she says, adjusting it over her shoulder, but I don't miss the smile that plays on her lips when she looks down.

"Of course," I agree. "Just a beautiful, chequered shawl with absolutely no meaning. Silly me."

"Silly you," she says breezily, hooking her arm through mine.

"And silly me too," Mustafa cuts in, waltzing in front of us from out of nowhere and grinning when he takes in the scowl on Muna's face.

"What do you want?" Muna asks curtly.

"Only to be the object of your desire." Mustafa sighs, leaning against the lamp post. "Is that too much to ask?"

"Have you considered joining a boyband, Mustafa?" I laugh. "Leaning all up on a lamp post is kind of a good look for you."

Muna rolls her eyes. "Don't feed his ego, Safiya."

Mustafa positions himself suggestively. "Not a boyband. But could be the cover art for a solo debut album, don't you think?"

I slide my phone out to take a picture because Yusuf *needs* to see this – his ridiculous friend doing some seriously ridiculous flirting – when I remember that I can't show him anything.

Muna grabs my arm, giving me an excuse to pocket that idea. "Look, Saf and I need to get going. Maybe we'll see you in form if you haven't already been scouted by then."

"Wait, I'll walk with you." Mustafa straightens. "I want to know how my boy is doing. His black eye looked horrendous yesterday."

"Excuse me?" I turn to Muna who's now looking daggers at Mustafa.

"Oh, damn…" Mustafa mutters, beginning to walk backwards.

"What does he mean, *black eye*?"

"Right, so, I think I'm going to head off now, ladies." Mustafa gives us a thumbs up. "This get-together has been fun, but it's getting late."

"Late?" Muna screeches as he retreats before breaking into a full-on sprint. "It's quarter past eight, you idiot! At least come up with a better excuse!"

I place a hand under her chin, turning her to face me. "Muna."

Muna is breathless with fury, so it takes a moment for her to reply.

"Yusuf…" she begins slowly, "*maybe* isn't sick… At least, not in the usual way."

"Okay," I prompt. "In what way *is* he sick?"

"In the way that one might be after getting beat up by Kyle." She sighs. "Yusuf was trying to figure out, you know, who planted those edibles in Halima's bag. I mean, everyone knew they weren't hers. He heard they were Kyle's, followed him until he could catch him in the act, and when he got proof, he told Ms Devlin. But then…" Muna bites her lip. "Then he got beat up."

"Are you kidding?"

Muna shakes her head. "It was a couple of days ago now. Someone must have figured out it was Yusuf and snitched to Kyle. He was alone and heading home after football when he got jumped by Kyle and his friend. The worst of it is a black eye, busted lip and a few bruised ribs, but he didn't break anything, Alhamdulilah."

"Why didn't anyone tell me?" I whisper, finding my way to Mustafa's lamp post, because I *have* to lean against something, anything. "Why didn't *you* tell me?"

Muna's face softens. "I'm sorry, Saf. I wanted to, but Yusuf made me promise not to say anything. That idiot never even told me what he was planning. I only found out after he got hurt." She sighs. "Maybe I should be glad Mustafa's such a blabbermouth. At least now you know."

I don't know how long I'm standing frozen for but, at some point, Muna grabs my hand and guides us to school.

She tries to speak to me, but I only hear the echo of Yusuf's voice.

*Safiya, I love you.*

My eyes swim with tears and my bruised heart shatters into a thousand pieces.

# HALIMA

Hooyo insists on accompanying me to school the next morning like I'm a child. I fight her the whole time before we leave the house, but she refuses to budge from her position.

When I ask why, Hooyo retorts with *"Halima, is it such a crime to want some quality mother-and-daughter time?"* But I know exactly what that means, especially in the context of my suspension.

I wonder if I should tell her to drop the act. That I overheard her speaking to the husband last night and there is no need to beat around the bush.

*"Halane,"* she had whispered on the landing when she thought I was asleep. *"Do you really think Halima would be accused out of the blue? It doesn't make sense. Something else must be going on."*

A small part of me wishes Hooyo is only doing this to look out for me in the wake of recent loss, but I know that certainly isn't true. Hooyo has not mentioned Abti Haroon since she found me sobbing in the toilet.

Her announcement this morning posed a problem for a different reason though because, while I'd donned my school uniform, my plan was never to get anywhere near Northwell High.

My plan was to start the journey to get as far away from it as possible – even if there were still a few holes in my clumsily put together scheme.

Hooyo drops me off outside the school gates, giving me a brusque kiss on the cheek. I wait for her to leave but she stays until she sees me walk through the gates, past the security guard, and into the building.

It briefly occurs to me that maybe Hooyo is also hovering close because she senses my imminent getaway. Or maybe, like a metal detector, she can sense what I have stolen. But I know that is impossible and Hooyo is only desperate to keep an eye on me for other reasons.

I pass through hallways and classrooms like a ghost. Every so often, I find reassurance in the treasures buried in my pocket, touching them for comfort. The handful of necklaces, rings and earrings I took from Hooyo's jewellery box and the passport I swiped from the husband's briefcase.

At some point, someone shakes me out of my trance. I look up to find Mr Croft, my maths teacher, openly staring at me, and the attention of most of the class on me too.

He points to a question on the board. "Halima, can you tell us how we'd start by answering this question?"

I look at the board and the question. See the answer that forms in my mind almost immediately.

"No," I reply. "I don't know anything."

Some kids in the class snigger. Thankfully, Mr Croft does not push for more.

My eyes catch Safiya's hunched back and deflated shoulders a few seats in front of me.

I have barely registered her presence in any of our classes. A far cry from our reality last week when I saw her nearly every day after being suspended.

I don't know what we are to each other but I know that, somehow, she has made me feel a little less of a stranger in this place. Taken away the heaviness in me, the loneliness that has been my shadow since I landed at the airport. Talking with her did something that I didn't even think was possible: made me forget that I ever wanted to leave.

I touch the gold in my pocket.

*Not this time,* I think. *Not ever again.*

The school bell rings, pushing everyone up and out of their seats.

In the hallway, I see a subdued Safiya once again. She is on her own, no Muna in sight, but I know where one is, the other can't be far behind.

An idea occurs to me then. Not perfect, but pragmatic.

Safiya does not know it, but she will be my ticket to getting out of here. She has to be, because I don't think I can do it easily myself.

While she may have been the distraction that preceded my whole world falling apart, Safiya will be the solution that rights it again.

# SAFIYA

The day feels sluggish and impossible to get through.

Even though Yusuf isn't here, he seems to be everywhere I look, and I can't help but miss him.

I miss seeing him in form. Catching sight of him playing football on the Astro at lunch or sharing a glance with him whenever Mustafa tries to ruffle Muna's feathers.

But most importantly I miss *him* and the way he always made me feel lighter whenever he was around. The friendly flirting and loaded words he would speak.

I miss him being a constant and a fixture. Someone who has always been here and who I imagined always would be.

But then I remember BANTRxpose and, in an instant, the Yusuf that I thought I knew disappears.

Is it possible to reconcile two polarizing sides of the same person? I sigh, burying my head in my hands. I wish that Muna was with me, but she's been whisked away for school councillor duties on the one day I need her most.

At lunch, I sit alone at the back of the canteen. Someone taps me on the shoulder and I turn, reluctantly, to find Halima.

I don't have it in me to smile or offer her a seat, but she takes one anyway.

"I need help," Halima announces, crossing her arms.

I scoff, pushing the potatoes around on my plate. "Don't we all."

She purses her lips. "I forgive you for lying about my picture," Halima says, interlocking her fingers. "So now you help me."

I raise my eyebrows at her before realizing what she's talking about. The picture of our mothers.

I take a bite of potato. "I don't owe you anything."

"Yes, you do," Halima insists. "And you will help."

Despite her seriousness, I can't help but laugh. "Why do you need my help?"

"Because I am leaving," she says. "Going back to Somalia. Today."

The second bite of potato that was destined for my mouth falls back onto the plate.

# *HALIMA*

Safiya and I sit in uncomfortable silence, prickly energy fizzing between us.

"*Waa baxooyaa,*" I tell her. "*I am leaving.*" The words feel like a weight off my chest, like a bird has swooped in, soared, and taken the load away. "*I am going back to Somalia. Today.*"

Her eyes widen in shock and she drops her potato.

"What are you talking about?"

There is a panic that sets in, that makes her eyes glow and fingers twitch. "Aabo's leaving again?"

I shake my head. "*No, aniga kaligey.*"

"Are you coming back?" she asks.

"No," I answer truthfully. "I am never coming again."

She looks down and I see the gears in her mind work overtime as she tries to make sense of what I have just said. I dig my fingers into my blazer, grazing the gold I have touched so many times today. I slide out a few pieces and present them to her.

"Look," I say, extending my hand. "I have gold, but I need money."

This seems to yank Safiya out of her thoughts. "Are you

silly?" she whispers angrily, placing her hand over mine. "You don't pull out this kind of stuff here!"

I extract my hand, rubbing the area where her nails dug into me, and hide the necklace and bracelet once more.

"You can't go without a passport," she says triumphantly.

I dig into my blazer again but think better of it. The same rule for the gold probably applies for something like this too.

"I have it," I respond, patting my chest.

Safiya's hands ball into fists and I sense she is angry for some reason. Upset with my declaration. But what reason does she have to be? Isn't this, my leaving, making her life easier?

I wish I could unburden myself more. Speak the reasons I'm leaving as well as the fact that I am. I wish I could say it is because my dearest friend, Abti Haroon, has departed from this life, stolen away from me by a lung-destroying disease that left him half the man that he was. That I made a promise to myself to see him one last time, but made a liar out of myself by forgetting it.

That Hooyo is not the person I want and need her to be, that she has become someone with too many secrets. That she has not batted an eyelid about forcing me to flee the home I was born in, grew up in, made lifelong friends in.

I wish I could say it is because Hooyo does not care about me any more and all I want is to go back home, where I belong, because I no longer belong with my family. Not since my mother married Safiya's father.

I wish I could say that this day has been a long time coming because, the truth is, I lost Hooyo the day she married her husband. The day she stopped being mine.

But I cannot say any of those things because it hurts too much.

"Safiya, I need money," I say, praying that she understands what I am doing without me needing to say why. "From *dahab*. And a ticket to fly.

"Please," I add when she remains silent. "Please."

She looks down at the table again. "If I do that for you, will you do something for me?"

"Yes," I say breathlessly, hope coursing through me. "Everything you want."

"Okay," she says thoughtfully. "We have a deal."

There is a twinkle in her eyes, something I can't quite describe, but I am too happy to care. I am going home.

# SAFIYA

I keep my face expressionless as I lie straight through my teeth. My mouth says, *"We have a deal"* but my mind is thinking something very different. I just hope I don't give anything away, because I can't afford to lose Halima's trust.

For now, I push all thoughts of Yusuf aside. I do not have the capacity to think about him and what's happened when I've got the enigma of my family to finally deal with.

A tentative plan begins to form in my head. One that will put me face to face with the person who has betrayed me and continues to. The man I have been running from ever since he moved back.

Too many people have been lying for far too long and seeing all those liars come together last night has very much pissed me off.

After school, we walk in the direction of Halima's house. I text Muna not to wait for me.

"No, I am not going there." Halima stops walking.

"You have to. Trust me. Just give me a bit of time."

"*Sababta?*" she replies, exasperated, and for a moment I feel like a mother dictating things to a child.

"Because I need to get your money and book you a ticket. I need time to get it ready."

"I will come with you," she answers simply. "We will go together."

"No!" At her raised eyebrows, I quickly walk back my outburst. "I need to go home first. I need to pee really bad and my mum can't see you. Obviously, she's not your biggest fan."

Halima hesitates, thinking it over.

"So you give me the gold and passport," I say, pressing on. "I'll sort it all out for you and see you in a bit."

Halima puffs out her cheeks. "When?"

I shrug my shoulders, getting impatient. "Soon. I'll be quick. You can wait at the newsagent's if you like. I'll text you when I'm on my way."

She narrows her eyes. I feel myself getting warmer under her gaze and I'm grateful today, more than ever, for my dark skin not being able to blush. I'm grateful my skin can keep a secret.

"*Hadaad iga xado, qabriga aan ku sugaa.*" Halima points a finger at my face.

I let myself relax.

"Don't worry, I won't steal anything. Keep your threats to yourself."

She hands over the jewellery and passport. I wonder if she's second-guessing herself and this irrational decision to fly halfway across the world, or, at the very least, the decision to hand over something so valuable to me, someone who she doesn't, and shouldn't, trust.

"Call me," she says, pointing that same finger in my face.

When I reach home, the sky is already inky blank. I slip into the warmth of my house, peeking my head into the living room, but Hooyo isn't here.

I bound upstairs to my room, grabbing the box from underneath my bed. I find the ultrasound and photograph inside and push them into my bag.

Regardless of what Muna says, I know there is truth still missing, but I intend on filling in the gaps of the puzzle tonight. I'm going to tell Halima about all of it, everything I have thought, the how and the why, and then the both of us will find and confront Aabo – the one person who connects both halves of our stories.

I see Hooyo's emergency credit card on my bedside table and grab that too, sliding it into my purse.

I text Halima that I'm on my way and head downstairs, wondering for the first time where Hooyo is. She wasn't home when I arrived. I wonder if she went to the interview she mentioned last week, because I can't think of any other reason she'd be gone.

Then I notice shoes in the hallway that weren't there before. She must have just come in.

I find Hooyo sitting silently in the living room and greet her, giving her a quick kiss on the forehead, but she sits rigidly, as if she doesn't want to be touched. I pull back, assessing her, deciphering her expression and posture like I've done so many times before when words have failed.

Has Hooyo already slipped back into the ghost of my mother? Did parents' evening last night take a bigger toll on her than I realized?

Of course, I always knew we'd end up here again – had prepared myself for it, like I always do – but the thought still hurts keenly, like acid to a paper cut. Though when I look at Hooyo properly, I don't see a ghost. I see anger. She is bubbling. She twists her fingers and taps her feet.

"Where are you going, Safiya?"

I think back to the last time Hooyo asked me a direct question about my comings and goings, weeks ago. How shocked I was that she'd paid attention to me, how easily I'd lied to her.

"To Muna's," I reply, shouldering my bag. "Just revising for some tests we have next week."

"That's all?" Hooyo asks, continuing her foot tapping. "Revising for some tests? With Muna?"

"Yeah, of course. What else would I be doing?"

Hooyo doesn't answer me. I use the opportunity to try to make my escape before she can ask any more questions.

"Don't you dare turn your back on me, Safiya Aden," Hooyo says, standing. "I know you're lying to me."

I whip around. "Hooyo…what are you talking about?"

That must be the worst thing I could say, because Hooyo explodes in a way I've never seen before.

For the last few years, since Aabo packed up and left, all I've seen is a mum who draws in on herself. So quiet and small she is almost invisible in this house. That's the Hooyo I know how to navigate.

I have no idea how to deal with a Hooyo who is staring daggers at me and who has tears streaming down her face.

"I just saw you with her!" Hooyo shouts, pointing at the window. "I saw you with that wretched girl from the family your father abandoned us for, walking home from school! After everything your father has put us through, here you are befriending her." Hooyo's voice creeps louder and, for a moment, I'm sure the house shakes with the reverberations of it. But it's not the volume that makes me flinch, it is her words. "Of all the things I thought you were capable of Safiya, I never imagined it would be this." She shakes her head. "How could you do that to me?"

Hooyo is accusing me of betrayal, of selling her out, and the truth is…she's right.

I knew from the moment I met Halima in the park that I was fraternizing with the enemy and, by doing that, I was driving a knife into Hooyo's back. I can't hide away from that truth, even if it's an ugly one, but seeing Hooyo look at me like this, with rage and disgust, as though she no longer recognizes me, I feel a swell of anger.

"How can you accuse me of betrayal when *you're* the one who has betrayed me all these years? Hooyo, you forgot about me the minute your husband walked out of the door! I have cared for you, cooked for you, *loved* you, even when you left me to fend for myself." My breathing turns heavy, and my vision blurs.

"Do you even remember the last time I was sick, Hooyo? Or that I broke my foot last summer? I mean, are you even aware that Muna's mum is my emergency contact at school? Do you know *anything* at all?"

I have never in my life spoken to Hooyo like this. Never told her how I really feel, because for so long she has been too fragile. But there is something rising inside of me now, some twisting fury I can't squash back down.

"How *dare* you speak to me like that, Safiya?" Hooyo demands, seething. "This disrespect – to your mother of all people – is unforgivable." She purses her lips, taking a deep breath in. "I know that our situation is far from ideal. I know that I am not blameless, but whatever I have done—"

"Far from ideal?" A mirthless laugh. "I have done more than any child should ever be expected to. I have paid bills, tried to hide your shame from this community, applied for jobs you don't even bother interviewing for. I have dealt with debt collectors and negotiated tabs, because most days we can't afford to pay for everything. I have scraped together something out of the *nothing* you provide. You're just a mother who has disappeared for the last five years and one that's lied to me my whole life!"

Now Hooyo is the one who flinches. "What are you talking about?"

"I'm talking about the fact that Aabo turns up, after all these years, with a woman who he's apparently known for quite some time, with a stepdaughter who looks more like him than I do. I'm talking about the fact that there is an ultrasound scan of a baby I've never heard about. And then there's the photograph of you and Halima's mum – a woman you led me to believe was a *stranger* to you. But she's not a stranger, is she? All of these lies, all of these secrets—"

Before I can process what's happening, Hooyo strikes me. Her right hand connects with my cheek. The contact of her skin on mine feels like it lasts an eternity.

I cup my face protectively. The tears that spring to my eyes come without warning, spilling over to fall onto my hijab. Hooyo gasps, covering her mouth.

A wail escapes me and then I run, slamming the door behind me, trying to get as far away from her as possible.

# HALIMA

I step out of my house, shutting the front door quietly behind me.

Though Safiya told me that I could wait at the newsagent's for her, I felt this sudden, insistent tug standing outside the shopfront. A pull to see my house and imagine my family behind its walls for the last time. To step inside, even fleetingly, and hear their voices carry in the hallway.

So I left and went home. Creeped inside and listened to the sounds of Hooyo in the kitchen making dinner for the boys.

I briefly wondered whether I could get away with going upstairs and packing a small bag but decided against it. Better to avoid anything that might draw attention to my already precarious presence in the house.

Just as I turned to leave, Abu Bakr caught me in the hallway and tried to climb on my back.

"*Anigana waa ku raacaa, Halima,*" he had whined. "*Please, please, please.*"

"Shush," I whispered, preparing to swing him off my back and tell him that screeching in people's ear is never the polite thing to do, but when I grabbed his arms a bolt of sheer terror coursed through me. I wouldn't be seeing him again. At least, not for a long time.

I gently slid him round, perching him on my hip. He lowered his head, leaning it against mine, the rise and fall of our chests mirrored.

*I love you, little brother*, I thought then. *I have loved you even when I thought I didn't.* But out loud, I whispered, *"I'll see you later, okay?"*

To my disbelief, Abu Bakr did not fight me on that, only nodding before shuffling off me.

*"Okay,"* he said, turning away, feet skipping down the hallway. He swung around again before he disappeared into the living room. *"Halima, can you help me with ABC later?"*

A lump formed in my throat. Seeing him, my small-framed brother, standing under the warm light of the hall. Letting him think he would see me again, letting him think I was coming back.

Hooyo's voice floated over to us.

*"Abu Bakr! Kamal! Hada imaada!"*

I cleared my throat.

*"Of course,"* I said to him. *"We'll figure it out later."*

I left without another glance back.


In the distance, I make out Safiya's silhouette. Her height, jacket, speed of walk and sway have all become familiar to me. Much too familiar.

Anticipation grows in my stomach.

Walking towards me is my ticket out of here and the reality of what I am about to do hits me suddenly.

I am leaving without Hooyo, without the protection of anyone. I have never travelled across cities on my own, let alone entire continents. What if I am not strong enough to do this?

Safiya gets closer. I can make out her face now and something about it calms me.

If Safiya did not think I was capable of this, I would not be going. She would have told me it was a bad idea and she would have let it die. Of course, I would have been furious with her for bringing my hopes crashing down, would have said *What do you know?* but, in the end, I may not have fought it.

*You are doing the right thing, Halima.*

Safiya finally reaches me. Her eyes are bloodshot and the skin around them looks darkened too, as if she has not slept in days.

"Hi," she says, sniffling.

"Hi," I reply cautiously.

She looks around, appearing slightly dazed.

*"You have the things?"* I prompt.

A dog barks from around the corner and Safiya startles. Her gaze focuses back to me. Distant, disorientated.

"Yes," she says monotonously. "I do."

*"Haye soo soco hee,"* I say, prompting her again.

Safiya looks at me vacantly. She shakes her head, as if clearing it from fog. "Yes, sorry. You're right." She looks over her shoulders, around the junction nearby. "Let's go to the train station."

"Okay," I reply, letting her take the lead.

# SAFIYA

Hooyo's hand still feels connected to my face even though I know that's impossible. Even if I feel the ghost of her hand lingering over my cheek, I know it is not real.

Halima walks by my side, unbothered. I can't help but notice the spring in her step too. She looks happy, I realize. In all the months I have known her, I don't think that I've ever seen her like this. It makes me wonder what happy looks like on me.

Above us, the black sky manages to grow even darker. I crane my neck upward, trying in vain to find some glimmer of a star across the gloomy expanse but I know, for London, that's like trying to find a winning lottery number. There are no stars penetrating the thick, polluting coat of this city. No stars to brighten up my sad life.

I look over to Halima again. I don't imagine I'll be able to keep up the pretence for very long. She's bound to ask me outright for what I promised, but I am empty-handed. I have no ticket for her. No gold converted to cash.

I was never planning on helping her anyway. All this time, I believed her desperation to run away was unreasonable, perhaps even a little attention-seeking.

But now I get it. All I want is to escape too. What do all these secrets matter if there is no happiness at the end of the line? Hooyo's slap, if anything, jolted me to reality. There is no happy-ever-after for me and my family, so what's the point in trying? All I wanted was the truth, but all I keep coming up against is more pain.

Halima can disappear and then I will go somewhere far, far away too, at least for a short while. Get away from this suffocating place and the struggles, lies and secrets it constantly breeds.

I will let her go because we both need this more than I need answers.

I may not have any gold-converted cash, but I do have a credit card nestled safely in my purse. Ordinarily, I never would have dreamed of doing something so reckless. I would have been tied up with reminders of debt and tabs and a million other money worries, but what does all that matter now?

How can I care about keeping my only family afloat when it's clear no one cares about me the same way?

We reach Northwell Abbey train station. I'm worldly enough to know which underground line to take, but clearly not enough to know there are four different terminals for Heathrow airport.

Halima points at the tube map on the wall. "Which one we going to?" she asks.

"That one," I say without thinking and my finger lands on terminal two. "Yeah, that's the one," I say again, more decisively.

Halima nods, oblivious to all the flaws in the plan I'm hastily putting together.

The announcement for the next approaching train rings from the platform. Halima whips her head forward, slightly bewildered.

"I can hear...but where is it?"

The screech of the approaching train intensifies. Its front lights cut through the dark tunnel on our left.

"There." I point, laughing when I notice she's covered her ears. "Don't worry, you'll get used to tuning it out quite quickly."

She grimaces.

When the train stops, Halima hesitantly steps forward. I indicate for her to follow as I wind through the bodies on the platform but, when I turn around, she still hasn't moved.

"Come on," I huff, grabbing her arm and dragging her along. "You're the one who wants to go home and we won't be getting to the airport if these doors shut."

We jump into the carriage seconds before the doors close. Halima yelps, yanking her bag out of the way. A tall man in a suit standing near us mutters something under his breath.

"Yes?" Halima asks, voice lined with provocation. "You want to speak?"

We find a free seat in the middle of the carriage. I tell Halima to take it. At least sitting down, she'll be at less risk of starting a train brawl.

I stand over her, gripping the handrail. Eventually, another seat frees up and I claim it.

The both of us sit in silence, the number of passengers dwindling the closer we get to the airport.

My hands begin to sweat. Either from the lies I must confess to about the money and ticket, or the fact that I'm running away from home – I'm not sure.

I turn over the budding plan in my mind.

Get to the airport – almost there.

Find a desk or approach a friendly employee.

Enquire about flights to Somalia.

Use Hooyo's emergency credit card to cover the cost.

Say goodbye to Halima.

But all of those are the easy steps. The hardest will be figuring out where I'll be disappearing to after that.

# HALIMA

I am not sure if the nausea I feel is due to the relentless jostling of this train or because we are not far from our destination now. If I understand the map correctly, there are only five more stops along this route to the airport.

Safiya sits beside me as the carriage empties. Both of us stare at the window opposite and our reflections, side by side, momentarily soothe the turbulence in my body. I may be alone for the rest of this journey but, for now, I have Safiya.

I look down at my watch and try to ascertain how much time I have before the funeral tomorrow. It will be starting at midday, giving me approximately fifteen hours of travel time to reach Mogadishu.

The disbelieving and unhelpful portion of my brain whispers it is impossible. That between unconfirmed flight times, transfers and general airport delays, fifteen hours could be cutting it close. The determined and optimistic portion of my brain tells me otherwise.

"Why the rush?" Safiya asks, leaning in close so she can be heard over the banshee-like screams of the train. "I knew you wanted to go home but it seems like...like you're running away or something." Her head dips with some emotion I can't understand.

"Not running away," I reply. "Running to."

She turns around in her seat to face me, eyes questioning.

"To Abti Haroon," I add, feeling my throat constrict. "He is gone. Dead."

Safiya gasps.

She takes me by surprise, enveloping me in a hug. "I'm so, so sorry, Halima," she whispers as the train slows. "I know how much he meant to you. What a great friend he was. I can't imagine what that loss feels like."

The fresh anguish from when I first heard the news blankets me again, the flimsy plaster I had covered the wound with disintegrating.

"He was great," I whisper into her shoulder, the warmth of my tears spreading over my face. "The best."

Safiya rubs my back as I cry all the tears that I have been holding back while trying to be strong. Through the meeting with Mrs Devlin and parents' evening. Through all these things that have no real bearing in my life, but I have had to perform for anyway.

I pull back suddenly with an idea. "Come with me," I say, wiping my face. "You and me in Mogadishu. You can see my home, see Khadija. We can do it together."

Safiya's eyes widen and she starts to shake her head, but I interject. "I know you running too. I can see in your face. I know what running looks like." I squeeze her arm, remembering her bloodshot eyes and dazed look as she came to meet me.

"We stop running in Somalia, Safiya. Really, you will never want to come back here again."

I cannot believe that I have asked her this. That I have offered a way out of whatever situation she is trying to flee. She, the girl who I blamed for making me forget my mission in the first place. But offering her this feels right.

At some point, Safiya stopped being the wedge I was trying to manoeuvre between Hooyo and the husband. She became something else in the process.

Safiya smiles a little sadly. I know her answer before she says it, but I am surprised by the hurt that it exacts.

"I can't," she replies. "Maybe one day. I've always dreamed of visiting home. When I was younger, I wished that Aabo would take me on one of his trips there, but that never happened." Safiya leans away again and stares at her reflection. "Anyway, I don't have my passport with me and, since I'm not sixteen yet, I think I'd need permission from my parents but they definitely won't be signing off on anything."

We stay quiet after that. Safiya stands to read the map and some of the other advertisements, but I know she could read them from her seat if she wanted to. She needs a break, a moment of quiet. I can understand that more than anyone.

But I sense something wrong when she suddenly retreats to our seats. She grabs my hand without warning and yanks me up. Safiya stares ahead, pointing at the other carriage through the window as I look on in confusion.

"Kyle," she says.

# SAFIYA

I let out a string of curse words under my breath.

If I'd been sitting in my seat, Kyle wouldn't have seen me from the other carriage and he wouldn't have noticed Halima either.

Just our bloody luck that we see Kyle Peters on the same train, today of all days.

I wonder what he's doing here, all the way on this side of the Piccadilly line. Then I notice we're near Hounslow, one of the last few stops before the airport. He must be headed there for his own thing, for reasons completely unrelated to vengeance.

I mean, this *has* to be a coincidence. If it wasn't, he would've done something already, right?

But he's seen us now and, whether coincidence or not, I'm sure Kyle won't let this slide.

I unceremoniously yank Halima up, keeping my eyes on him. Ordinarily, I wouldn't think twice about dealing with Kyle in public or even squaring up to him, but knowing what he did to Yusuf worries me now. And seeing his anger soar when he noticed Halima definitely scares me.

I may have my words to spit but I'm no physical fighter, which is why we have no choice but to run.

I pull Halima along to the door separating us from the next carriage. The train rattles on, screeching, and I push down on the handle to open it. A few sparks fly below and the train tracks gleam dangerously. The few passengers left in our carriage side-eye us, probably chalking up this behaviour to a couple of silly kids playing a dodgy game.

Halima tries to wriggle out of my grip, but I hold on tightly.

"Halima, you don't understand," I say in a rush. "I don't think Kyle is messing around." I indicate his carriage and the door he's struggling to open. "He's going to try to hurt you. He beat up Yusuf when he defended you and he's going to do the same to you now. We need to *go*."

She stops fighting then. I see the question in her eyes about Yusuf. *What do you mean he defended me?* But there's no time to answer her questions now.

I rattle the door of the next carriage and open it too before swinging myself through. I look up to see Kyle about to enter our carriage and pull Halima's arm, encouraging her to follow my lead.

She hesitates and then the train lurches, pushing her forward. She whimpers, holding tightly to the wall.

"Together," I say urgently, extending a hand to grip her elbow. I use my other hand to hold the wall on my side of the carriage. "You can do it."

Halima says something underneath her breath. Then she swings herself over too. She nearly collapses into my arms but I hold her steady, shutting both doors of the carriage as Kyle makes a run for us.

We have two more stops until our final destination. Heathrow terminal two.

I lead us to the next set of doors, praying as hard as I can.

# HALIMA

Safiya's grip on my sweaty hand does not loosen.

We move through another carriage before the train stops at the next station. I look over my shoulder to see Kyle ready at the main doors, waiting for them to open like we are too.

Once they do, Safiya and I bolt.

We fly across the platform, pushing by other passengers disembarking, to get to the carriage that will put us furthest away from Kyle.

But even without looking over my shoulder, I know he cannot be far behind. So, I slide my hand into my bag, without slowing my pace, and locate my half-empty water bottle. As Safiya yanks me into a carriage, I turn, aim, then hurl the bottle at Kyle. It clips him just above the eye.

"Bitch!" he screams, drawing the attention of some people around us.

"You too!" I yell, wishing I had another bottle to throw.

My foot slips into the gap between the train and platform as the doors start to shut. Kyle realizes his window of opportunity on the platform is closing too so he jumps into the carriage behind us. Safiya drags me up and in before my foot gets caught, then leads us again to the next set of carriage doors.

"Only one more stop to go," she says, panting hard. "If we can get to the airport, I think we can lose him there."

Just then, the voice of an irritated train driver carries over the speakers. Some warning about danger, but the train is too loud to hear it clearly.

We make it through to the next carriage without Kyle getting any closer as the announcement rings for the next stop. Heathrow terminal two.

We get off the train along with several other passengers lugging suitcases or carrying large holdalls. Snaking speedily through the crowd, Safiya taps her travel card on the reader, then pulls us both through once the gate opens. We faintly hear someone shout at us, but we are already too far away to pay much attention.

My breaths come quick and heavy. I focus on Safiya as we climb the stairs. She zigzags through every obstacle with precision and grace, and I can't help wondering whether she has had to run from trouble before.

I stupidly decide to look back. Kyle is gaining on us, taking three stairs at a time where Safiya and I can only manage two.

I do not know what he intends to do if he catches us, but I would rather not find out.

We reach the terminal. Trolleys with towering suitcases flow in all directions. Travellers are harried and haggard before they've even begun their journeys. Babies are crying, with mothers and fathers who look as though they wish to cry too.

Safiya pulls on my hand, drawing my attention. Her eyes

dart about the place. She leads us to the ladies' toilets at the far end of the terminal.

"We need to hide here," she announces with an air of calm, drawing us into an empty cubicle. "At least until he gets bored and leaves us alone."

*But I do not have time*, I want to cry out.

Instead, I say, "*Let me deal with him. I can fight. I want to fight.*"

Safiya snorts, taking a seat on the toilet lid. "You're hilarious."

"Not a joke. I can do it. *Khadija and I have fought enemies before.*"

"I don't care how many fist fights you've had in Somalia, we're not taking that chance," Safiya grits out. "You don't know what Kyle is capable of. You don't know what he did to Yusuf."

But I cannot accept that. I have come too far and sacrificed too much to have my dreams foiled by anyone, let alone Kyle.

"What he want with me anyway?" I ask, throwing my hands up in the air. "*I'm the one who should be angry. He's the one who framed me.*"

Safiya lets out the biggest groan I have ever heard in my life. "Yes, but now he's the one who got caught, suspended and questioned by the police! You're off the hook because Yusuf got the evidence to prove your innocence. So I am pretty certain Kyle is angry at you too. Maybe he thinks you had something to do with it."

The story stops me in my tracks. Yusuf is the one who saved me? Why?

357

But, like before, it only takes one look at Safiya for me to piece it together.

"Yusuf did it for you…" I say with a small, disbelieving smile. "Right?"

Safiya shifts uncomfortably. "Look, can you drop it? Let's just stay in the toilet for another twenty minutes and go from there."

"Fine," I reply, crossing my arms.

"Do you want to share the seat with me?"

"No."

"Fine."

We stay like that – me, standing at the cubicle door, and Safiya, head bent and sitting on the toilet – for exactly twenty minutes.

When the time is up, I unlock the door and leave, not waiting for her to catch up.

I head in the direction of nowhere for all of ninety seconds before giving in. I turn around to find a smug-faced Safiya right behind me.

That's when I see him, over her shoulder.

Kyle looks to his right, then to his left, and spots us through the gaps between the crowd. He sprints towards us at full speed from about ten metres away.

This time, I am the one who grabs Safiya's hand and runs.

# SAFIYA

We leg it to the toilets for a second time, dodging people as best as we can and trying to avoid tripping over any suitcases. I can see a long line forming outside the ladies' loos and hope we don't run into any trouble by cutting in.

About five metres away is when I start to realize Kyle is going to reach us before we get there.

Four metres when I look over at Halima and let go, telling her with my eyes that I need her to keep running.

She is the one Kyle really wants and without her, he just might lose interest.

Three metres before I stop running and turn to face him.

Two metres before Yusuf comes out of nowhere and socks him in the face.

# SAFIYA

I almost sob with relief.

Yusuf stands in front of me, cradling his reddened fist as Kyle lies on the floor, clutching his face. Whatever fight the boy had in him, it's clearly been knocked out.

Yusuf rubs his knuckles and turns to face me. The skin around his left eye is blackened and his bottom lip split. His face looks as though it's beginning to heal from the trauma inflicted on it, but it still looks raw and painful.

He smiles at me and for a moment it feels as though nothing has gone wrong between us. That we are still Safiya and Yusuf – two friends with the promise of something more between them.

I think back to the last time I saw him. When his face wasn't bruised like this. When we were standing in his back garden and he told me he loved me.

"You got new glasses?" I ask out of nowhere.

He barks a small laugh of surprise. "We fall out and the first words you say to me are 'You got new glasses'?" He shakes his head.

Yusuf turns to Kyle – who is still on the floor, groaning, but looks as though he's starting to recover – saving me from further embarrassment. People nearby murmur and begin to gather around. I wonder how long before someone alerts security.

Yusuf bends to speak to Kyle. I'm not sure what the hell he could ever say to get him to stop this crazy crusade, but I stop wondering when familiar arms encircle me from behind.

I lean into Muna. Her shawl tickles my cheek.

"How did you find us?"

"A journalist never reveals their secrets," she replies and I sense her smiling.

"You know, those words sound exactly like something Mustafa would say. Oh sorry, *has* said."

She growls, swinging me around to face her. "You're infuriating. I save you, and this is how you repay me?"

I give her a small smile. "Thank you," I say, feeling the gratitude well up in my eyes. "Like, seriously. Kyle is unhinged. I don't know what he would have done if you and Yusuf hadn't turned up."

"Oh, stop it." Muna lightly slaps my arm. "You should be saying that about your mum. She's the one who called me."

"What?"

Muna's expression grows serious. "She said you'd had a fight. A big one. She was really worried about you. So she called me to see where you were."

"And, sorry…" I take a step back, the improbability of this situation finally hitting me. "*How* did you know where I was?"

Muna digs into her pocket and waves her phone in my face.

"My phone tells me where to find my friends," she says, laughing. "I mean, granted, it was a bit tricky when you went underground and your internet was only on intermittently, but it was enough to tell me which line you were taking. And which direction you were headed in." She grins like she's solved the greatest mystery in the world. "Yusuf and I were only coming to see if you were okay. We had no idea you were coming to the airport, or that Kyle was after you." Muna takes a step back, crossing her arms. "Wait, *why* are you at the airport?"

I bite my lip and look over to Halima, unsure about where to start.

Muna rolls her eyes. "Of course." She sighs. "Of course this is about your conspiracy theories!"

"This has nothing to do with that," I insist. "We're here for a different mission entirely. Getting Halima home. Right, Halima?"

Muna rubs her forehead as if she's just developed a migraine. Halima doesn't respond, watching the unfolding scene with Yusuf and Kyle instead, who are both standing up now. Kyle says something to Yusuf, throwing Halima and I one final withering look before he leaves. Yusuf tracks his exit out of the terminal, coming over once he's confirmed Kyle is gone.

"How did you get rid of him?" I ask, raising a disbelieving eyebrow.

Yusuf shrugs his shoulders. "Kyle's not stupid. He knew if this ever got out it wouldn't end well. Not a good look to stalk two girls when he's already involved with the police. There's CCTV everywhere too, so it's not like it would be hard to prove it."

"You're telling me he was happy to walk *away* after you punched him?"

"Well, he wasn't *happy*." Yusuf smirks. "But like I say, he's not stupid. He only jumped me last time because he had a friend with him. Kyle knows he wouldn't actually win a fair fight."

Though his words are threatening, his eyes are soft. I feel my heart quicken, my chest constrict. Yusuf is staring at me too long with those soft eyes, so I look away.

He clears his throat awkwardly, turning his attention to Halima.

"Halima, I really don't know if this is the right time…" he says, eyes downcast. "But I need to apologize to you. For everything. I know that sorry doesn't cut it, but I did an awful thing and it led to some worse stuff that I didn't mean to happen." He pushes his glasses up the bridge of his nose. "I hope…I don't know. Maybe you can forgive me one day. I'm going to keep apologizing to you for as long as it takes."

Halima smiles. "Thank you, Yusuf," she says. "I appreciate."

Everyone pointedly looks to me then, but something has clamped my tongue.

Maybe it's the fact that this is the first time I've been this close to Yusuf since that night in his back garden. Or that I'm only now starting to process Kyle chasing us across a train and airport. I don't know what it is, but my eyes find Muna's and she saves me instinctively.

"So from what I understand, the plan is to get Halima on the next flight to Somalia, right?"

"Yes." I nod. "Exactly. That's the plan." I look around at our motley crew of four. "Any questions?"

Muna raises a hand. "It's really more a piece of information I would like to share than an actual question."

"What is it?"

"If Halima's going to go, you need to do it before your dad gets here. Safiya, we told him you were heading to the airport and he knows Halima has gone AWOL too. He's probably going to be here soon."

# HALIMA

"Okay, that's fine," Safiya says, nodding her head vigorously. "Yep, that's fine. Just a minor hiccup, but nothing we can't deal with." She points to Muna and Yusuf. "I need you two on door duty. If you spot my dad, call me immediately."

"But there's multiple doors," Yusuf says, pointing at the exits. "And the terminal is huge."

Safiya grins. "Looks like you two are really going to get your steps in then."

Muna narrows her eyes. "You owe me *big* time for this."

Yusuf gives in more readily, bidding goodbye with a two-finger salute, and pulling his cousin along with him. They split up to cover more ground.

Then Safiya turns to me.

"All right," she says with an attempt at breeziness. "Now let's find you a ticket."

It takes me a few moments to process her words.

"*Maxaa ka wadaa?*" I ask, spinning her around to face me as she makes a beeline for an airport worker. "You have not found my ticket?"

"We're finding it now. I couldn't get you a ticket before

because I didn't know how. But anyone can buy a ticket at an airport, right?"

I narrow my eyes at her. "You said you knew."

"I lied," she says, without so much as a hint of apology. "And we can stand here fighting about it or we can get a move on. You don't have much time."

"Where is the gold?" I cross my arms. "You stole?"

Safiya rolls her eyes but pulls the jewellery pieces out of her blazer and deftly places them in my hand.

"Happy now?" she asks, re-initiating her mission to flag down an airport worker.

The employee receives us warily.

"You'll want Ethiopia or Turkish Airlines," he advises, the look of disapproval weighing heavy on his eyebrows as he takes in our school uniforms. "There are no direct flights to Mogadishu."

Safiya thanks him and then both of us head to the other end of the terminal.

Only one of the airline desks appears to be open, boarding for a flight to Ethiopia.

"This one," I say. "When we came from Somalia, we stopped in Ethiopia. In Addis Ababa."

"Are you sure?" she asks, craning her neck to presumably look for another airport worker.

"Yes." I pull her face towards me. "Yes. I am sure."

"Cool." Safiya grins. "Well, that was easy."

The both of us join the snaking line. The flight is departing in a couple of hours. I do the maths in my head again.

If I get on this flight, and if the stopover in Ethiopia is less than four hours, I'll be in Mogadishu by midday, perhaps even an hour before that. That is, if everything goes according to plan and the flight isn't already full. But we are here now. We have made it this far, which means that my duas have nearly been answered and my fate today, hopefully, will be to return home.

We reach the front of the queue. The woman sitting at the desk does not bat an eyelid when we ask to buy a ticket to Mogadishu. She requests my passport, which Safiya hands over, scrutinizing my date of birth. She requests payment, to which Safiya responds by waving a card in the air.

Safiya looks over at me and grins.

"You're going home," she whispers.

My heart swells with warmth and giddiness.

*I am going home,* I think. *Finally, finally, finally.*

But my stomach squeezes when I realize there will be no more rendezvous in the park. No more stories swapped about our lives. No more laughs and language shared.

It is with that realization that I come to understand what we are to each other.

"My sister," I say to her as she punches numbers for the card in the keypad. "You are my sister."

The woman at the desk raises an eyebrow but I do not care.

Safiya turns around as she pushes the last button. She extends a hand, gripping mine. Her eyes fill with tears that I never imagined to see.

"You are my sister too," she whispers, squeezing my hand.

She looks as though she wants to say more, but the woman interrupts.

"Sorry, love," she says, sliding the passport across. "Can't help you. Your card's been declined."

# SAFIYA

"No, no," I say, jamming the card in the reader again and punching more numbers. "That can't be right. This card is for emergencies. I've used it before. I swear, it works."

The woman shrugs, standing to wave the next customer forward. "The cost of the ticket has probably exceeded your card's limit. Sorry – next!"

"No, wait." I shake Halima's blazer desperately, avoiding her eyes. "Look, we can pay with this. We have gold and it's more than enough to cover everything." I dump the ring, necklace and bracelets on the counter, going against the very advice I gave Halima earlier about hiding valuable goods.

"It's enough," I say, sliding them closer to her. "You can trust me."

The woman takes a moment to sympathize. "Look, the airport isn't a pawnshop and even if I wanted to help you, the policy is card or cash, not gold."

I groan loudly, digging my fists into my eyes. "Please, you don't understand. This girl *needs* to get back home. Her friend died and he's being buried tomorrow—"

My voice hitches, turning slightly hysterical. It draws the

attention of some of the other staff at the desk and the security officer several metres away.

I know that I'm making a scene, but I can't help it. Everything is going spectacularly wrong right at the finish line.

Halima stands stoically, arms crossed, expression neutral, but I know that it is all for show. The flame of anger in her eyes burns hot.

"Can you reserve a seat for her, maybe? Give us enough time to get the money?"

The woman shakes her head apologetically.

The security officer shifts closer and, before I realize it, he's right next to us and reaching for my arm.

"Do not touch me!" I shout. "Look, we're going, okay? We're leaving."

Then we turn around and come face to face with Aabo.


My breathless, flustered father. He is here, standing in front of us.

I blink and wonder if he's a hologram, if he is the ghost of anger that appears whenever I lose my cool, but he defiantly remains when my eyes reopen.

Aabo sags with relief, leading me and Halima to a corner. We are too stunned to react, to do anything but allow him to guide us. He leans in, drawing me and Halima into an embrace. I catch her panicked look before Aabo's arms engulf us.

"Why? Why are you here?" he asks, emotion catching his voice. "What are you running from?"

I pull back from him then, wanting to look him in the eyes.

All I wanted was to escape. To get out of the farce that is my life, because it has been built on too many lies. But if Aabo is here, if he is asking this sincerely, then there are questions I need to ask too.

I slide out the evidence from my pocket, what I have been carrying since I left home. My plan – before everything with Hooyo and Halima – had been to confront Aabo. Show him the photograph, the ultrasound, the diary. Make him answer for everything. Because he is the convergence. Because all roads lead to him.

"You need to tell us the truth."

Aabo's arms immediately drop from our shoulders. His eyes widen as fear floods his face. He looks from me to Halima, and then back to me again.

"The truth." He drops his head in resignation. "Oh my girls…I wish the truth were a simple one." Aabo sighs, looking up at us through tears. "It's not, but you have both been owed it for a long time and I will not keep it from you any longer."

Then Halima and I receive the story we never knew we'd been waiting our whole lives to hear. In the middle of a busy airport terminal, everything is laid bare and the truth is finally illuminated.

# THE SEASON
# OF TRUTH

In the year of a persistent drought, a boy married his young love in secret, against the wishes of his family. She was a housemaid but, much worse than that, she was of a tribe looked down on, sneered at, laughed about.

Though their love was powerful, the strength of it was not enough to withstand the onslaught of disapproval from every corner of his family and so, eventually, with great reluctance, they dissolved the union of their love.

Of course, they would come to carry that regret with them for the rest of their lives, but the girl of that lowly tribe came to carry something else too. A baby. A child borne of their love.

She told no one of this truth, not even the boy she loved more than life itself. He was already gone. Flown away to a different country, driven far away from her and from what everyone considered to be the devilish nature of their connection.

The girl, now a woman, found another prospect not long after. A man who could provide for her and who she could use to also mask her secret. A man who she did not love but a man who was necessary.

And the man who had flown away a boy settled with someone

else too. A match his family were pleased with, one they cried through the streets of home about. One they had expected him to pursue from the very beginning.

She loved him fiercely, this new woman. Tried to scrub his heart down, take away the pain that he carried with him from that lost love. She thought she could re-make this man into one she had always dreamed about. She pushed him, focused him, grew his ambition, moulded him into the very image of success, and their child – a daughter – helped to create something of a love between them at the start.

There were highs and lows through their marriage. The highs were dizzying, and the lows were brutal. They wanted, over time, to create more love between them and so they tried for more children, but with every try came more loss. One early miscarriage, two later ones.

They came to realize that their daughter was the reason they loved one another, and, without her, there would have been nothing at all.

Even across oceans, in the motherland, loss reared its ugly head too. The woman, with her secret baby, lost the man who had provided for her. Five years into that marriage, she was widowed, and she crumbled without him. Not because she loved him – no, there would only be one love for her, in this life – but because she had lost what she needed to survive.

She picked up the phone to tell her first love about the daughter they had created and, though it was never the woman's intention, that phone call, that day, changed everything…

# HALIMA

I melt on the dirty airport floor without regard for anyone or anything. The husband's words ring in my ears.

*You are both my daughters.*

I close my eyes. See flashes of the man I believed, all my life, was my father. Flashes of a life lived in lies.

Did Aabo die thinking I was his daughter? I wonder. Did he lie to me too or was he only a victim of someone else's deception?

I want to ask him about all of this, but I can't. Aabo is dead, just like Abti Haroon.

I look up at Safiya who somehow pieced this together. She is my sister, I think. My real, blood sister.

*No.* I scratch that thought.

She was my sister before my whole world imploded.

# SAFIYA

Halima is on the floor, thrown off course. My heart hurts for her but I can't comfort her now. Tears bubble in my eyes and track down my face, but I am too angry to wipe them away.

"Why did you all lie? Why did you have to keep this a secret for so long?"

Aabo looks away, dragging a hand over his face. "There were so many times we wished to explain, but as the years went on, I suppose we always found a reason to stay quiet." He looks down at the photo of Hooyo and Halima's mum, grazing his thumb over it.

"Back home, Rahma and Idil were the best of friends. So inseparable, not even a crowbar could pull them apart. When I fell in love with Rahma, it ruined their friendship but also the plan my family had for me." He takes a long, deep breath, turning the photo over. "Your mother and I were destined for each other, Safiya. Our families had arranged our marriage years before, but, of course, love can't be trusted to follow the rules.

"Idil moved to England ahead of me. She knew that my

heart belonged to Rahma, but she was still willing to marry me. I was due to meet her shortly after, but Rahma and I eloped. It was very impulsive..." Aabo swallows. "There are times when I imagine what life might have looked like if Rahma and I had only resisted. If we'd decided to dream of a future instead of secretly putting one together." He pauses, looking down at Halima who is still on the floor. "But even if I regret certain actions...well, the truth is, I do not regret everything that came out of them. I would not wish either of you out of existence."

Halima stiffens at that and Aabo must notice because he looks away, dragging another breath in.

"I never knew about Halima," he continues, "until a few months after her father died. Rahma had kept that a secret from me too and, for a while, I was livid with her. For hiding my own flesh and blood from me. But that revelation eventually led to us connecting again. It reignited something I thought I had buried so deeply and intensified all the troubles Idil and I were already having in our marriage. When your mother found out I had been speaking to Rahma, she was furious, as she had every right to be. She told me then that she no longer wanted to be married to someone who would keep choosing another." A solitary tear falls down Aabo's cheek, landing in his henna-coloured beard. "She asked me to leave. She said that I owed her that after...after destroying her life and taking away her closest friend."

The blood in my veins turns to ice.

Hooyo asked Aabo to leave?

All these years, I thought her anguish was because Aabo decided to abandon us, but, clearly, it was never that simple.

Hooyo's despair was everywhere, unending. For years.

Despair because she felt no choice but to drive Aabo away, into the arms of another woman. Despair because she was left without an inheritance. Left a single mother, without a husband or a best friend.

My hands tremble and I draw them into my pockets as though that will stop the shaking from clutching my entire body.

"Then why did you come back?" I whisper.

Aabo smiles but it feels distant, faint. The smile of someone standing metres away.

"For you," Aabo says simply. "I should never have left you, Safiya. You were too young and you were left with too much responsibility. I returned a few years ago because I wanted to see you and your mother, try to start making amends, insist on financial support, but…" Aabo pauses, clearing this throat. "But Idil was still too hurt, and she didn't want anything to do with me."

My mind reels – with illuminated truth, with the picture of my new and burgeoning family tree – but I push that away and chase the clarity I'm still looking for. I point to the evidence Aabo holds in his hand. At the ultrasound beneath the photo.

Muna's words ring in my ears.

*That ultrasound scan you're referring to might not be Halima,* she'd said. I'd thrown that theory right out the window without a second thought.

"What about this scan then? If you didn't know about Halima until way after she was born, whose baby is this?"

Aabo shakes his head. "Safiya, I'm sorry…I cannot answer that. Certain lines are not mine to cross. Those answers lie with your mother."

He turns his attention to Halima then, bending down to whisper something. She is frozen but slowly thawing. Aabo helps her to stand. He hesitates when she is on her feet, uncertain about his next movements.

Halima turns around to face me. She throws herself in my arms and I throw myself at her too.

We hold the weight of truth together, sharing that burden as sisters in spirit and now in blood.

Whatever comes next, I know we will face it together.

# SAFIYA

The drive home is quiet, but not uncomfortable.

Halima sits at the front with Aabo, and I sit at the back with Muna and Yusuf. Muna grips my hand tightly all the way home and I am grateful for the physical touch that I don't have the words to ask for.

"We did a pretty bad job, didn't we?" Muna whispers, leaning in. "At looking out for your dad in the airport."

I snort. "The worst. You two are horrible at surveillance." I shrug my shoulders. "On the bright side, we got a free ride home out of it."

We fall into silent laughter then. Yusuf raises his eyebrows at us, but we've already reached home so I am saved from having to speak to a boy I've forgotten how to be normal around.

We say our goodbyes and then Aabo and Halima drive off.

At home, I remove my shoes, waving goodbye to Muna and Yusuf before quietly shutting the front door.

I wonder where Hooyo is. If she's shut herself in her room or if she's still angry about the words we exchanged before I ran away.

I hear murmuring and walk into the living room. Hooyo is sitting on the floor, head bent low, wrapped in her prayer jilbaab. She whispers in Arabic feverishly, making the same dua over and over again.

*"Allahumma rahmataka arju fala takilni ila nafsi tarfata 'aynin wa aslih li sha'ni kullahu la ilaha illa anta…"*

I know that dua. I've read it enough times myself over the years. The meaning rings in my head without any effort.

*O Allah, I hope for Your mercy. Do not leave me to myself even for a blink of an eye. Correct all my affairs for me. There is none worthy of worship except You.*

I drop on the floor next to Hooyo and wrap my arms around her. Hooyo jumps, pulled out of her spiritual spell. She gives a cry of joy when she realizes who it is.

The two of us fall to the ground together, limbs entangled, and Hooyo cups my cheek, smoothing it over.

"I am so sorry, Safiya," she says tearfully. "I am so, so sorry. For hurting you and abandoning you. Leaving you to be a mother when I should have raised you as a child." She kisses my cheek. "I am sorry a thousand times over."

I tell Hooyo that she has my forgiveness and that she will always have it, but the flow of apologies from her lips continues like a prayer and a promise.

Hooyo and I speak long into the night and, for the first time, she doesn't hold anything back.

"Being Halane's wife was never easy for me, Safiya," Hooyo

begins, staring at the clock in the living room, long since broken. "I knew, even from the beginning, I was playing second fiddle to someone he loved long before he became mine, but I was so determined to make him forget her. To make him love and choose me, because, after all, we had been promised to each other. I thought that I could do that by making him successful in every part of his life. So successful and so grateful to me, that he would have no choice but to forget about her. For a while, that was easy. Your father was building his business with my help, he was becoming more prominent in our community, everything I hoped for was coming true. I even sold the land my father gave me to help him. As if that was the greatest show of commitment for my love." Hooyo laughs quietly under her breath. "But, of course, life has a funny way of reminding you you're not in control. You were too young to remember any of this, but your father and I lost children. Three children, in fact. Our first baby we lost four months into the pregnancy, before you were born, and the other two were after you, before we even got to the first scan."

I blink, trying to make sense of Hooyo's words.

"After the last miscarriage, our marriage really began to take a dive. Halane and I were at each other's throats whenever you were at school. He would take business trips, or trips he insisted were for business, at least, several times a year. And the phone calls." Hooyo laughs bitterly. "The phone calls were the worst, because he took them in this very house. Speaking to his old flame from Mogadishu, the woman who was once my closest friend, under my roof, without a care in the world for me. Rahma was a housemaid in your father's house, which is how both of us came to know her. She knew Halane was promised to me…and she still took him anyway." Hooyo sighs. "Anyway, at this point, after the last miscarriage, I was in pain and beyond broken. I knew the marriage wasn't sustainable, so I asked Halane to leave."

Hooyo looks at me, angling her body so she can hold my gaze.

"I knew about Rahma; I knew that he married her when he left us and came to have children with her. I will not lie about that. It may have been too painful for me to think about, let alone share with you, but, Safiya, it was only when they came to this country and I saw the girl, his stepdaughter, that I suspected there was something I wasn't quite connecting. I remembered the times he would always send so much money back home, always telling me it was for this, that or the other, but, when I saw them in the park that Eid…"

Hooyo closes her eyes, blinks back tears.

"Whether or not she is your sister, I want you to know that you do have three other brothers and sisters too. They're not here with us but they are yours. I should have told you about them years ago, but I didn't think I was strong enough to carry your pain along with mine."

She opens her eyes again, smiling sadly. "I used to feel that I was alone in this life, but I forgot, for a long time, that there was someone to love me. Someone who has loved and cared for me all along." Hooyo leans in to kiss my forehead, tears streaming down her face.

"You, my most beautiful, precious daughter."

# *HALIMA*

I lean down to smell Abu Bakr's head. He snores softly on my lap while Kamal sleeps at my feet.

I am still a little overwhelmed by the reception I received when I returned home. I would be lying if I said I expected everyone to be overjoyed by my departure, but I had not expected this sadness, this fear and worry on my family's faces when I walked back in.

It had taken Hooyo about thirty minutes before she was able to detach herself from me. Abu Bakr, another twenty.

Sitting on the sofa now, smelling Abu Bakr's hair and surrounded by the warmth of my brothers, I cannot remember why I ever ran away.

What was it that made me so single-minded about fleeing in the night?

But, in an instant, it comes crashing back and I remember what drove me.

Abti Haroon.

The funeral will still be tomorrow, at midday, but Khadija has promised to call me at the janazah prayer. I feel a pang of gratitude for having this girl in my life, for all that she has done for me and continues to do. The devastation from my aborted travel plans hurts deeply, but I know it would be unbearable without her.

I look across the living room. Hooyo is sitting at the table, head buried in her hands. I shuffle out from under Abu Bakr, careful not to step on Kamal, and make my way over to her.

Since finding out the husband is my biological father, a torrent of emotions has been let loose inside me. Some are easier to name than others. It will take more time than this night can give me to work through them all but, right now, I need to hear from Hooyo.

Hooyo looks up at me when I take a seat at the table. Her eyes, red and swollen, reflect the fear and anxiousness that line the rest of her.

I spend the next several hours listening to the story of their forbidden love, their secret marriage, and their secret child. Of the father I knew and loved, and the secrets kept from him too.

I listen to stories that leave me spinning. Hooyo holds my hands through it all.

"*I'm so sorry, Halima,*" she says at the end of it. "*The truth is, the older you got, the more afraid I was of telling you. I feared it would leave you feeling bitter and disgusted by me…*" Hooyo swallows. "*That it would drive you away if you knew that I had betrayed my friend and lied to the men in my life.*"

"*That's not your choice to make, Hooyo,*" I reply, wiping the tears from my face. "*You should never have kept this from me or Aabo. He died thinking I was his daughter.*"

"*You are your father's daughter,*" Hooyo says fiercely, gripping my hands tighter. "*Never, for a second, doubt that, Halima.*"

Hooyo draws me into an embrace and, in her arms, I remember the words the husband whispered to me in the airport.

"*I may be your father, Halima,*" he had said. "*But I am second-in-line. No one will ever replace your first.*"

# SAFIYA

Hooyo and I sleep on the floor of the living room that night. We wake to pray Fajr, but we're both too wired to return to sleep.

Morning light streams through the curtains as we talk. About school, my upcoming exams, the subjects I'm worried about and the ones I could pass in my sleep. I tell Hooyo about Yusuf and Muna. I tell my mum my life and she does not retreat the way she once would have. Hooyo is alert and attentive and questioning. She looks hungry for all these details and says she will never tire of them again.

After breakfast, there's a knock on the door.

"I'll get it," I say, putting my tea down. "It's probably Muna, but I'll tell her I'm not going to school today."

I open the front door, expecting her to wade through and start ranting at me, but there is only silence. A very uncharacteristic non-Muna silence.

I peer around the door to find Aabo standing with Halima's mother, Rahma. My mouth gapes but she only smiles, leaning in to gently peck me on the cheek.

"*Salaam, Safiya,*" she says. "*Is your mother home?*"

Hooyo emerges from the living room. She freezes when she sees who it is.

"*Rahma?*" she says, in question more than in greeting. Her eyes widen in shock when she sees Aabo behind her too.

"*Idil, can the three of us talk?*" Halima's mother asks. She hovers in the doorway, awaiting permission to cross the threshold.

I look to Hooyo. Whatever signal she gives me, whatever instructions she hands out, I will be here to follow through. I will slam this door in their faces – in anybody's face – if it means protecting her, because Hooyo has had to endure too much. I refuse to see her suffer for a second longer now that I know the truth.

Hooyo smiles, dropping her guard. "*Of course, please, come in.*" She looks to me for a brief moment before turning her attention to her guests. "*I suppose we all have a lot to discuss if we're going to make this work. We owe it to our girls at the very least, don't we?*"

# HEXPOSE
## Musings of The Investigative Hijabi

### Special Edition
### Edibles: Behind the Smokescreen

Well, fellow Northwellers, it certainly has been a very tumultuous time. I can only apologize for my recent absence, which appears to have left a gaping void in the gossip fabric of this school. But I can assure you, loyal readers, that shall be no more. The musings of your fave investigative Hijabi have returned.

I send out this special HEXPOSE edition to publicly announce that the NWHS Edibles Fiend has been identified and brought to swift justice. As most of you will remember, one innocent student was suspended following a police search that identified drugs in their bag last half-term. That student has now been cleared of any and all wrongdoing. Hooray! Of course, it is now my hope (and expectation) that they will receive a much warmer welcome than they have done so far.

The police have charged Kyle Peters under the Misuse of Drugs Act. Due to the ongoing investigation, that is all the information publicly available to us, but you will, of course, be kept updated with any further developments.

I would like to send out a special thank you to the student who single-handedly uncovered this and managed to bring this Edibles Saga to an end.
To that student, now an Honorary Editor-in-Chief of this publication, you know who you are. But I leave you with the warning that there is only one Investigator in town and you better not step on her toes again...

Signing off here and leaving you all with a little bit of HEXPOSE magic to get you into the mood for the rest of this term. As always, I hope our exposés put a hex on you.

**HEXPOSE Editor-in-Chief**

# SAFIYA

At the newsagent's, Muna waits outside. When I step out, Halima is already there, the two of them chatting away.

"Hi, sis," I interrupt them, giving Halima a quick hug.

"Hi, sis," she echoes, with a twinkle in her eyes. "For me?" Halima indicates the ice cream in my hand but I shake my head. Muna smirks and I shove her light-heartedly.

At King Eddy's Park, we find Yusuf on the swings, bicycle on the ground, wheels still gently spinning.

Muna tells me he's been spending a lot of time here lately despite the drops in temperature. He smiles when he notices us.

Even from a distance, I can still see the purple bruises on his face, intermingled with his dark skin. I wonder how long it will take for the hurt to fully heal.

I walk over and sit on the swing next to him, waving goodbye to Muna and Halima as they embark on a stroll around the park.

"Hey," I finally say, staring ahead at the climbing frame.

He glances at me over his shoulder. "Hey yourself."

I kick off from the ground, swinging at a gentle pace. My mind runs through a million conversation-starters, each one worse than the last. "So, what's cooking with you?" I come up with eventually, but my insides cringe the second the words leave my mouth.

Yusuf chuckles. He stares up at the sky as if his answers are there.

"A storm," he answers. "Cooking up a storm."

"Really?" I scrunch my face, leaning into this weird exchange. "That's all?"

He snorts in disbelief. "Safiya, do you know what a storm is? If I'm cooking one up, trust me, there's no time to be doing anything else."

Now it's my turn to laugh. "What the hell is that supposed to mean?"

"It's pretty self-explanatory," Yusuf says, kicking off from the ground to match my swings. "I mean, you'd have to be pretty clueless not to get it."

My head falls back as laughter overwhelms me. I look across to see him already staring at me. His smile is wide and warm and comforting.

"I miss you, Yusuf."

The words roll off my tongue without design, but I don't berate myself.

It's true. I do miss him. I have missed him. And if Yusuf could be honest and brave about his own feelings, then why can't I?

He stops swinging, coming to a gentle stop and I stop then too. Yusuf shifts one of his legs so he's straddling the seat and facing me directly.

"Saf," he says after an agonizing minute of silence. "I really need you to know how sorry I am. About everything. I've said that word a lot lately, but I haven't said it to you yet."

Yusuf leans forward. There is fog lining the edges of his glasses, but I can still see his hot-chocolate eyes.

"I want you to know I'm sorry for thinking I could solve your problems or that you wanted them to be solved in the first place. For using my...my feelings for you as a weapon to hurt someone and pretending that was all okay." He runs a hand through his hair and lets out a sigh. "I'm sorry for telling you I loved you when you were angry with me, but, most of all, I'm sorry for ever messing with our friendship. Because that's one thing I don't ever want to lose."

Yusuf looks away to stare at the rubber mulch under our feet. I know he's waiting for me to respond without the pressure of his gaze, but I already have my words.

I knew what I was going to say before I even stepped into this park. The truth that I tried to deny but have known from the very beginning.

When Aabo left, I grew up believing that love couldn't be trusted. That it could be here one minute and gone the next.

And maybe love can't be trusted, but I'm starting to think that is the way it's *supposed* to be.

Because maybe what we're meant to do is trust the person it comes from.

"Yusuf...I love you." His head shoots up so fast it nearly throws me. "And not just friend love, but real love."

I see his eyes widen and I stand up from the swing to continue my declaration.

"I mean, I tried not to. I tried convincing myself whatever I was feeling was a silly crush, because what kind of predictable idiot falls in love with her best friend's cousin? A cousin who also happens to be her next-door neighbour?"

Yusuf's laughter booms when he hears his own words thrown back at him. "*Wow*, so it's going to be like that, is it?"

I grin. "Well, how am I supposed to outdo such a great monologue? You should actually be flattered, you know."

His dimples rise into his face as his smile stretches.

I slide the Magnum out of my pocket, hoping it hasn't melted by now.

"Here," I say, presenting it to him. "To commemorate my promise to you."

He immediately throws it over his shoulder.

I hear the *crack* of the chocolate shell splintering with the impact and shout in protest. "What's your problem? I got that for you!"

I make to retrieve the packet, now lying on the ground a little way behind the swings, but Yusuf stands to block me.

"Saf…" Yusuf says, holding my gaze intensely this time. "I don't need an ice cream to commemorate anything. I am already yours and I *always* will be."

# WINTER
# JOURNEYS

In the district of Yaaqshid, Mogadishu, a man returned to the homeland with two young daughters in tow. The first, born out of a wild and passionate love, and the second, born out of a love promised.

For the daughter of passion, the journey was both a return to roots and an opportunity to honour a great loss.

For the daughter of promise, the journey was an awakening, a chance to live and breathe in the land where her ancestors once had.

And for the man, the journey was a chance to prove that he could be a father that both daughters could look up to and be proud of.

All three found what they were looking for.

And all three found some peace and a sprinkling of something new between them.

# ACKNOWLEDGEMENTS

It feels surreal that I get to sit down and pen another set of acknowledgements after already being blessed with a first book. Alhamdulilah. I pray that this gratitude never leaves my heart.

Thank you, first and foremost, to Allah for the light and love I experience in my life that's allowed me to write.

The greatest of thanks to my wonderful parents: Farxiyo Roble Xuseen and Abuukar Macalin Maxamuud. I write stories because I want to share something with this world, but, more importantly, I write to make you proud.

Thank you to my aunt Sahra Roble Xuseen for all that you have done for me and continue to do.

To my youngest sisters, Ibtisam, Ibtihaj and Imaan, this story of sisterhood and friendship is for you. While we may be sisters by blood, we are friends by choice, and I remind myself every day what an honour that is. (Special shout-out to Ibtihaj for being the first of the girls to read this book!)

Thank you to Asli and Jibreel for always picking up the phone when I called. I am so lucky to have you both be so charitable with on-demand creative validation and listen to my rambling updates.

To the best of friends – Naima, Saima, Sharon, Chevonne and Feyi – thank you for all your warmth, love and support. Thank you for not just being friends, but sisters too. The journey has been long but it would have been even lengthier and tougher if not for your kindness and endless excitement about the words I somehow manage to string together.

To Clare Wallace, dream agent, I don't know what I would do without you. Thank you for always steering me in the right direction; your guidance is invaluable and treasured and I am forever grateful for it. But thank you, above all, for making me feel like my voice and writing matters. And to the rest of the wonderful DACBA team – Becca, Chloe, Kristina and Lydia – I am so fortunate to count myself among you.

I am forever indebted to everyone at Usborne for giving me the space to tell stories that I truly care about. To Sarah Stewart, my brilliant editor, thank you a million times over for helping to shape this book. I'm continually in awe of your ability to cut straight through to the heart of the story and understand what it needs. I feel safe when my words and stories are with you.

A huge and overdue thank you to Rebecca Hill for helping me step onto the publishing stage. Beth Wetherfield for reading the early drafts of this story (and for leaving the most entertaining comments throughout). Hannah Featherstone for some serious eagle-eyed copyediting; I really don't know how you do it but the timeline thanks you! Thank you to Will Steele and Wasima Farah for the most gorgeous cover design and illustration. I could not imagine a more perfect Halima and Safiya. I am also incredibly grateful to Beth Gardner and

Jess Feichtlbauer for their marketing and publicity magic, Sarah Cronin for the text design, and Gareth Collinson and Charlotte James for proofreading.

Writing and publishing is a gift and a privilege. Thank you to children's writers past, present and future. Young people's literature is an inspiring and extraordinary space and I am so thankful to be contributing in some small way to that. And thank you, especially, to the readers who keep us writing.

A heartfelt thank you to my English teachers, Ms Shapiro and Ms Soskice-Gandhi, both of whom inspired me creatively and encouraged my early writing; I don't think I would be here without you and I am so very grateful to have been taught by you both.

Finally, while this sentiment is woefully inadequate, I would like to acknowledge the writers, journalists, poets and artists who continue to share truth in a deeply divided and unforgiving world. Thank you for your fortitude, compassion and humanity. Thank you for writing with such courage.

To share the haunting words of Refaat Alareer, a Palestinian poet and writer killed in an Israeli airstrike in Gaza in December 2023:

*If I must die / let it bring hope / let it be a tale*

I hold onto these words as a reminder to write with hope and love. To write with humanity. A clarion call to write stories that matter.

# ABOUT THE AUTHOR

Ayaan Mohamud wrote her first ever book in lockdown and during NaNoWriMo, while also studying as a medical student, and it became her debut novel, *You Think You Know Me*. It was inspired by her own experiences of Islamophobia and a desire to write about Somali culture, and went on to become a World Book Night title and be shortlisted for the Waterstones Book Prize and the Branford Boase Award. She lives in London and can usually be found either writing or complaining about writing.

◎ 𝕏 @ayaan_moham

SILENCE IS SAFE. MY TRUTH IS LOUD
YOU THINK YOU KNOW ME
AYAAN MOHAMUD

*People like me are devils before we are angels.*
Hanan has always been good and quiet. She accepts her role as her school's perfect Muslim poster girl. She ignores the racist bullies.

*A closed mouth is gold – it helps you get home in one piece.*
Then her friend is murdered and every Muslim is to blame.
*The world is angry at us again.*

How can she stay silent while her family is ripped apart?
It's time for Hanan to stop being the quiet, good girl. It's time for her to stand up and shout.

**READ ON FOR AN EXTRACT FROM AYAAN'S STUNNING DEBUT NOVEL...**

Since Andrea's running late, I ride the bus to school alone. The seat next to me remains empty the whole time, as if I'm sending out a silent signal to ward everyone off. The bus is packed to the brim and the eagle-eyed passengers, whose radars are forever on the hunt for any free seat, glance at the coveted space, but it remains empty for the rest of the ride. Not only that, a few people actually look *nervous* when they board the bus and lock eyes with me. I quickly look over my shoulder to see if there's anyone scary-looking behind me, but there's only a group of nursery kids being hushed by a dishevelled woman.

I walk into form alone, winding through the tables, chairs and clustered bodies to get to Nasra, Lily and Isha, who are chatting about Lily's weekend trip to Switzerland. I muted the group chat this weekend after the phone call with Andrea, not really in the mood to hear about Swiss Alps and skiing, so I'm a little out of the loop.

"Hey, guys," I mumble, leaning in reluctantly to Nasra's open arms before sitting down.

"What's up with you?" Isha asks, raising her eyebrows.

"It's a Monday morning," Lily replies, sighing dramatically. "That's what's wrong with all of us." She digs for something in the inside pocket of her blazer and hands it to me. "But I'm sure this gorgeous keyring will make you feel better, Hanan."

If I was going to be real with Lily, I'd tell her there's not a single keyring in the world that could magically make everything better, but I know that this is tradition and that she's just being nice, so I dutifully take out my keys and swap out the last keyring she gave me – one from a weekend trip to Paris – for this one, a slice of dangling Swiss cheese.

Lily beams at me and jumps straight into another story about her adventures with her mum but my mind just isn't there.

Nasra must notice because she pulls on my sleeve to get my attention. "You sick or something?" she asks, concern colouring her face.

"No, it's not that," I say uncertainly. I look down and fiddle with my planner, wanting to avoid her gaze. A small part of me is worried that if I give words to my feelings, it might make them more real.

The weekend had been hard enough already. I'd barely gotten any sleep because my nightmares had come back in full force. Except this time, the nightmares had been much, much worse. They weren't just fuzzy images and unrecognizable screams. They were the face and screams of Mr Fleming. And my dad. Always, my dad. And, because of that, Hussein had barely gotten any sleep either. Though, luckily for him, that meant I'd decided to let him off the hook for lying to me – for now, anyway. I'll just have to find the perfect time for an interrogation later.

"These last few days have been weird," I start to say, still fiddling with the loops of my planner's spine. "I can't even tell you why exactly. Just a feeling that something's off, you know. The vibe on the bus was really weird this morning too." I pause, fingers still on the planner.

"You know what? Never mind. I'm being dumb."

In my sleep-deprived state, of course everything is going to be *off*. How can I expect to feel normal and fine when Mr Fleming is dead?

"You aren't being dumb, Hanan. I get what you mean." Nasra drops her voice lower, speaking in a half-whisper even though there's no way anyone's going to hear over Lily squealing about the quality of Swiss hot chocolate.

If I'm being honest, I'm starting to feel like this conversation might not be for them anyway.

"Things have been starting up since what came out on Saturday," Nasra adds soberly.

"What do you mean?" I turn my body so I'm completely facing her. Our closeness makes it feel like it's just us in the classroom, like there's no one else around. "What came out on Saturday?"

Nasra looks at me incredulously. "Girl, do you have amnesia or something? I'm talking about the Muslim guy who stabbed that ex-school caretaker, Mr Fleming, on Faren? It's been all over the news."

*Shit.* I'd avoided the TV, my phone, everything over the weekend, because I know how these things usually go. Photos of Mr Fleming, words from family members, shots of the crime scene. Rinse, repeat. I hadn't wanted to see any of that because it would have made things a thousand times more difficult to bear.

"What do you mean he was Muslim? One of those 'death to the disbelievers' crazies?"

"Nope," she replies, shaking her head. "I mean, they're really trying to make him look like that, but he was just a regular guy.

A regular criminal, I mean." She laughs, once, but it's not her usual laugh. There's something darker in it, something that sounds a little hopeless. "You know it's funny –" she continues – "they'll really claim us when Mo Farah is out here winning gold, but they won't even let us have normal criminals. Everyone's got to be an extremist." She sighs dramatically and looks away. "I'm just tired."

"But maybe it's not about that." I pull her back to look at me. "Just forget what I said. It's probably a coincidence. Me over-thinking or—"

"Let me just stop you there," Nasra says. She quickly looks over to Mr Foster and pulls out her phone. "I'm sending you a video. Watch it later. You'll see what I'm talking about."

I pull a face at her and imitate her seriousness. She scowls back at me.

Andrea hurries in seconds before Mr Foster calls her name on the register. He gives her a disapproving look but gestures for her to sit down.

"Alarm emergency," she whispers to us after she's caught her breath. "My mum changed the code again and forgot it so the bloody thing wouldn't shut up."

When the register's done, Mr Foster stands at the front of the class and calls for our attention. He clasps his hands loosely in front of him, and looks down sombrely, leaning back against his desk. I feel a twinge of pity for the five people sitting at the table nearest to him. They'll be getting a front row seat to another one of Mr Foster's regular spit-storms.

"It's very saddening, this morning, to have to stand here and discuss something with you all that's truly come as a shock to the school and our local community over the last few days," Mr Foster begins, "but I also believe it is necessary." He clears his throat. "What happened last week was a hugely tragic and unexpected event and it's one that has certainly left a mark on this school. For those of who you aren't already aware, Mr Fleming, the victim of last week's attack on Faren High Street, was an integral part of the Grafton Grammar community serving as our caretaker for over twenty years." Mr Foster paces a few steps around his desk before leaning on it again. "I know most of you will have seen Mr Fleming around the school before his retirement last year. Perhaps some of you even got to know him well in the years you've been here."

I close my eyes, wanting him to stop talking, wanting the bell to ring right this very second, so I can leave and pretend like nothing's changed. So, I can pretend that Mr Fleming's still at home, enjoying his retirement.

Andrea lightly pats my leg. She texted me a few times over the weekend to check up on me. I don't think she believed me each time I told her I was fine, even though I'd tried to be as convincing as possible.

"There's support at the school for anyone who feels like they need to talk to someone. Please don't be ashamed to seek it if you need to," Mr Foster continues. "There should be more information soon about a memorial service we'll be holding for Mr Fleming so please keep an eye out for that, as well, if you'd like to come." He gazes around at us. "Does anyone have any questions about what I've said or would like to share anything?"

The class is silent for a couple of beats. I look down at my planner, waiting for us to move onto something else. We're almost there, almost over the awkward hump of silence, when Jessica breaks it.

"I have something I'd like to say, sir. If that's okay."

"Of course," Mr Foster says, sitting back down. "Go ahead, Jessica."

I look up, sure this can't be anything good.

Jessica sits up straighter. I'm not quite sure how to describe her expression. It's like a cross between real sadness and her usual savagery. "This situation with Mr Fleming... It's really shaken me, sir. I'm sure it's shaken a lot of people."

She looks around the room, taking in the nodding heads and murmurs of quiet agreement.

"He was obviously a big part of the school before he retired," she continues, "and I just think it was such a shame that he, you know, was killed the way he was. That someone could just kill him in broad daylight. What kind of person would do something like that?"

Somehow, all in the space of a minute, the atmosphere in the class has changed. Not in any obvious way, but in a way I can feel, and in a way I know Nasra can feel too because, when I glance at her, she's already looking my way.

Mr Foster nods solemnly, eyes cast down as he listens to Jessica. He looks up when she's done talking.

"I can appreciate that, Jessica, thank you for sharing that with us. It is, of course, a more difficult loss, given the..." Mr Foster clears his throat again. "Given the circumstances of his passing and…and it is something that may take some time for people to come to terms with. Again, if there's anyone who feels they'd like to speak to me in private, or would like any kind of support, please do let me know." He nods at Jessica and then looks to the rest of the class. His gaze circles to our table in the back. I wait for him to drag his gaze around the rest of the class, like he always does, but he doesn't. Seconds elapse and I begin to wonder if this now constitutes outright staring, when Mr Foster speaks again.

"Is there anything else that anyone wants to share?"

I look back down again, praying we can finally move onto something else, but then I see Nasra's back straighten in the corner of my vision.

"No, sir, Hanan and I don't have anything to say if that's what you mean."

My head shoots up.

Mr Foster stammers a reply. "No, I wasn't, I'm not—"

"Don't worry about it, sir. We all get a bit tongue tied sometimes, just shake it off."

I reach over to pull on Nasra's arm. *What are you doing?* I say with my eyes. There's a fine line between acceptable sass and unacceptable sass. For some reason, Nasra always likes to walk the dangerous line between the two.

"It's not my fault," she whispers angrily across the space between us. "He was the one staring at us!"

Mr Foster quickly regains his composure, expression set in displeasure. "You'd better be careful what you say next, Nasra, or you'll find yourself in Mr Davies's office."

Nasra rolls her eyes but doesn't push her luck. I put a hand on her shoulder and hope that she doesn't say anything else.

Lily squirms uncomfortably, not looking at either of us. Isha stares hard at the lines of her palms, like there's something important in them she can't decipher. Next to me, I can feel Andrea quietly seething. She leans back in her chair, crossing her arms with a snort.

I catch sight of Jessica and her co-Braids smirking across the room. The rest of the class just looks at us with disdain.

I feel my skin prickle with awkwardness. I've made it through most of my years at Grafton without having to make proper eye contact or even interact with most of these people, but now it's all eyes on us.

And they're not kind eyes either.

"Mr Foster," Jessica says curtly. "I think it's only fair that one of them *does* say something though. I'm sure it's not just me who wants to hear it. That murderer was one of theirs after all—"

My hold on Nasra breaks. Before Mr Foster can respond to Jessica, Nasra jumps up, slamming both hands on the table.

"Bitch, I will beat your ass—"

"Nasra!" Mr Foster shouts. I've never heard his voice this loud before. It shakes the room for a moment. "That's enough. To the Head's office. Now!"

Nasra's body trembles with everything she's keeping a lid on, but she does it. She doesn't speak back to Mr Foster or Jessica. She packs her things away as quickly as she can, and I help her. There is only silence around us.

Her hand grabs mine after she zips up her bag. She bends down to whisper in my ear. "The cycle begins again, sis. Don't say I didn't warn you."

Nasra looks at me intently for a second before she leaves, letting the door slam shut behind her. The sound of it echoes in my ears long after she's gone.

### READ

# YOU THINK YOU KNOW ME

## TO DISCOVER HOW HANAN'S STORY CONTINUES

 @usborneya